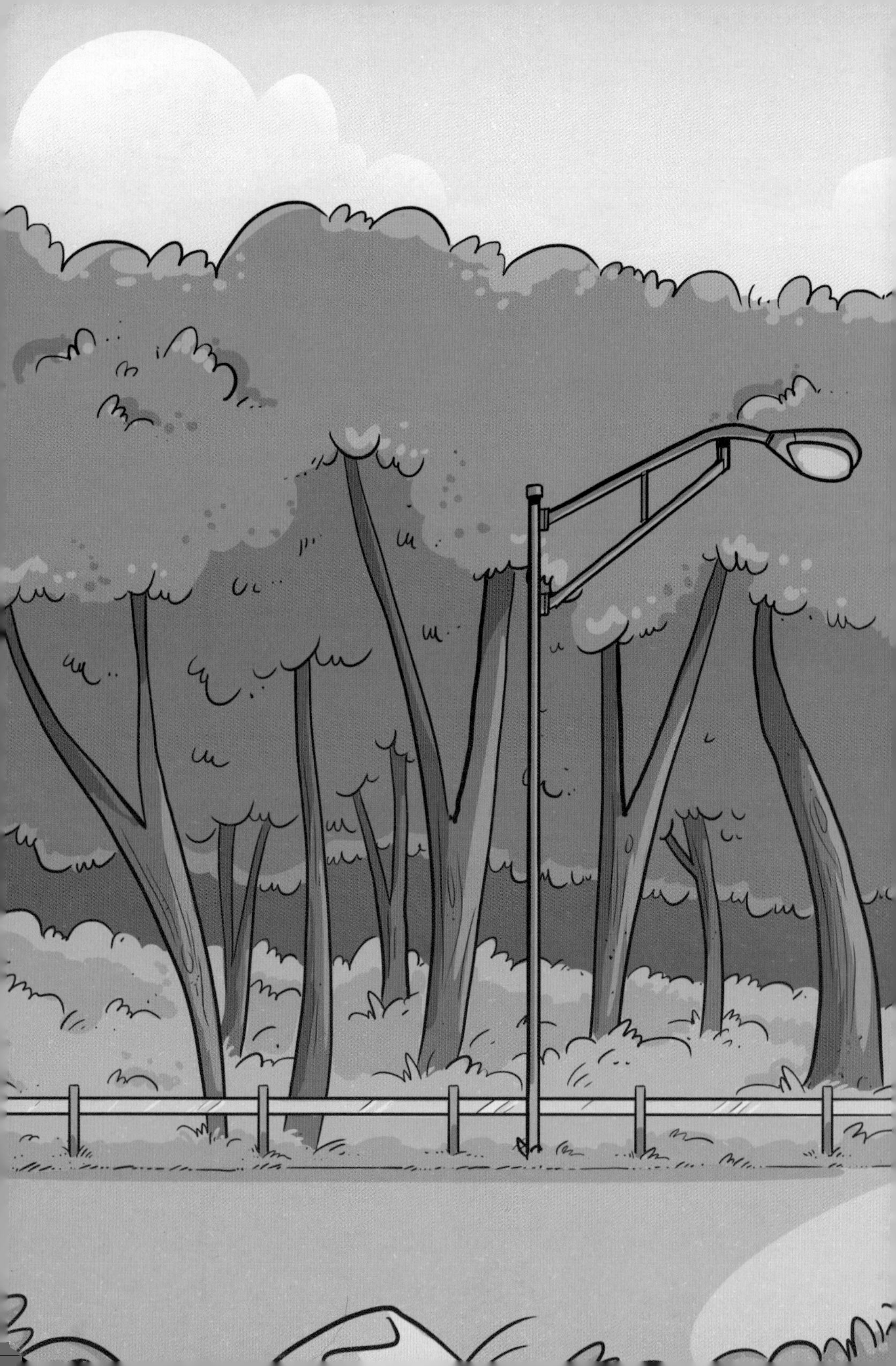

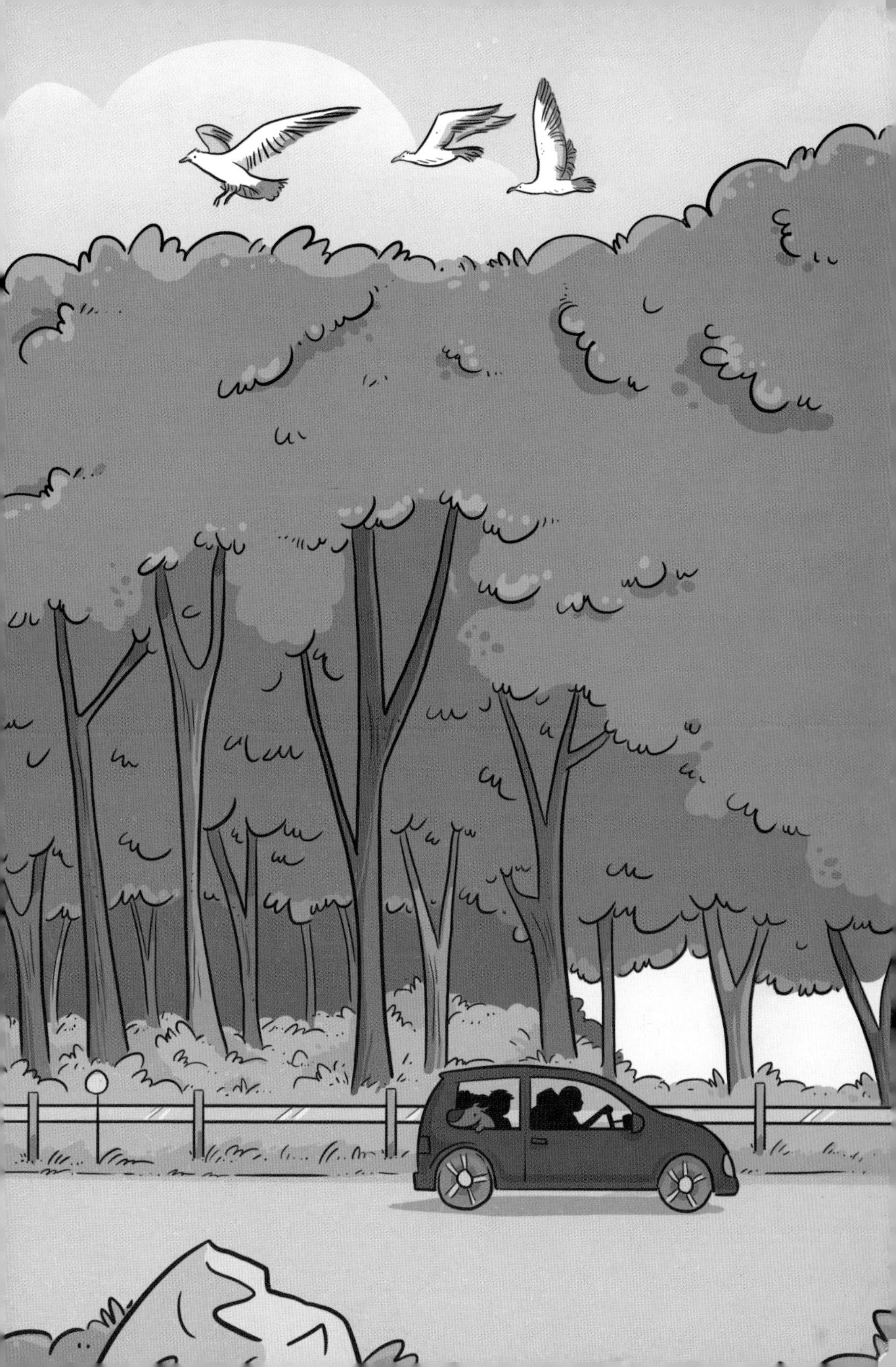

A special thank you to the crew at FableVision,
especially Didi Hatcher, Hannah O'Neal, Ellen Crenshaw,
Keith Zulawnik, and to the many interns who all had a
hand in helping illustrate this book!
— R. K.

𝒜
atheneum

ATHENEUM BOOKS FOR YOUNG READERS
An imprint of Simon & Schuster Children's Publishing Division
1230 Avenue of the Americas
New York, New York 10020

This book is a work of fiction. Any references to historical
events, real people, or real places are used fictitiously. Other
names, characters, places, and events are products of the
author's imagination, and any resemblance to actual events or
places or persons, living or dead, is entirely coincidental.

ATHENEUM BOOKS FOR YOUNG READERS is a registered trademark of Simon & Schuster, Inc.

Atheneum logo is a trademark of Simon & Schuster, Inc.

For information about special discounts for bulk purchases,
please contact Simon & Schuster Special Sales at 1-866-506-1949
or business@simonandschuster.com.

The Simon & Schuster Speakers Bureau can bring authors to your live event. For more information or to
book an event, contact the Simon & Schuster Speakers Bureau at
1-866-248-3049 or visit our website at www.simonspeakers.com.

FableVision

Also available in an Atheneum Books for Young Readers hardcover edition
Book design by Renée Kurilla and Sonia Chaghatzbanian
The text for this book is set in Slappy and space cowgirl.
The illustrations for this book are inked and colored digitally.
Manufactured in China
First Edition
2 4 6 8 10 9 7 5 3 1

Library of Congress Cataloging-in-Publication Data

Emerson, Sharon.
SPF 40 / written by Sharon Emerson : drawn by Renée Kurilla . — 1st ed.
p. cm. — (Zebrafish)
At head of title: Peter H. Reynolds and FableVision present
ISBN 978-1-4169-9708-5 (hardcover)
ISBN 978-1-4169-9709-2 (paperback)
ISBN 978-1-4424-5034-9 (eBook)
1. Graphic novels. [1. Graphic novels. 2. Camps — Fiction. 3. Rock groups — Fiction. 4. Charities — Fiction.]
I. Kurilla, Renee, ill. II. Reynolds, Peter, 1961– III. FableVision Studios. IV. Title. V. Title: SPF forty. VI.
Title: Peter H. Reynolds and FableVision present.
PZ7.7.E47Spf 2013
741.5'973 — dc23   2012014883

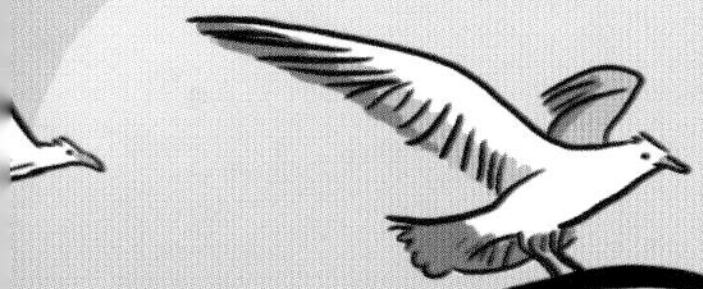

ZEBRAFISH

SPF 40

Written by Sharon Emerson

Illustrated by Renée Kurilla
with help from Didi Hatcher and
the team at FableVision

atheneum
Atheneum Books for Young Readers
New York · London · Toronto · Sydney · New Delhi

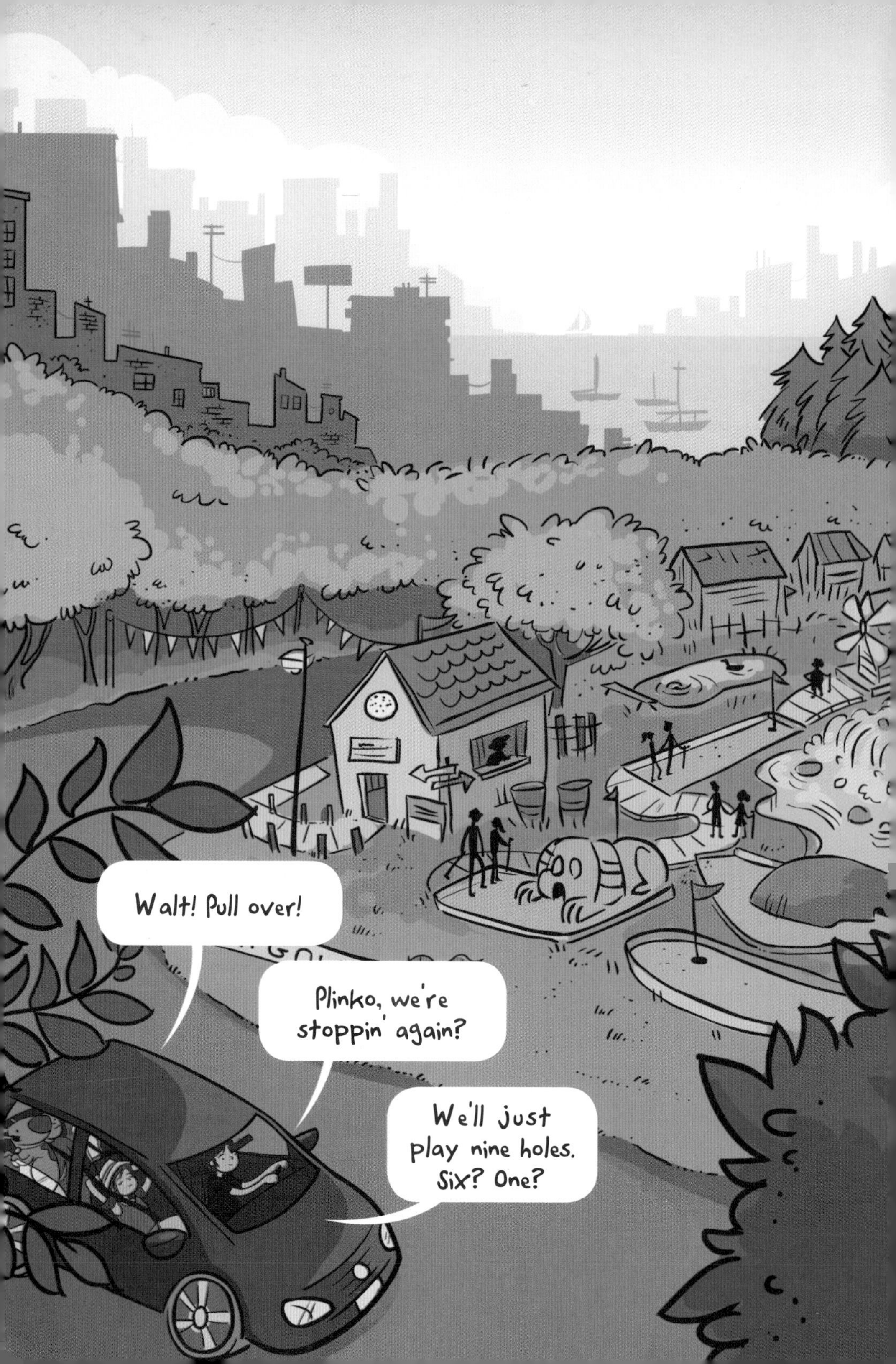
Walt! Pull over!
Plinko, we're stoppin' again?
We'll just play nine holes. Six? One?

Contents

"In the long history of humankind (and animal kind,
too), those who learned to collaborate and improvise
most effectively have prevailed."
—Charles Darwin

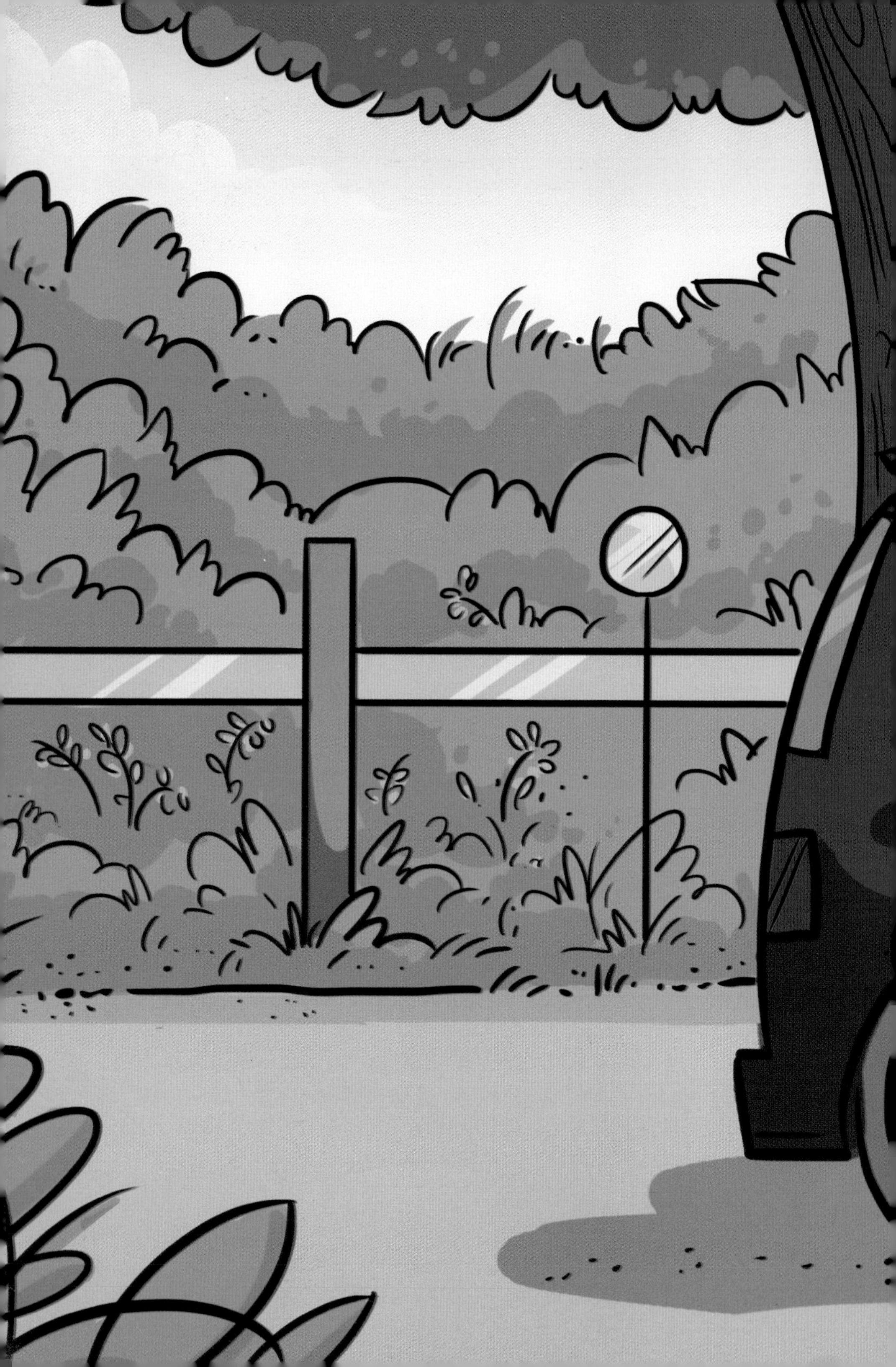

1. Road Trip
If turtles lay hundreds of eggs, why isn't the beach crawling with them?
I hope we see a sea turtle. They nest in the dunes.
They don't hatch until late summer. And then usually at night.

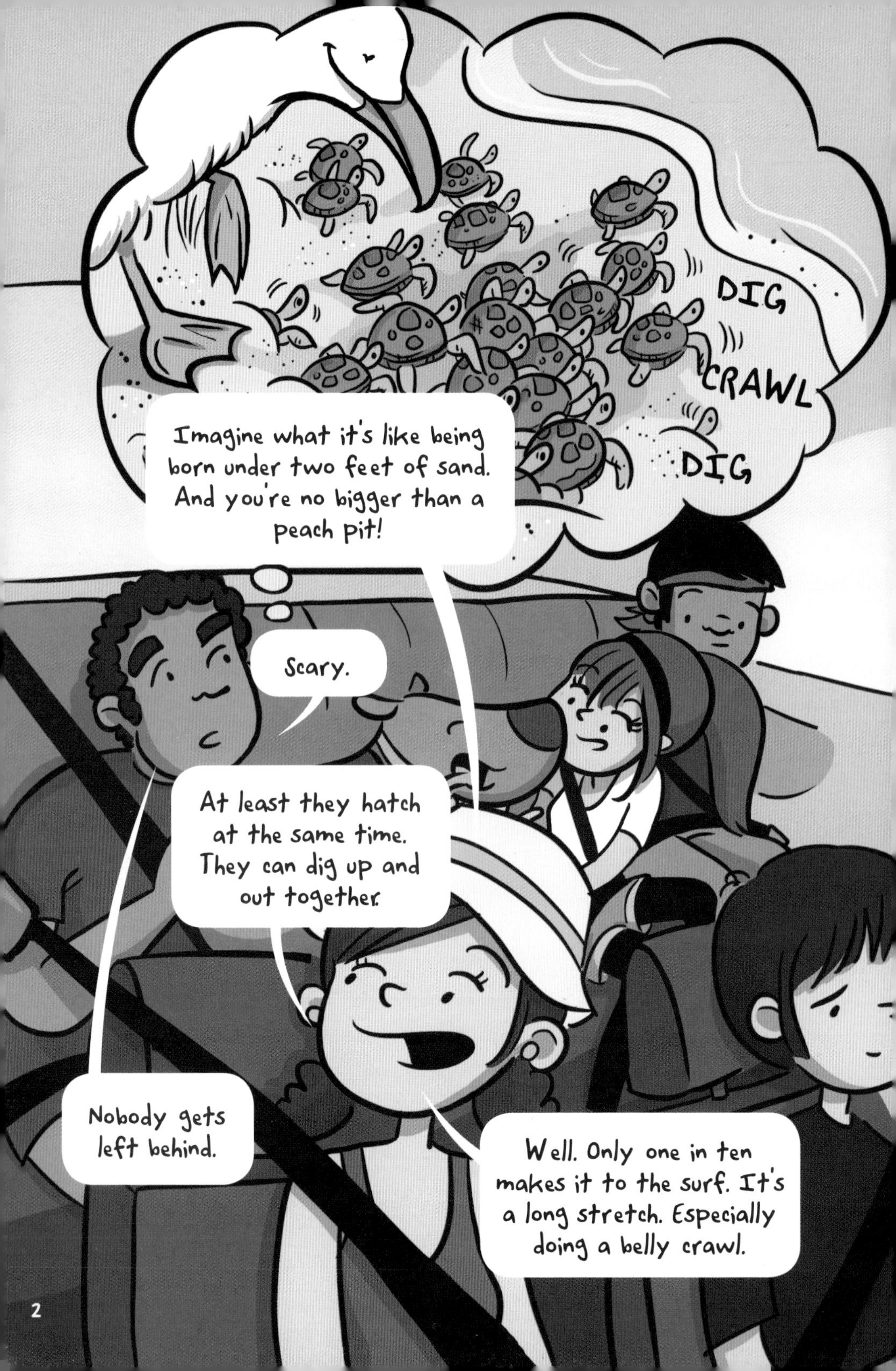
DIG
CRAWL
DIG
Imagine what it's like being born under two feet of sand. And you're no bigger than a peach pit!
Scary.
At least they hatch at the same time. They can dig up and out together.
Nobody gets left behind.
Well. Only one in ten makes it to the surf. It's a long stretch. Especially doing a belly crawl.

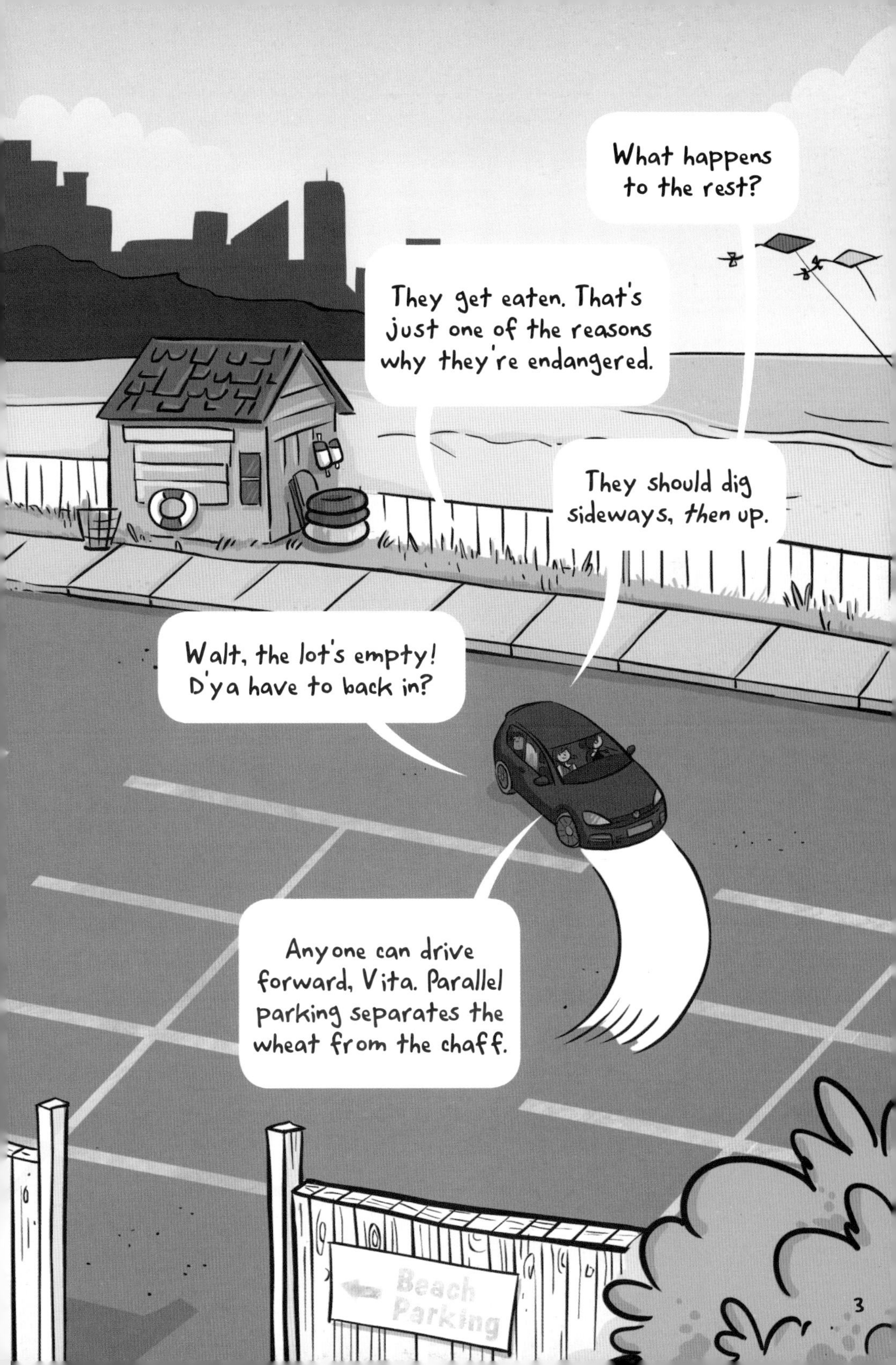
What happens to the rest?
They get eaten. That's just one of the reasons why they're endangered.
They should dig sideways, *then* up.
Walt, the lot's empty! D'ya have to back in?
Anyone can drive forward, Vita. Parallel parking separates the wheat from the chaff.
Beach Parking

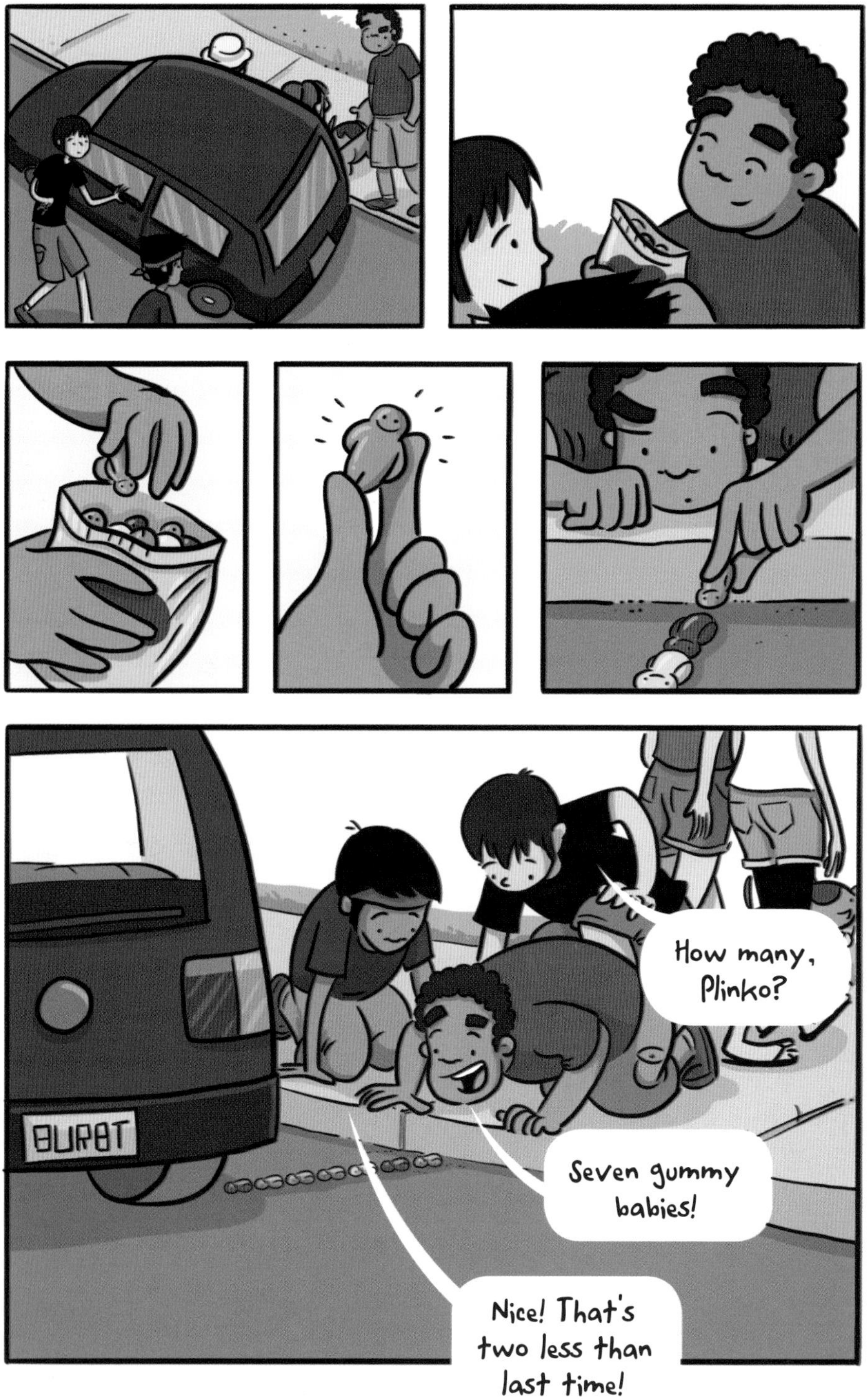
How many, Plinko?
Seven gummy babies!
Nice! That's two less than last time!

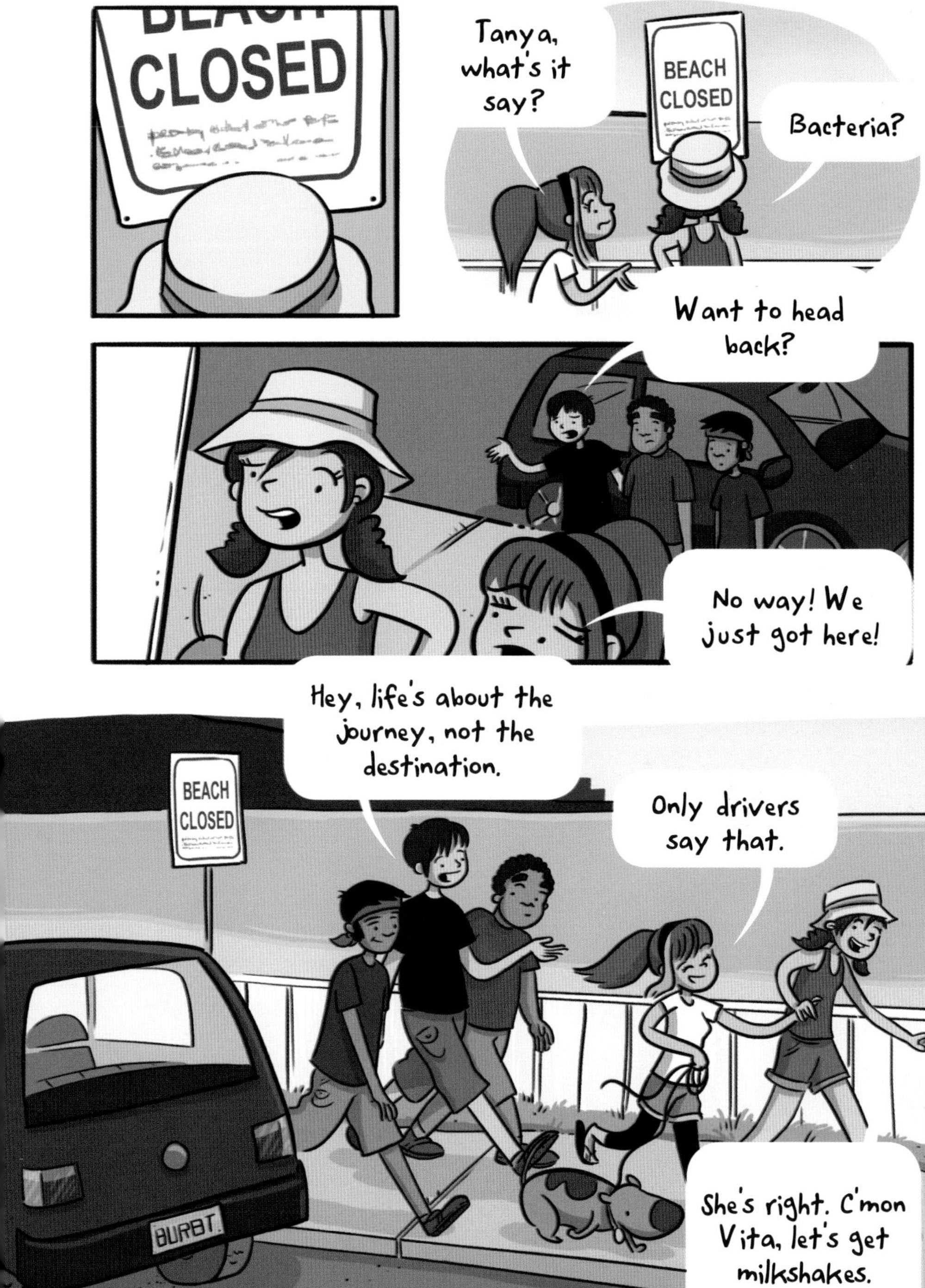
BEACH
CLOSED
Tanya, what's it say?
BEACH
CLOSED
Bacteria?
Want to head back?
No way! We just got here!
Hey, life's about the journey, not the destination.
BEACH
CLOSED
Only drivers say that.
She's right. C'mon Vita, let's get milkshakes.
BURBT

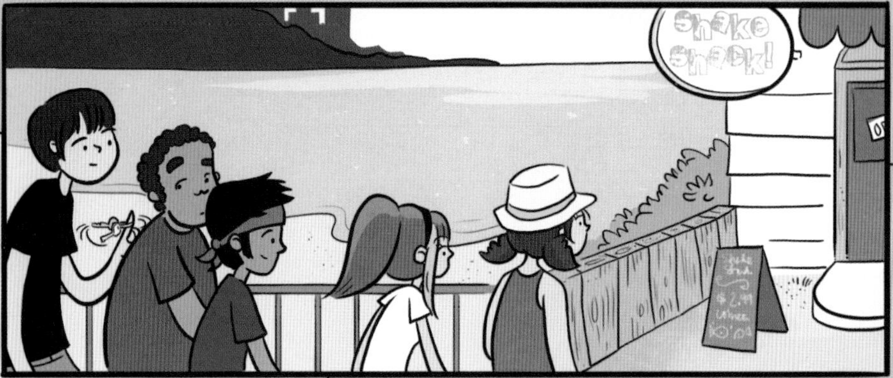
Shake Shack!

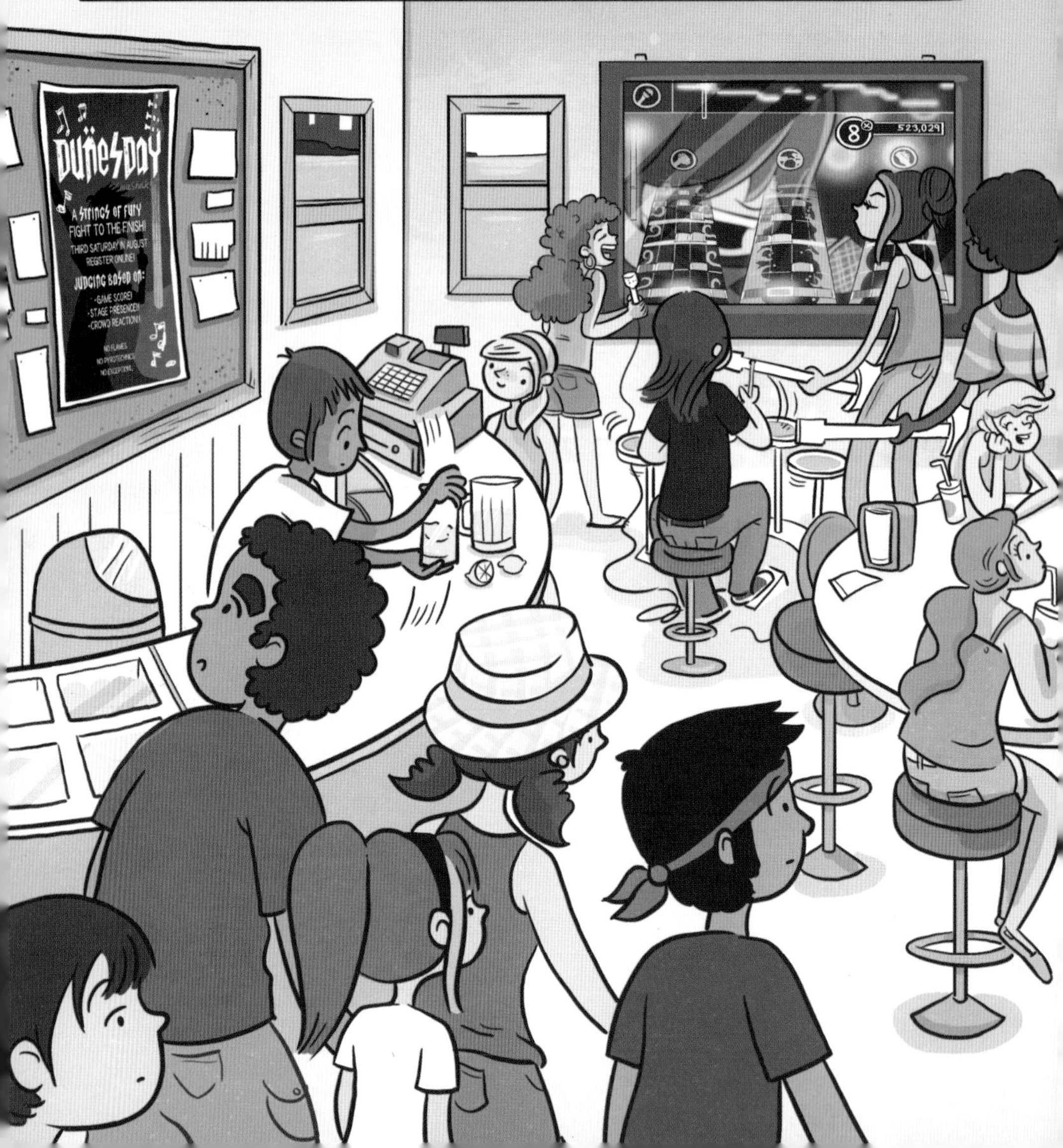
523,029
DUNESDAY
A STRINGS OF FURY
FIGHT TO THE FINISH!
THIRD SATURDAY IN AUGUST
REGISTER ONLINE!
JUDGING BASED ON:
-GAME SCORE!
-STAGE PRESENCE!!
-CROWD REACTION!!!
NO FLAMES
NO PYROTECHNICS
NO EXCEPTIONS

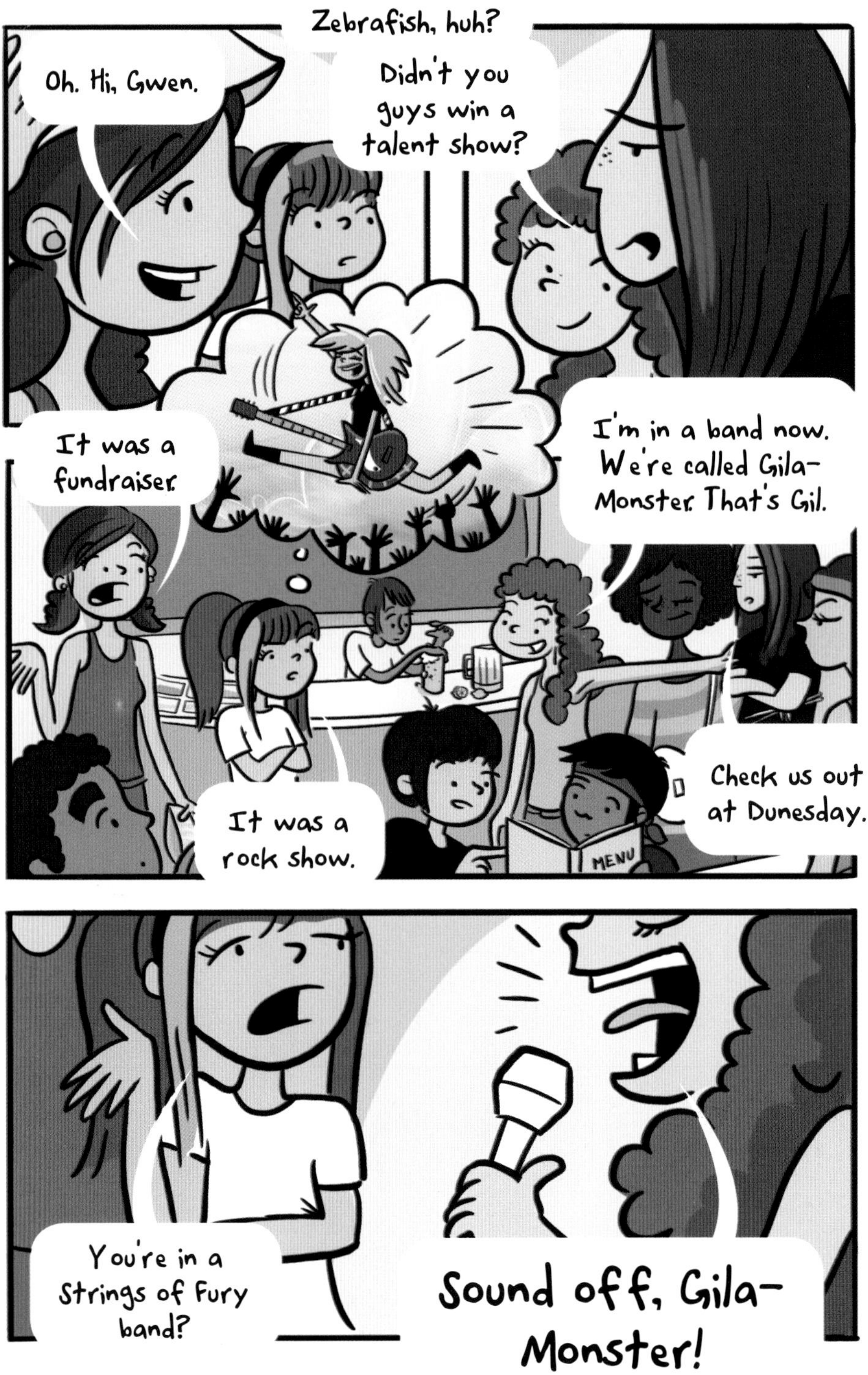
Oh. Hi, Gwen.
Zebrafish, huh?
Didn't you guys win a talent show?
It was a fundraiser.
I'm in a band now. We're called Gila-Monster. That's Gil.
It was a rock show.
MENU
Check us out at Dunesday.
You're in a Strings of Fury band?
Sound off, Gila-Monster!

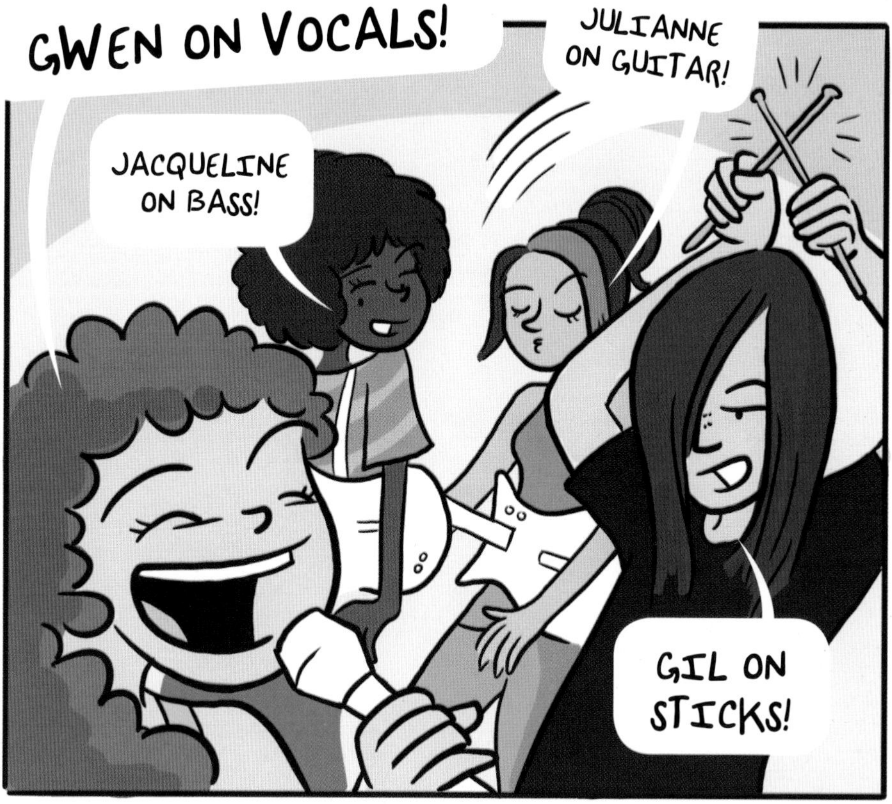
GWEN ON VOCALS!
JULIANNE ON GUITAR!
JACQUELINE ON BASS!
GIL ON STICKS!

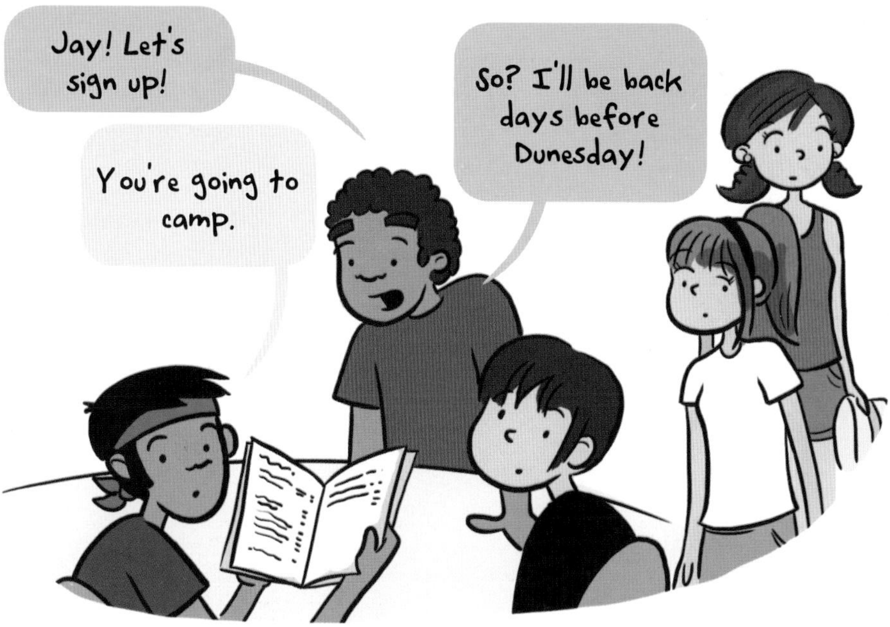
Jay! Let's sign up!
You're going to camp.
So? I'll be back days before Dunesday!

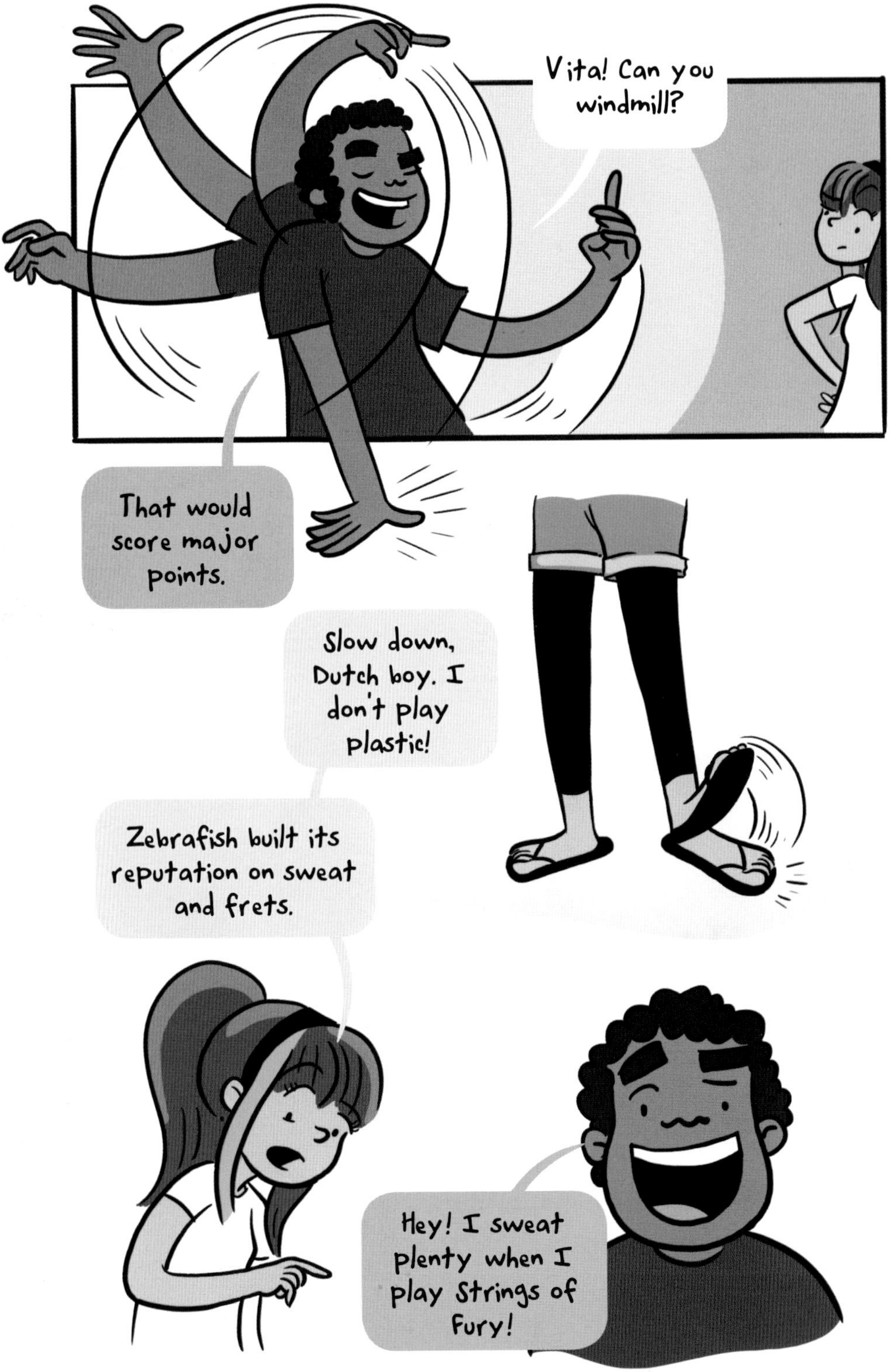
Vita! Can you windmill?
That would score major points.
Slow down, Dutch boy. I don't play plastic!
Zebrafish built its reputation on sweat and frets.
Hey! I sweat plenty when I play Strings of Fury!

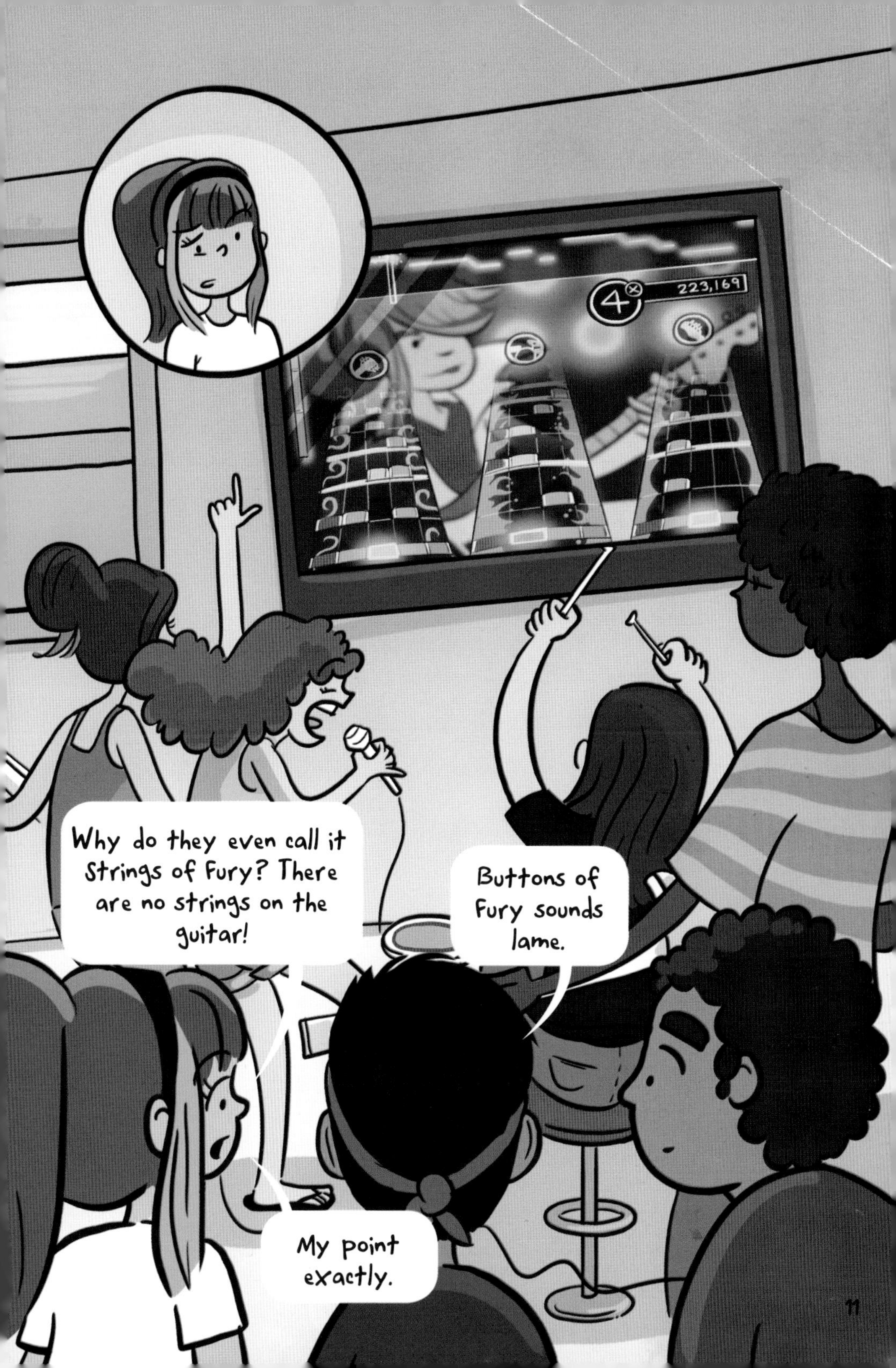
223,169
Why do they even call it Strings of Fury? There are no strings on the guitar!
Buttons of Fury sounds lame.
My point exactly.

That Night . . .

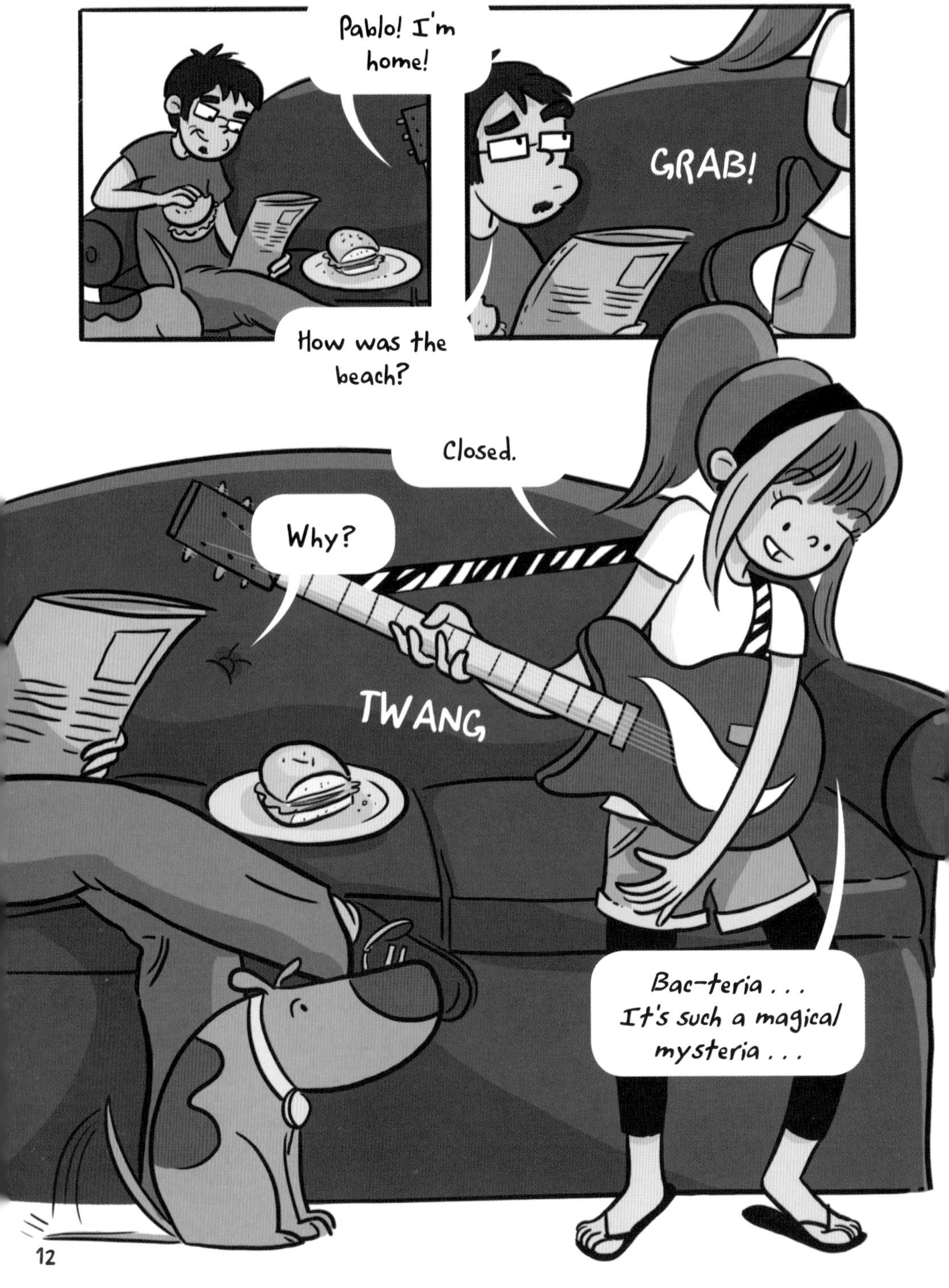

Pablo! I'm home!
GRAB!
How was the beach?
Closed.
Why?
TWANG
Bac-teria . . . It's such a magical mysteria . . .

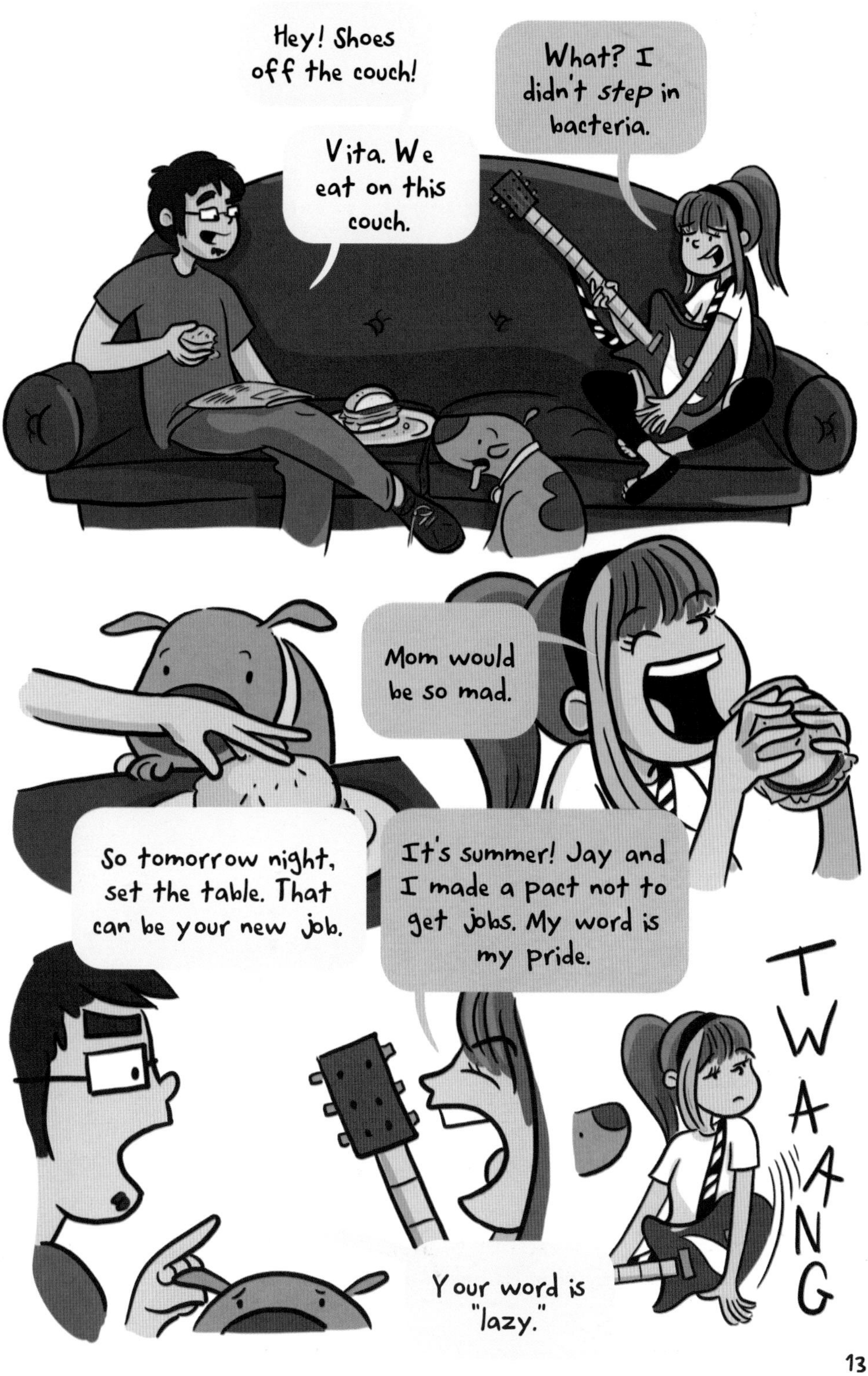
Hey! Shoes off the couch!
What? I didn't step in bacteria.
Vita. We eat on this couch.
Mom would be so mad.
So tomorrow night, set the table. That can be your new job.
It's summer! Jay and I made a pact not to get jobs. My word is my pride.
TWANG
Your word is "lazy."

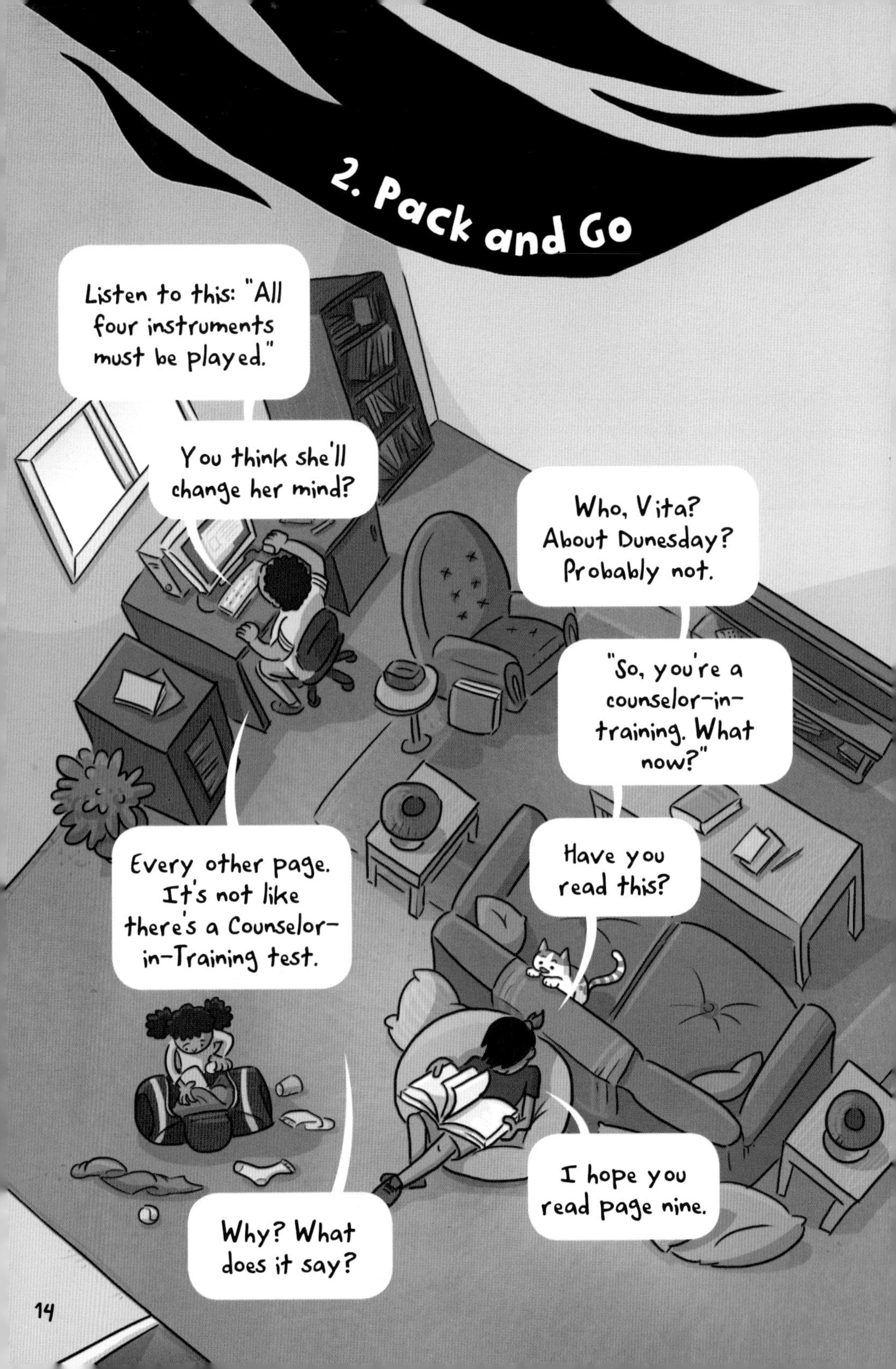
2. Pack and Go
Listen to this: "All four instruments must be played."
You think she'll change her mind?
Who, Vita? About Dunesday? Probably not.
"So, you're a counselor-in-training. What now?"
Every other page. It's not like there's a Counselor-in-Training test.
Have you read this?
I hope you read page nine.
Why? What does it say?

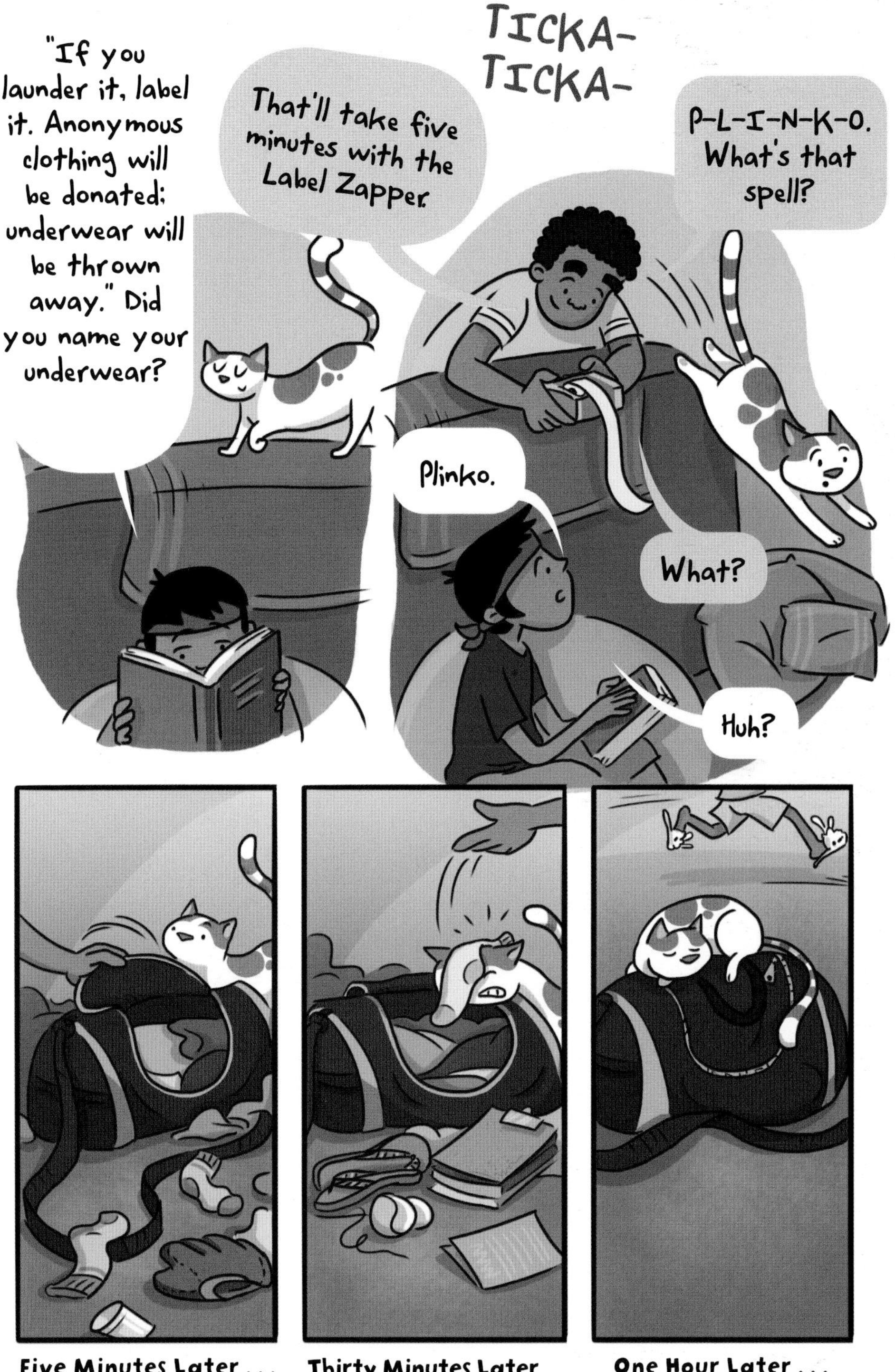
"If you launder it, label it. Anonymous clothing will be donated; underwear will be thrown away." Did you name your underwear?
That'll take five minutes with the Label Zapper.
TICKA-TICKA-
P-L-I-N-K-O. What's that spell?
Plinko.
What?
Huh?
Five Minutes Later . . .
Thirty Minutes Later . . .
One Hour Later . . .

Ten Minutes After That . . .

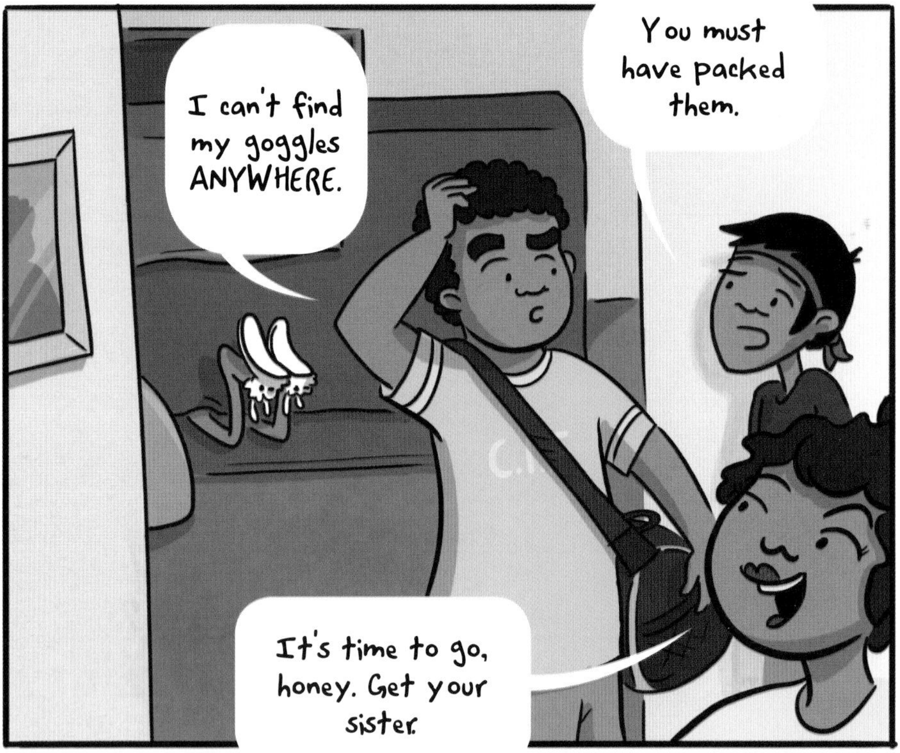
I can't find my goggles ANYWHERE.
You must have packed them.
It's time to go, honey. Get your sister.

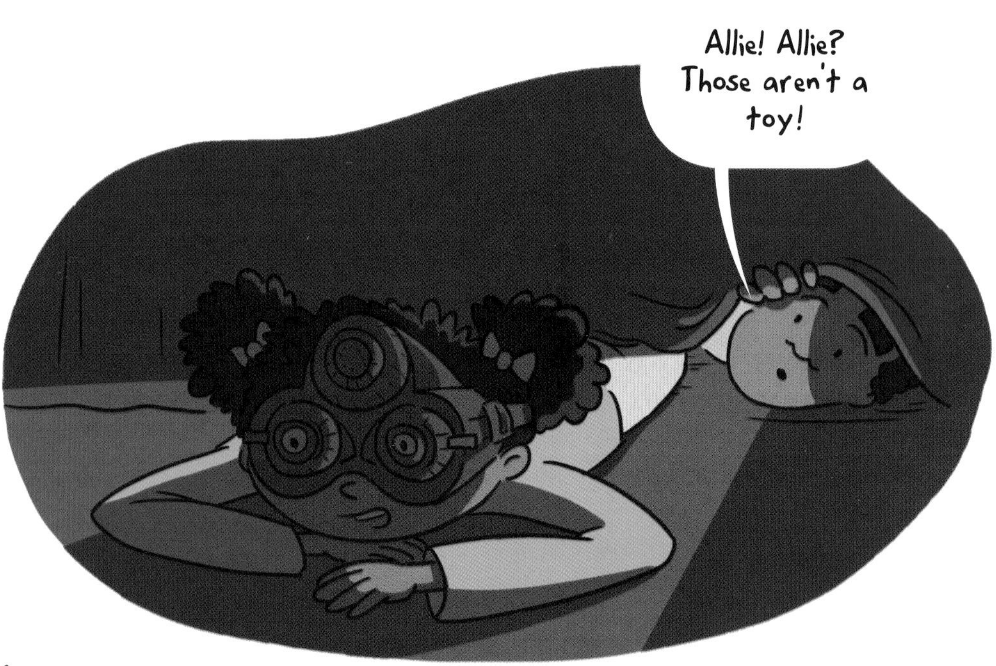
Allie! Allie? Those aren't a toy!

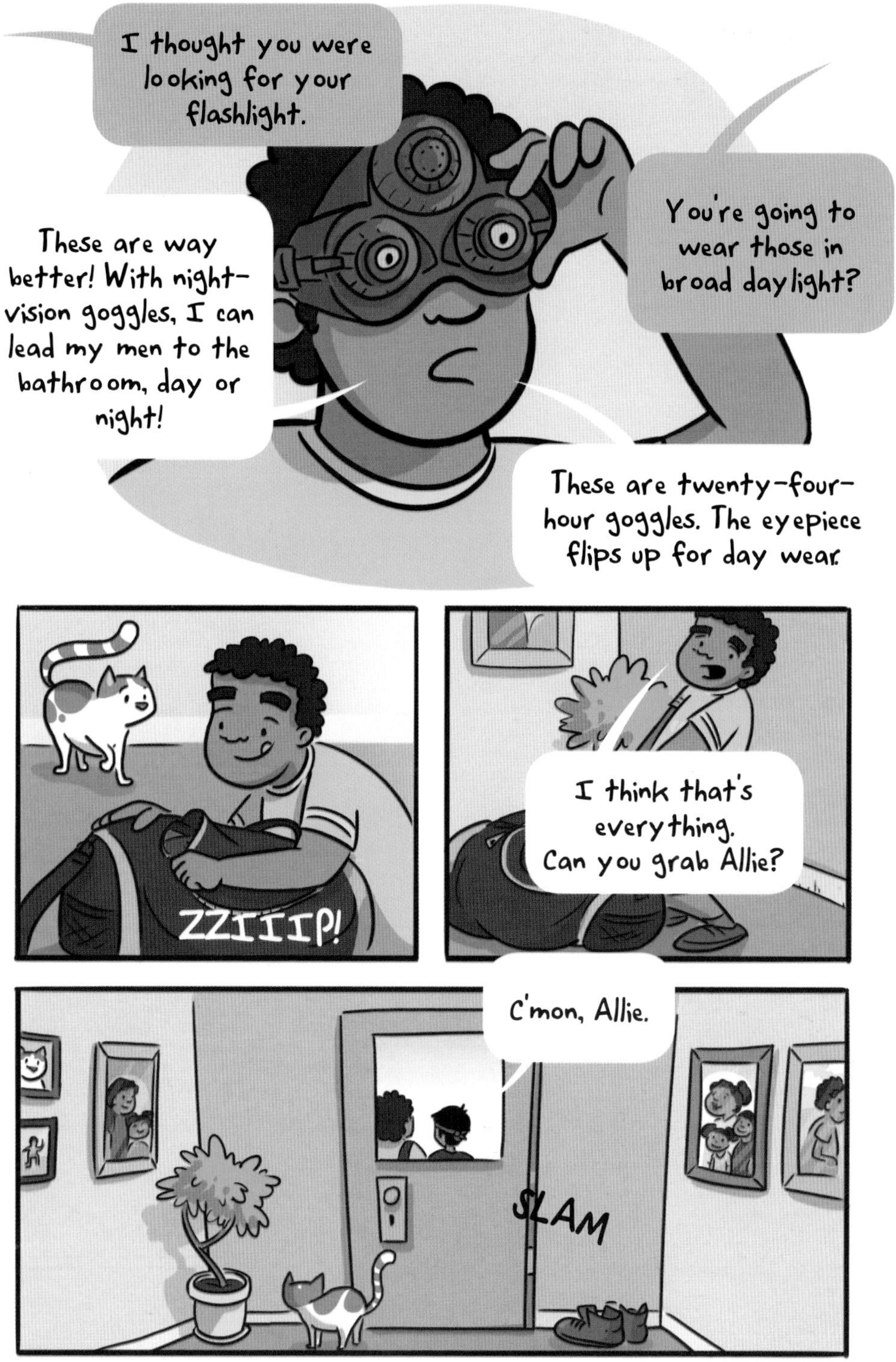
I thought you were looking for your flashlight.
These are way better! With night-vision goggles, I can lead my men to the bathroom, day or night!
You're going to wear those in broad daylight?
These are twenty-four-hour goggles. The eyepiece flips up for day wear.
ZZIIIP!
I think that's everything. Can you grab Allie?
C'mon, Allie.
SLAM

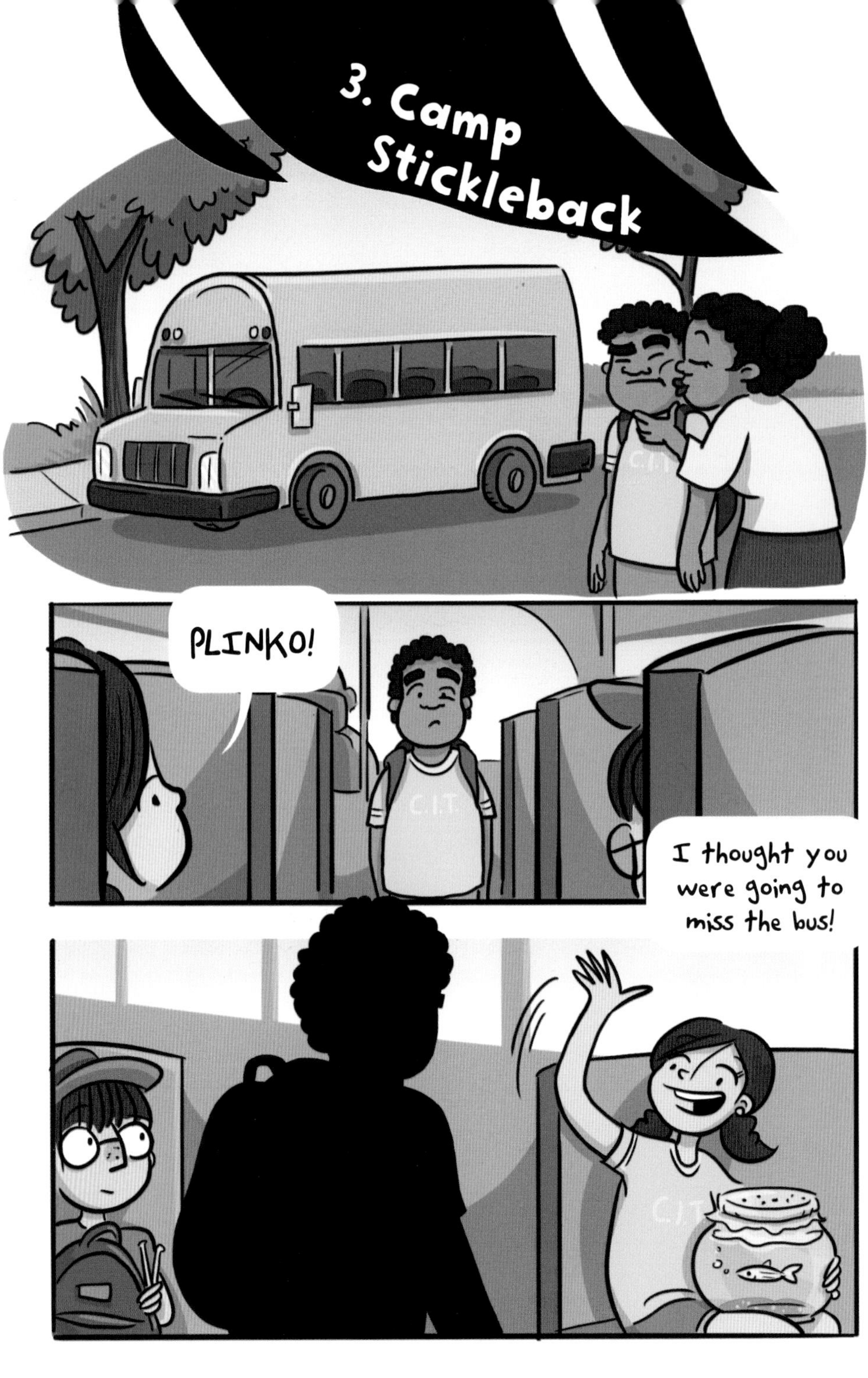
3. Camp Stickleback
C.I.T.
PLINKO!
C.I.T.
I thought you were going to miss the bus!
C.I.T.

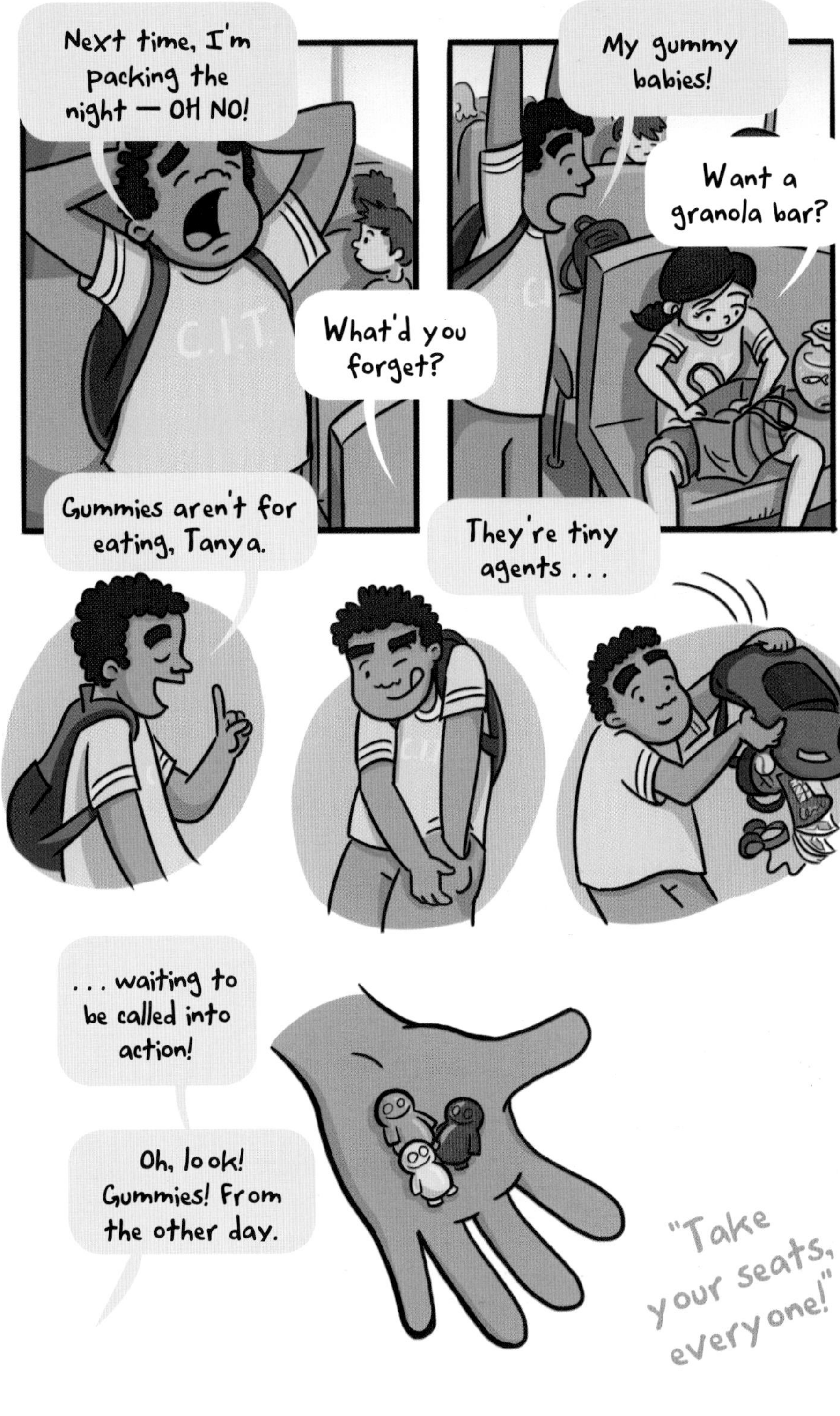
Next time, I'm packing the night — OH NO!
What'd you forget?
My gummy babies!
Want a granola bar?
Gummies aren't for eating, Tanya.
They're tiny agents . . .
. . . waiting to be called into action!
Oh, look! Gummies! From the other day.
"Take your seats, everyone!"

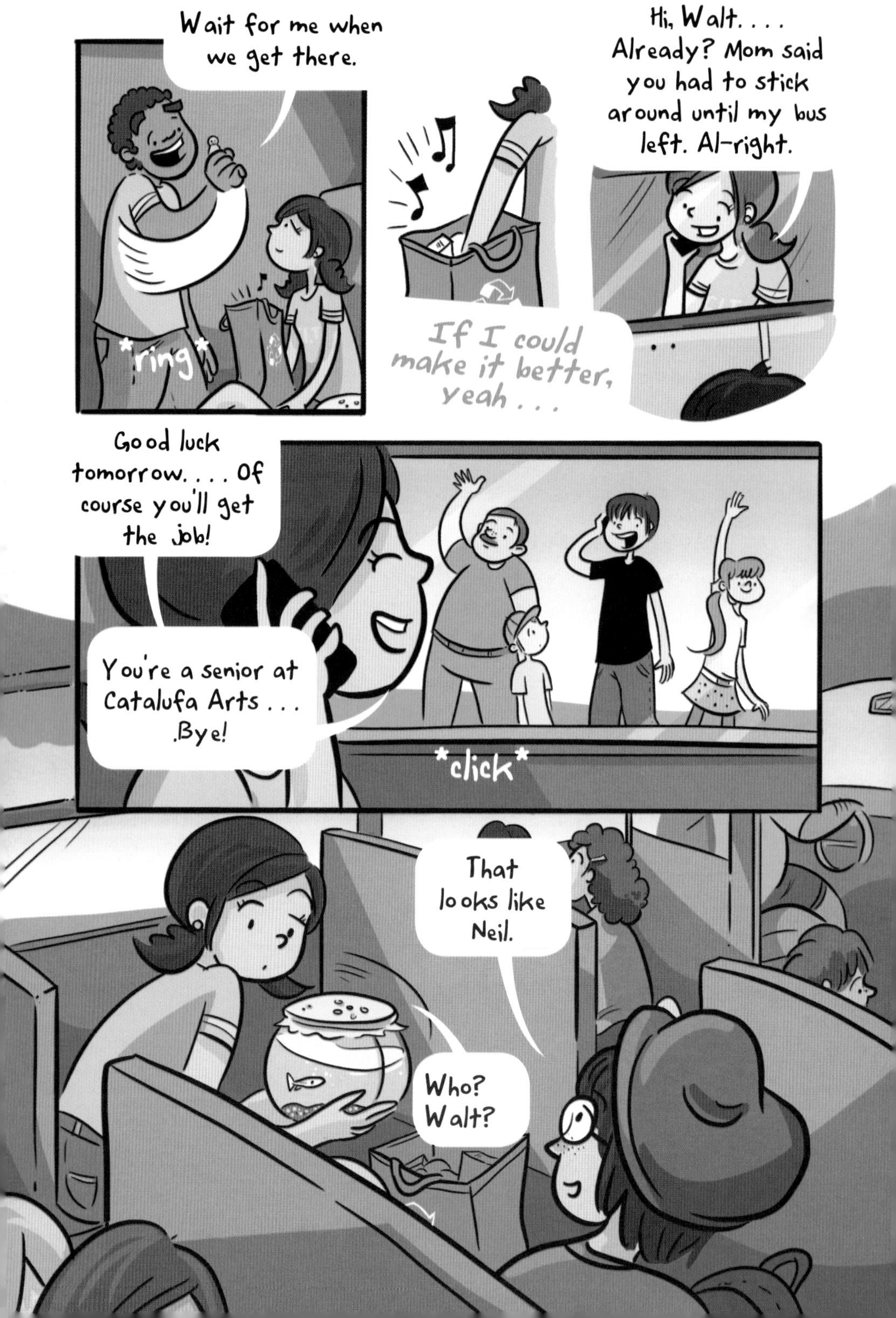
Wait for me when we get there.
ring
If I could make it better, yeah . . .
Hi, Walt. . . . Already? Mom said you had to stick around until my bus left. Al-right.
Good luck tomorrow. . . . Of course you'll get the job!
You're a senior at Catalufa Arts . . . .Bye!
click
That looks like Neil.
Who? Walt?

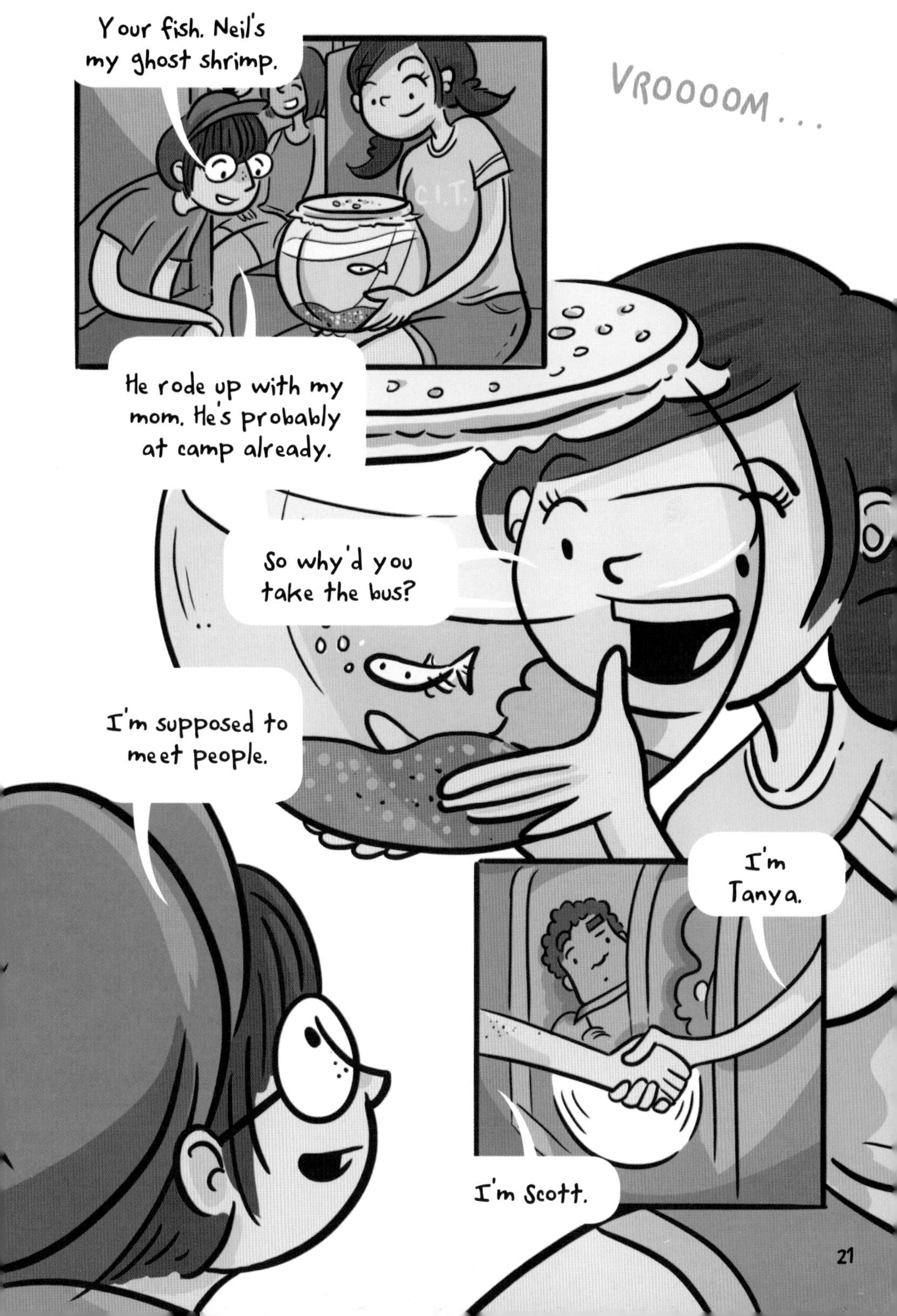
Your fish. Neil's my ghost shrimp.
VROOOOM . . .
He rode up with my mom. He's probably at camp already.
So why'd you take the bus?
I'm supposed to meet people.
I'm Tanya.
I'm Scott.

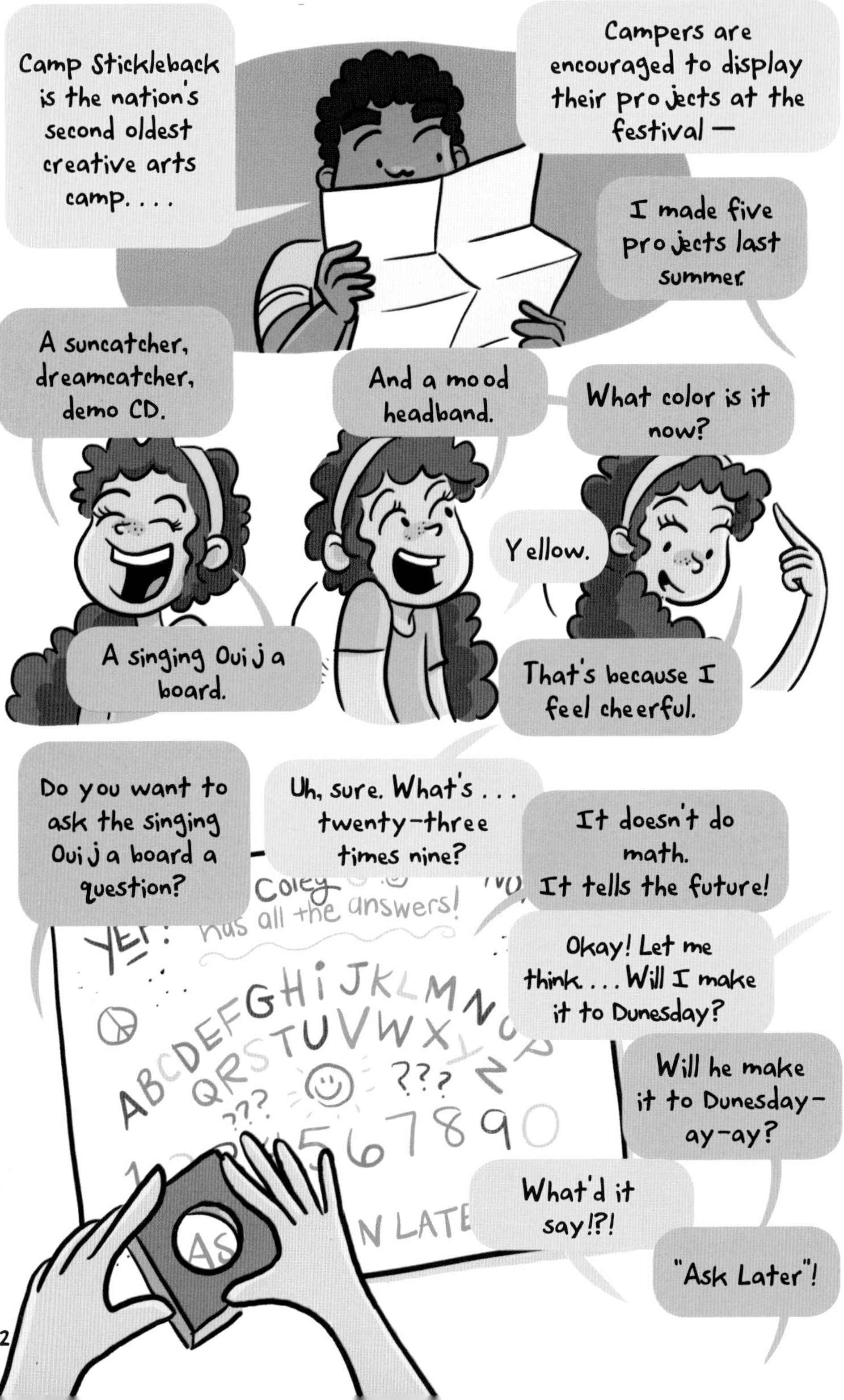
Camp Stickleback is the nation's second oldest creative arts camp. . . .
Campers are encouraged to display their projects at the festival —
I made five projects last summer.
A suncatcher, dreamcatcher, demo CD.
And a mood headband.
What color is it now?
Yellow.
A singing Ouija board.
That's because I feel cheerful.
Do you want to ask the singing Ouija board a question?
Uh, sure. What's . . . twenty-three times nine?
It doesn't do math. It tells the future!
Coley has all the answers!
Okay! Let me think. . . . Will I make it to Dunesday?
Will he make it to Dunesday-ay-ay?
What'd it say!?!
"Ask Later"!

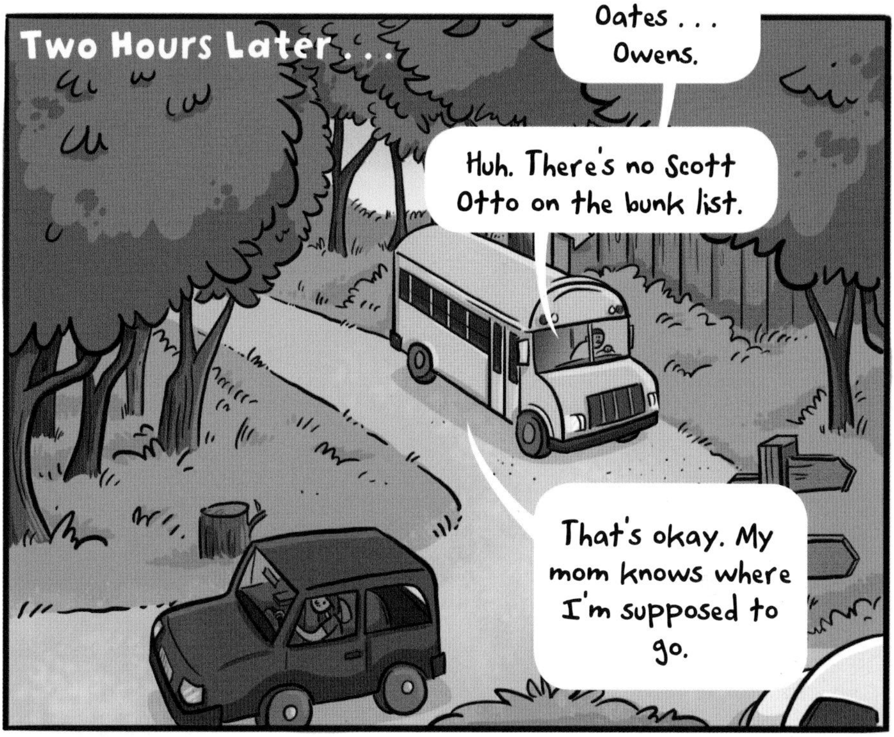
Two Hours Later . . .
Oates . . . Owens.
Huh. There's no Scott Otto on the bunk list.
That's okay. My mom knows where I'm supposed to go.

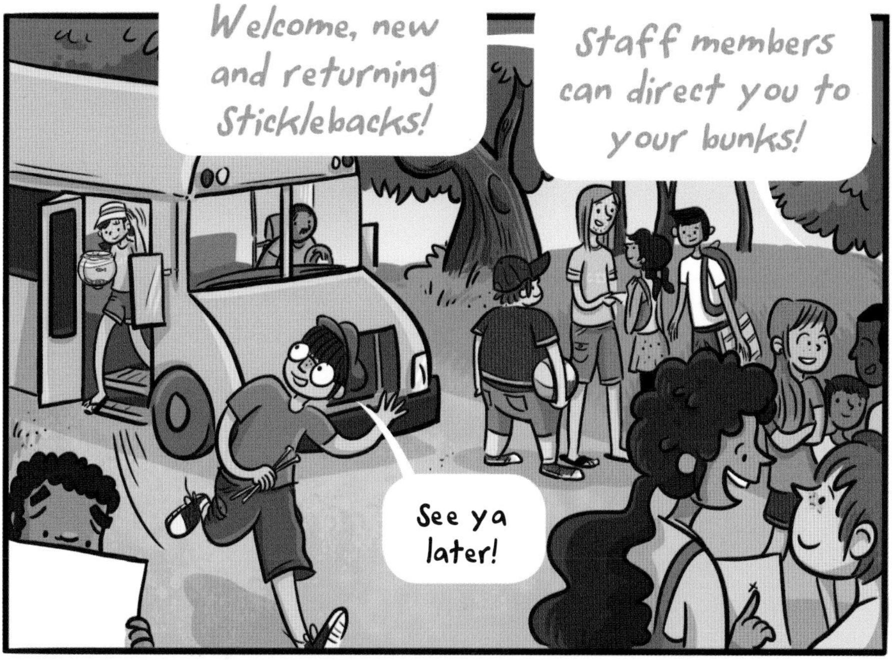
Welcome, new and returning Sticklebacks!
Staff members can direct you to your bunks!
See ya later!

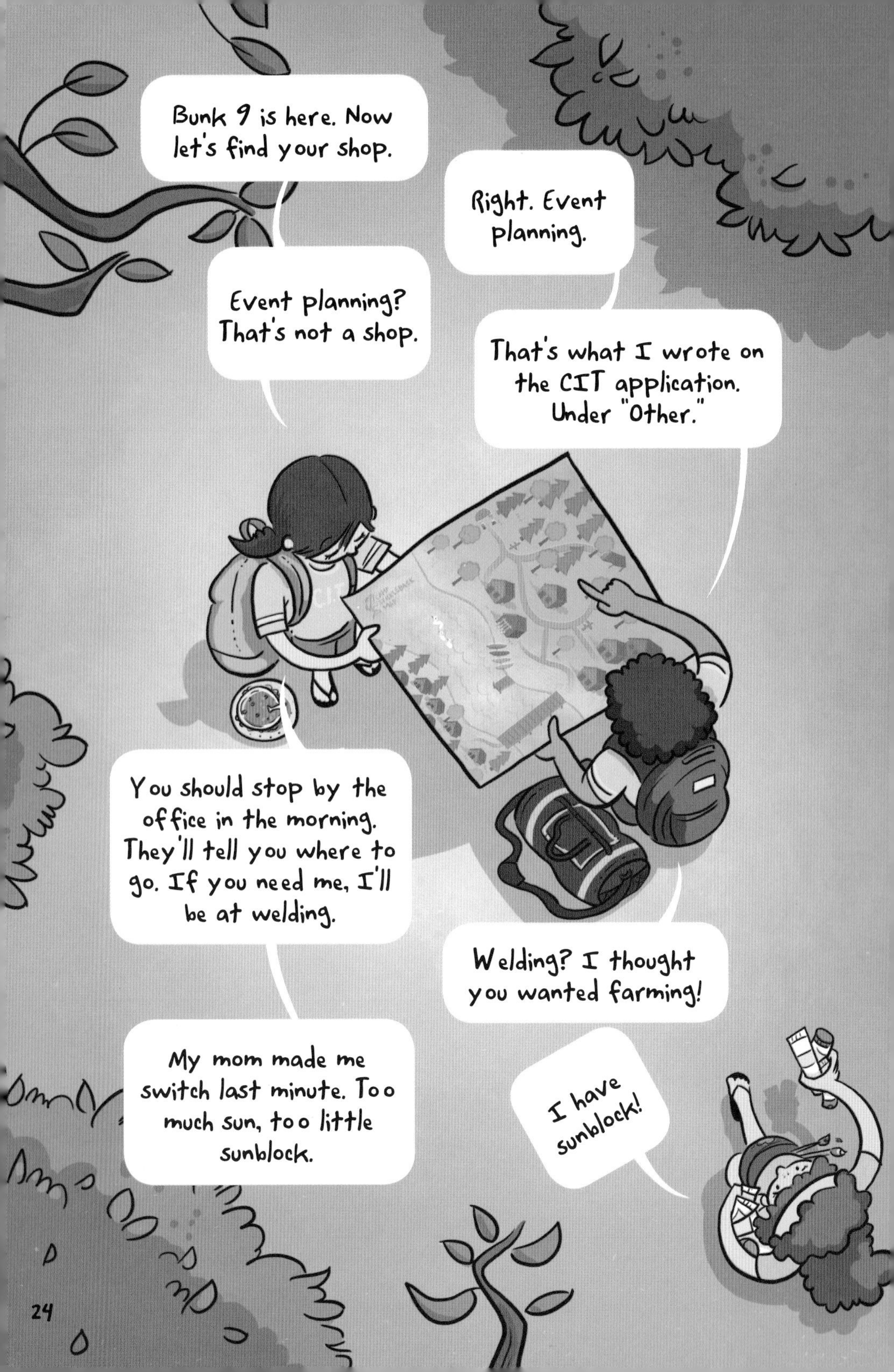
Bunk 9 is here. Now let's find your shop.
Event planning? That's not a shop.
Right. Event planning.
That's what I wrote on the CIT application. Under "Other."
You should stop by the office in the morning. They'll tell you where to go. If you need me, I'll be at welding.
Welding? I thought you wanted farming!
My mom made me switch last minute. Too much sun, too little sunblock.
I have sunblock!

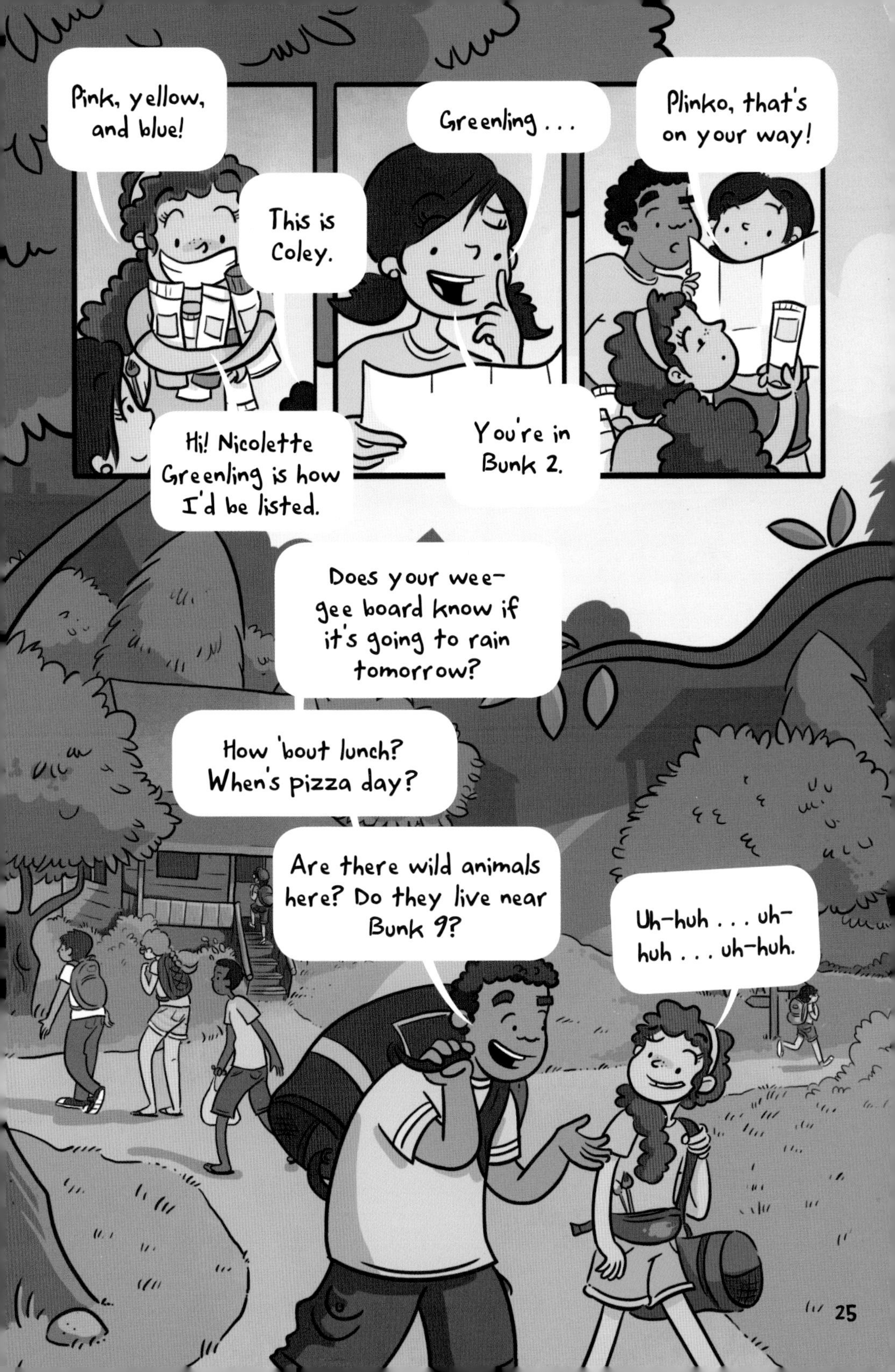

Pink, yellow, and blue!
This is Coley.
Hi! Nicolette Greenling is how I'd be listed.
Greenling . . .
You're in Bunk 2.
Plinko, that's on your way!
Does your wee-gee board know if it's going to rain tomorrow?
How 'bout lunch? When's pizza day?
Are there wild animals here? Do they live near Bunk 9?
Uh-huh . . . uh-huh . . . uh-huh.

4. Bookmobile

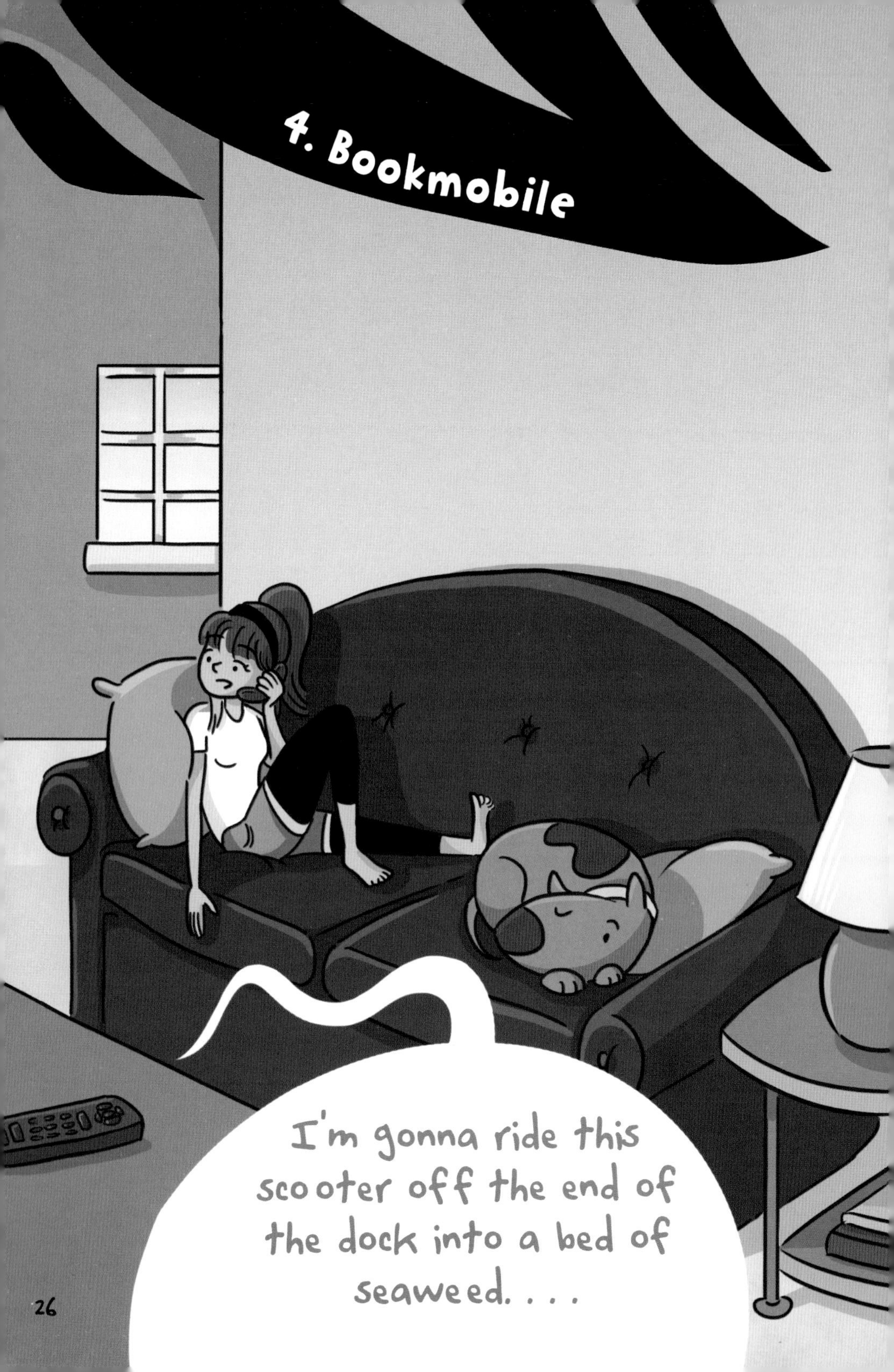
I'm gonna ride this scooter off the end of the dock into a bed of seaweed. . . .

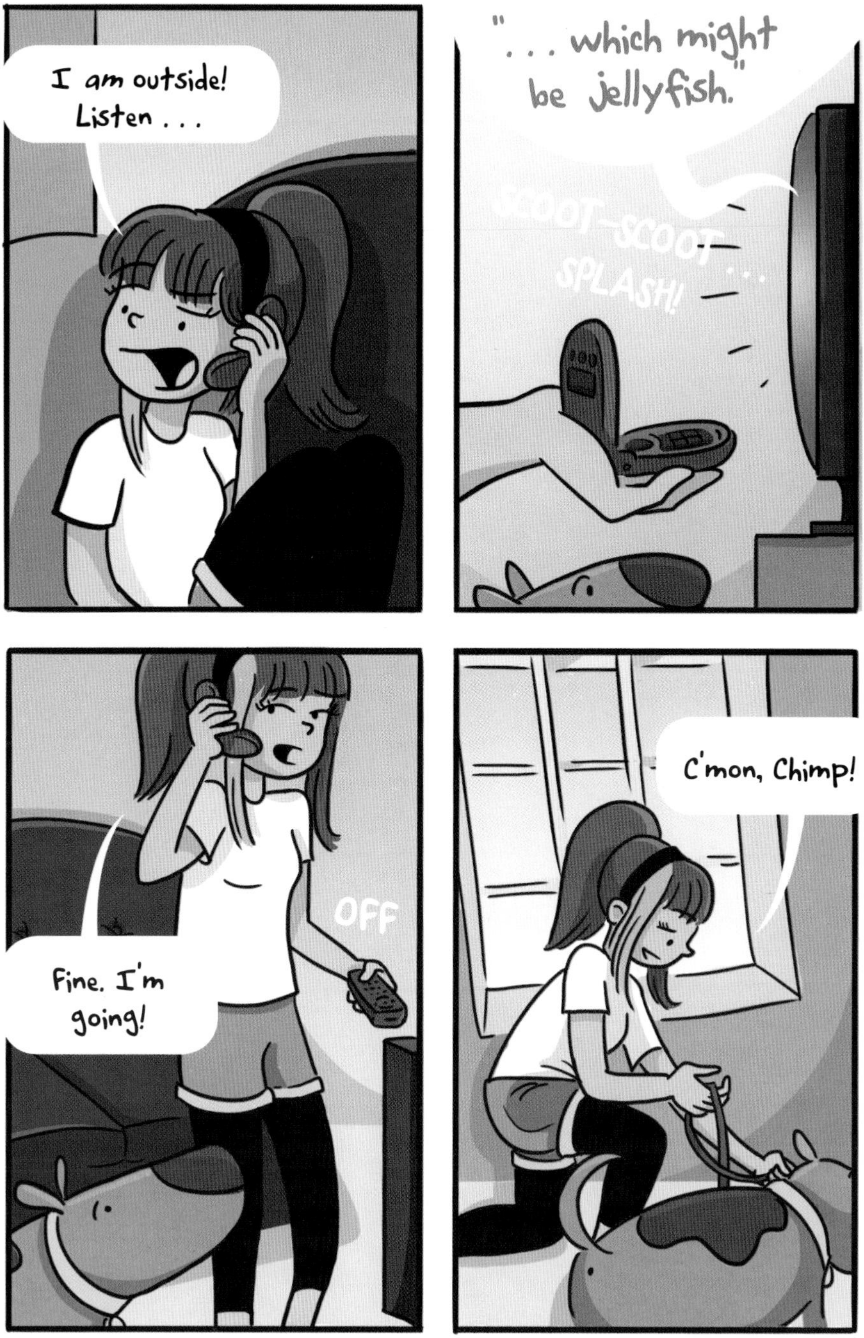
I am outside! Listen . . .
". . . which might be jellyfish."
SCOOT-SCOOT . . .
SPLASH!
OFF
Fine. I'm going!
C'mon, Chimp!

One Hour Later . . .

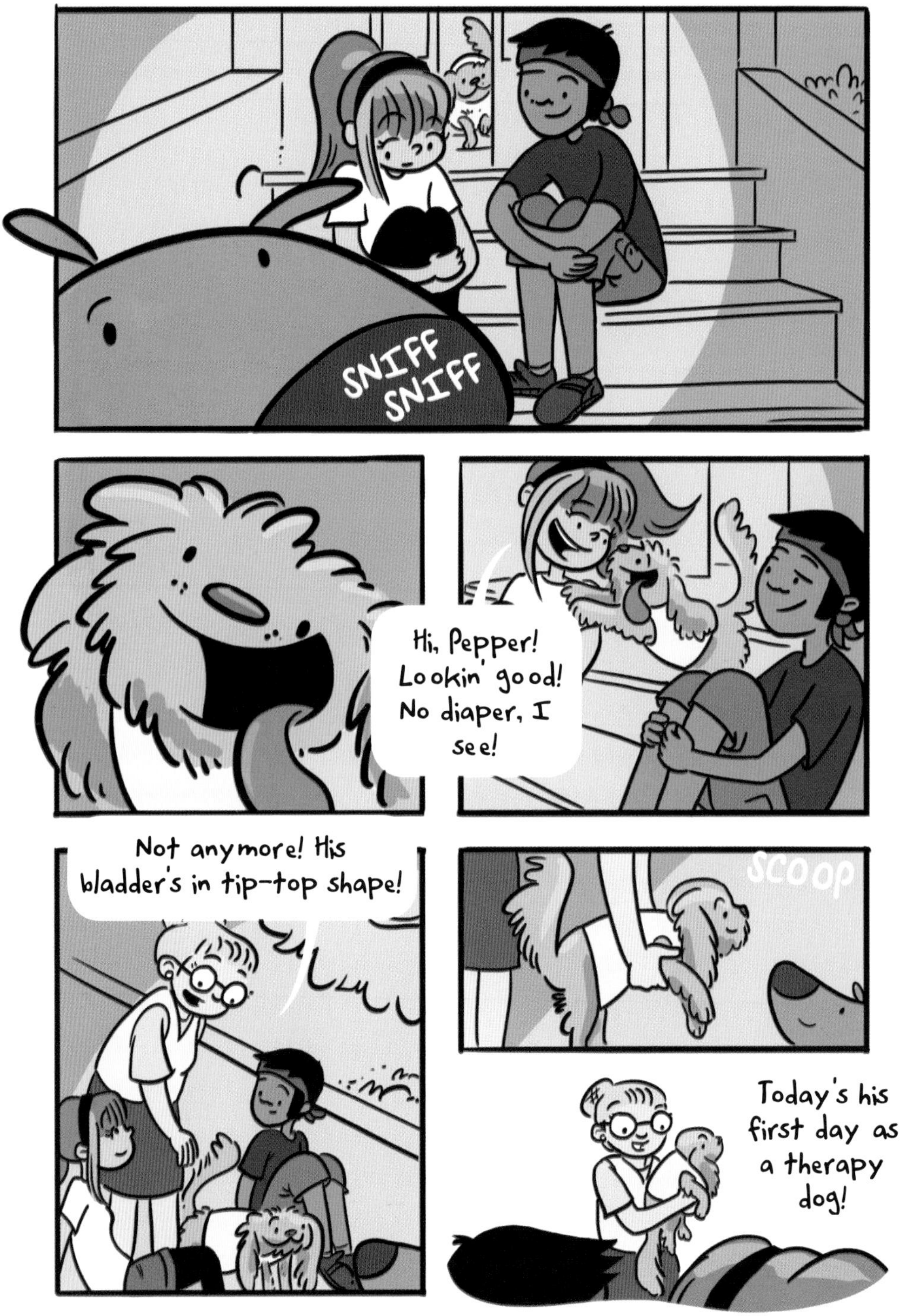
SNIFF SNIFF
Hi, Pepper! Lookin' good! No diaper, I see!
Not anymore! His bladder's in tip-top shape!
SCOOP
Today's his first day as a therapy dog!

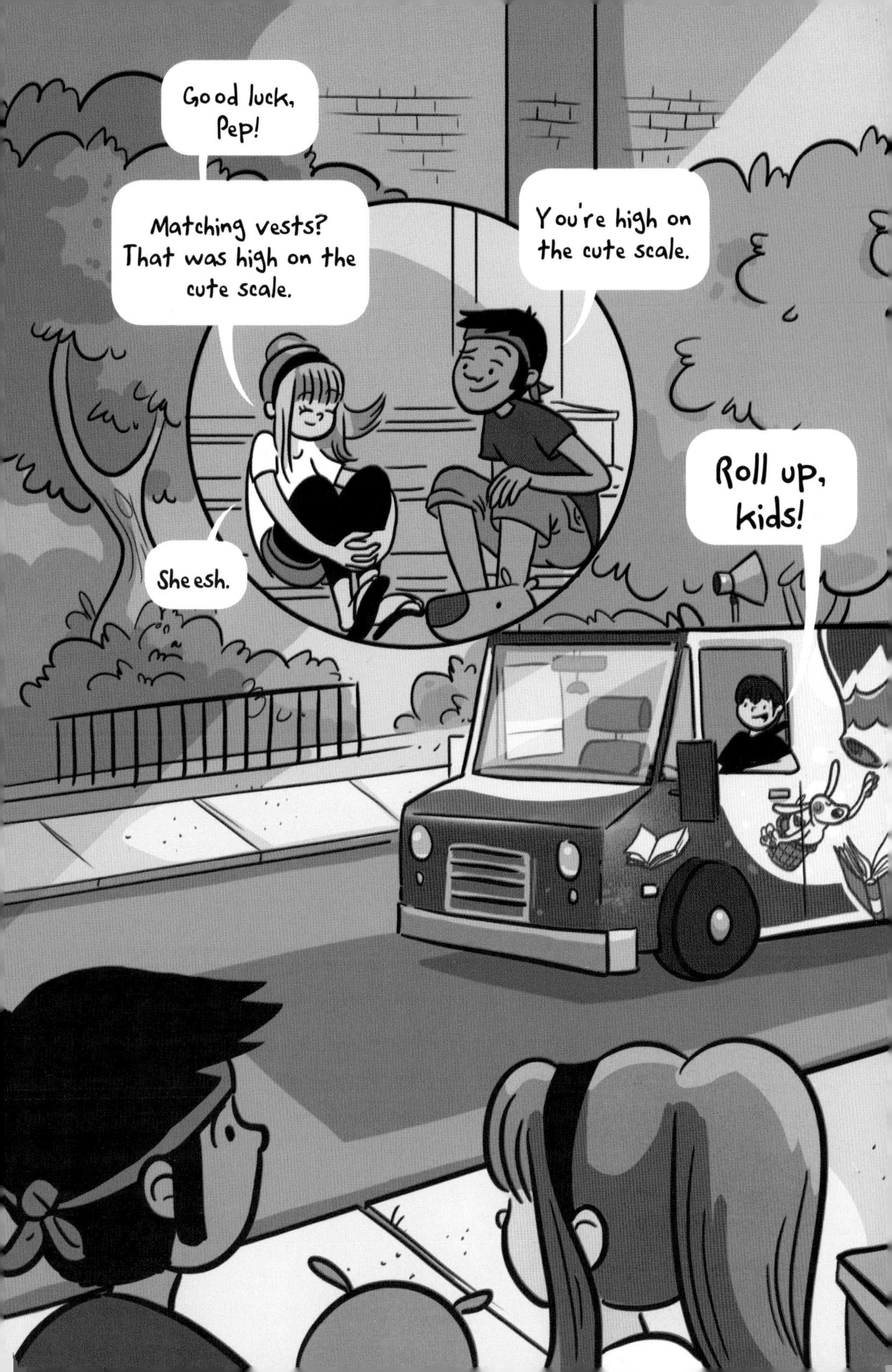
Good luck, Pep!
Matching vests? That was high on the cute scale.
You're high on the cute scale.
Sheesh.
Roll up, kids!

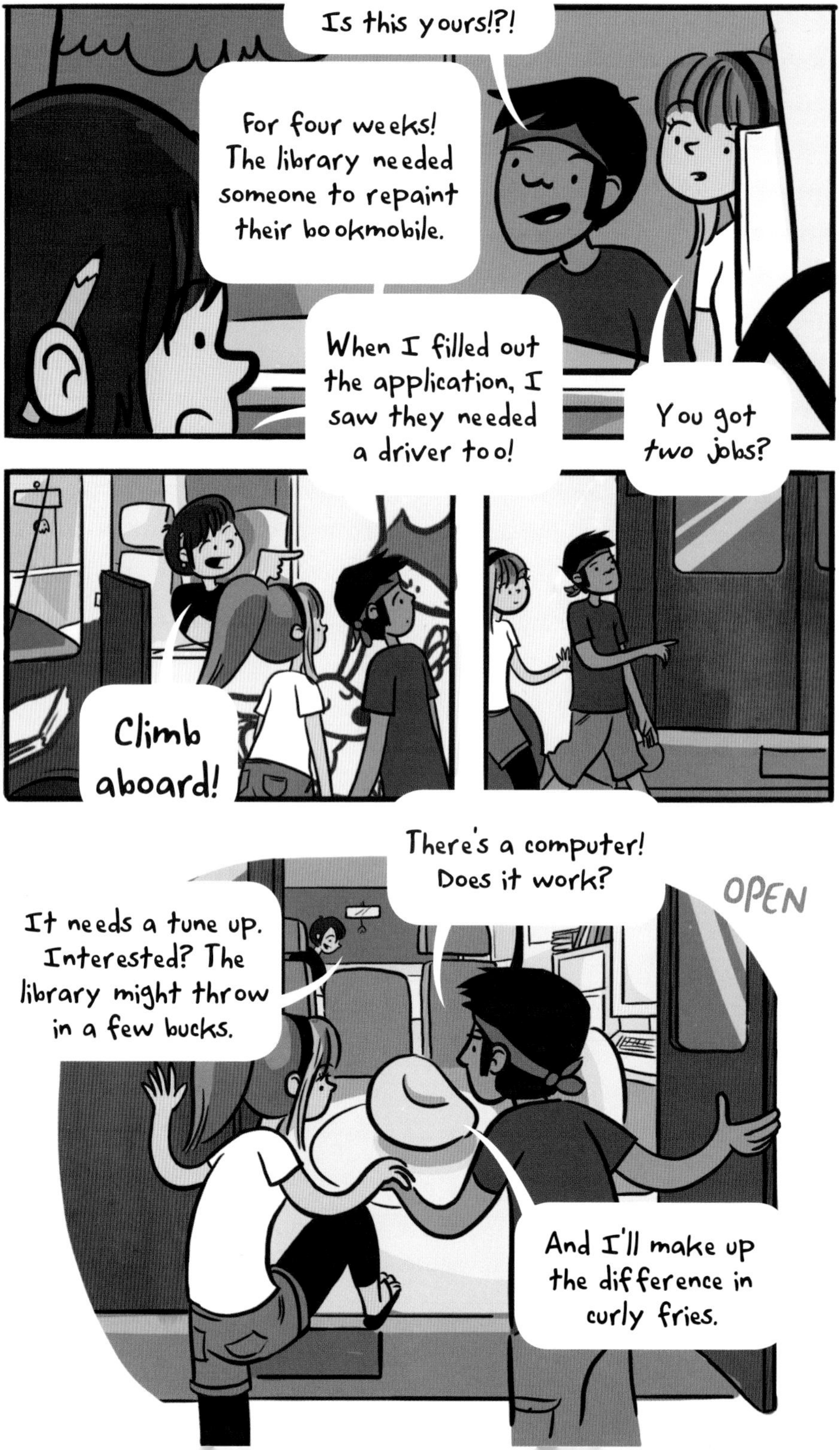
Is this yours!?!
For four weeks! The library needed someone to repaint their bookmobile.
When I filled out the application, I saw they needed a driver too!
You got two jobs?
Climb aboard!
There's a computer! Does it work?
OPEN
It needs a tune up. Interested? The library might throw in a few bucks.
And I'll make up the difference in curly fries.

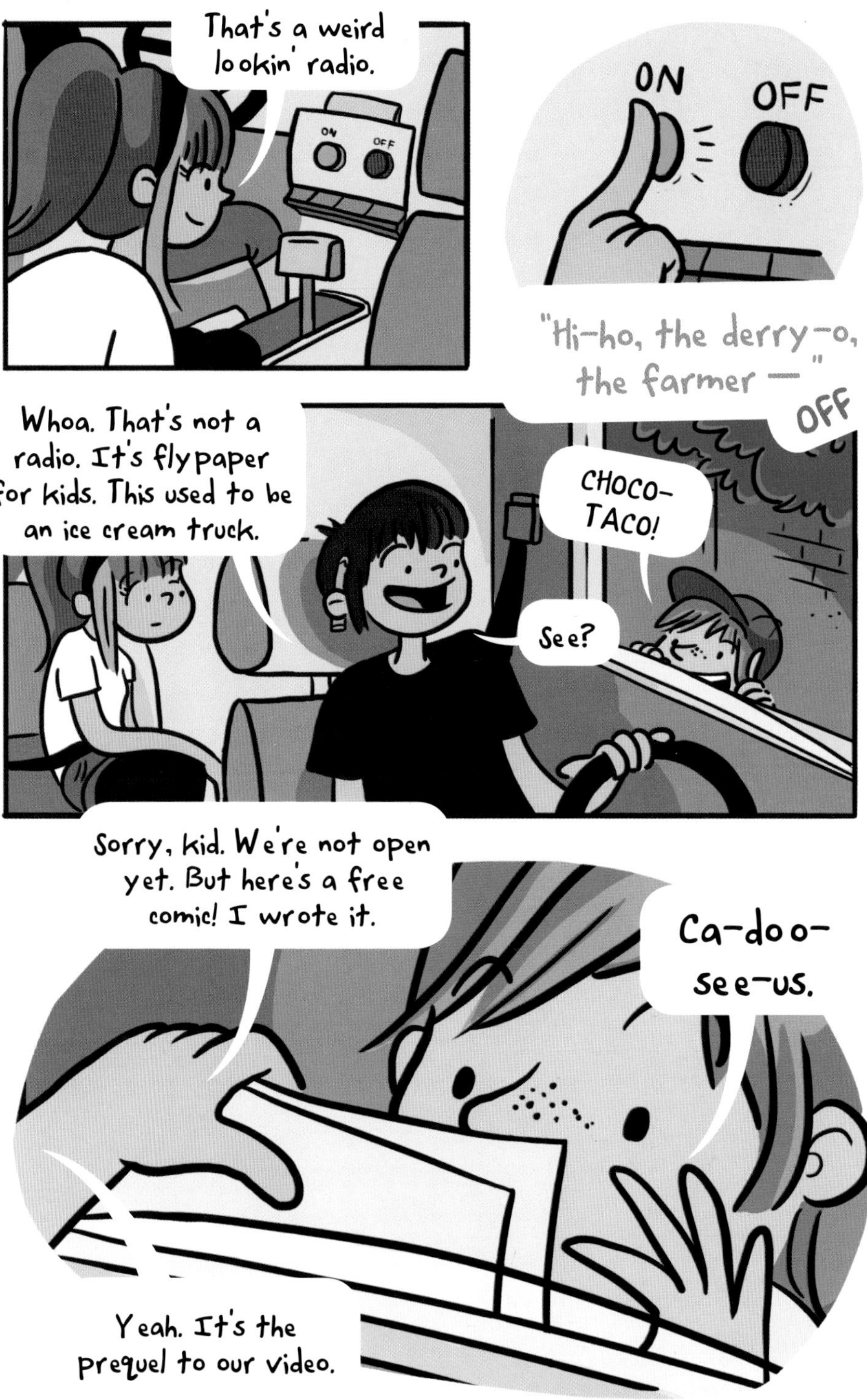
That's a weird lookin' radio.
ON
OFF
ON
OFF
"Hi-ho, the derry-o, the farmer —"
OFF
Whoa. That's not a radio. It's flypaper for kids. This used to be an ice cream truck.
CHOCO-TACO!
See?
Sorry, kid. We're not open yet. But here's a free comic! I wrote it.
Ca-doo-see-us.
Yeah. It's the prequel to our video.

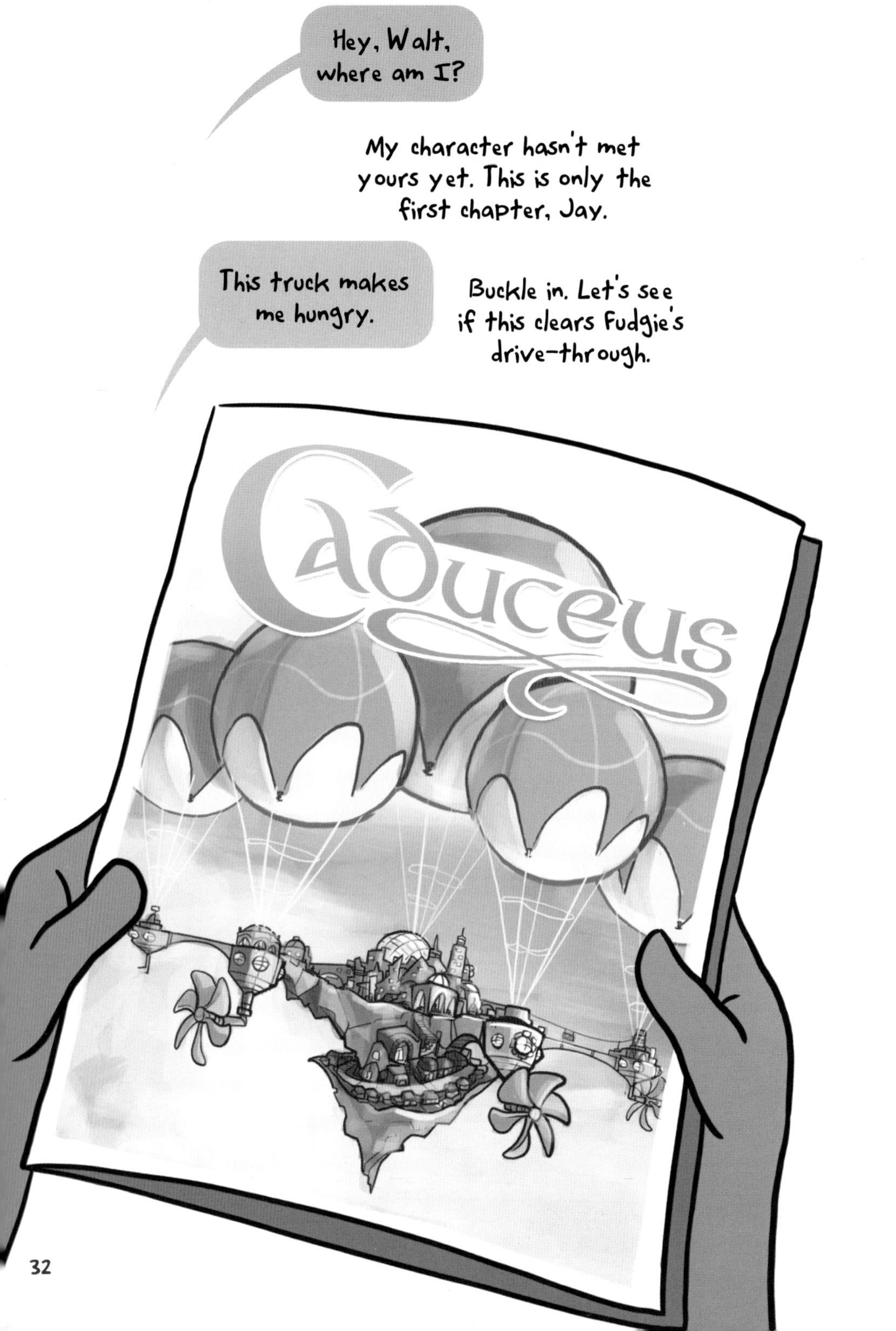
Hey, Walt, where am I?
My character hasn't met yours yet. This is only the first chapter, Jay.
This truck makes me hungry.
Buckle in. Let's see if this clears Fudgie's drive-through.
Caduceus

5. Spoonyard

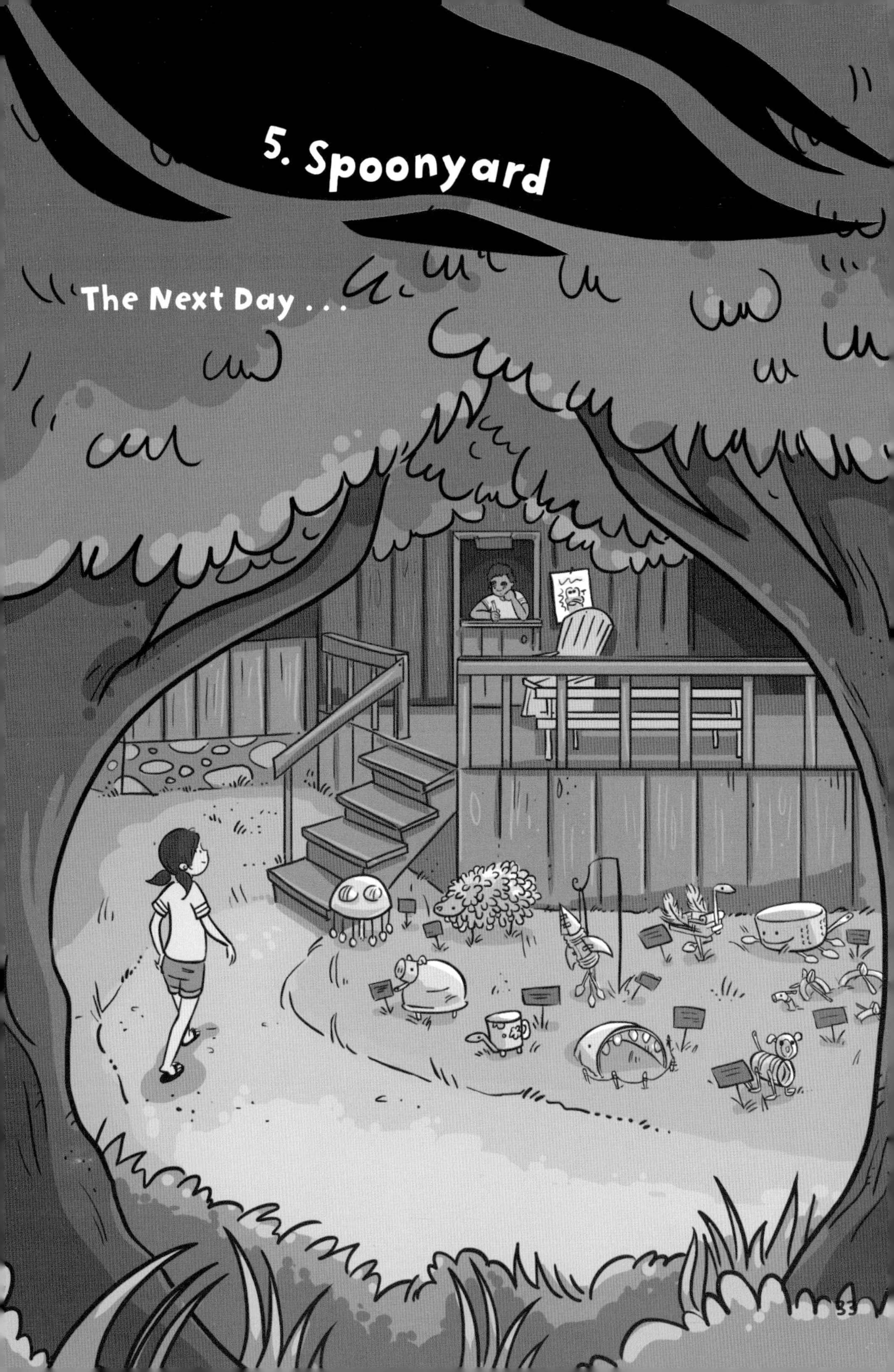
The Next Day . . .

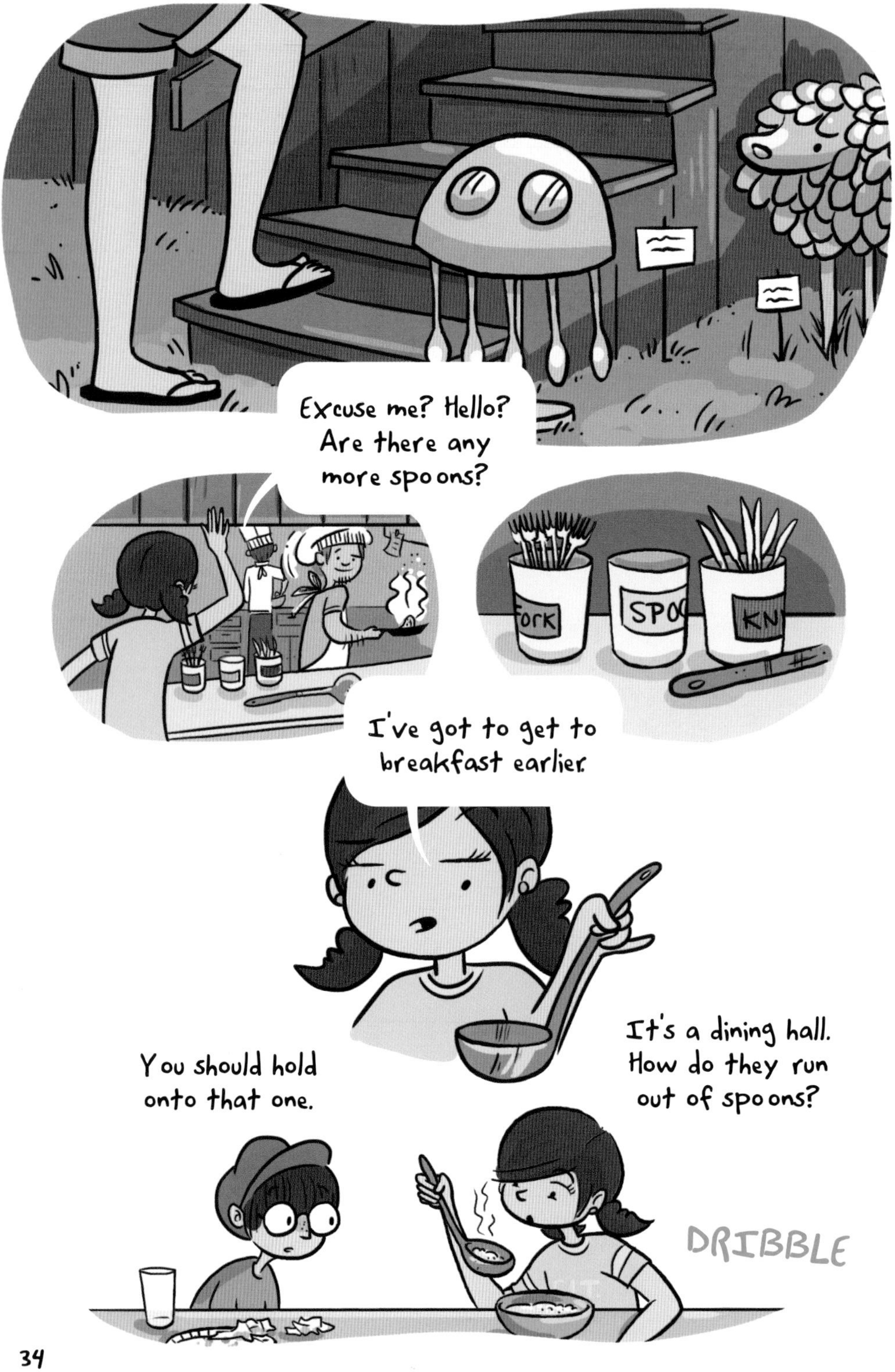

Excuse me? Hello? Are there any more spoons?
FORK
SPOO
KNI
I've got to get to breakfast earlier.
You should hold onto that one.
It's a dining hall. How do they run out of spoons?
DRIBBLE

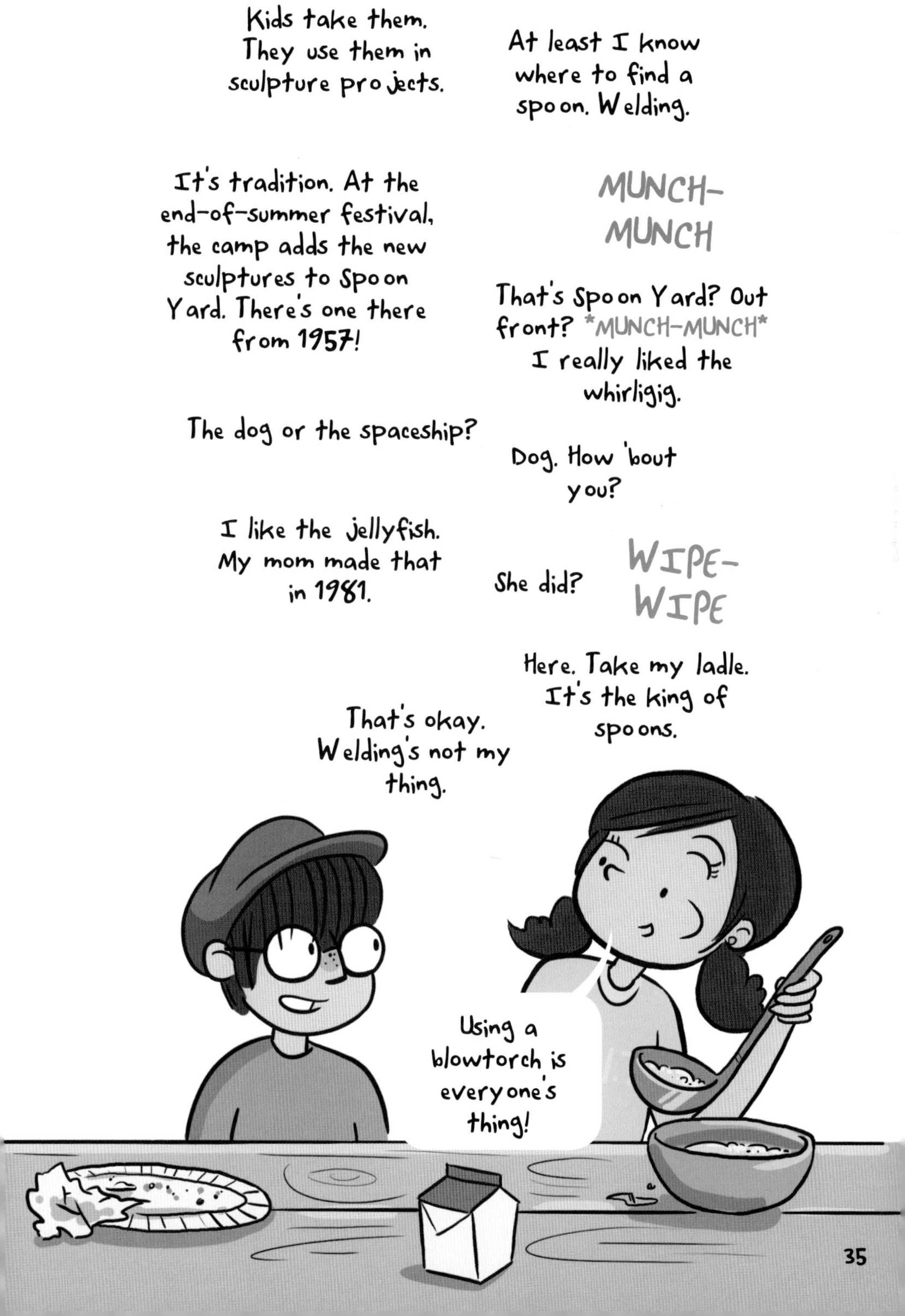
Kids take them. They use them in sculpture projects.
At least I know where to find a spoon. Welding.
It's tradition. At the end-of-summer festival, the camp adds the new sculptures to Spoon Yard. There's one there from 1957!
MUNCH-MUNCH
That's Spoon Yard? Out front? *MUNCH-MUNCH* I really liked the whirligig.
The dog or the spaceship?
Dog. How 'bout you?
I like the jellyfish. My mom made that in 1981.
She did?
WIPE-WIPE
Here. Take my ladle. It's the king of spoons.
That's okay. Welding's not my thing.
Using a blowtorch is everyone's thing!

Later That Day . . .

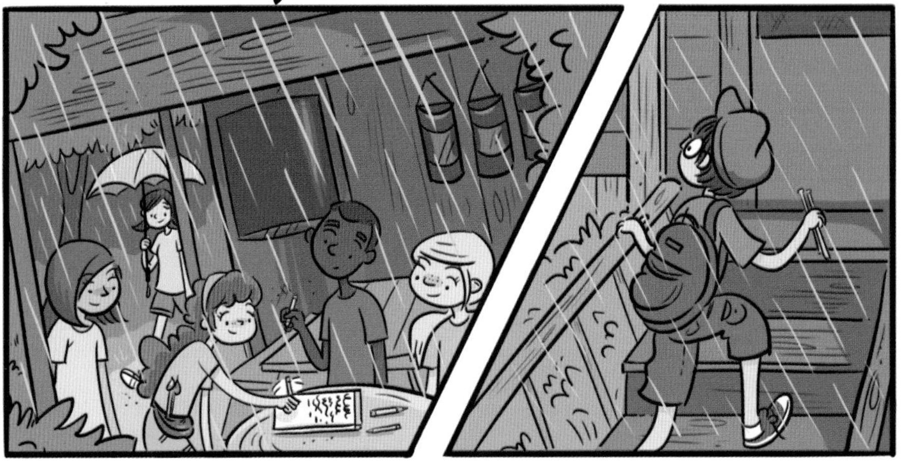

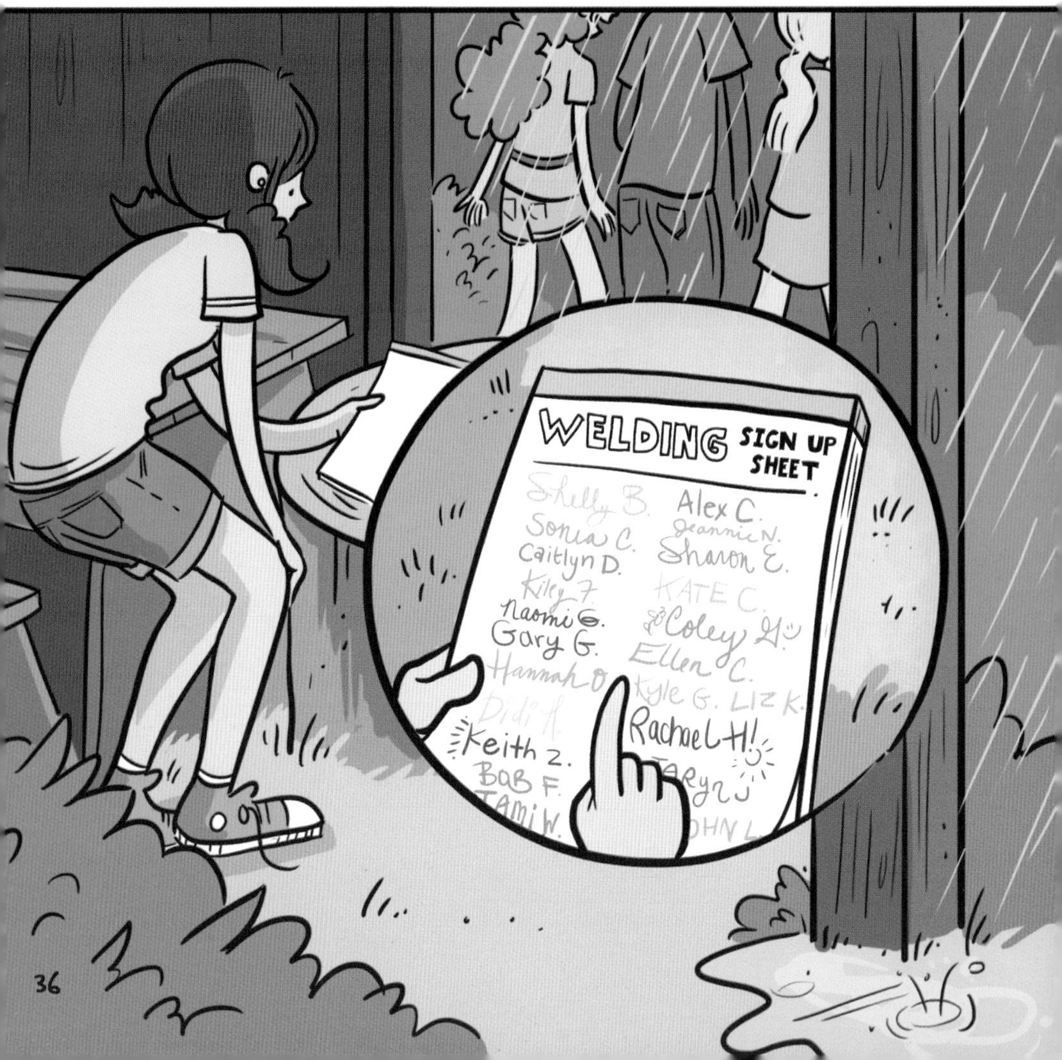
WELDING SIGN UP SHEET
Shelly B.
Alex C.
Sonia C.
Jeannie N.
Caitlyn D.
Sharon E.
Kiley Z.
KATE C.
Naomi G.
Coley G.
Gary G.
Ellen C.
Hannah O.
Kyle G.
LIZ K.
Rachael H!
Keith Z.
BOB F.
TAMI W.

6. Go, Team

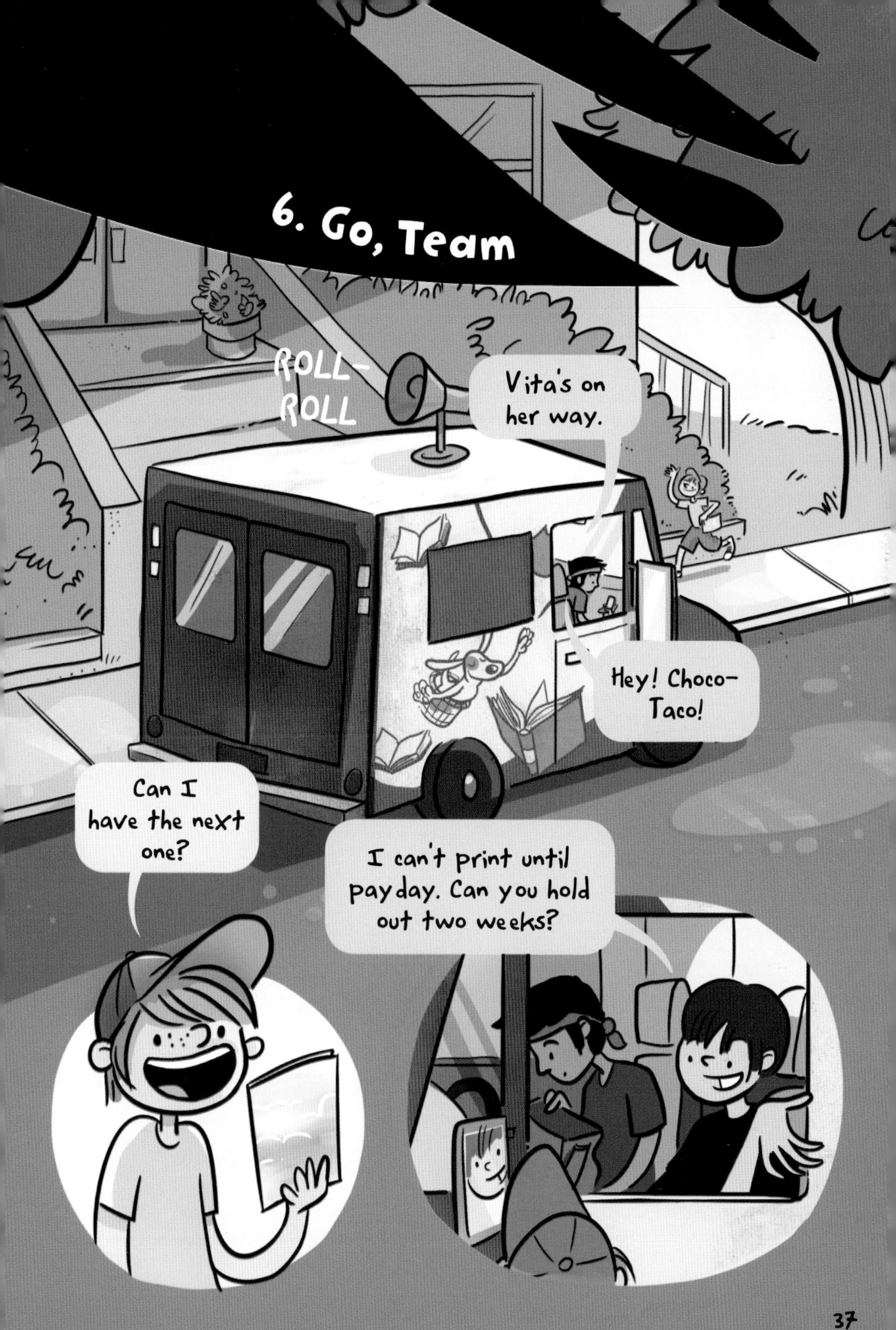

ROLL-
ROLL
Vita's on her way.
Hey! Choco-Taco!
Can I have the next one?
I can't print until payday. Can you hold out two weeks?

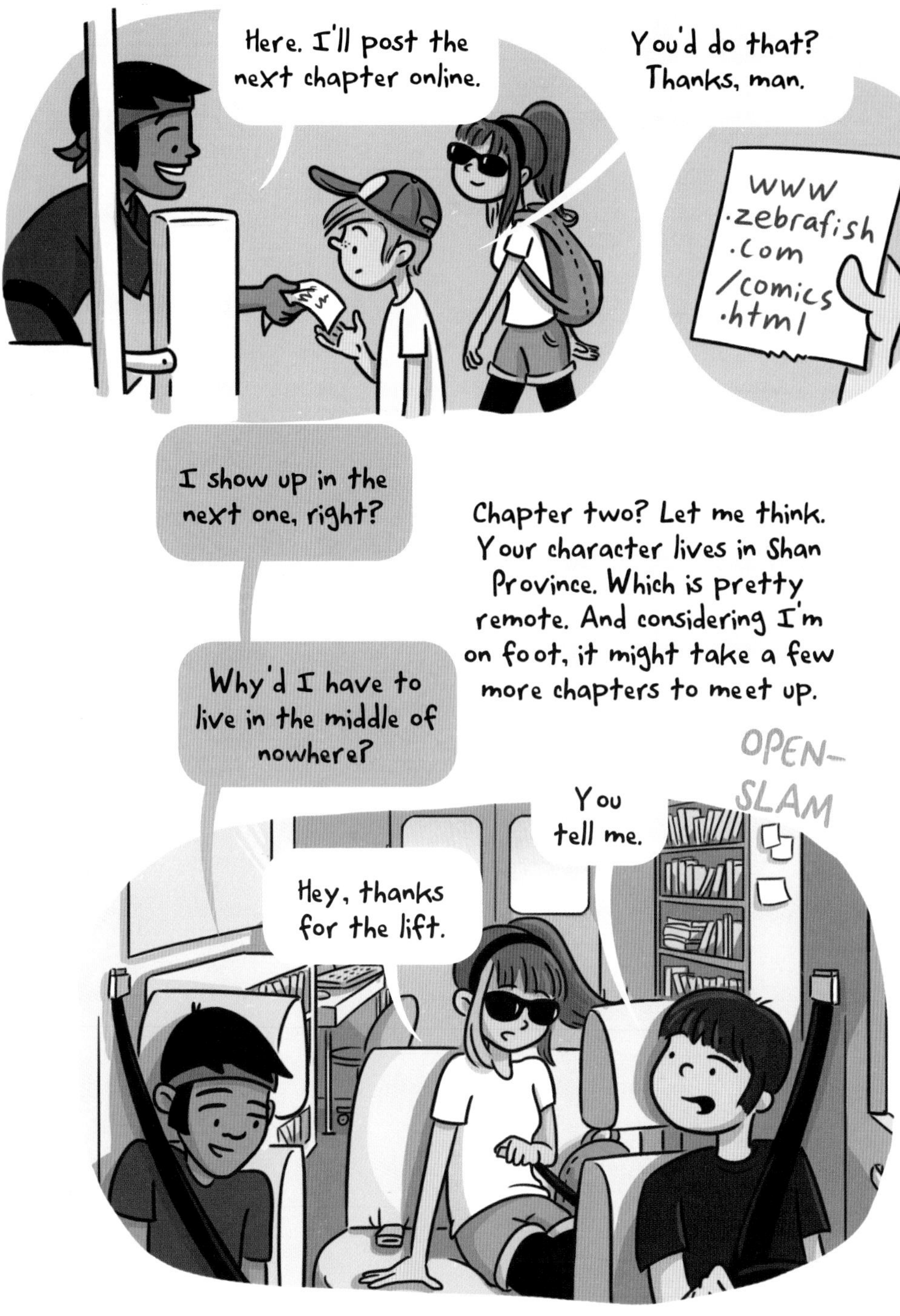
Here. I'll post the next chapter online.
You'd do that? Thanks, man.
www .zebrafish .com /comics .html
I show up in the next one, right?
Chapter two? Let me think. Your character lives in Shan Province. Which is pretty remote. And considering I'm on foot, it might take a few more chapters to meet up.
Why'd I have to live in the middle of nowhere?
OPEN-SLAM
You tell me.
Hey, thanks for the lift.

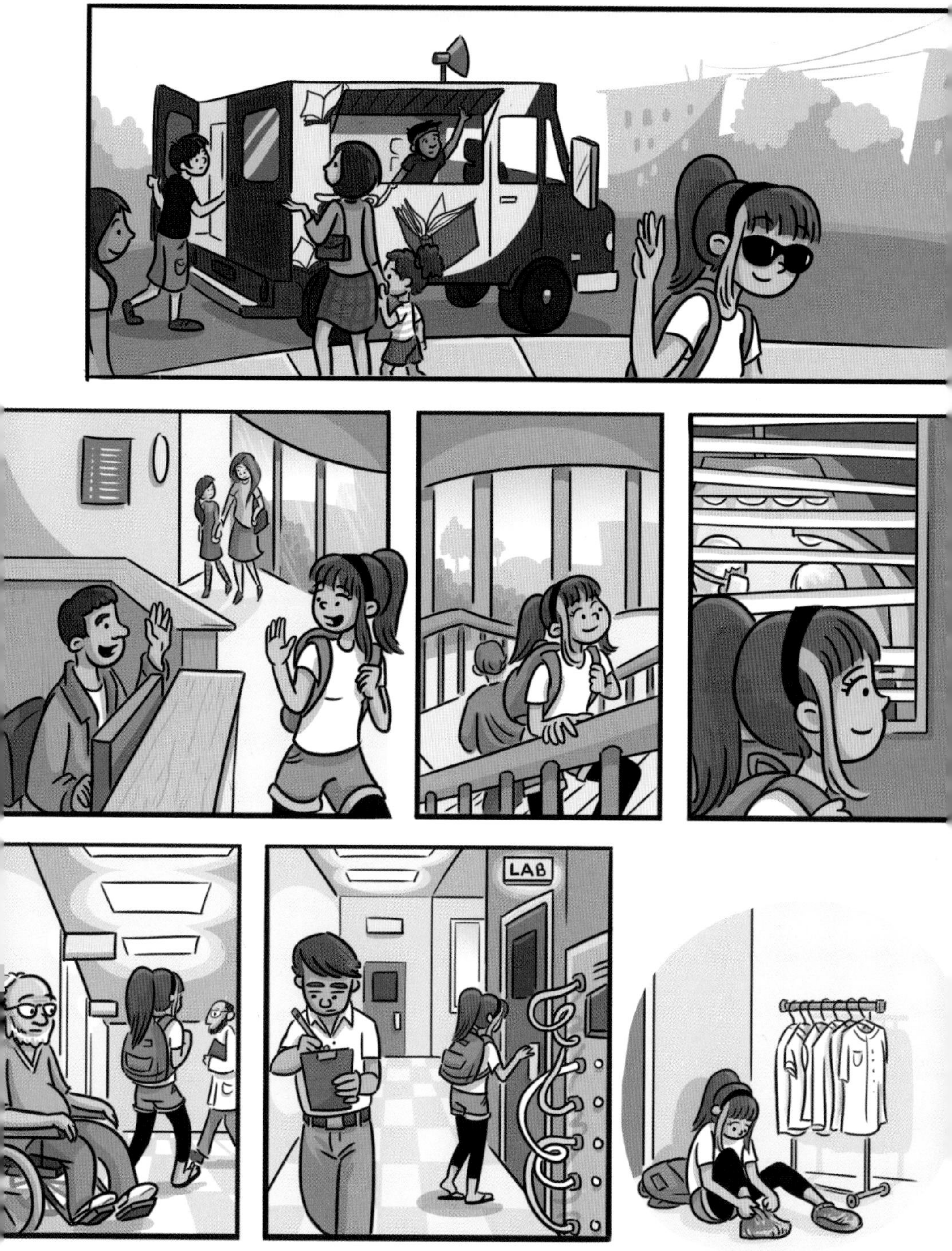
LAB

Hi, Pablo.

Look who's here! *Before* noon! Can you stick around for lunch?

I'm on a tight schedule. If I ride the bookmobile in the morning, I can be back home in time for *Double Dog Dare*.

GROAN

What? I'm getting fresh air. Isn't that what you wanted?

Can you combine fresh air with another activity?

Does walking count?

Now there's an idea! You could be a dog walker.

Oh, you mean a job.

Why not? Jay found work.

The bookmobile job fell into his lap. Walt doesn't need me.

He might. Think about what you can bring to the table.

What is this?

That's the new zebrafish.

He's glowing! Would my hand glow under the microscope?

No. I have a toolkit that lets me attach fluorescent proteins to cells. I can make any cell glow in any color I want: green, red, yellow—

Purple?

And purple. Once the cell's glowing, I can see what's going on in and around it.

Nothin's going on.

Keep looking.

See that pack of green tumor cells? They're trying to bust into the bloodstream. Usually they can, no problem.

So what's stopping them?

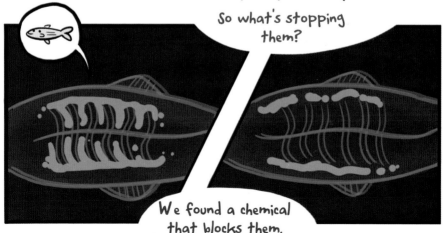

We found a chemical that blocks them.

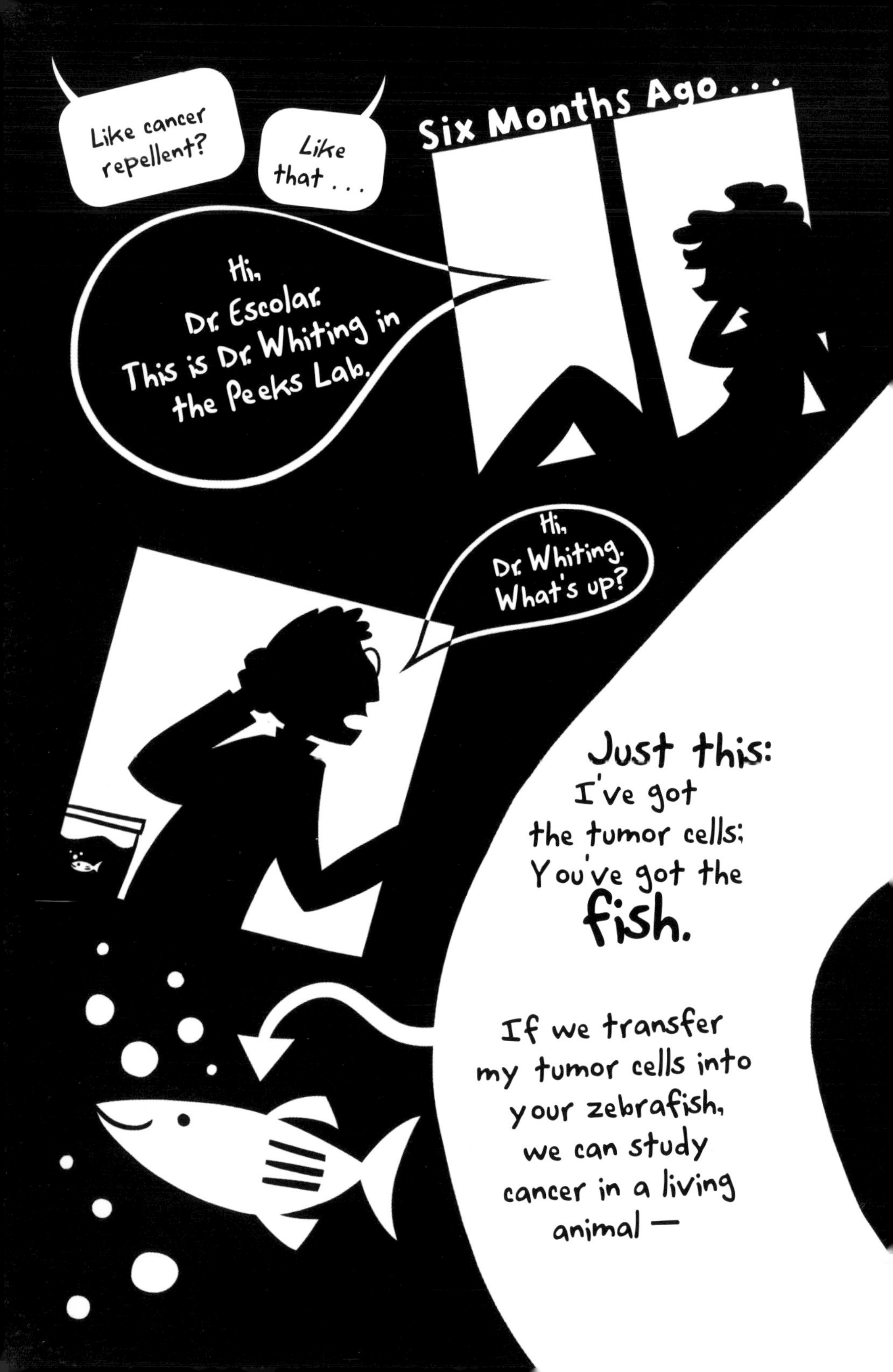
Like cancer repellent?
Like that . . .
Six Months Ago . . .
Hi, Dr. Escolar. This is Dr. Whiting in the Peeks Lab.
Hi, Dr. Whiting. What's up?
Just this: I've got the tumor cells; You've got the fish.
If we transfer my tumor cells into your zebrafish, we can study cancer in a living animal —

of course!
If we find a drug that'll beat cancer in zebrafish,
there's a good chance it'll work in mice.
Then humans!
We can identify promising drugs faster!
Bingo!

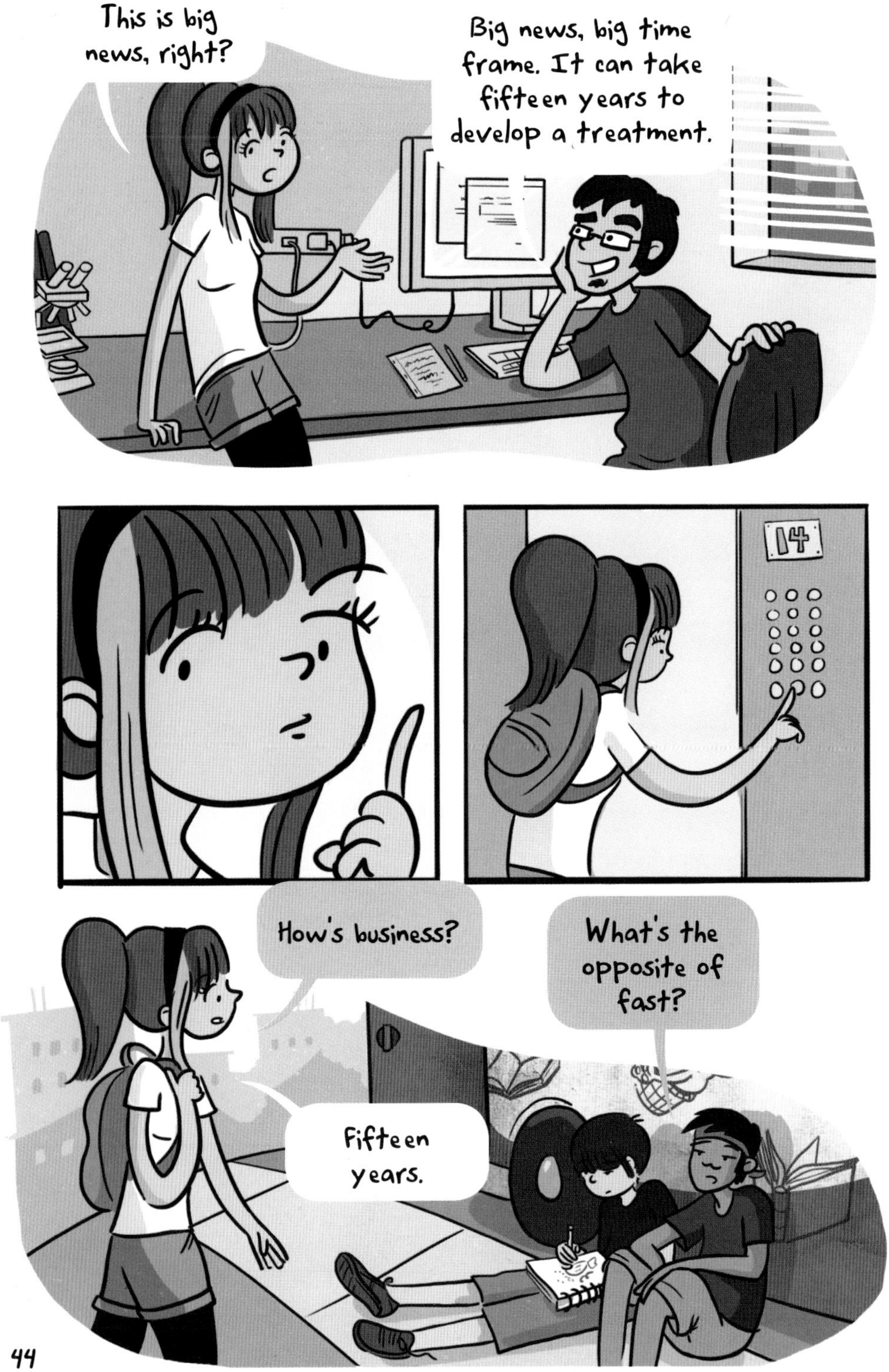
This is big news, right?
Big news, big time frame. It can take fifteen years to develop a treatment.
14
How's business?
Fifteen years.
What's the opposite of fast?

7. Lost and Found

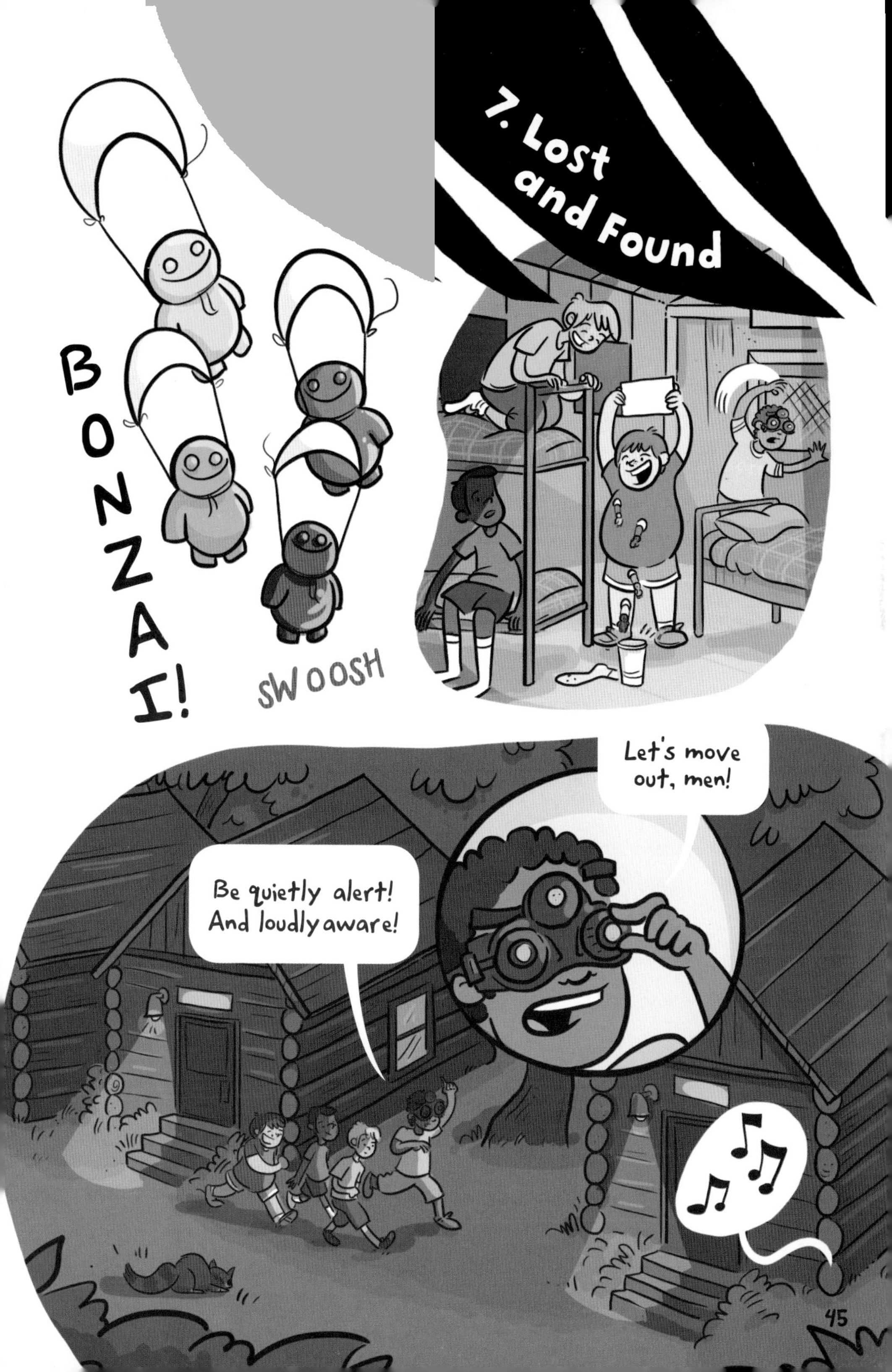
BONZAI!
SWOOSH
Let's move out, men!
Be quietly alert! And loudly aware!

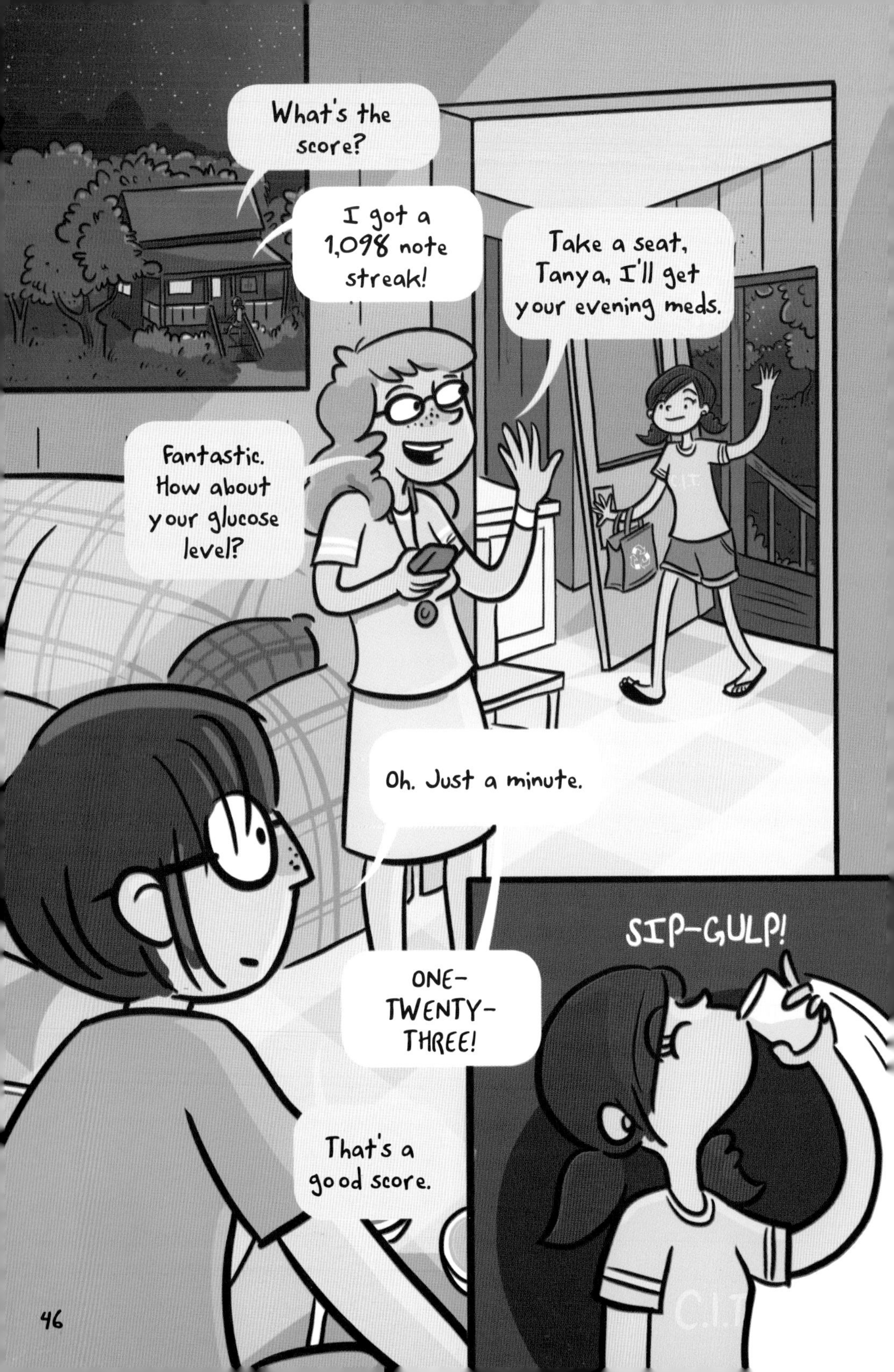
What's the score?
I got a 1,098 note streak!
Take a seat, Tanya, I'll get your evening meds.
Fantastic. How about your glucose level?
Oh. Just a minute.
ONE-TWENTY-THREE!
That's a good score.
SIP-GULP!
C.I.T.

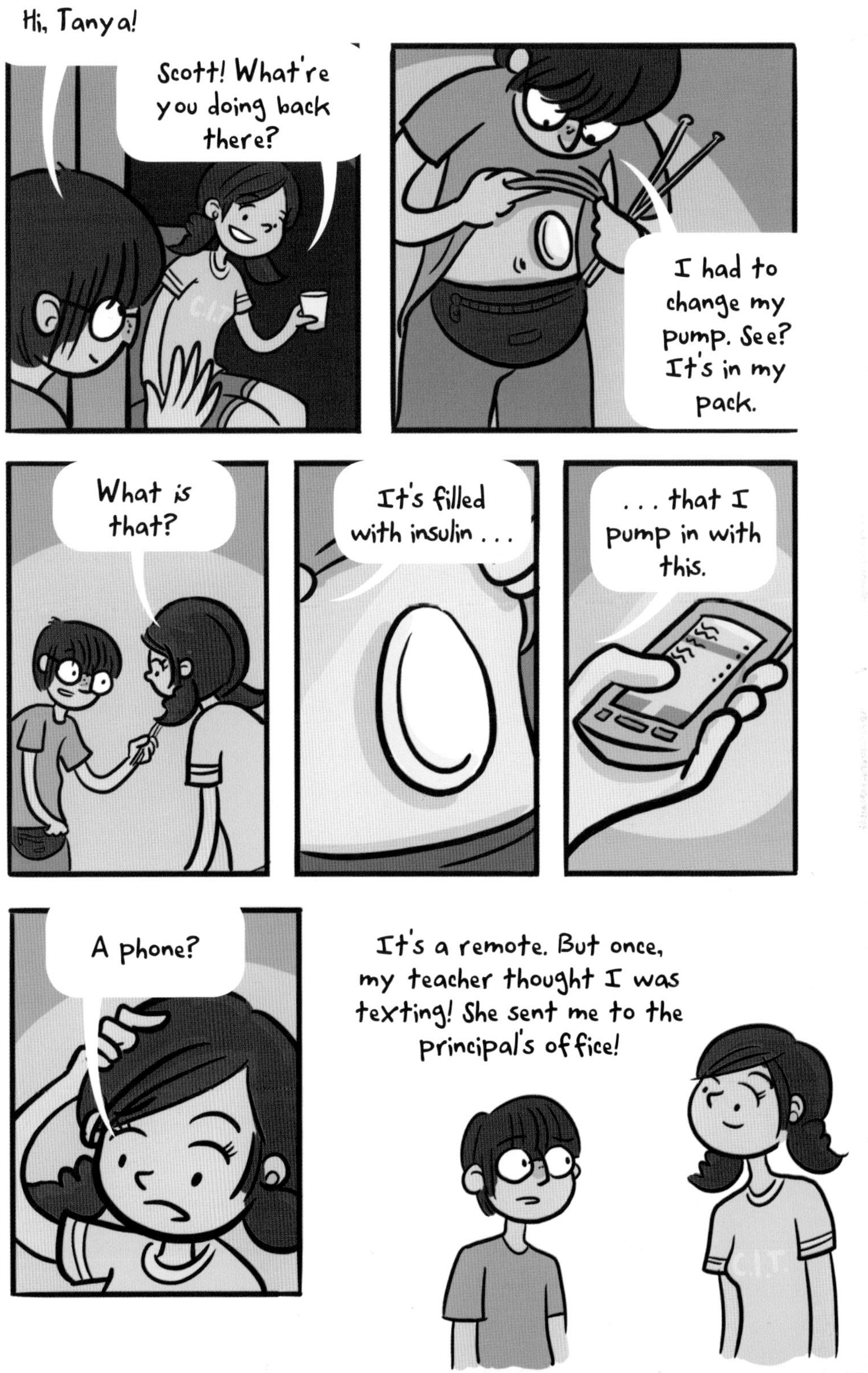
Hi, Tanya!
Scott! What're you doing back there?
I had to change my pump. See? It's in my pack.
What is that?
It's filled with insulin . . .
. . . that I pump in with this.
A phone?
It's a remote. But once, my teacher thought I was texting! She sent me to the principal's office!

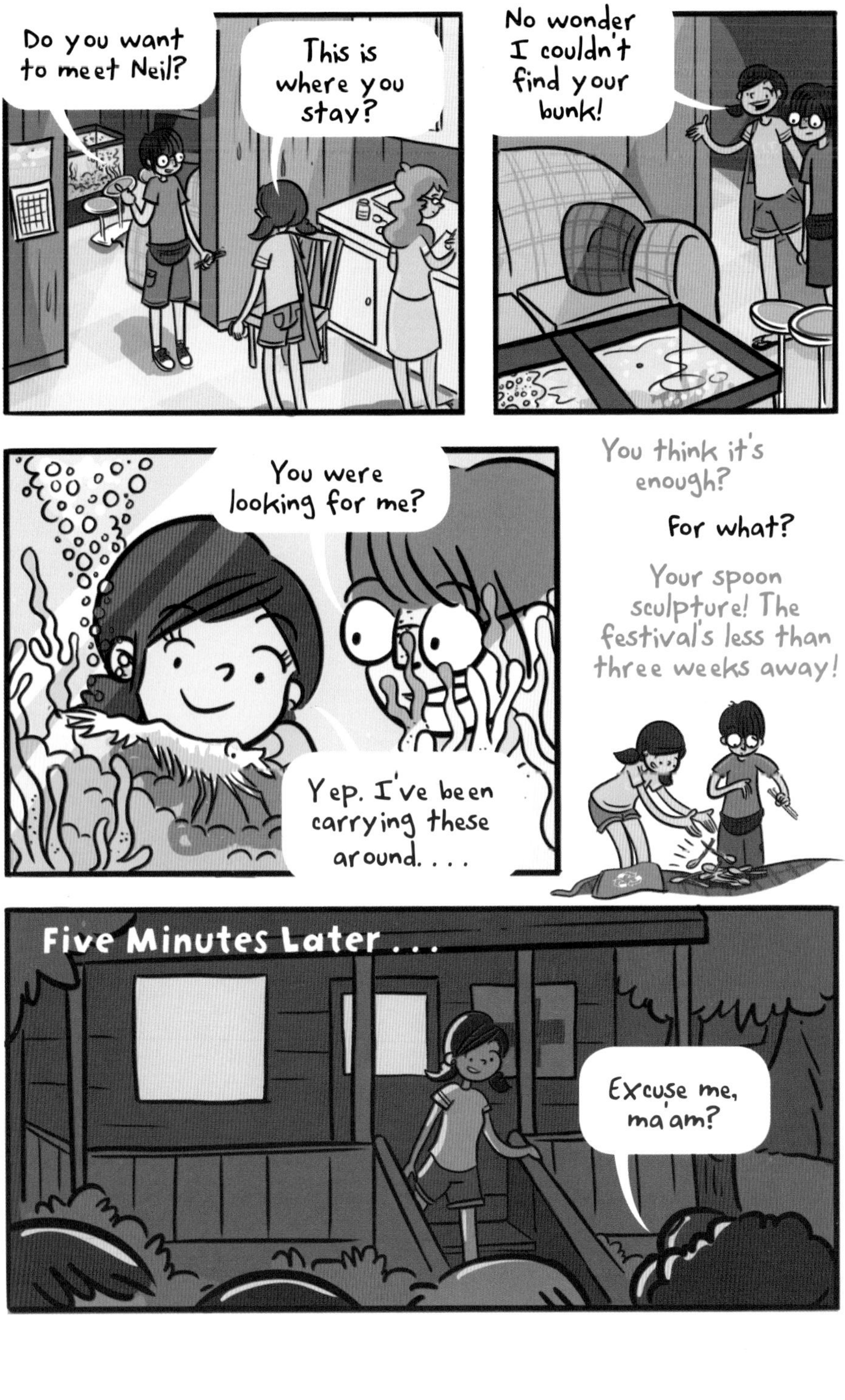
Do you want to meet Neil?
This is where you stay?
No wonder I couldn't find your bunk!
You were looking for me?
Yep. I've been carrying these around. . . .
You think it's enough?
For what?
Your spoon sculpture! The festival's less than three weeks away!
Five Minutes Later . . .
Excuse me, ma'am?

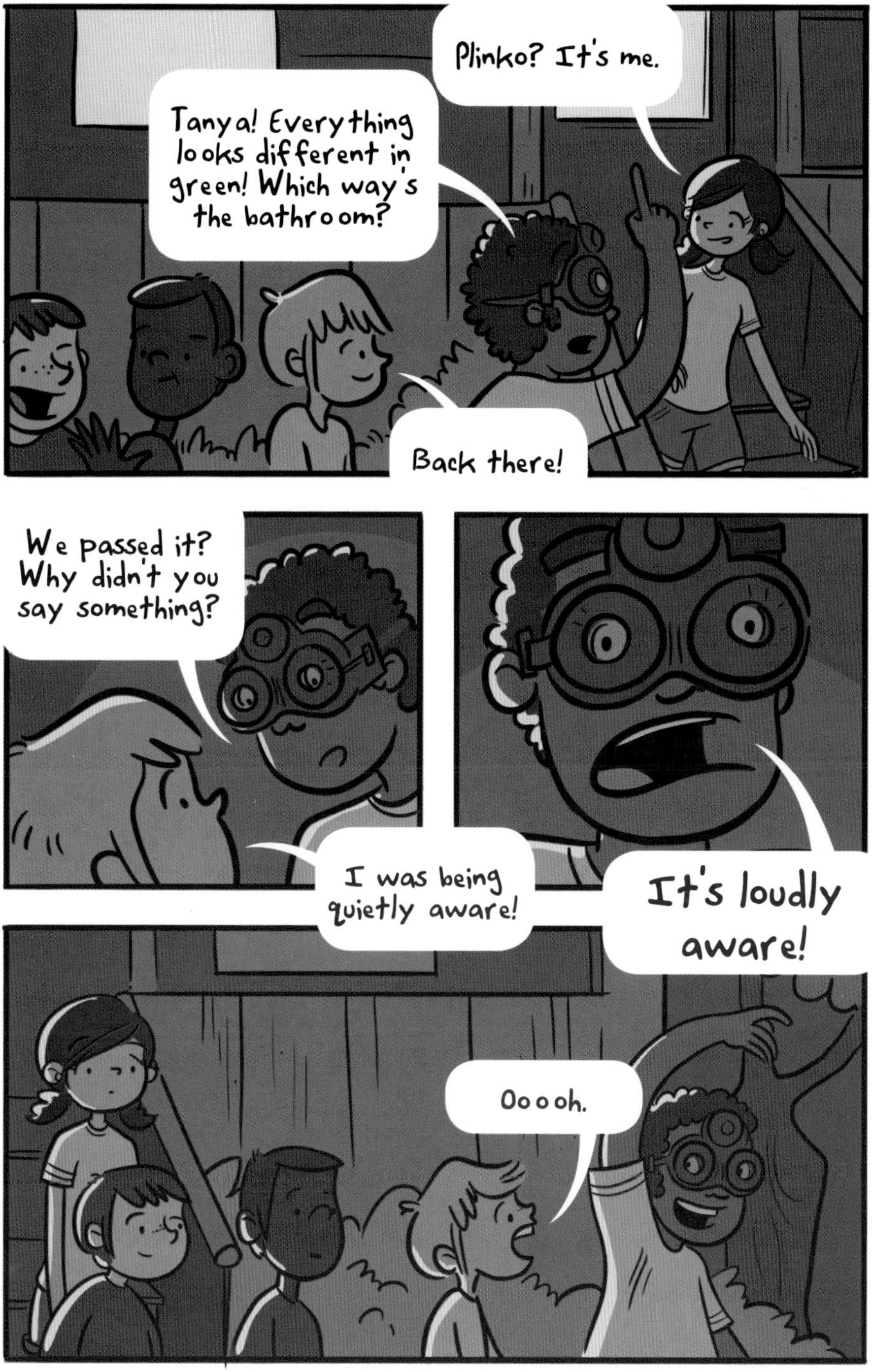
Plinko? It's me.
Tanya! Everything looks different in green! Which way's the bathroom?
Back there!
We passed it? Why didn't you say something?
I was being quietly aware!
It's loudly aware!
Ooooh.

8. Abandon Shop

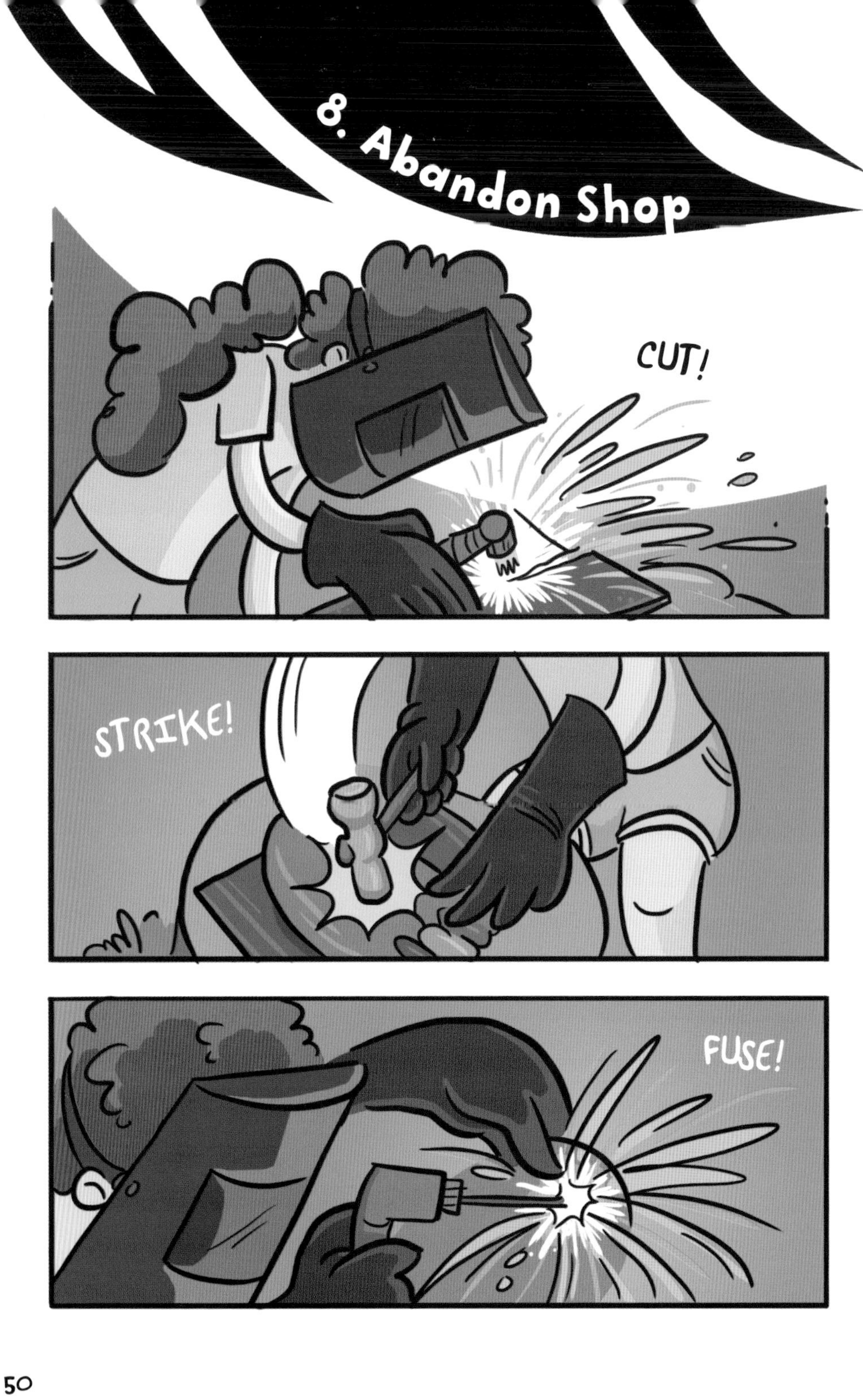
CUT!
STRIKE!
FUSE!

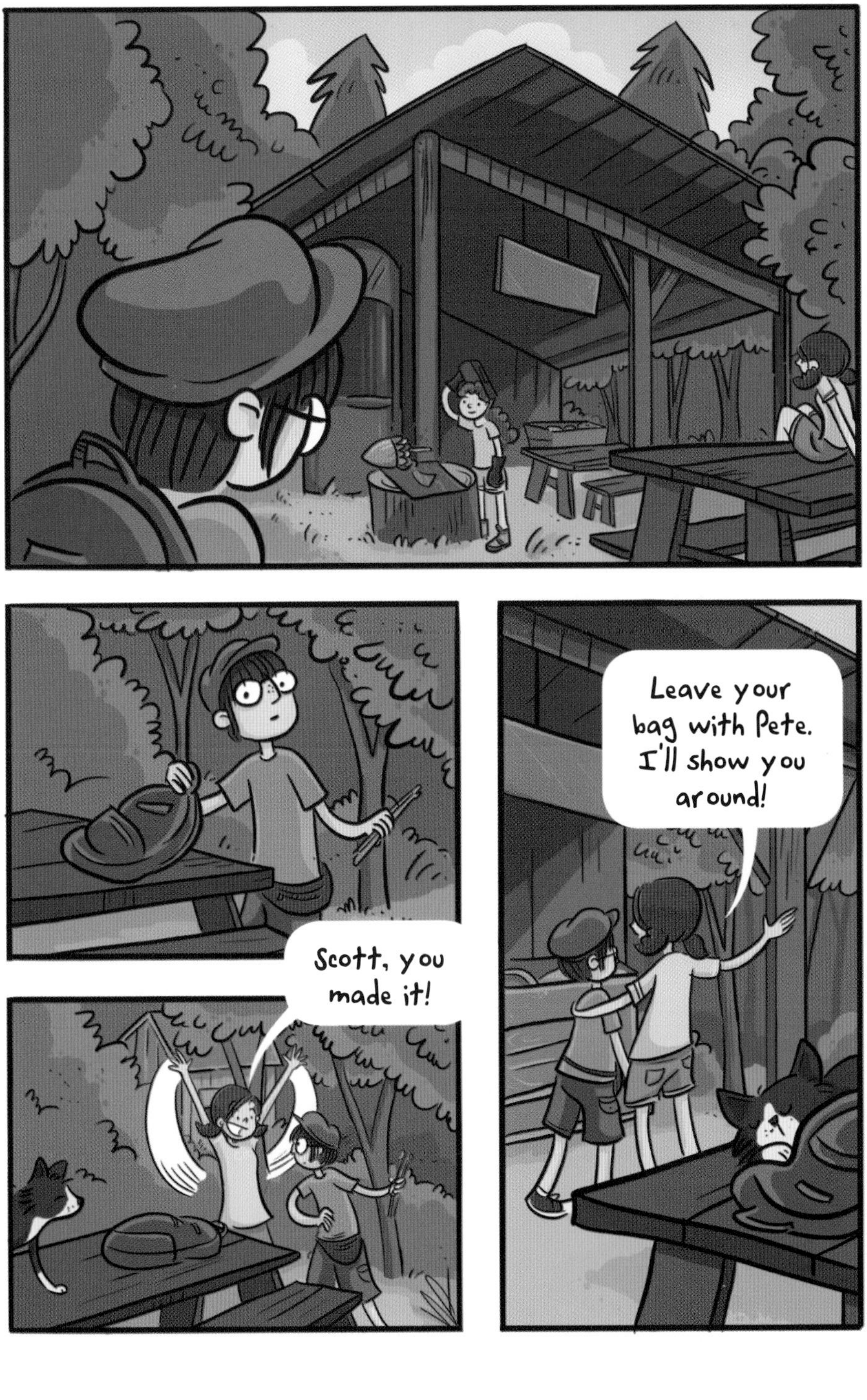
Scott, you made it!
Leave your bag with Pete. I'll show you around!

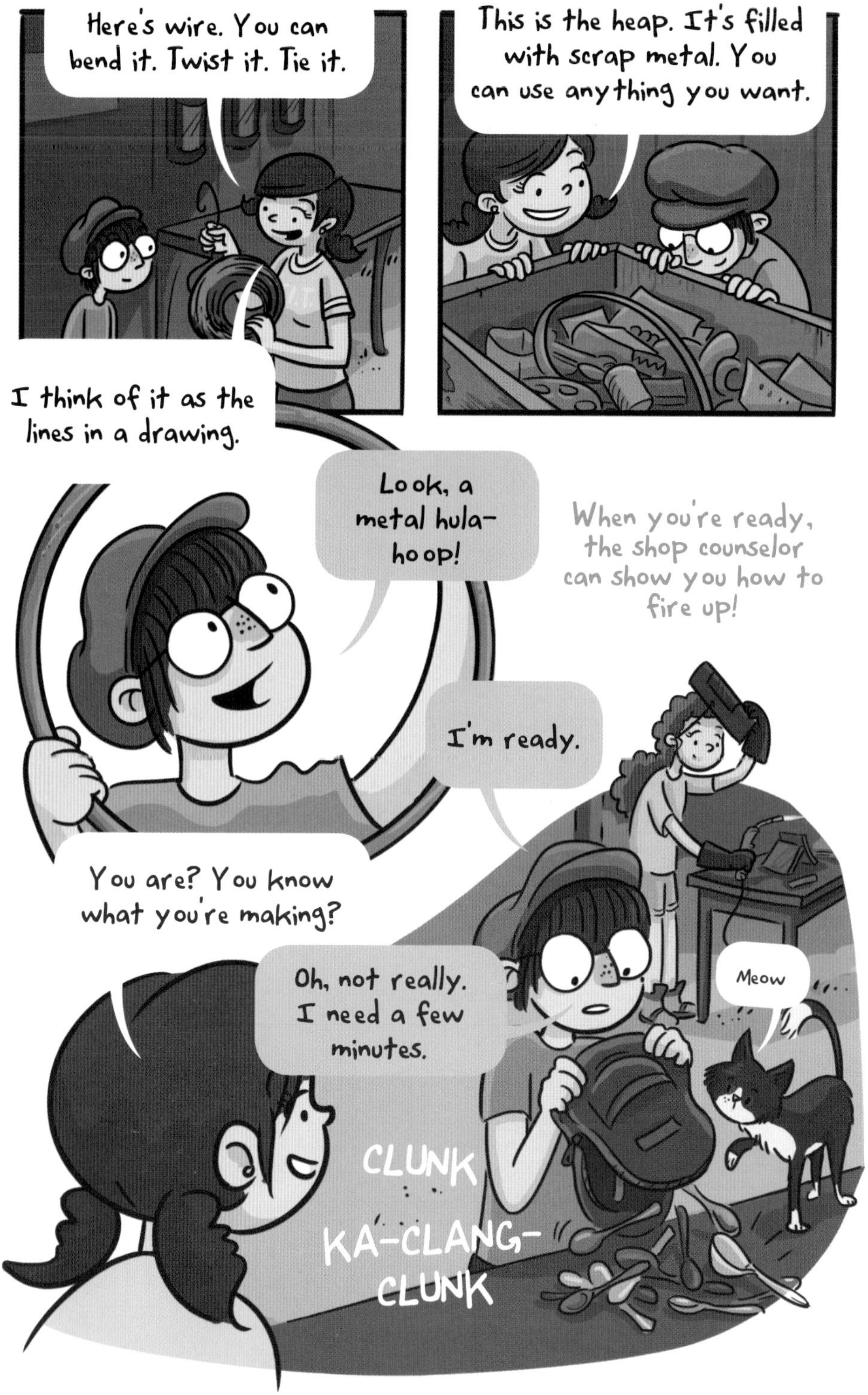
Here's wire. You can bend it. Twist it. Tie it.
This is the heap. It's filled with scrap metal. You can use anything you want.
I think of it as the lines in a drawing.
Look, a metal hula-hoop!
When you're ready, the shop counselor can show you how to fire up!
I'm ready.
You are? You know what you're making?
Oh, not really. I need a few minutes.
Meow
CLUNK
KA-CLANG-CLUNK

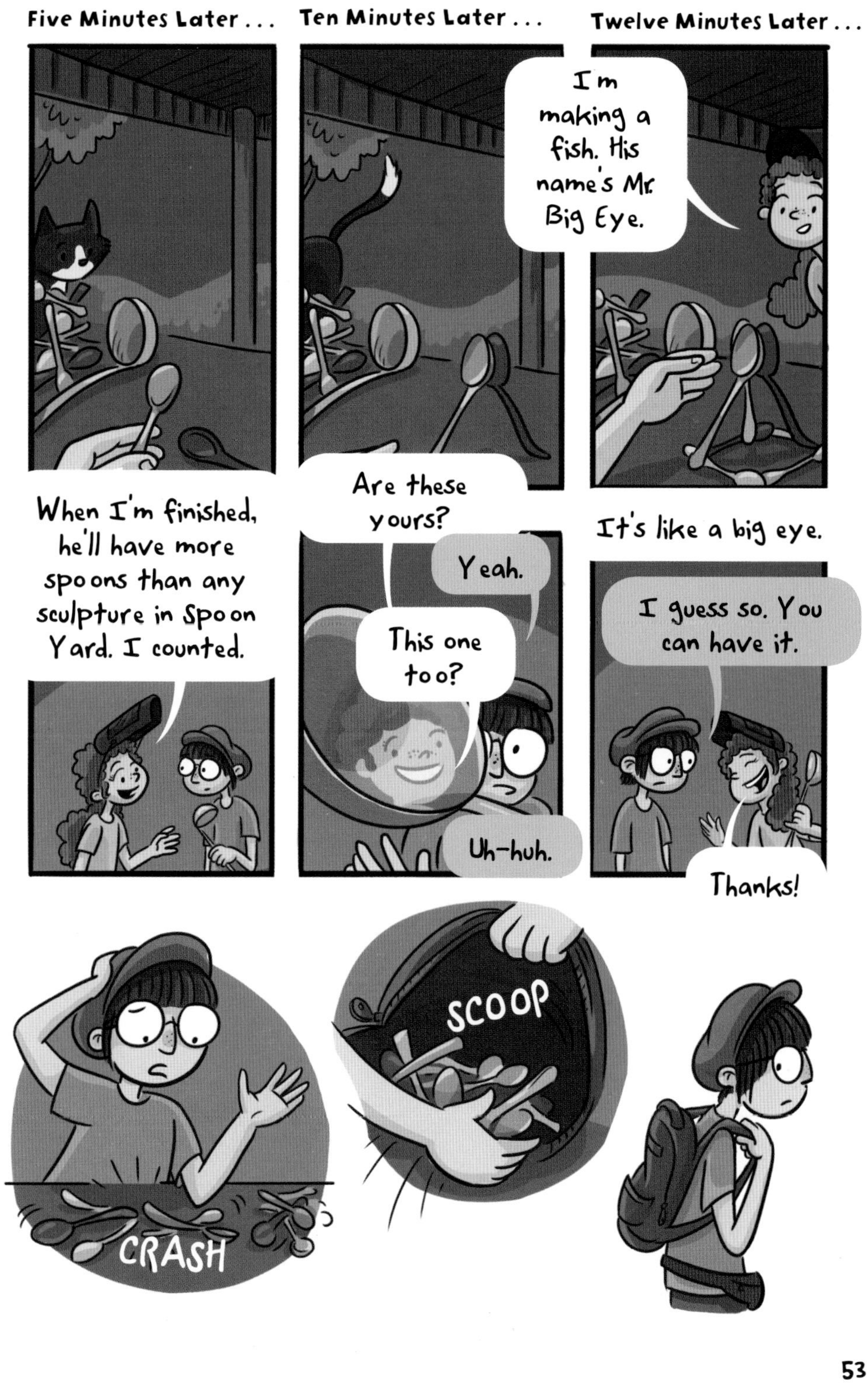
Five Minutes Later . . .
Ten Minutes Later . . .
Twelve Minutes Later . . .
I'm making a fish. His name's Mr. Big Eye.
When I'm finished, he'll have more spoons than any sculpture in Spoon Yard. I counted.
Are these yours?
Yeah.
This one too?
Uh-huh.
It's like a big eye.
I guess so. You can have it.
Thanks!
CRASH
SCOOP

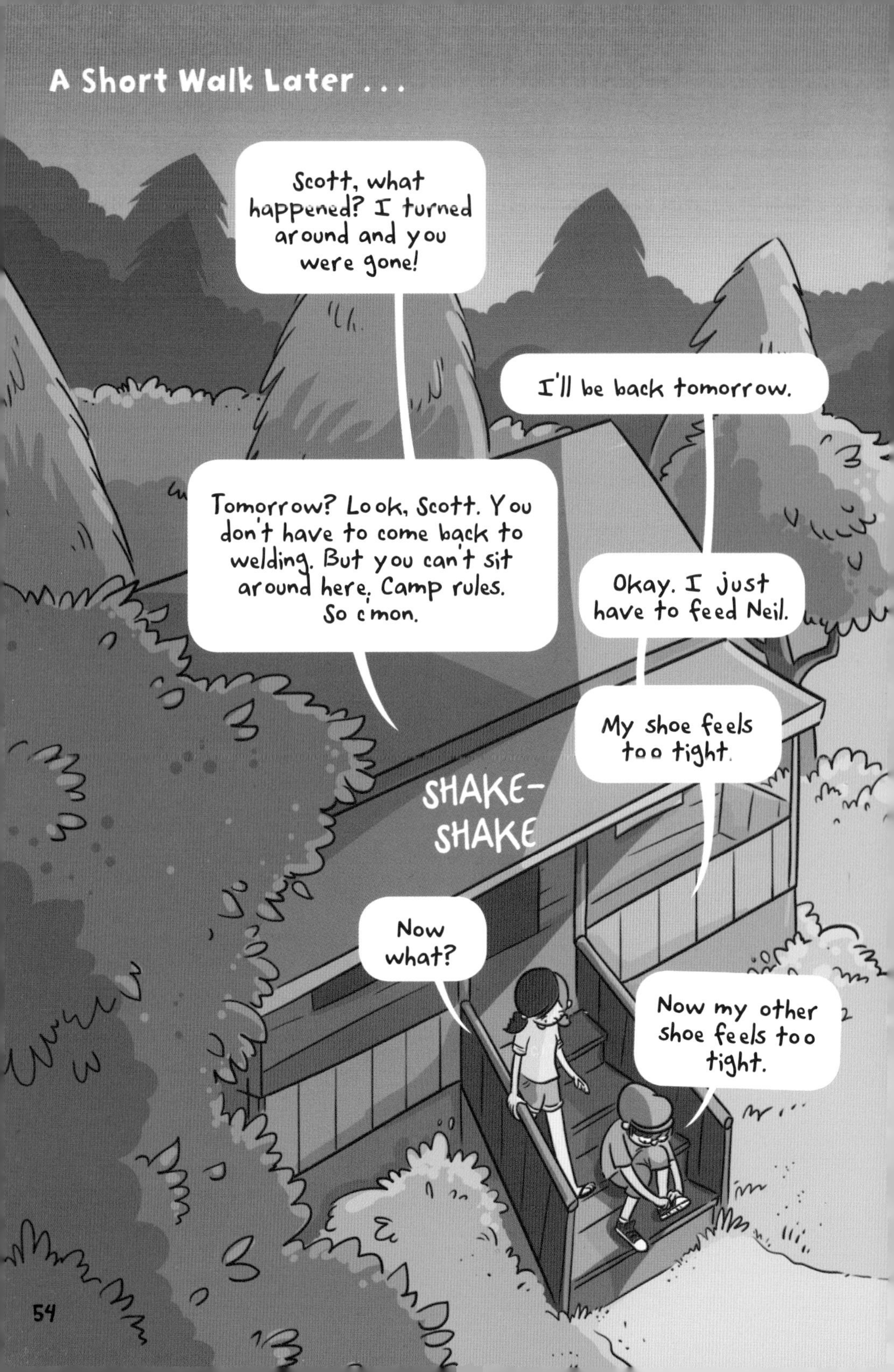
A Short Walk Later . . .
Scott, what happened? I turned around and you were gone!
I'll be back tomorrow.
Tomorrow? Look, Scott. You don't have to come back to welding. But you can't sit around here. Camp rules. So c'mon.
Okay. I just have to feed Neil.
My shoe feels too tight.
SHAKE-SHAKE
Now what?
Now my other shoe feels too tight.

9. Backtrack

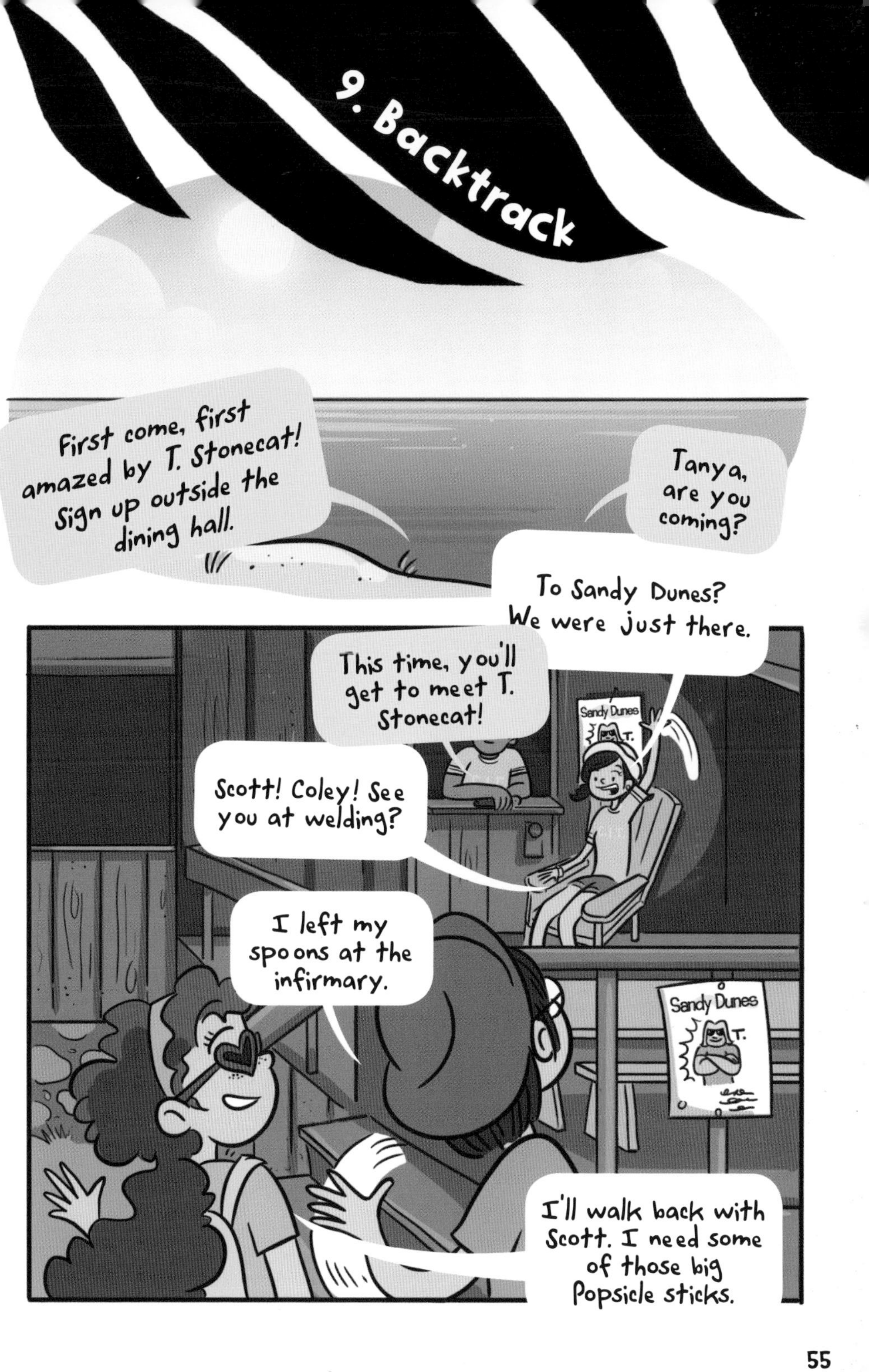

First come, first amazed by T. Stonecat! Sign up outside the dining hall.
Tanya, are you coming?
To Sandy Dunes? We were just there.
This time, you'll get to meet T. Stonecat!
Sandy Dunes
T.
Scott! Coley! See you at welding?
I left my spoons at the infirmary.
Sandy Dunes
T.
I'll walk back with Scott. I need some of those big Popsicle sticks.

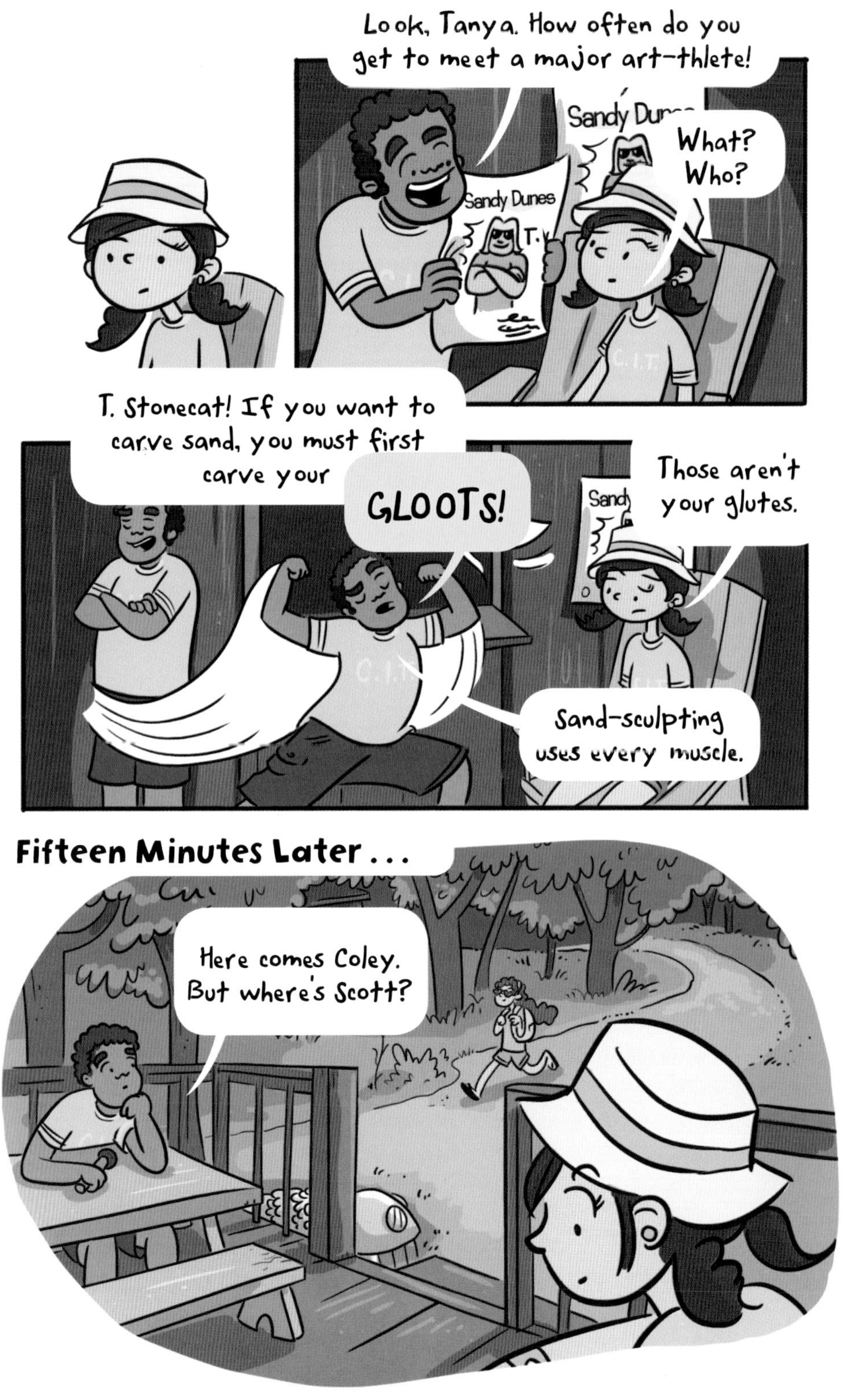
Look, Tanya. How often do you get to meet a major art-thlete!
Sandy Dunes
What? Who?
Sandy Dunes
T.
T. Stonecat! If you want to carve sand, you must first carve your
GLOOTS!
Those aren't your glutes.
Sandy
Sand-sculpting uses every muscle.
Fifteen Minutes Later . . .
Here comes Coley. But where's Scott?

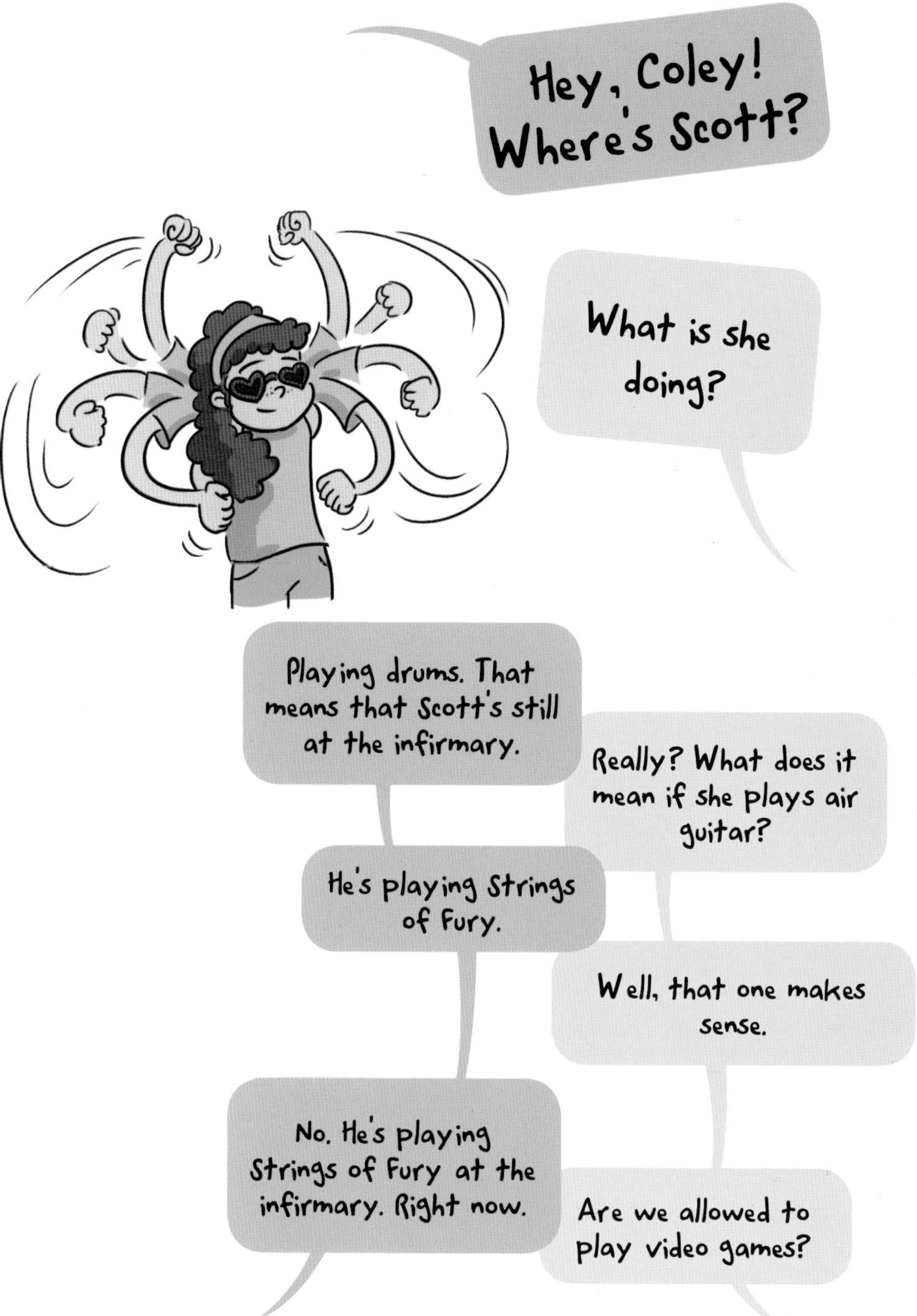
Hey, Coley! Where's Scott?
What is she doing?
Playing drums. That means that Scott's still at the infirmary.
Really? What does it mean if she plays air guitar?
He's playing Strings of Fury.
Well, that one makes sense.
No. He's playing Strings of Fury at the infirmary. Right now.
Are we allowed to play video games?

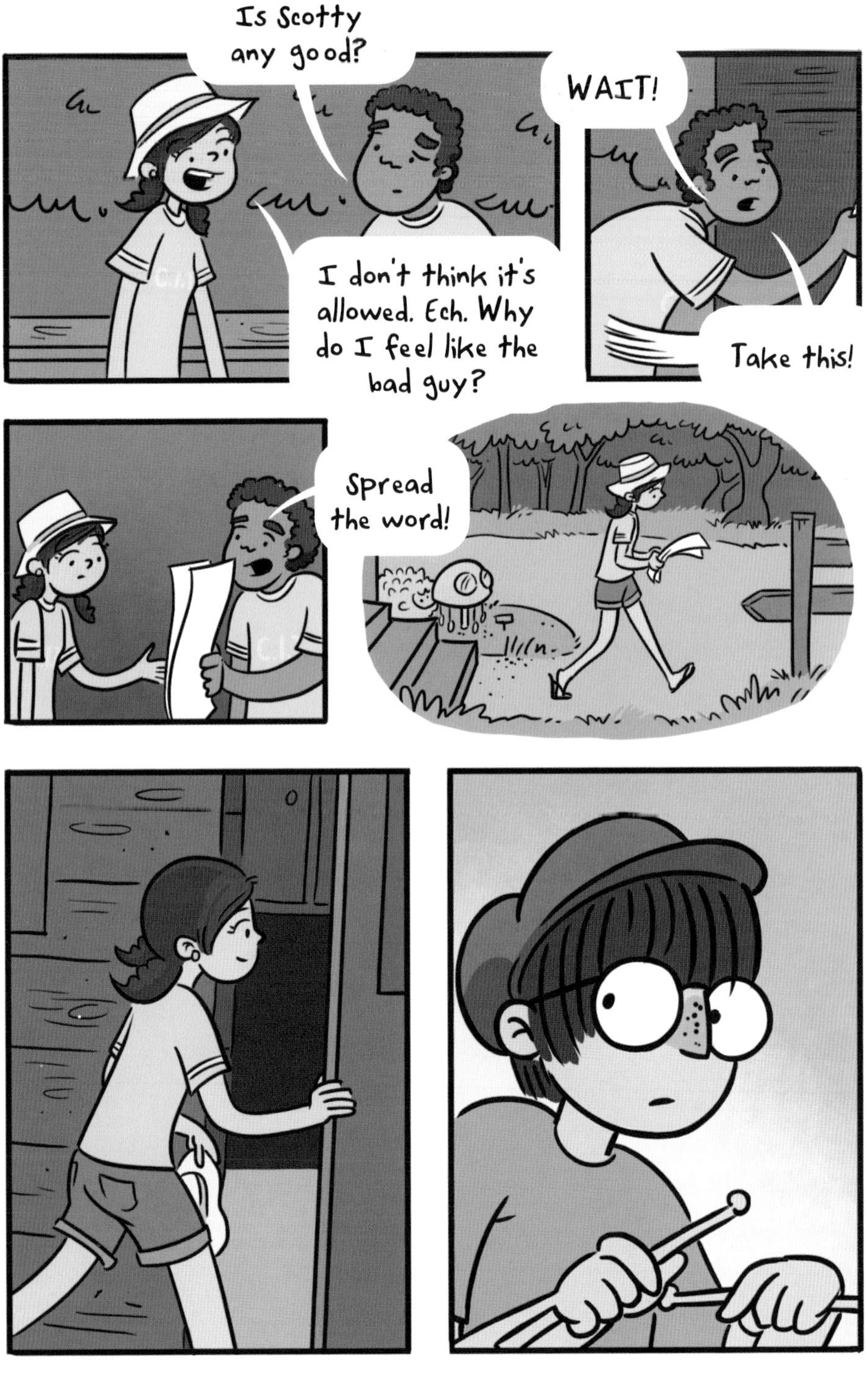
Is Scotty any good?
I don't think it's allowed. Ech. Why do I feel like the bad guy?
WAIT!
Take this!
Spread the word!

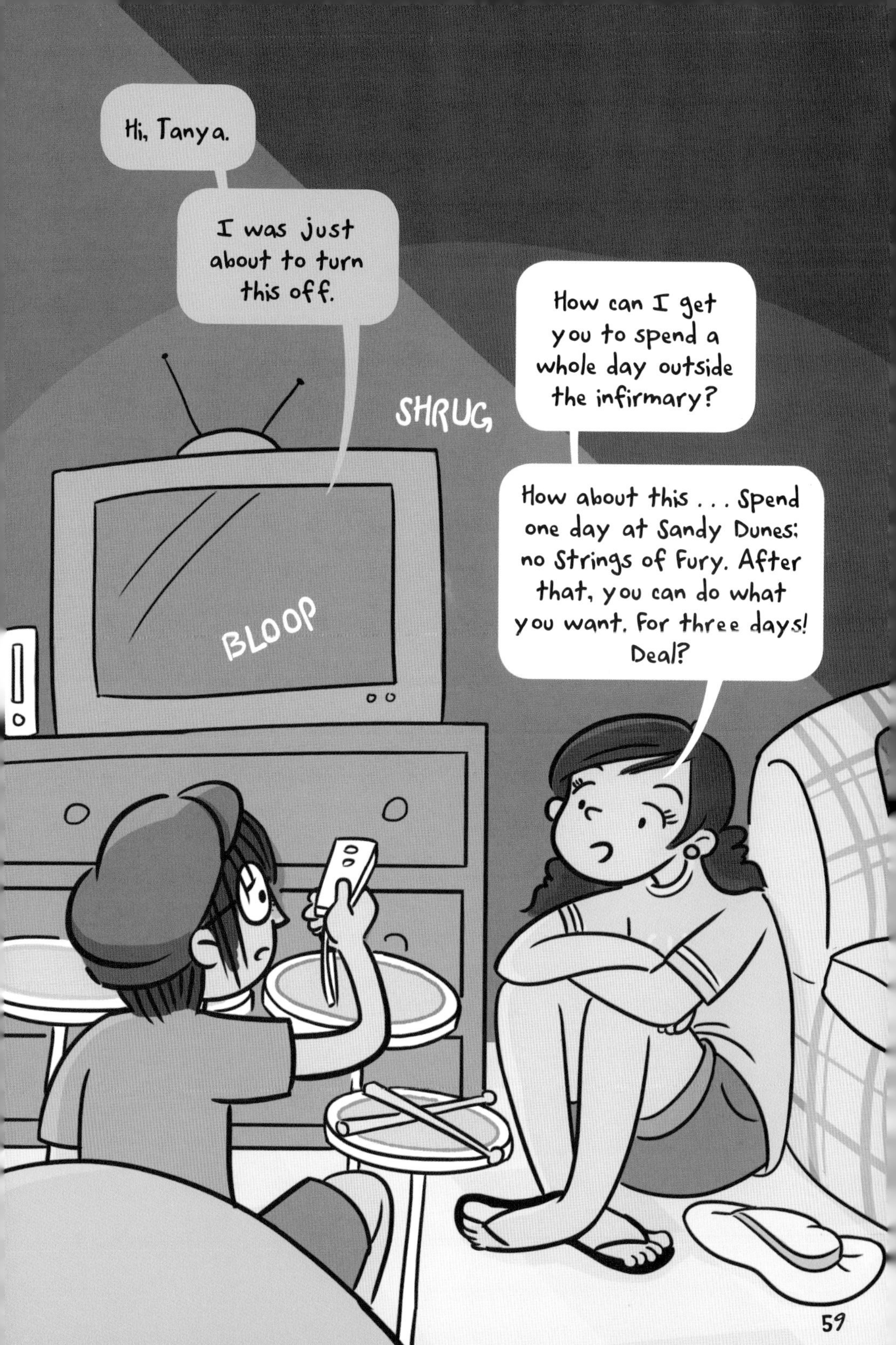
Hi, Tanya.
I was just about to turn this off.
SHRUG
How can I get you to spend a whole day outside the infirmary?
How about this . . . Spend one day at Sandy Dunes: no Strings of Fury. After that, you can do what you want. For three days! Deal?
BLOOP

10. Highs and Lows

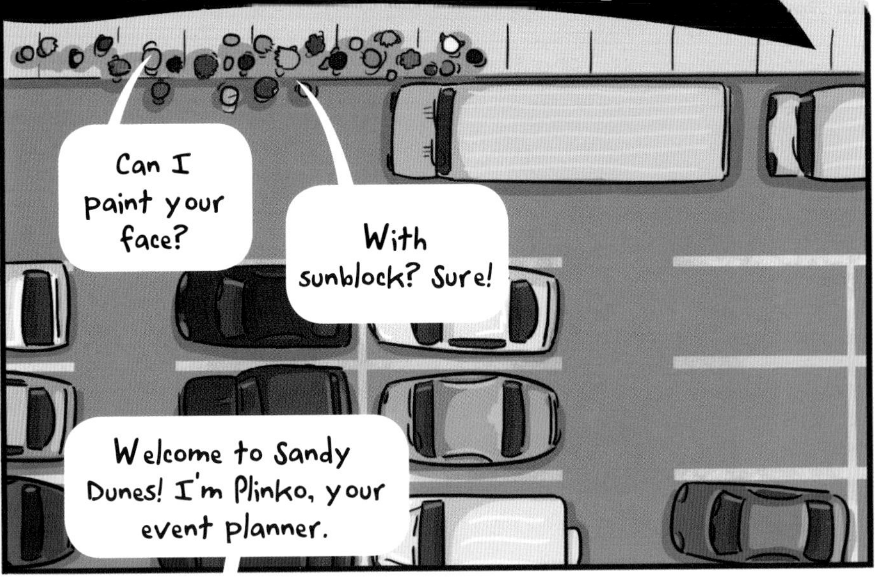

Can I paint your face?
With sunblock? Sure!
Welcome to Sandy Dunes! I'm Plinko, your event planner.

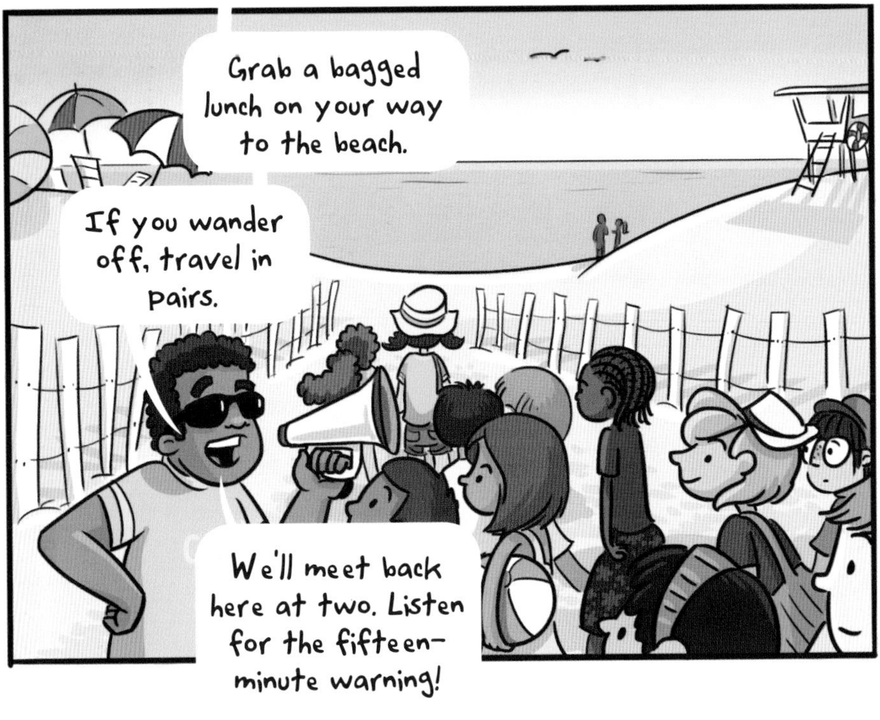

Grab a bagged lunch on your way to the beach.
If you wander off, travel in pairs.
We'll meet back here at two. Listen for the fifteen-minute warning!

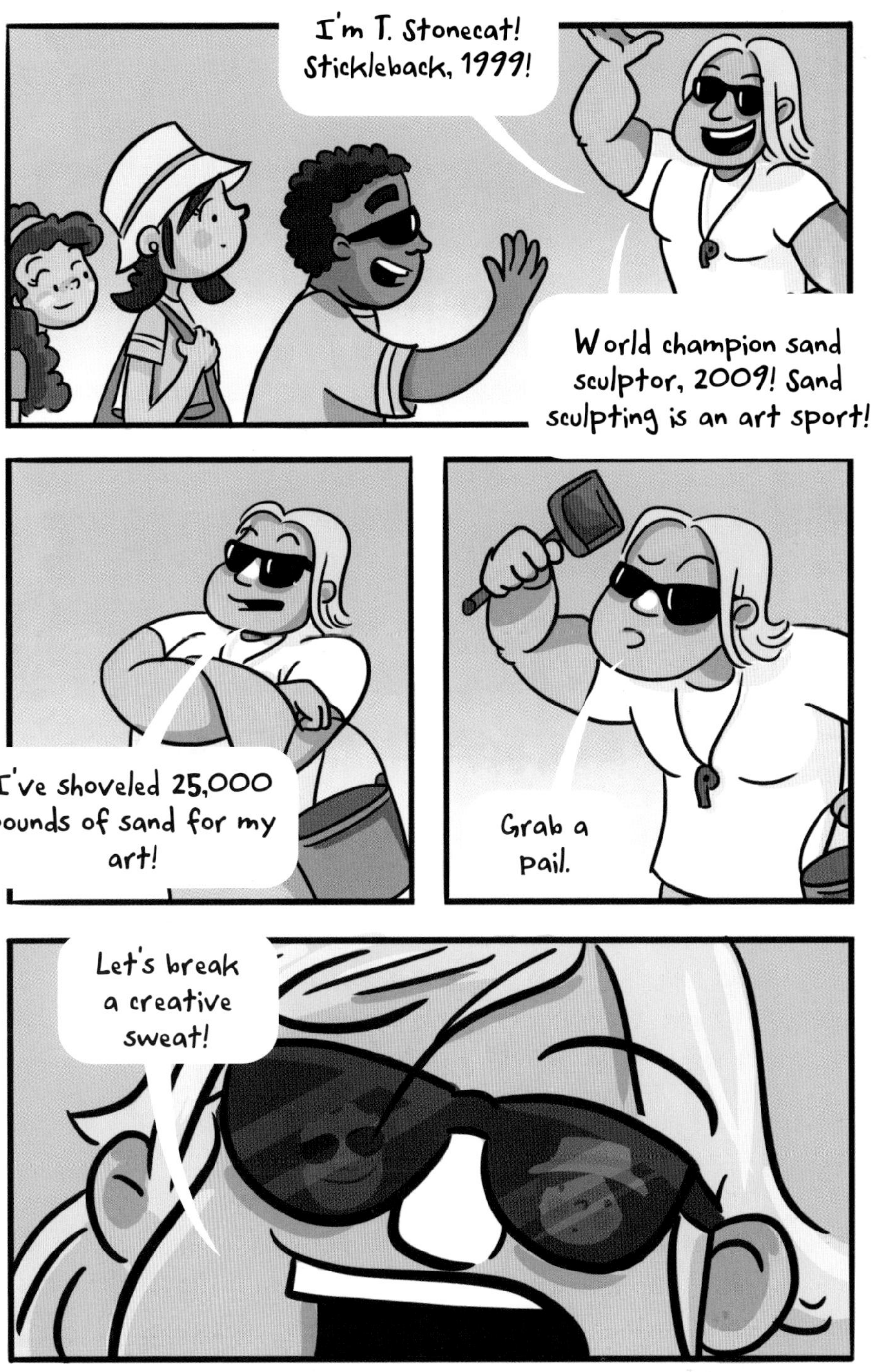
I'm T. Stonecat! Stickleback, 1999!
World champion sand sculptor, 2009! Sand sculpting is an art sport!
I've shoveled 25,000 pounds of sand for my art!
Grab a pail.
Let's break a creative sweat!

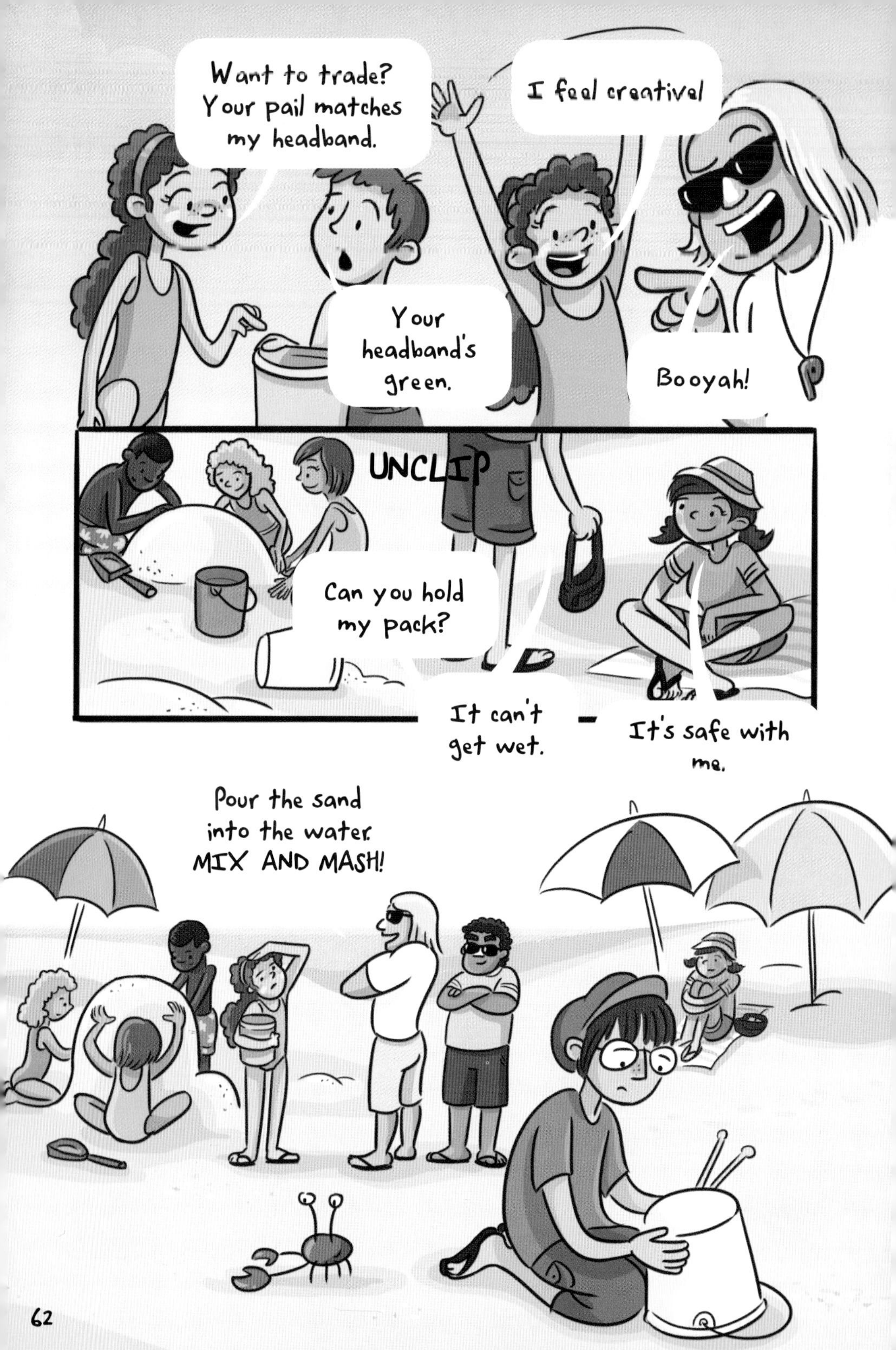
Want to trade? Your pail matches my headband.
I feel creative!
Your headband's green.
Booyah!
UNCLIP
Can you hold my pack?
It can't get wet.
It's safe with me.
Pour the sand into the water. MIX AND MASH!

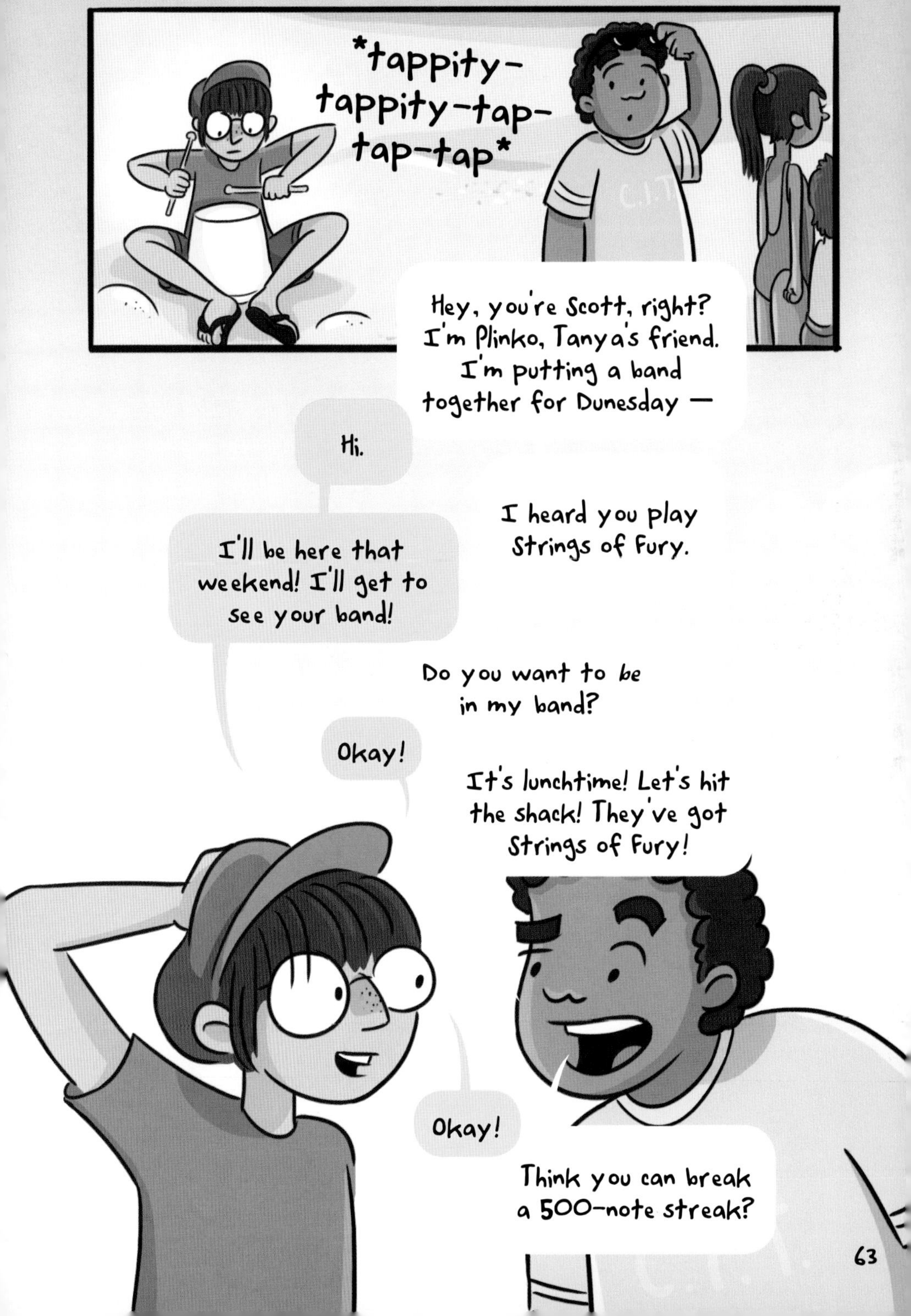
tappity-tappity-tap-tap-tap
C.I.T.
Hey, you're Scott, right? I'm Plinko, Tanya's friend. I'm putting a band together for Dunesday —
Hi.
I heard you play Strings of Fury.
I'll be here that weekend! I'll get to see your band!
Do you want to *be* in my band?
Okay!
It's lunchtime! Let's hit the shack! They've got Strings of Fury!
Okay!
Think you can break a 500-note streak?

One, Two, Three Hours Later . . .

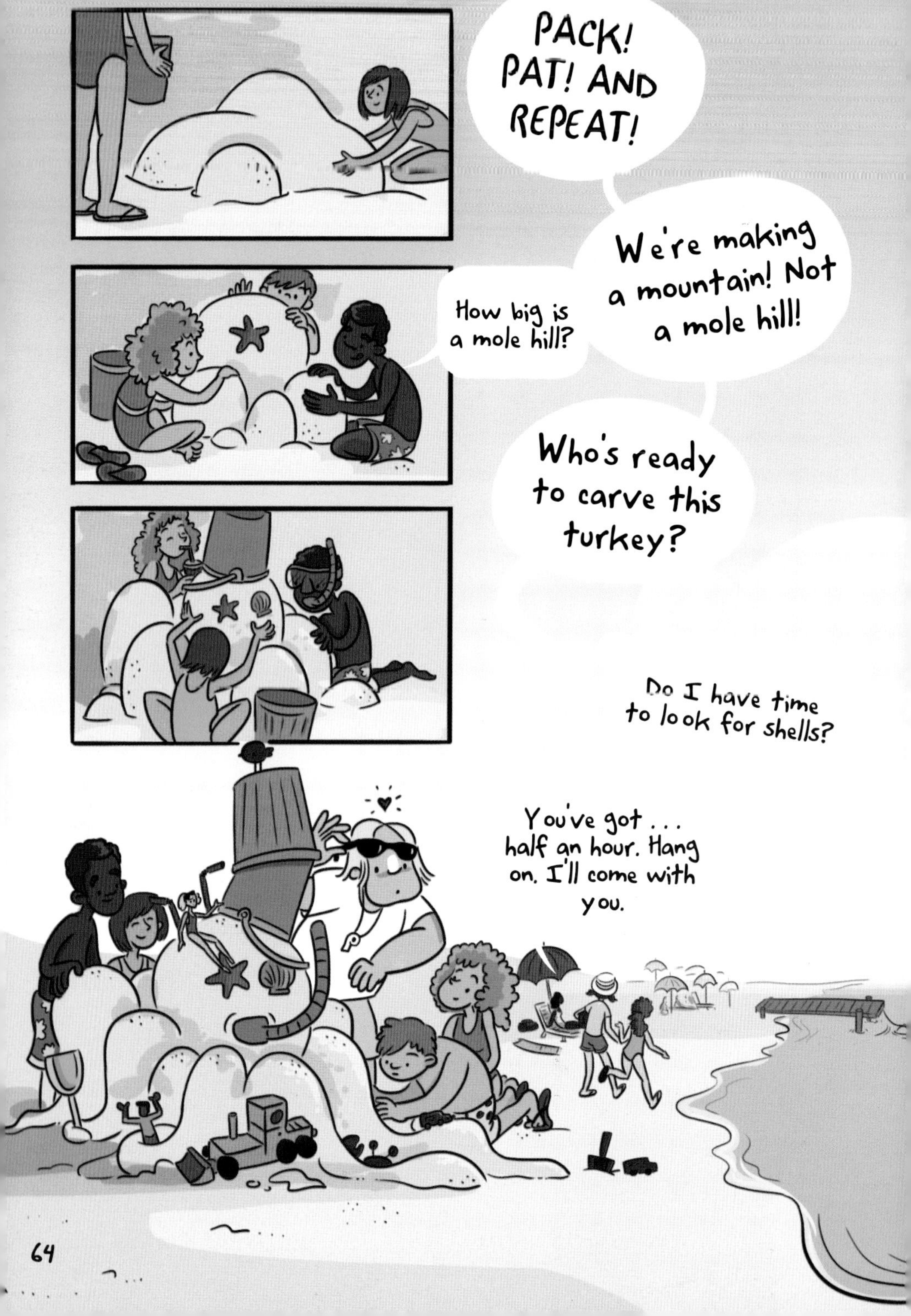
PACK! PAT! AND REPEAT!
We're making a mountain! Not a mole hill!
How big is a mole hill?
Who's ready to carve this turkey?
Do I have time to look for shells?
You've got . . . half an hour. Hang on. I'll come with you.

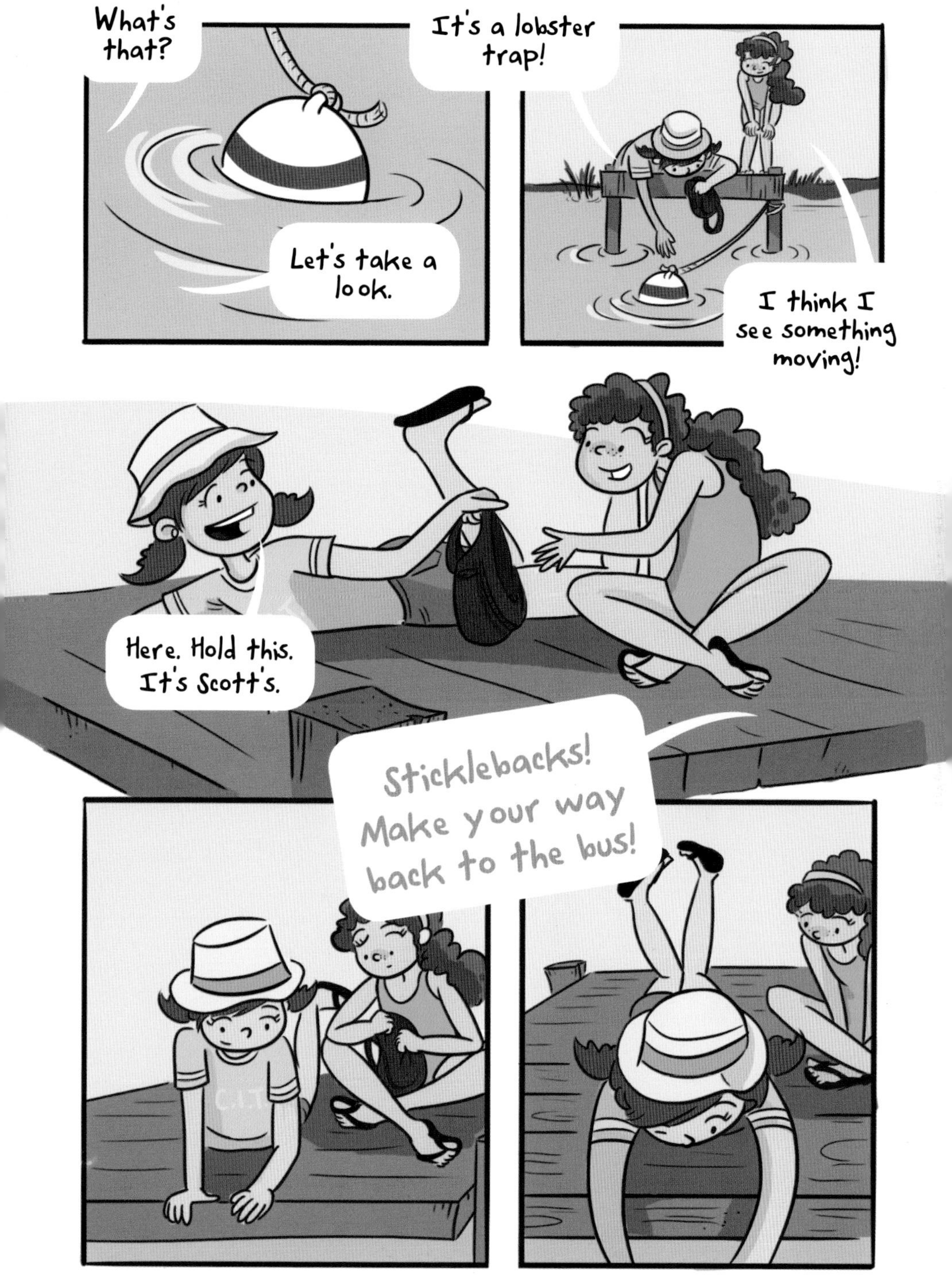
What's that?
It's a lobster trap!
Let's take a look.
I think I see something moving!
Here. Hold this. It's Scott's.
Sticklebacks! Make your way back to the bus!
C.I.T.

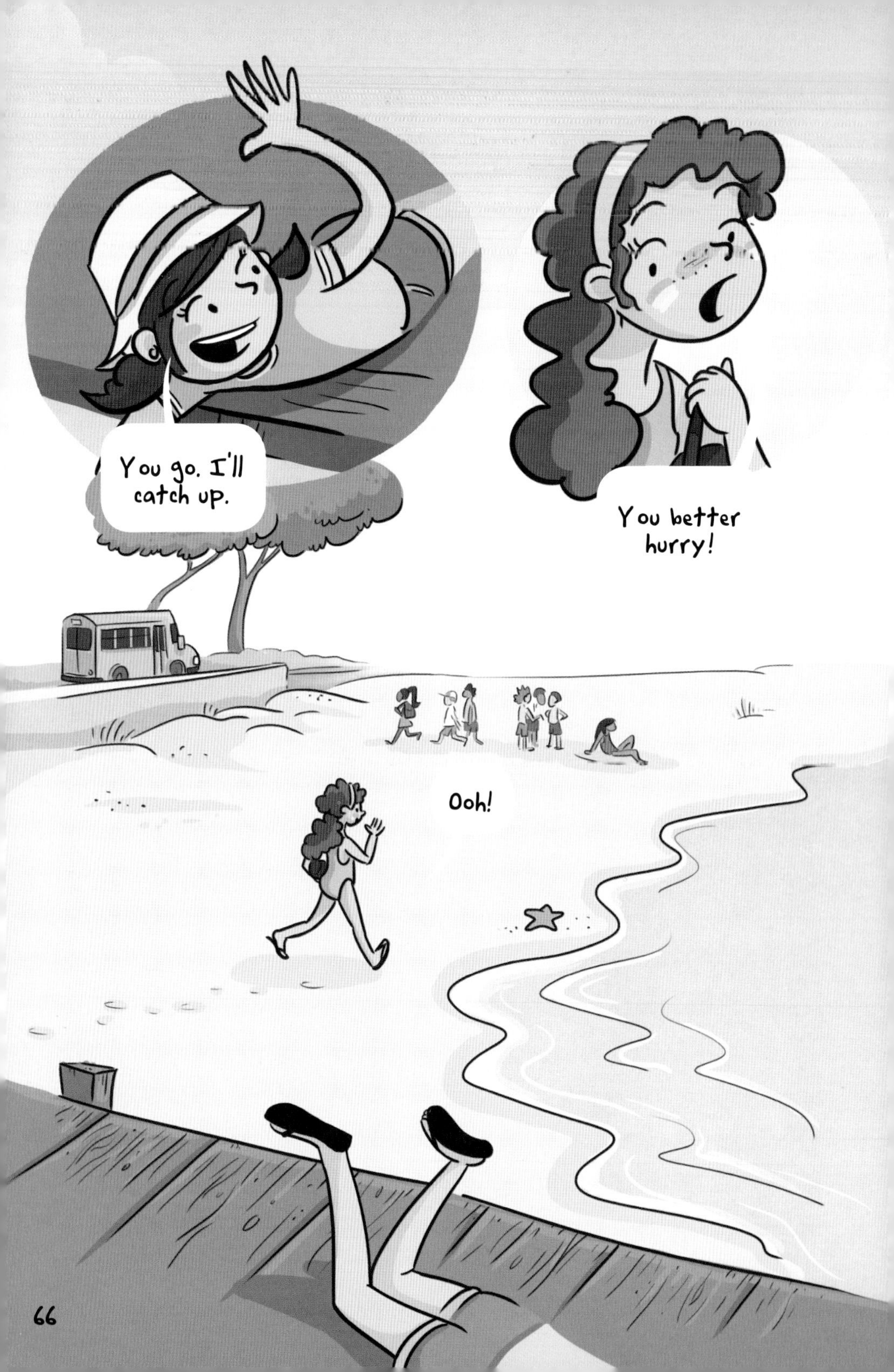
You go. I'll catch up.
You better hurry!
Ooh!

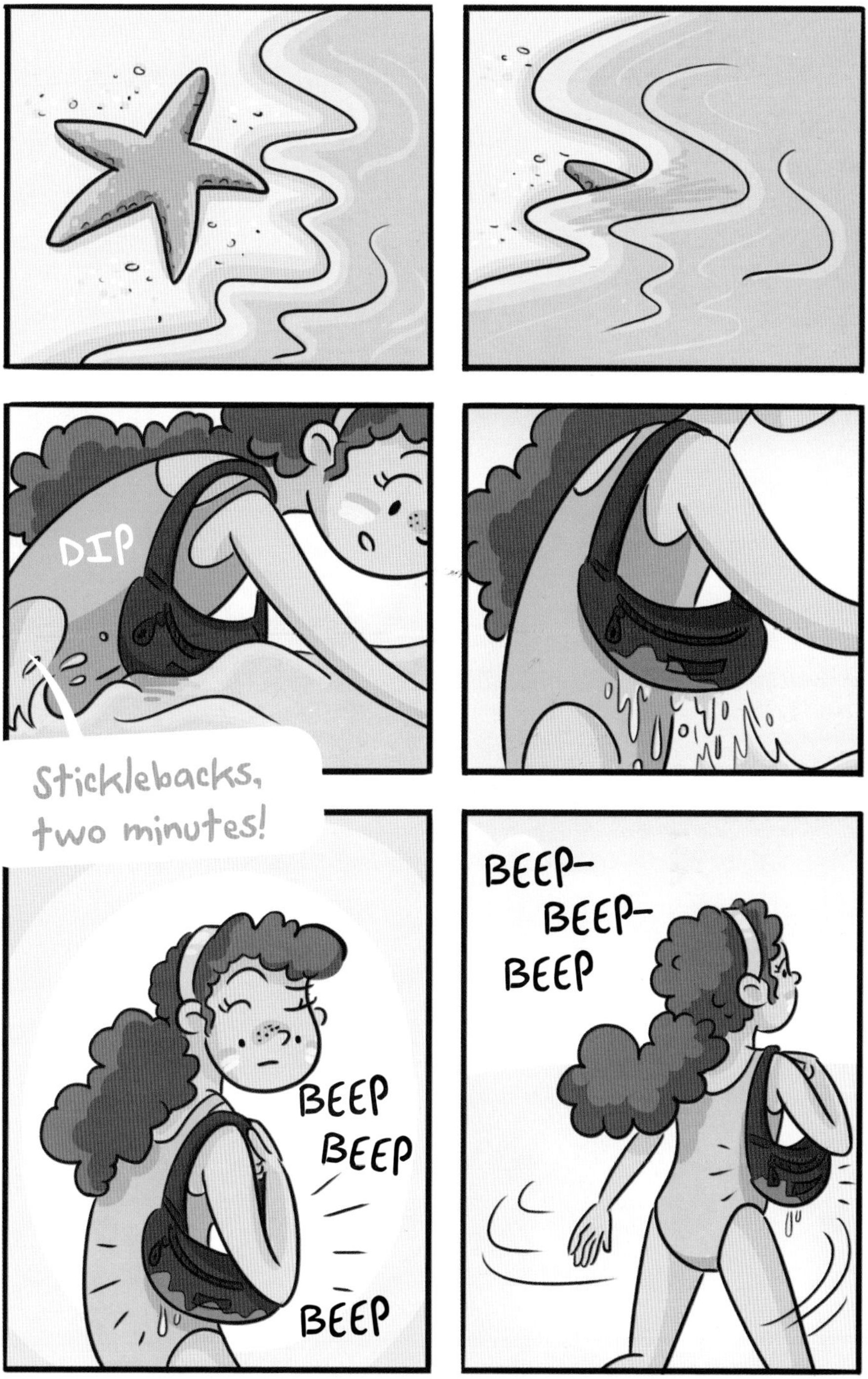
DIP
Sticklebacks, two minutes!
BEEP
BEEP
BEEP
BEEP-
BEEP-
BEEP

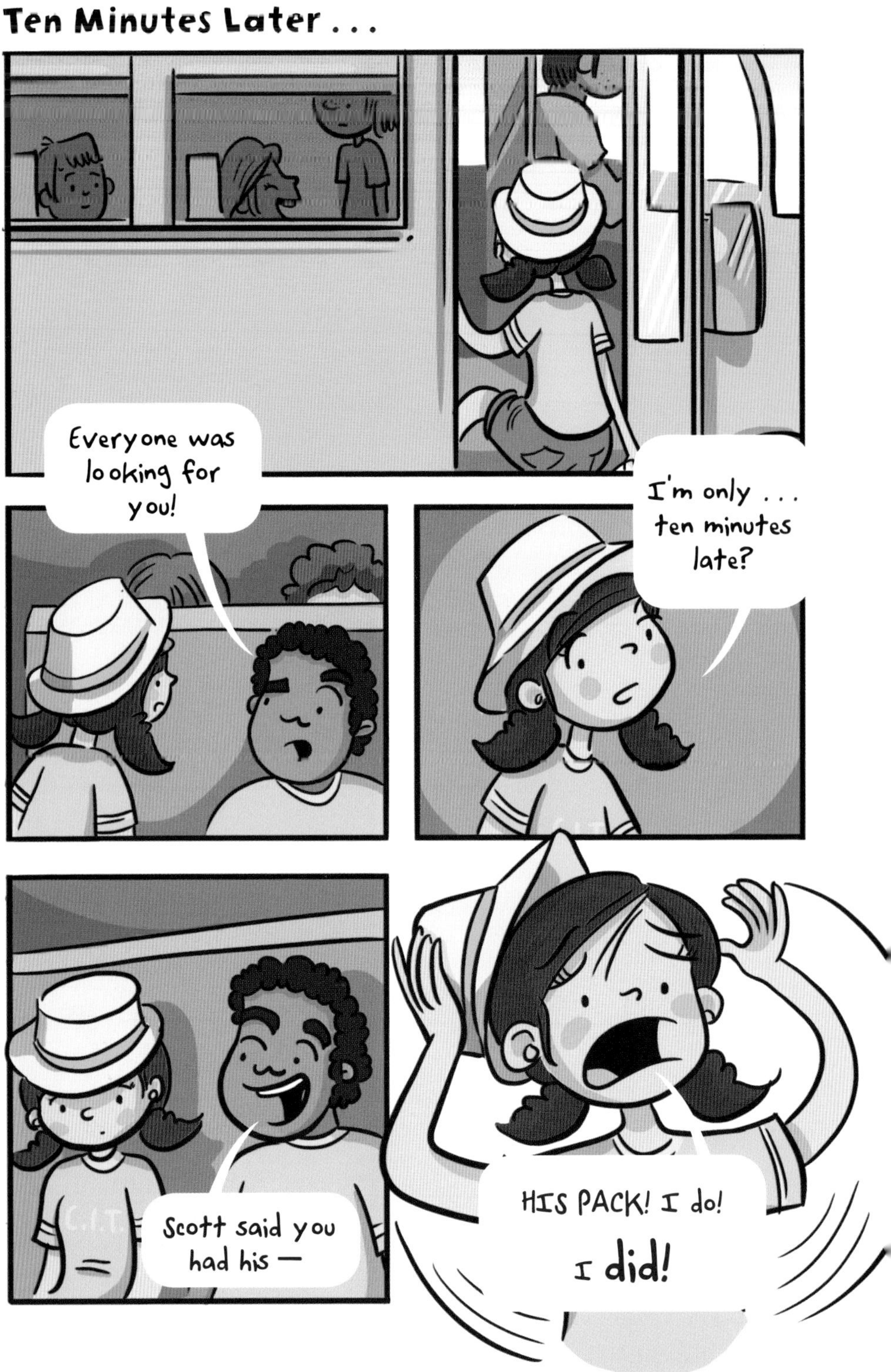
Ten Minutes Later . . .
Everyone was looking for you!
I'm only . . . ten minutes late?
Scott said you had his —
HIS PACK! I do!
I did!

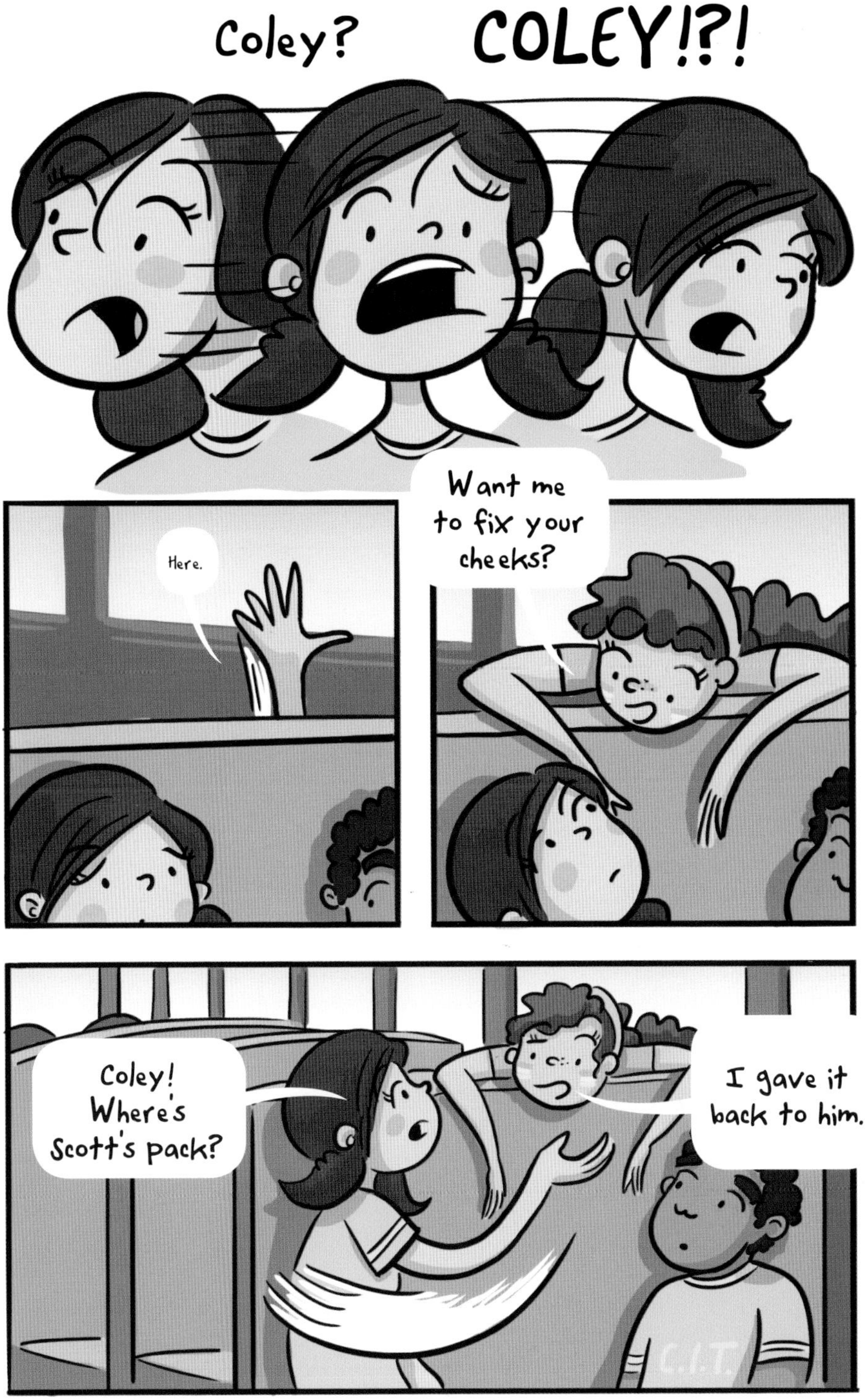
Coley?
COLEY!?!
Here.
Want me to fix your cheeks?
Coley! Where's Scott's pack?
I gave it back to him.
C.I.T.

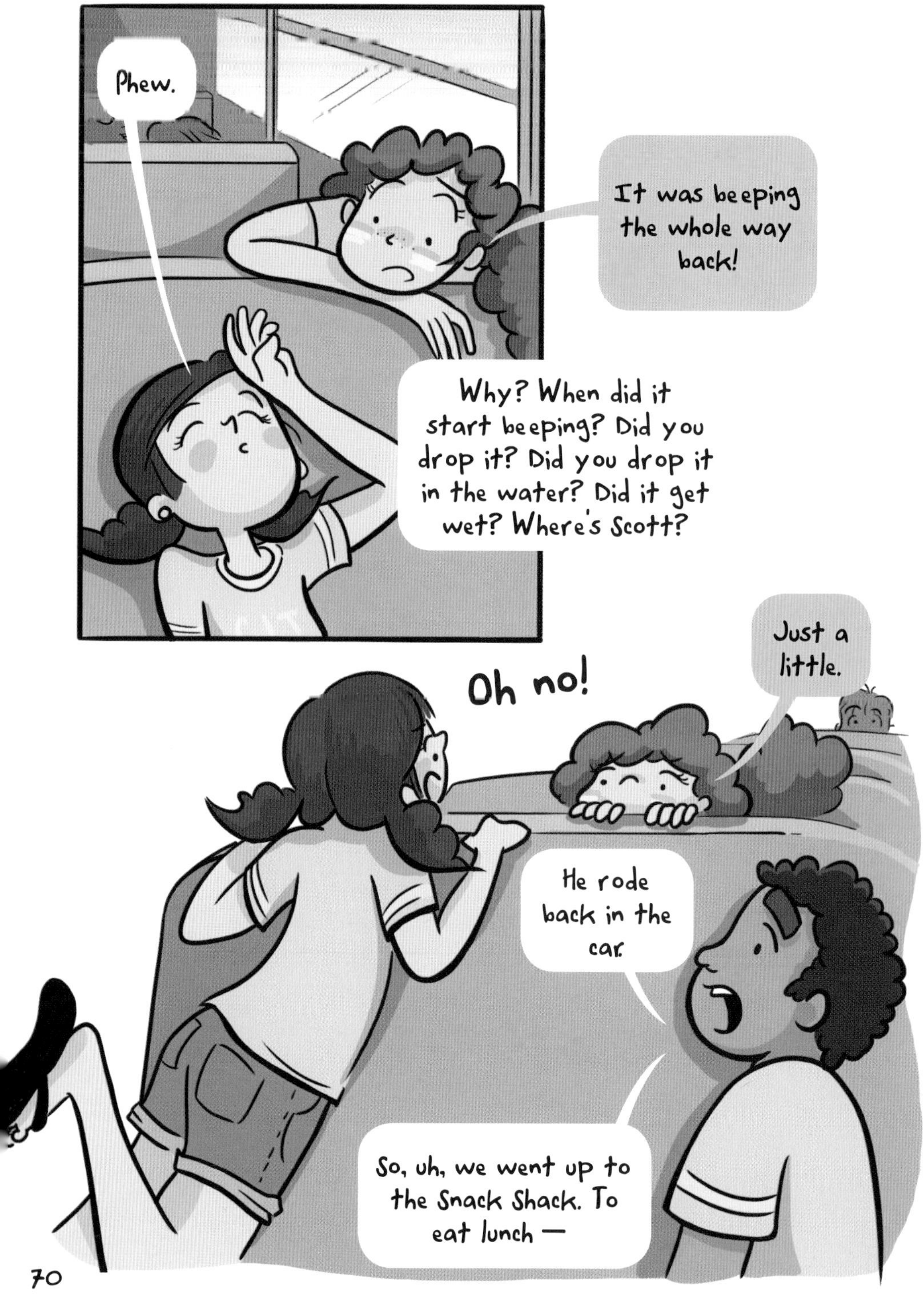
Phew.
It was beeping the whole way back!
Why? When did it start beeping? Did you drop it? Did you drop it in the water? Did it get wet? Where's Scott?
Oh no!
Just a little.
He rode back in the car.
So, uh, we went up to the Snack Shack. To eat lunch —

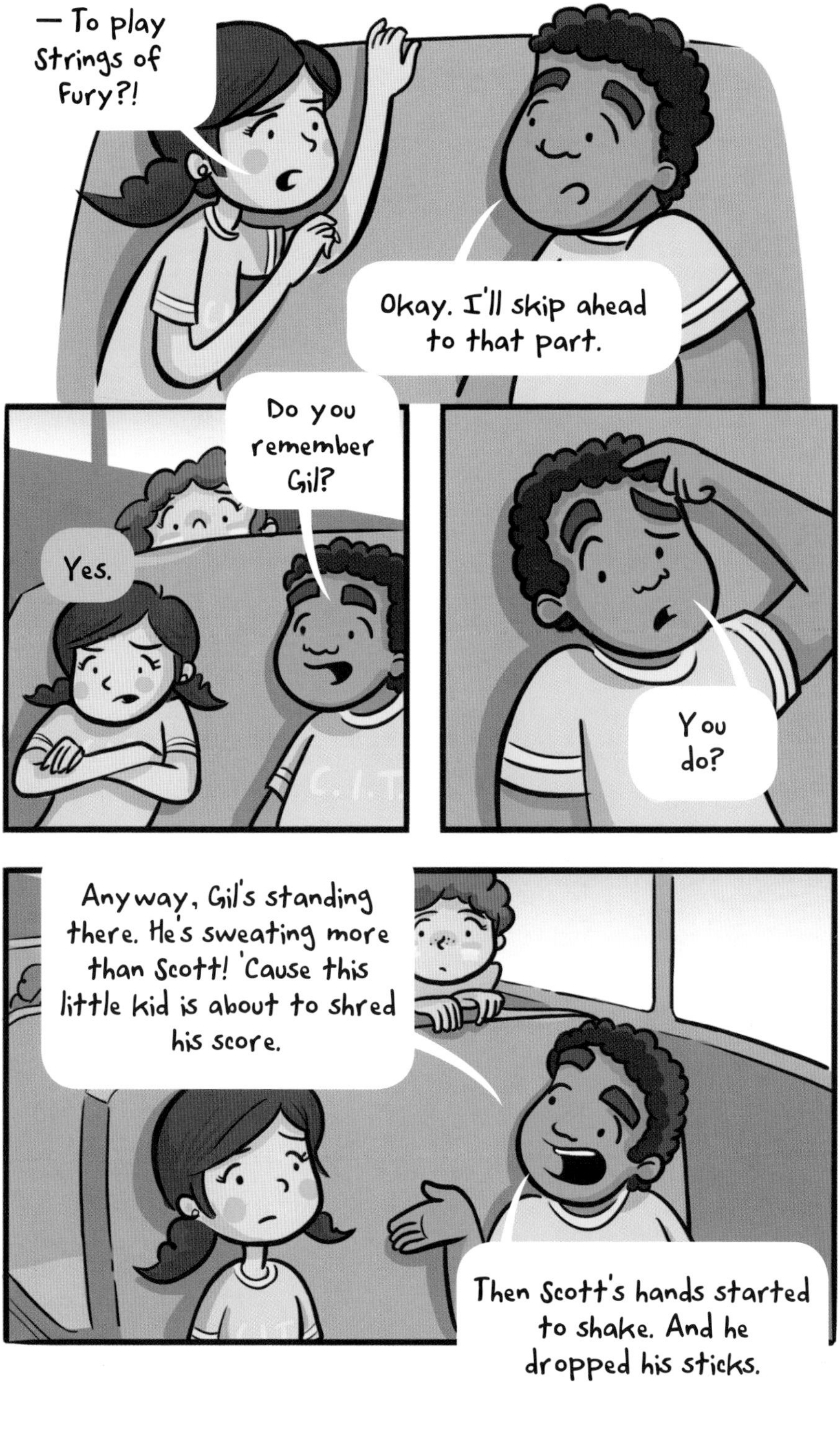
—To play Strings of Fury?!
Okay. I'll skip ahead to that part.
Do you remember Gil?
Yes.
You do?
Anyway, Gil's standing there. He's sweating more than Scott! 'Cause this little kid is about to shred his score.
Then Scott's hands started to shake. And he dropped his sticks.

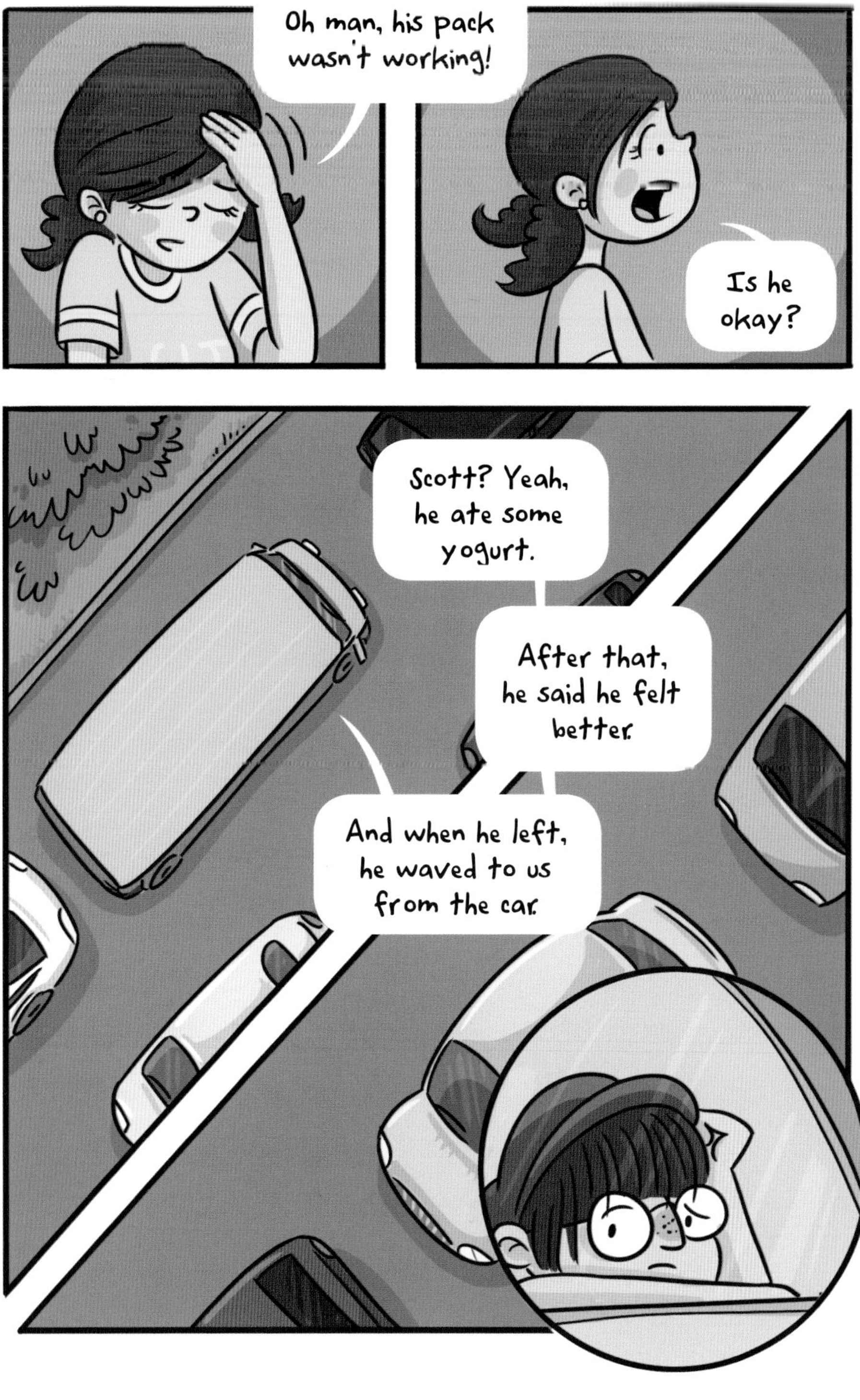
Oh man, his pack wasn't working!
Is he okay?
Scott? Yeah, he ate some yogurt.
After that, he said he felt better.
And when he left, he waved to us from the car.

11. Safe House

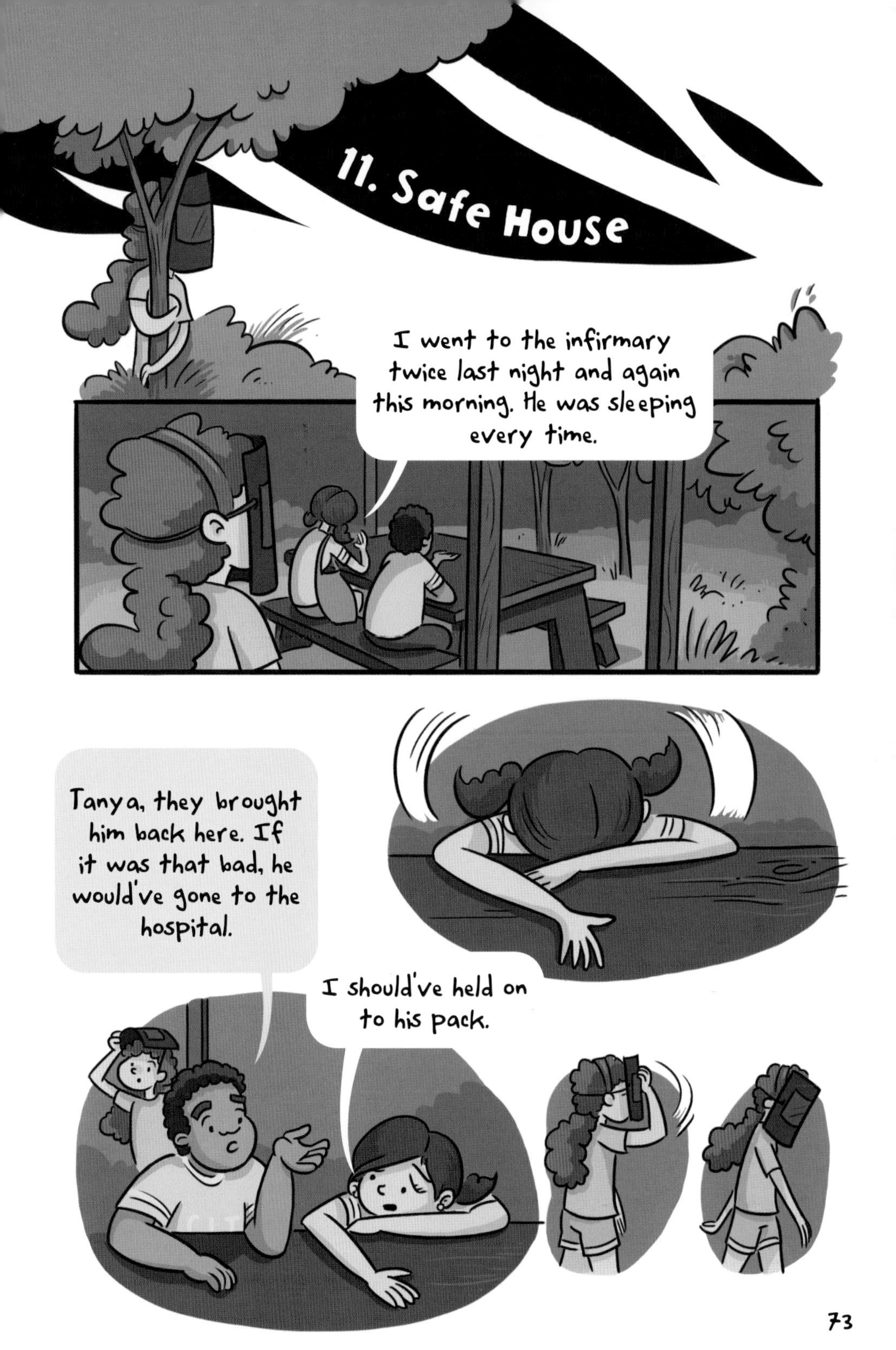
I went to the infirmary twice last night and again this morning. He was sleeping every time.
Tanya, they brought him back here. If it was that bad, he would've gone to the hospital.
I should've held on to his pack.

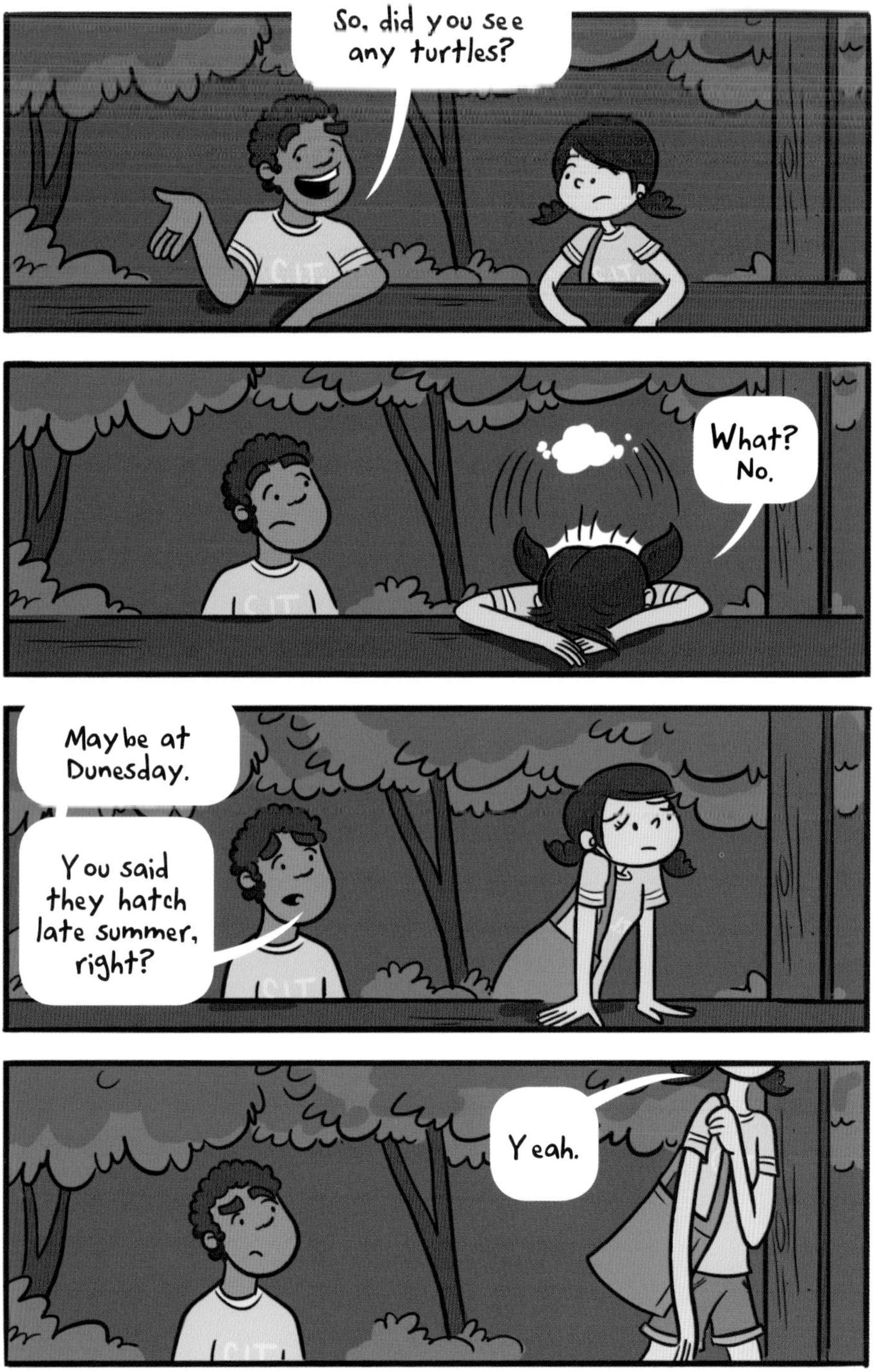
So, did you see any turtles?
What? No.
Maybe at Dunesday.
You said they hatch late summer, right?
Yeah.

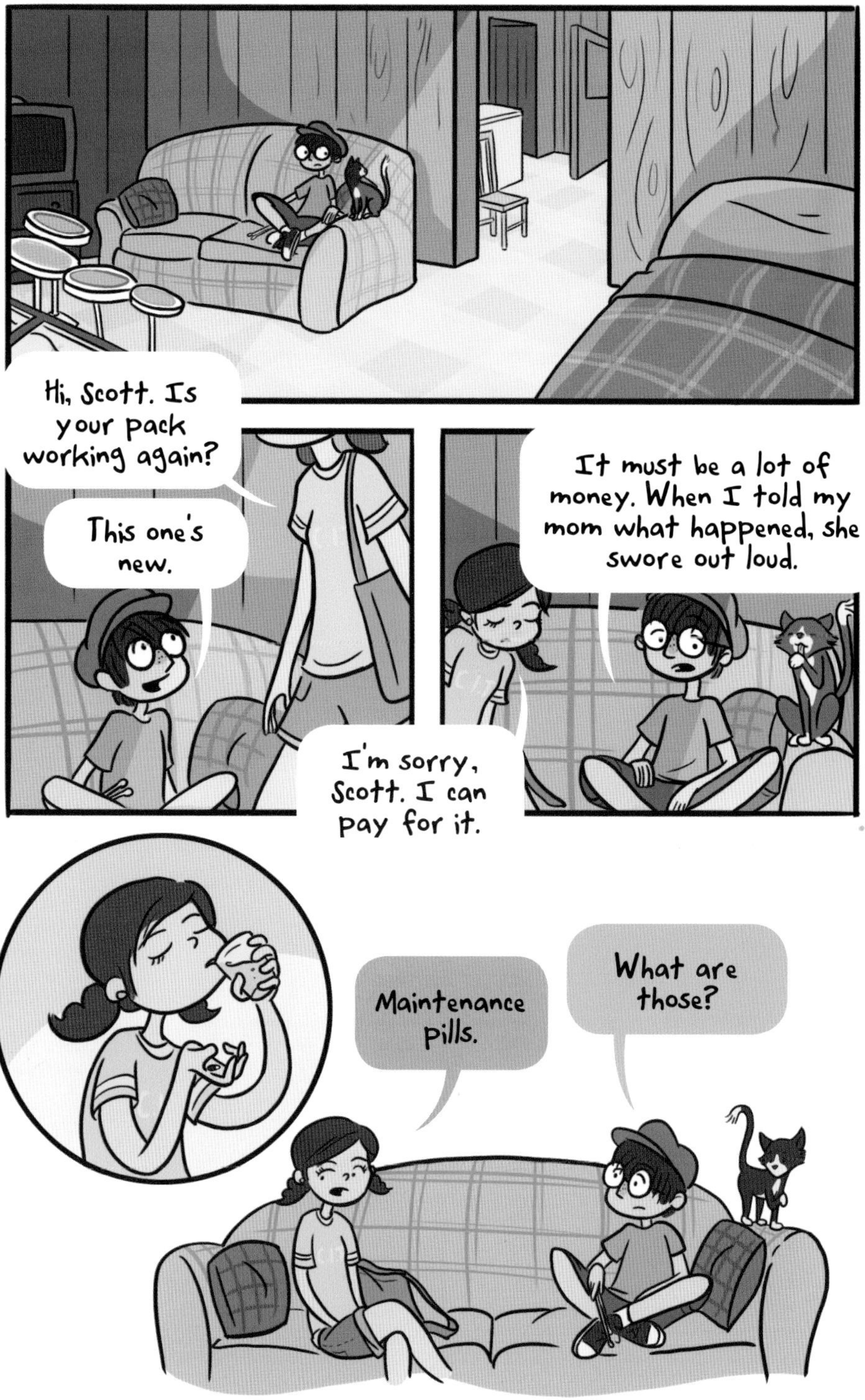
Hi, Scott. Is your pack working again?
This one's new.
It must be a lot of money. When I told my mom what happened, she swore out loud.
I'm sorry, Scott. I can pay for it.
What are those?
Maintenance pills.

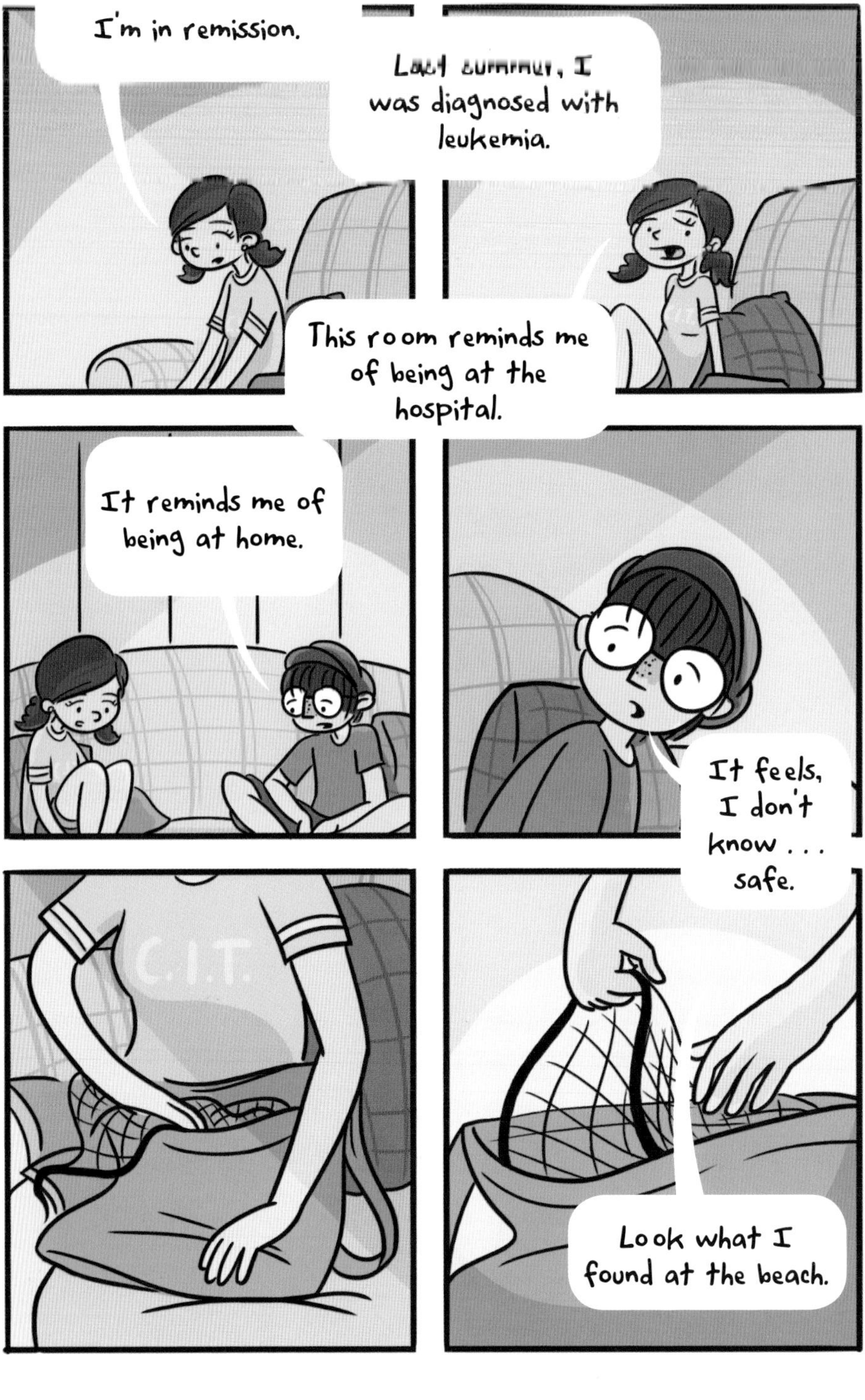
I'm in remission.
Last summer, I was diagnosed with leukemia.
This room reminds me of being at the hospital.
It reminds me of being at home.
It feels, I don't know . . . safe.
Look what I found at the beach.

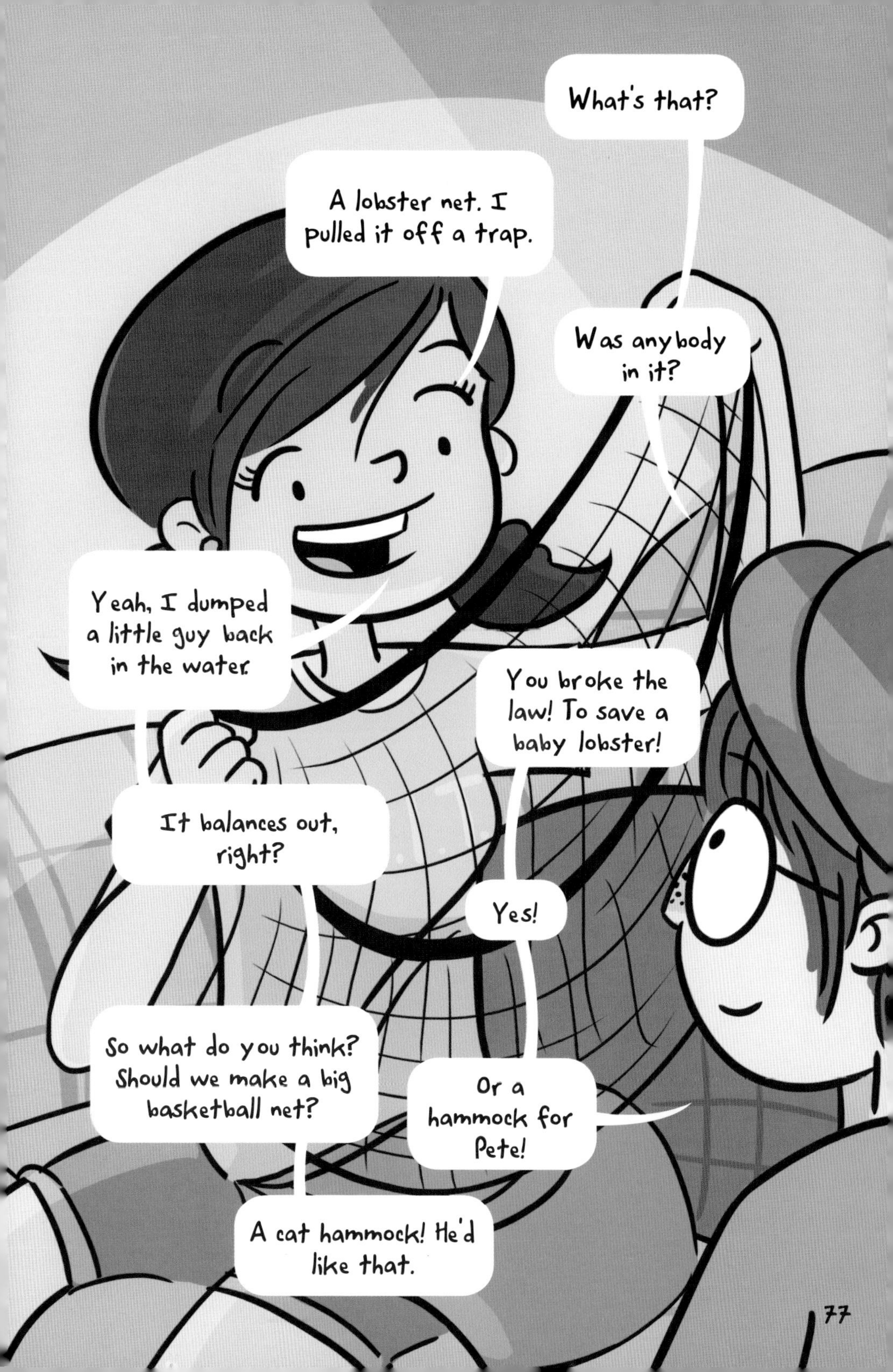
What's that?
A lobster net. I pulled it off a trap.
Was anybody in it?
Yeah, I dumped a little guy back in the water.
You broke the law! To save a baby lobster!
It balances out, right?
Yes!
So what do you think? Should we make a big basketball net?
Or a hammock for Pete!
A cat hammock! He'd like that.

12. Hoop Dream

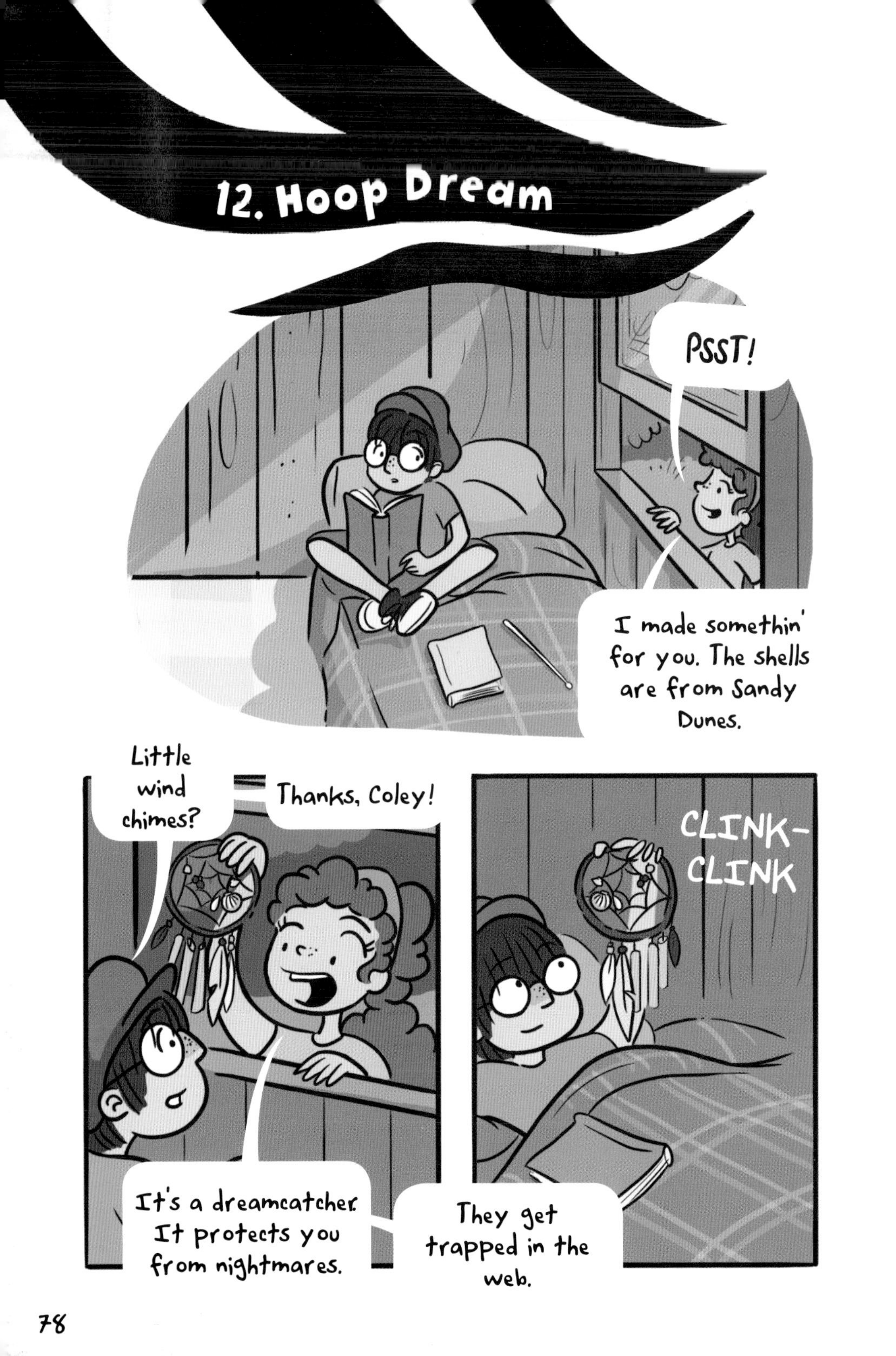
PSST!
I made somethin' for you. The shells are from Sandy Dunes.
Little wind chimes?
Thanks, Coley!
It's a dreamcatcher. It protects you from nightmares.
They get trapped in the web.
CLINK-CLINK

The Next Day . . .

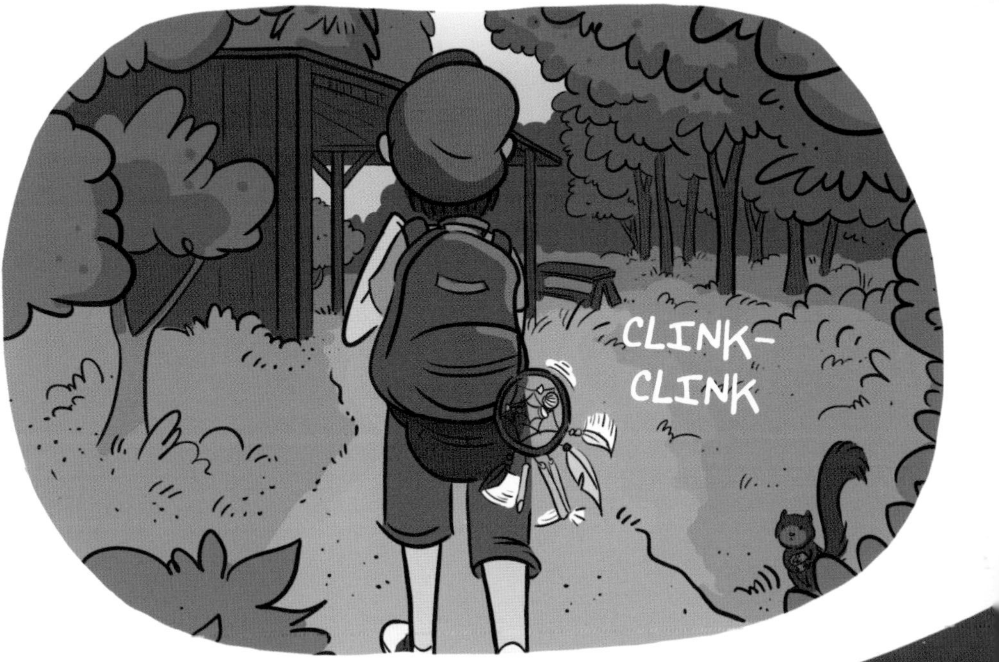
CLINK-
CLINK

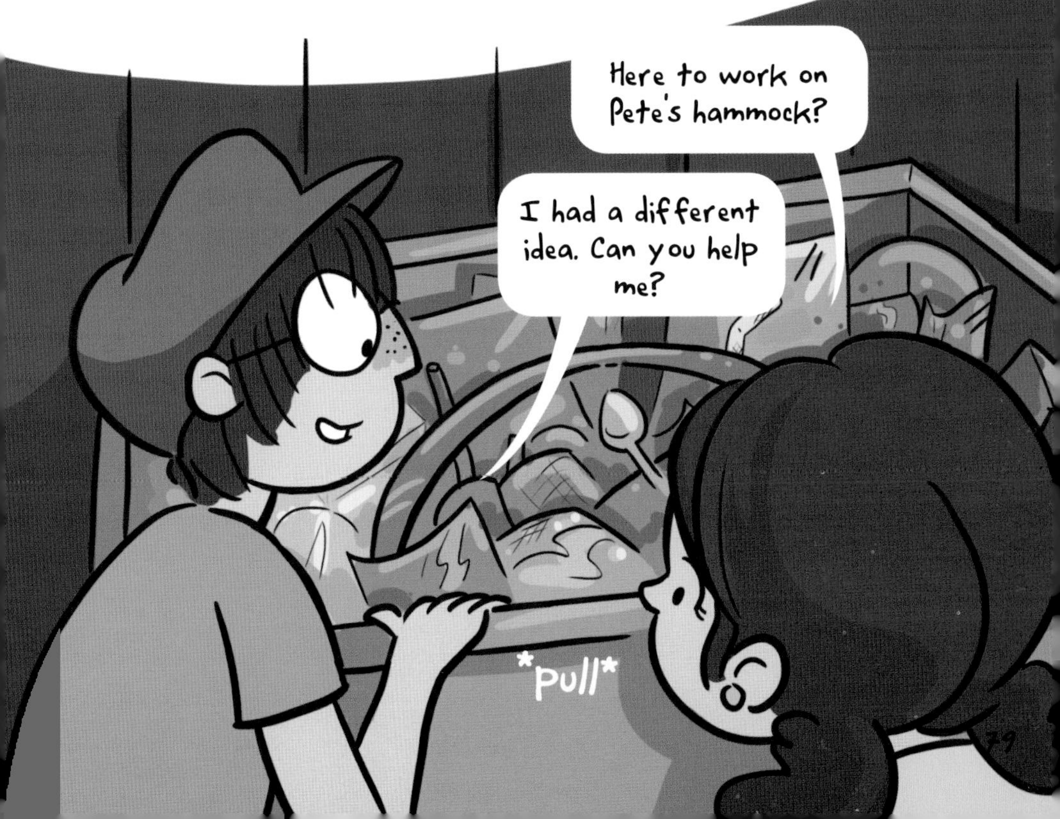
Here to work on Pete's hammock?
I had a different idea. Can you help me?
pull

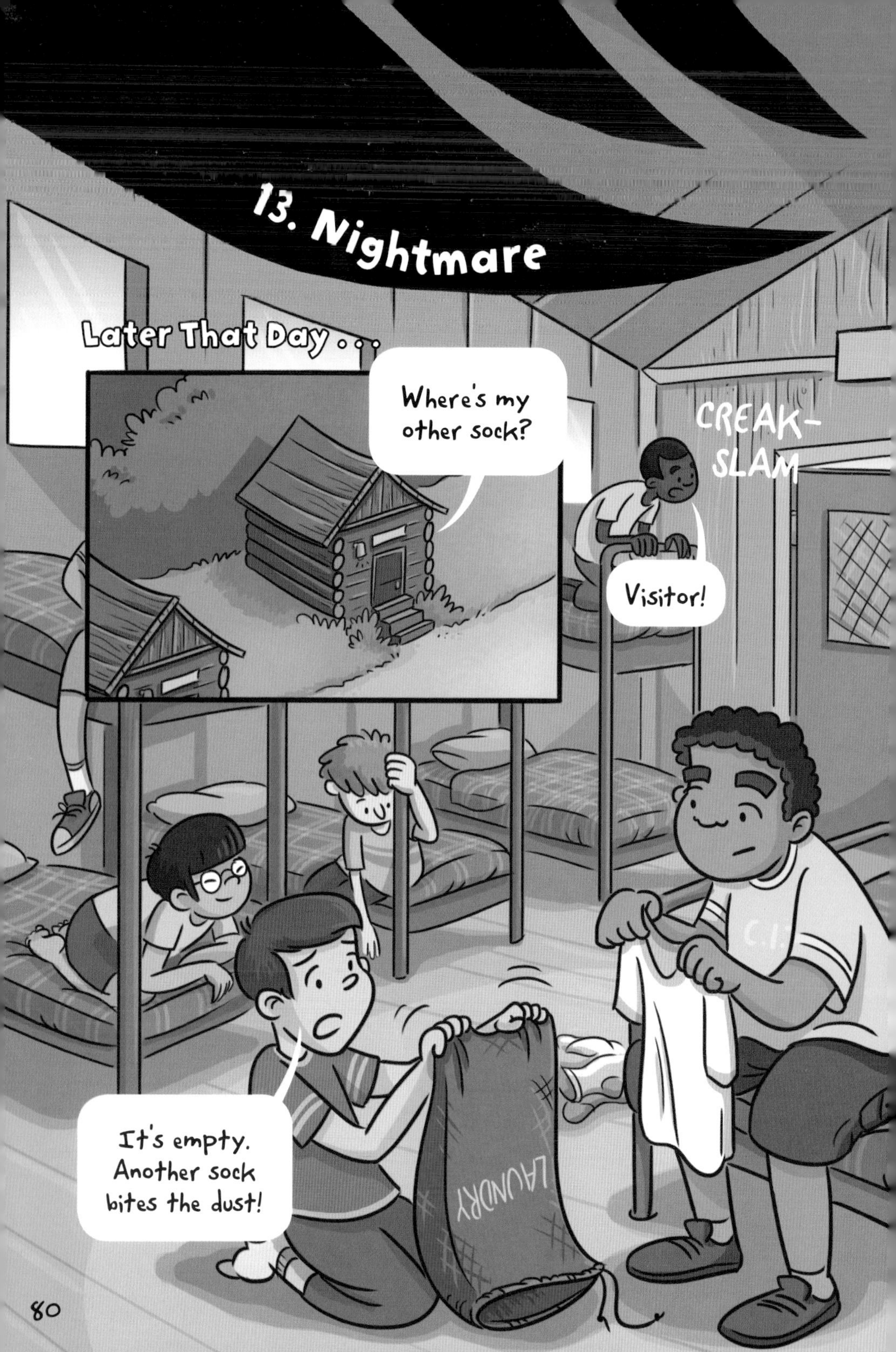

13. Nightmare
Later That Day . . .
Where's my other sock?
CREAK-SLAM
Visitor!
It's empty. Another sock bites the dust!
LAUNDRY

Scott! Come on in!

Is that Tanya?

Yeah, that's from April. We put on a show at our school.

MAKE IT BETTER
CONCERT TONIGHT

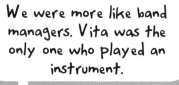

You guys were in a band?

We were more like band managers. Vita was the only one who played an instrument.

Is she in our Dunesday band?

Good question. Oh! I have something that belongs to you.

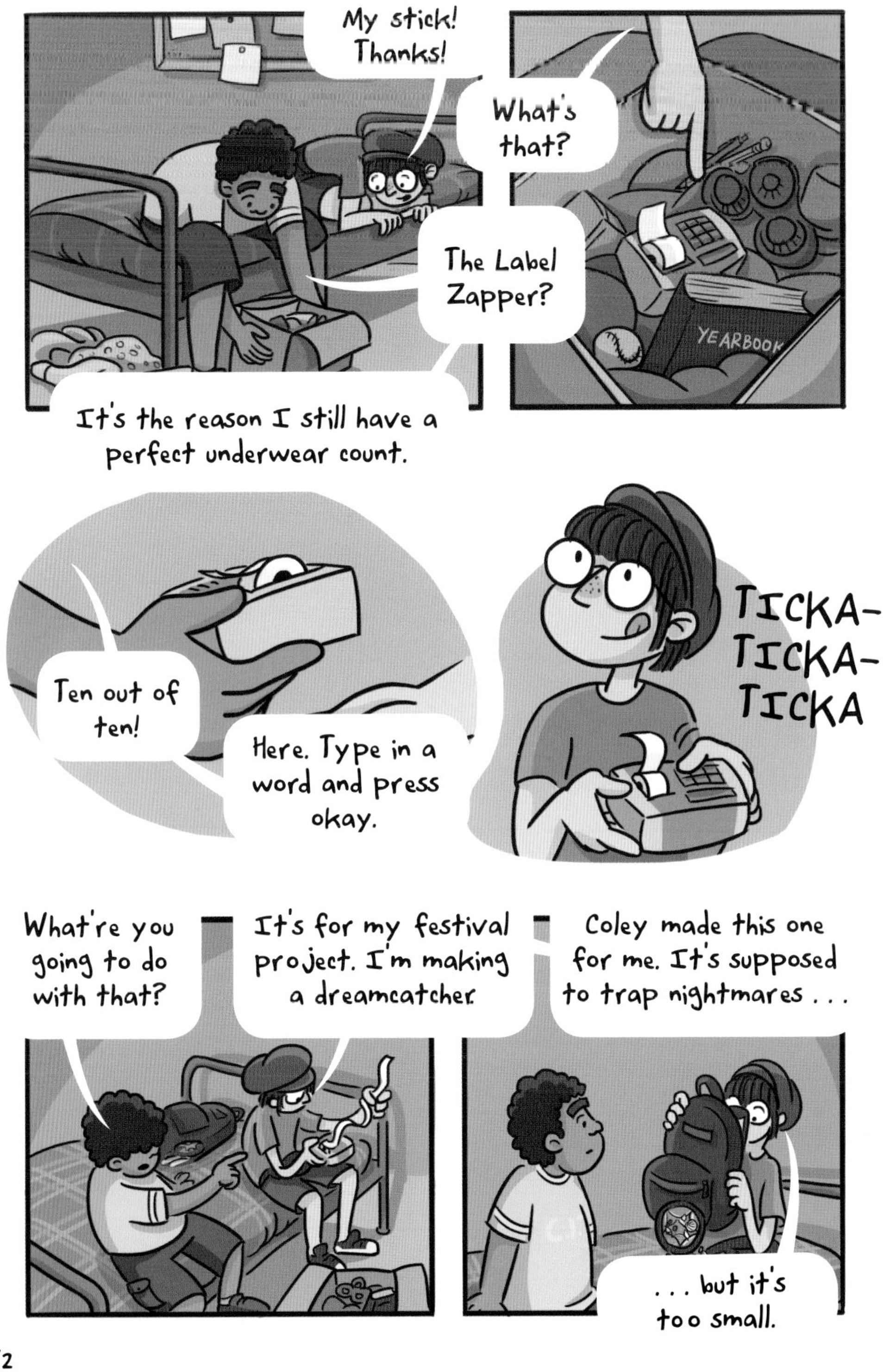
My stick! Thanks!
What's that?
The Label Zapper?
YEARBOOK
It's the reason I still have a perfect underwear count.
Ten out of ten!
Here. Type in a word and press okay.
TICKA-TICKA-TICKA
What're you going to do with that?
It's for my festival project. I'm making a dreamcatcher.
Coley made this one for me. It's supposed to trap nightmares . . .
. . . but it's too small.

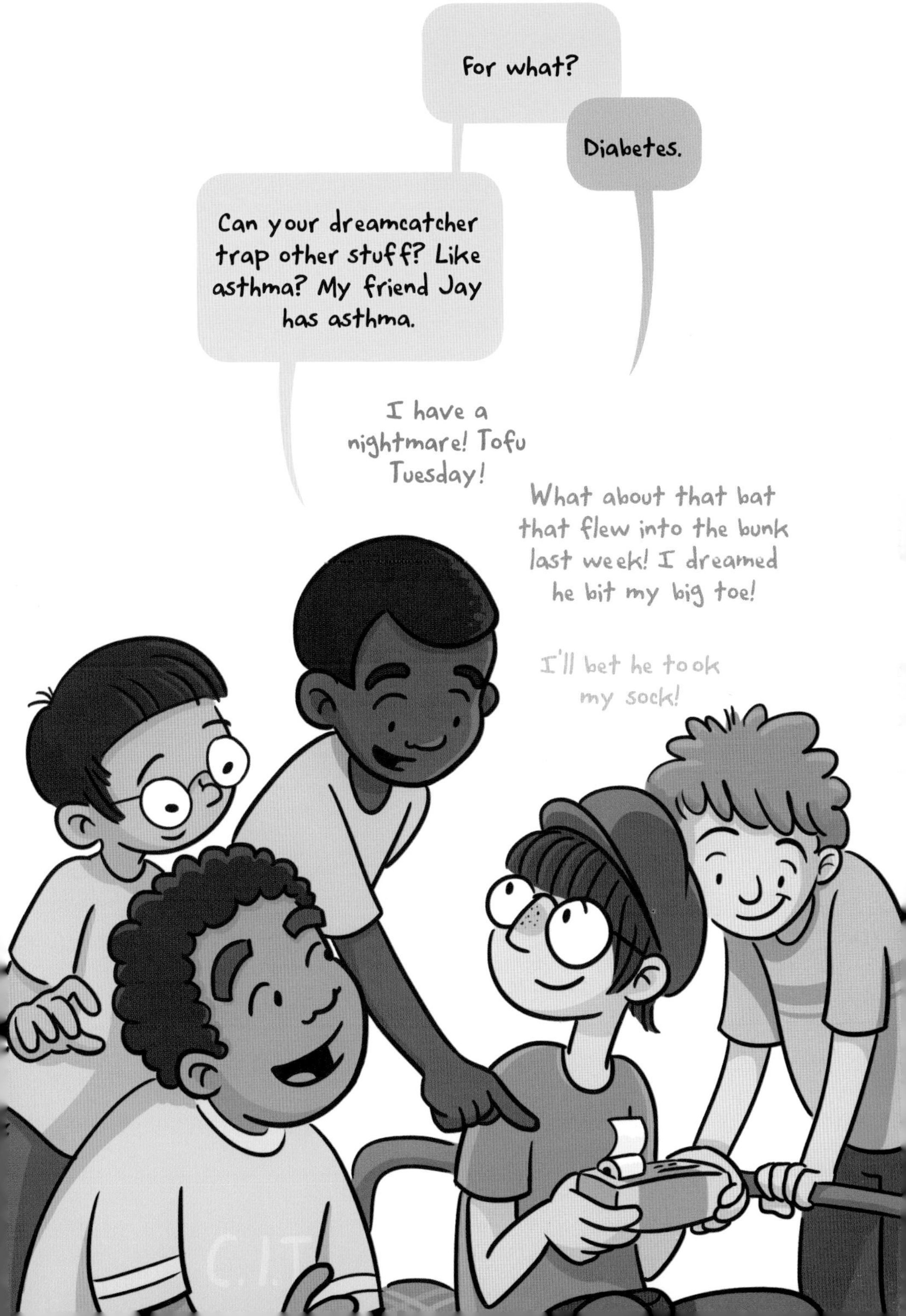
For what?
Diabetes.
Can your dreamcatcher trap other stuff? Like asthma? My friend Jay has asthma.
I have a nightmare! Tofu Tuesday!
What about that bat that flew into the bunk last week! I dreamed he bit my big toe!
I'll bet he took my sock!
C.I.T.

14. Dog Day

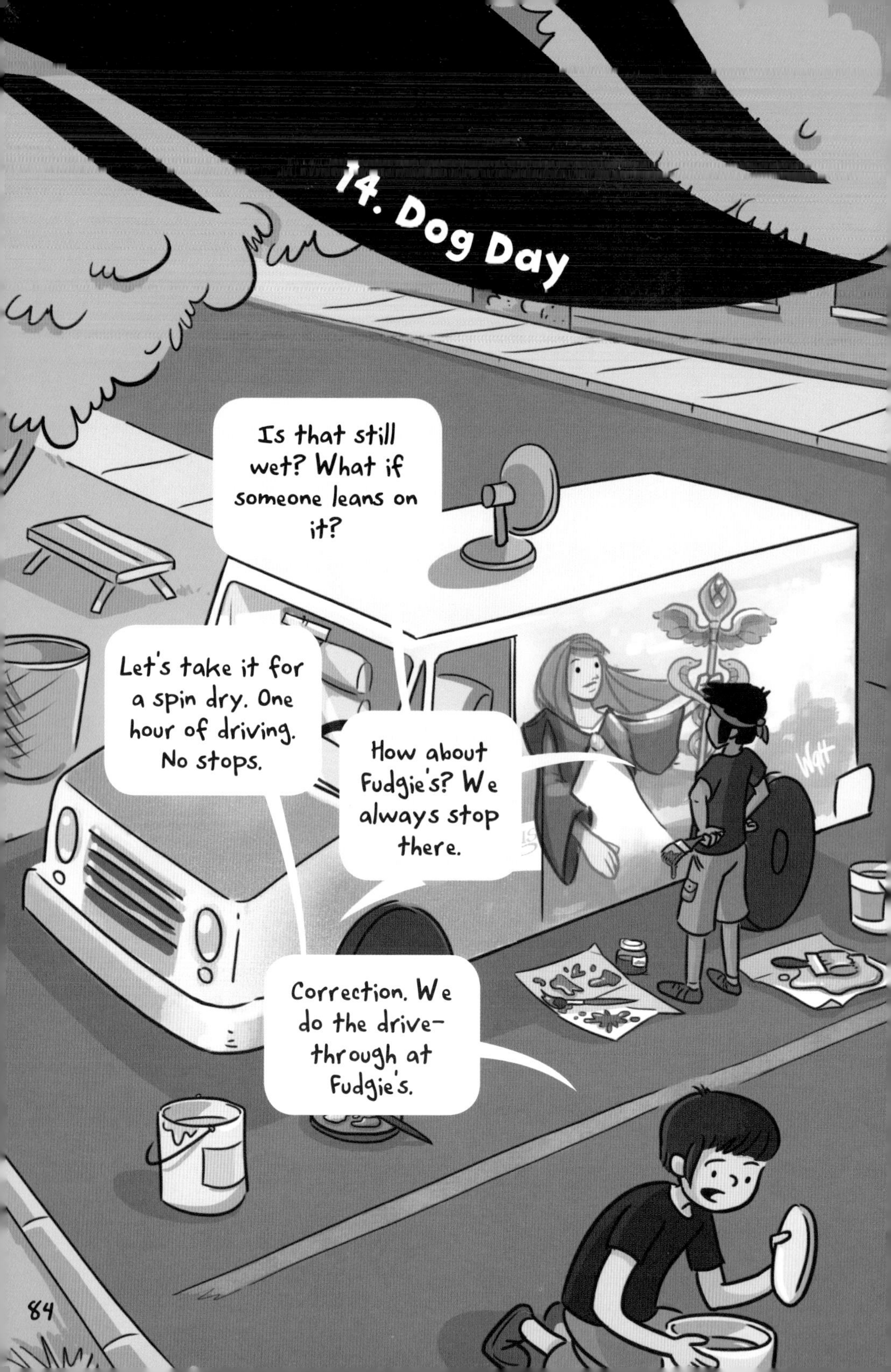

Is that still wet? What if someone leans on it?
Let's take it for a spin dry. One hour of driving. No stops.
How about Fudgie's? We always stop there.
Correction. We do the drive-through at Fudgie's.

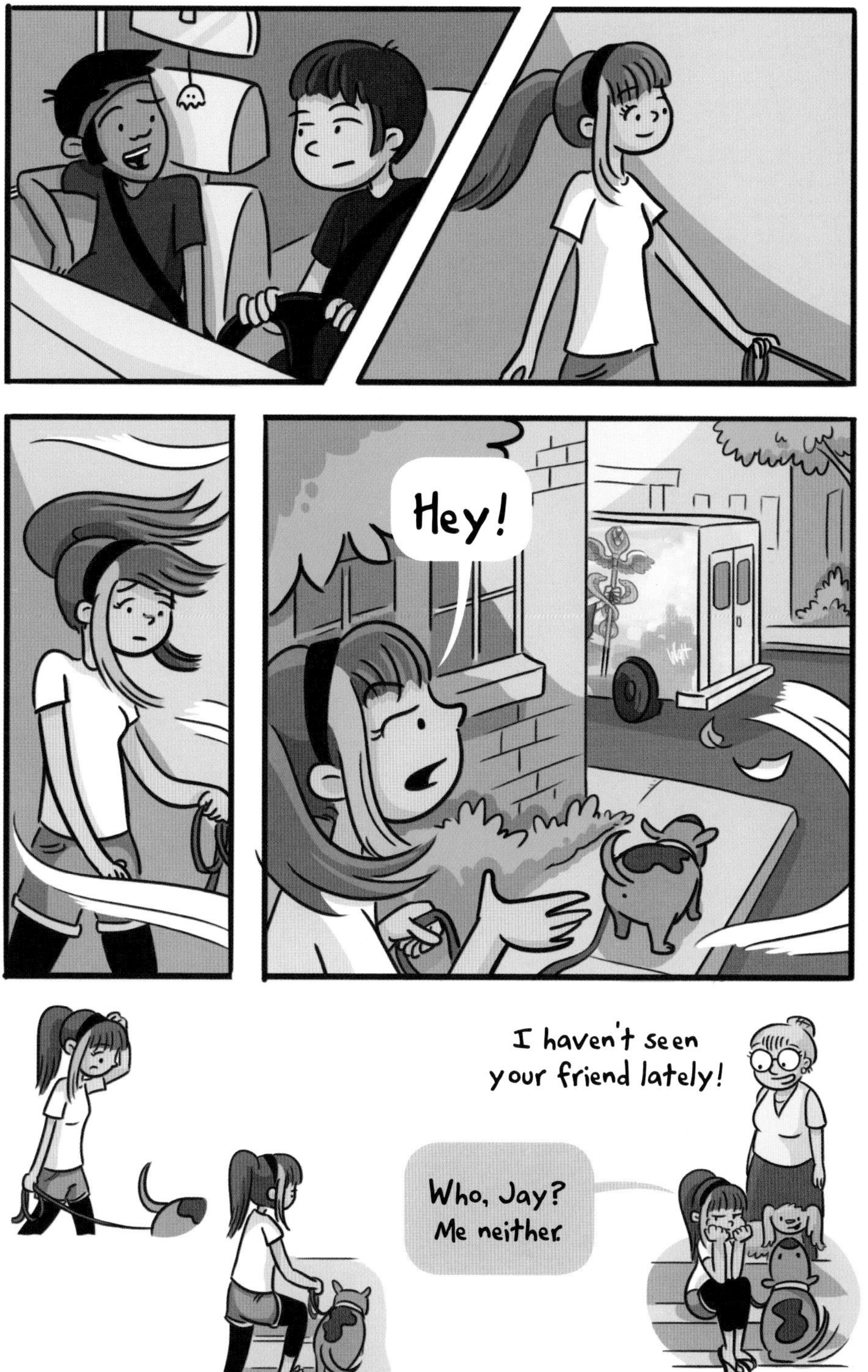
Hey!
I haven't seen your friend lately!
Who, Jay? Me neither.

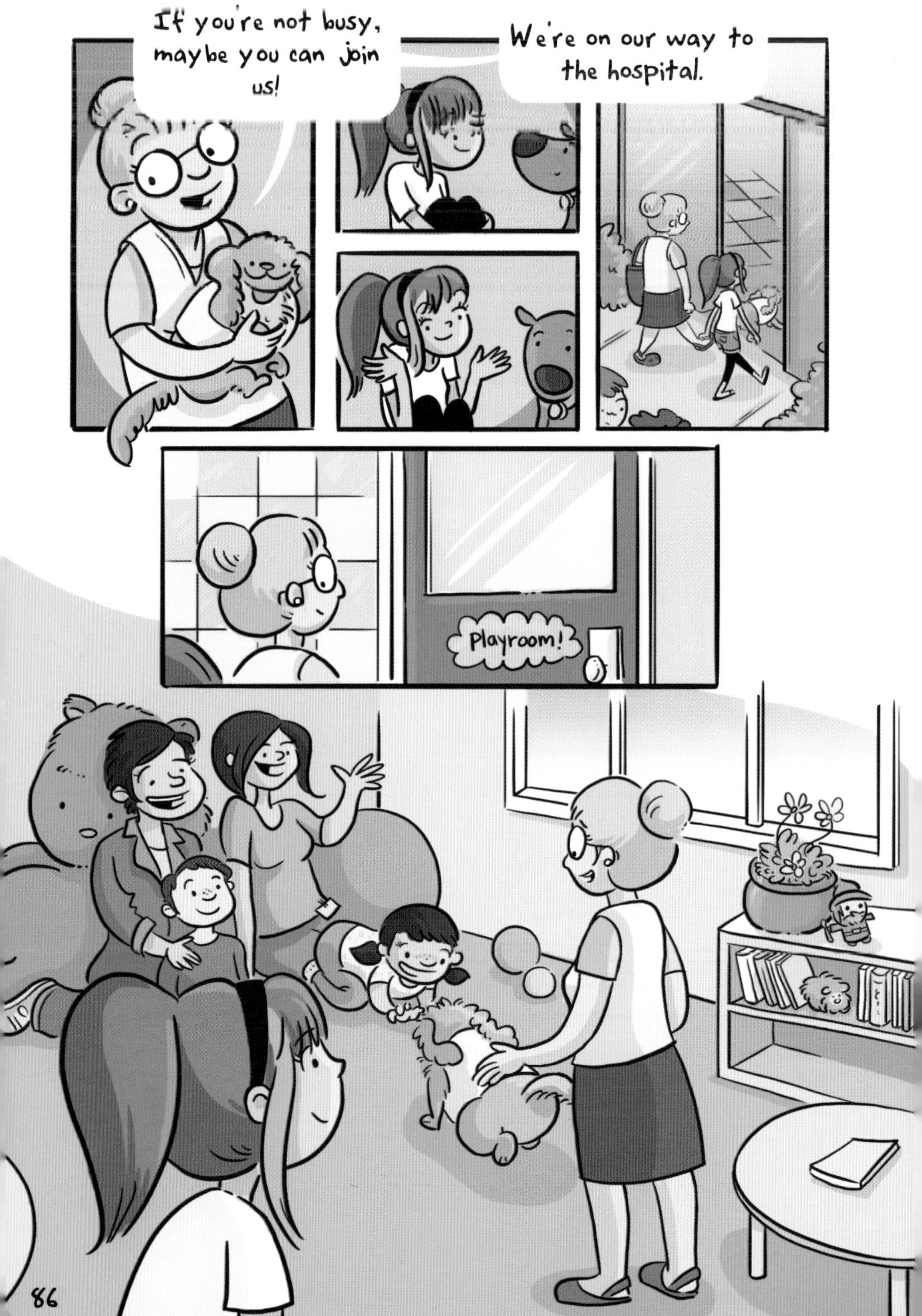
If you're not busy, maybe you can join us!
We're on our way to the hospital.
Playroom!

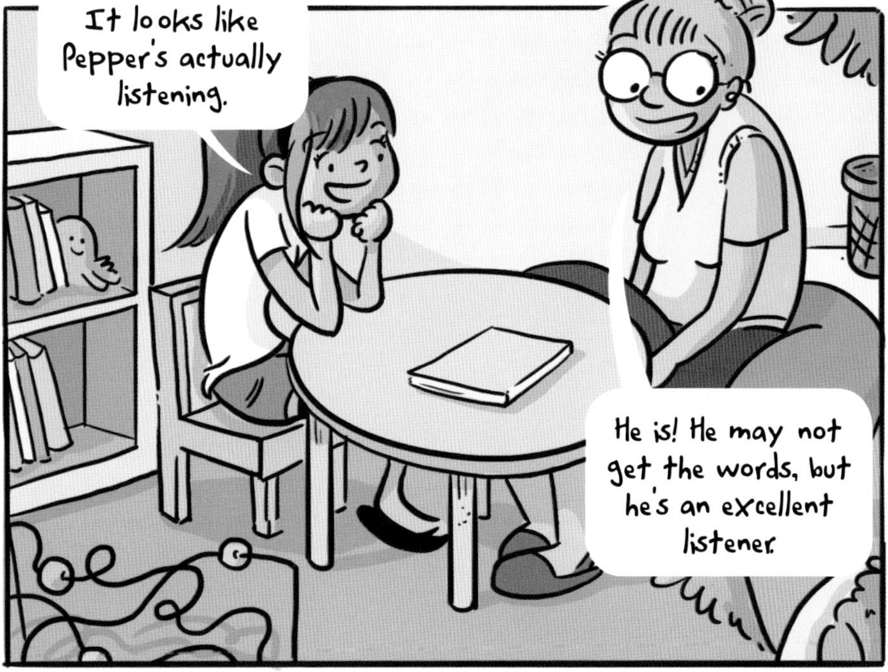
It looks like Pepper's actually listening.
He is! He may not get the words, but he's an excellent listener.

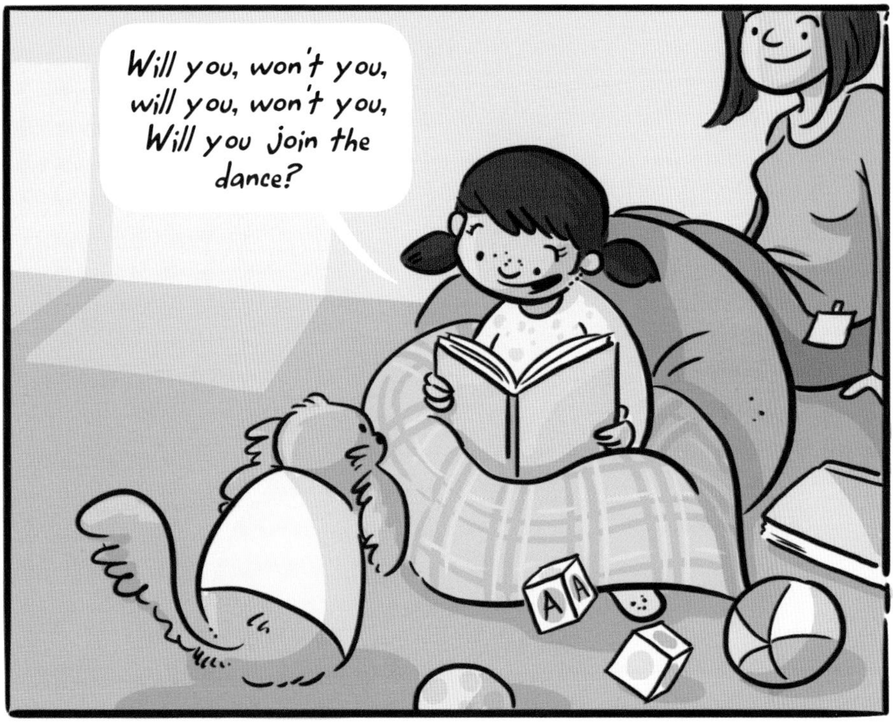
Will you, won't you, will you, won't you, Will you join the dance?

Meanwhile . . .

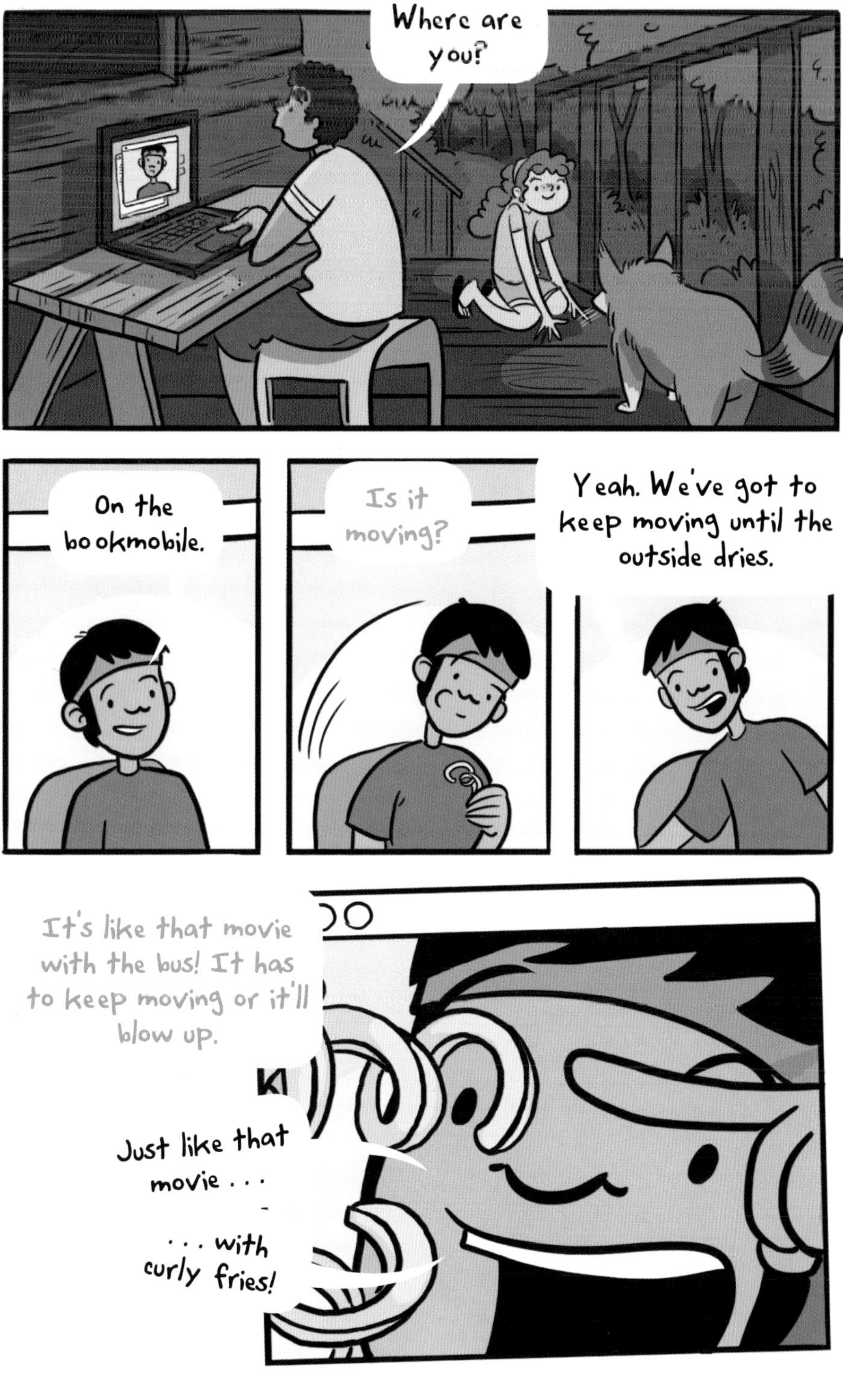
Where are you?
On the bookmobile.
Is it moving?
Yeah. We've got to keep moving until the outside dries.
It's like that movie with the bus! It has to keep moving or it'll blow up.
Just like that movie . . .
. . . with curly fries!

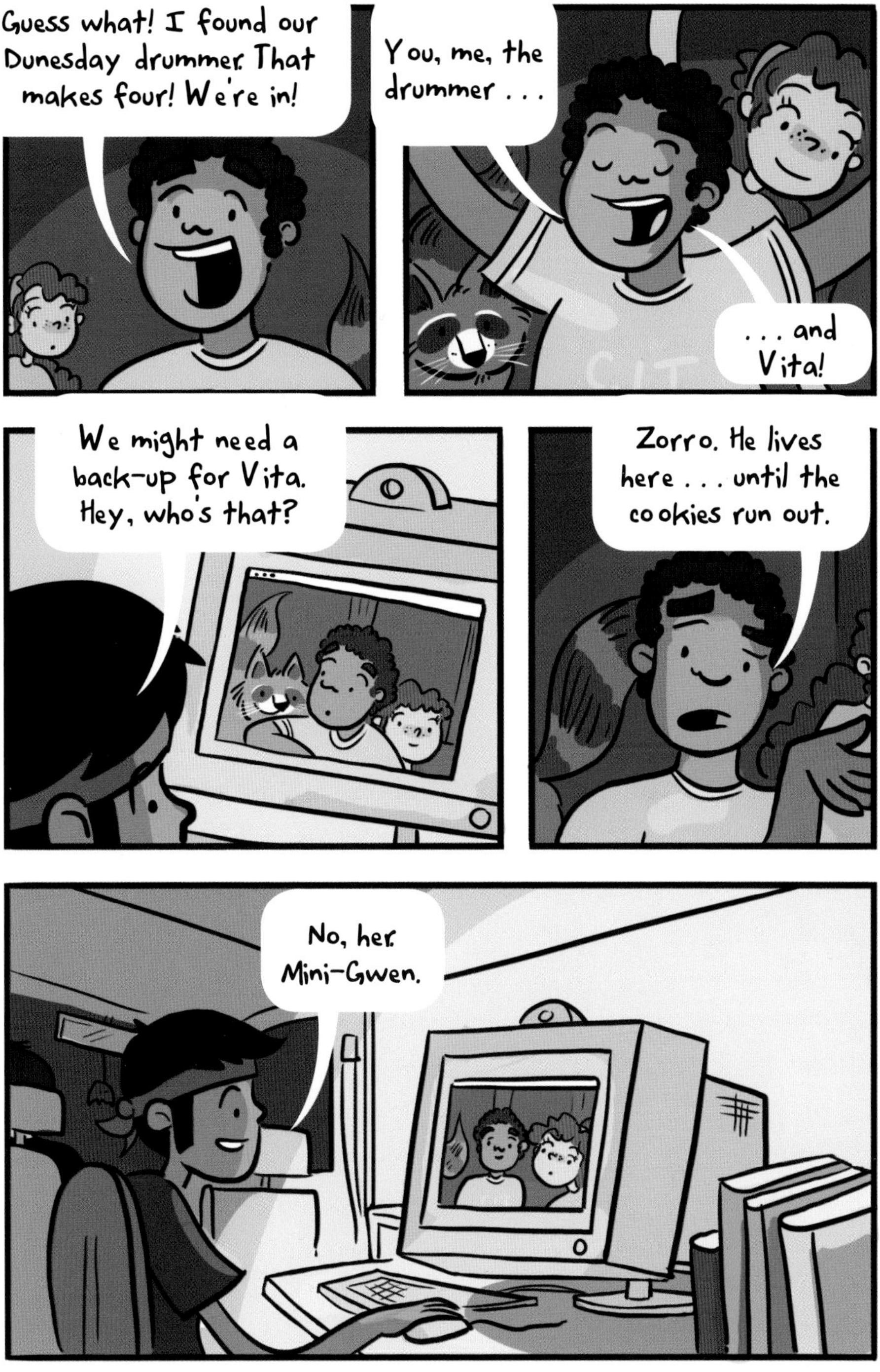
Guess what! I found our Dunesday drummer. That makes four! We're in!
You, me, the drummer . . .
. . . and Vita!
We might need a back-up for Vita. Hey, who's that?
Zorro. He lives here . . . until the cookies run out.
No, her. Mini-Gwen.

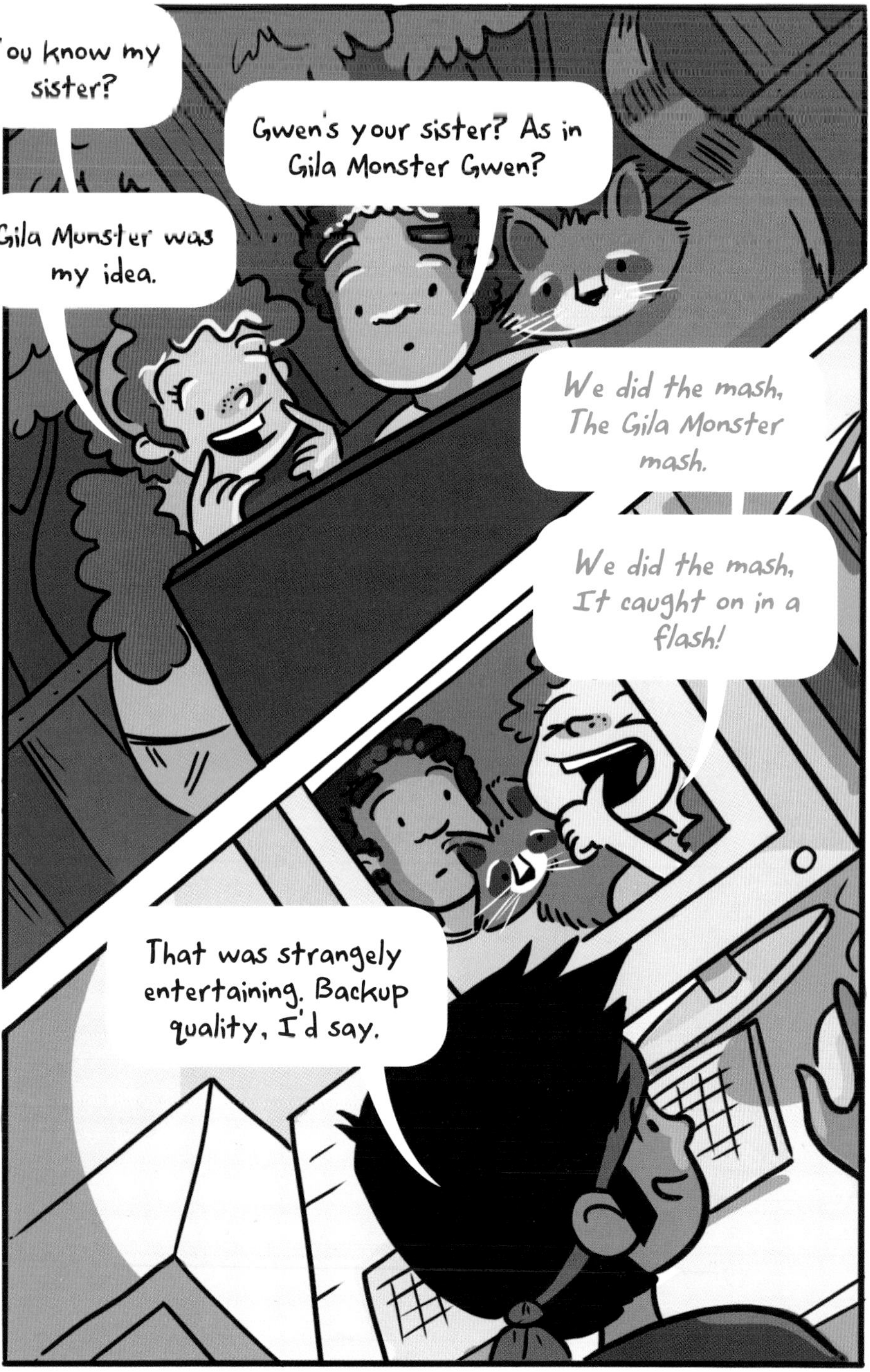
You know my sister?
Gwen's your sister? As in Gila Monster Gwen?
Gila Monster was my idea.
We did the mash, The Gila Monster mash.
We did the mash, It caught on in a flash!
That was strangely entertaining. Backup quality, I'd say.

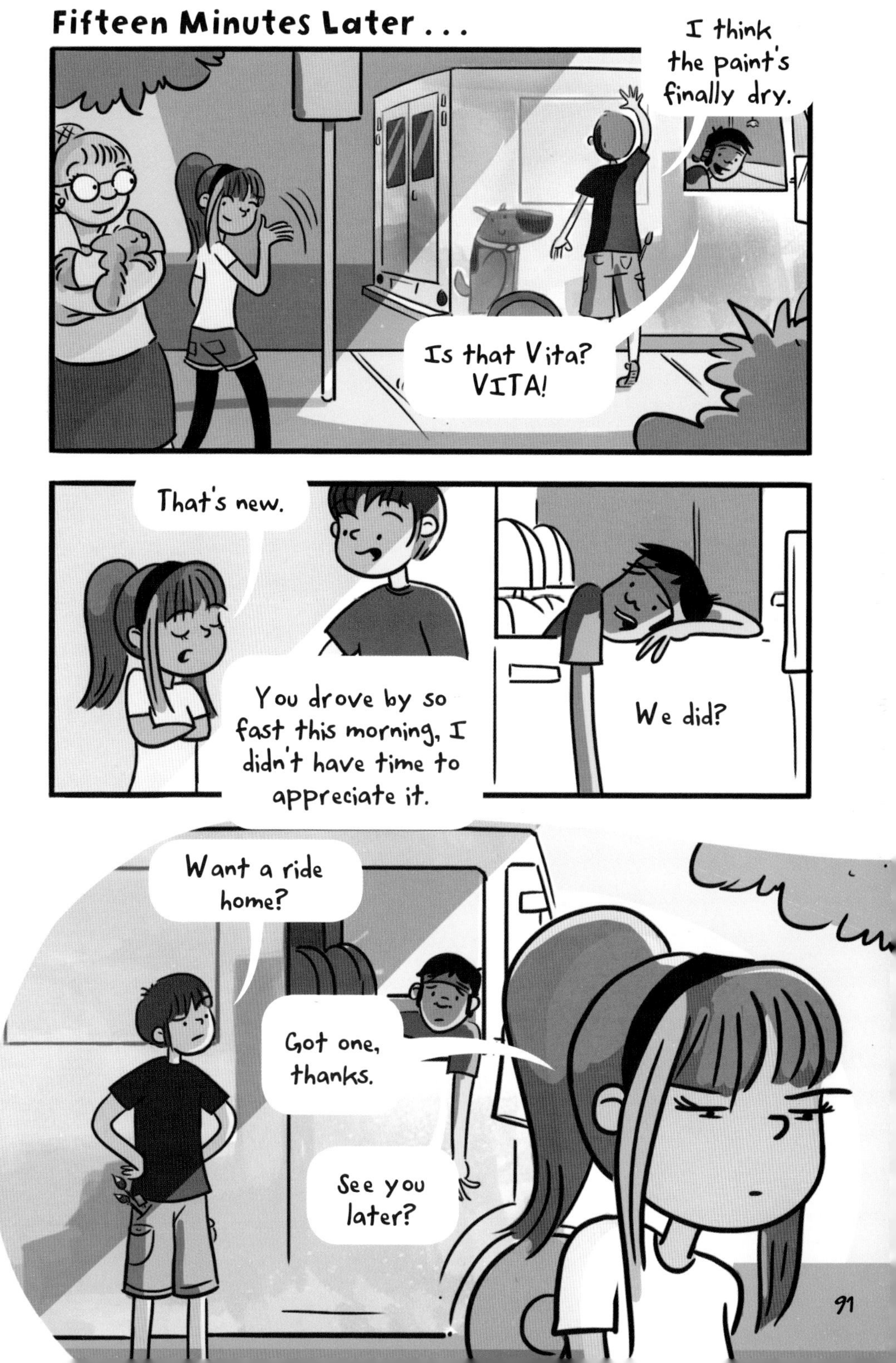
Fifteen Minutes Later . . .
I think the paint's finally dry.
Is that Vita? VITA!
That's new.
You drove by so fast this morning, I didn't have time to appreciate it.
We did?
Want a ride home?
Got one, thanks.
See you later?

Later That Evening . . .

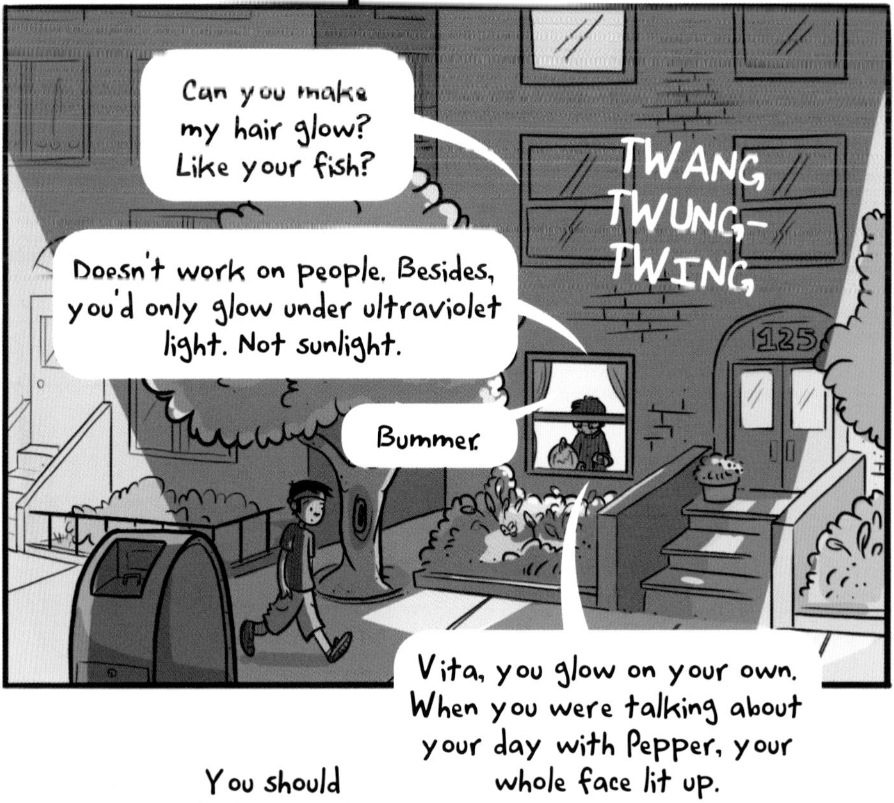
Can you make my hair glow? Like your fish?
TWANG TWUNG-TWING
Doesn't work on people. Besides, you'd only glow under ultraviolet light. Not sunlight.
125
Bummer.
Vita, you glow on your own. When you were talking about your day with Pepper, your whole face lit up.

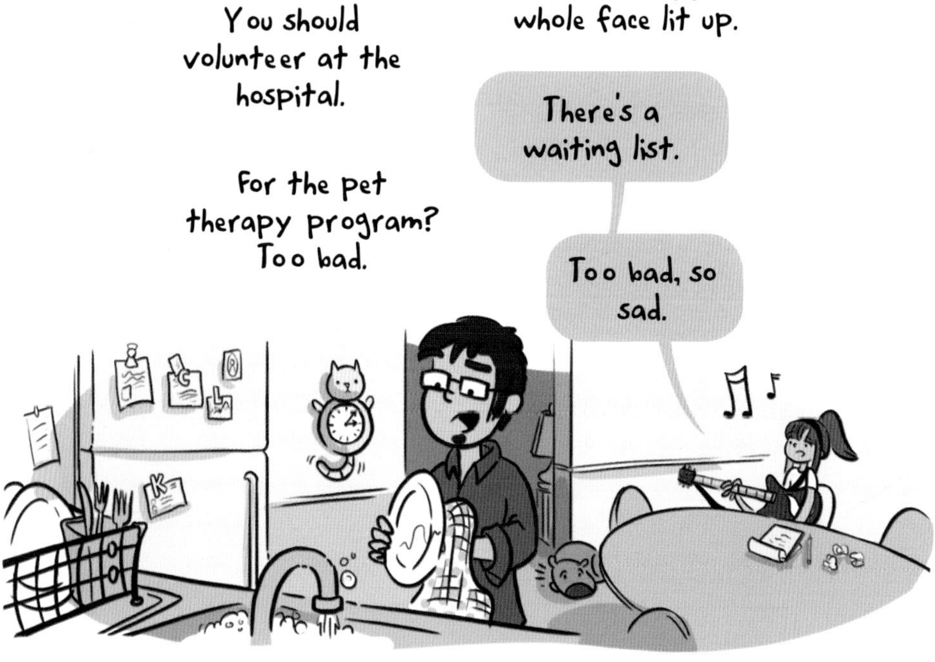
You should volunteer at the hospital.
There's a waiting list.
For the pet therapy program? Too bad.
Too bad, so sad.

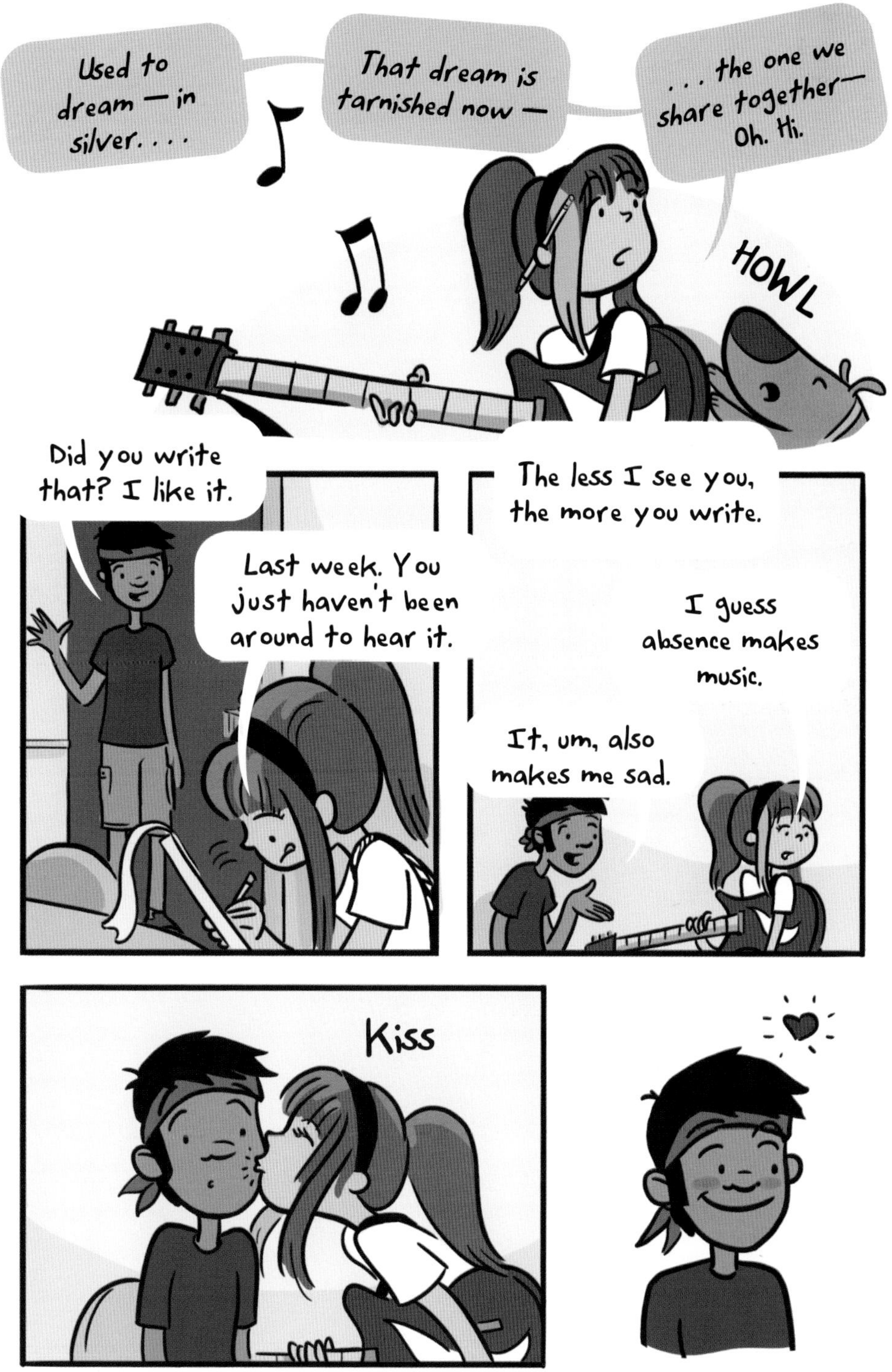
Used to dream — in silver. . . .
That dream is tarnished now —
. . . the one we share together— Oh. Hi.
HOWL
Did you write that? I like it.
Last week. You just haven't been around to hear it.
The less I see you, the more you write.
I guess absence makes music.
It, um, also makes me sad.
Kiss

15. Festival

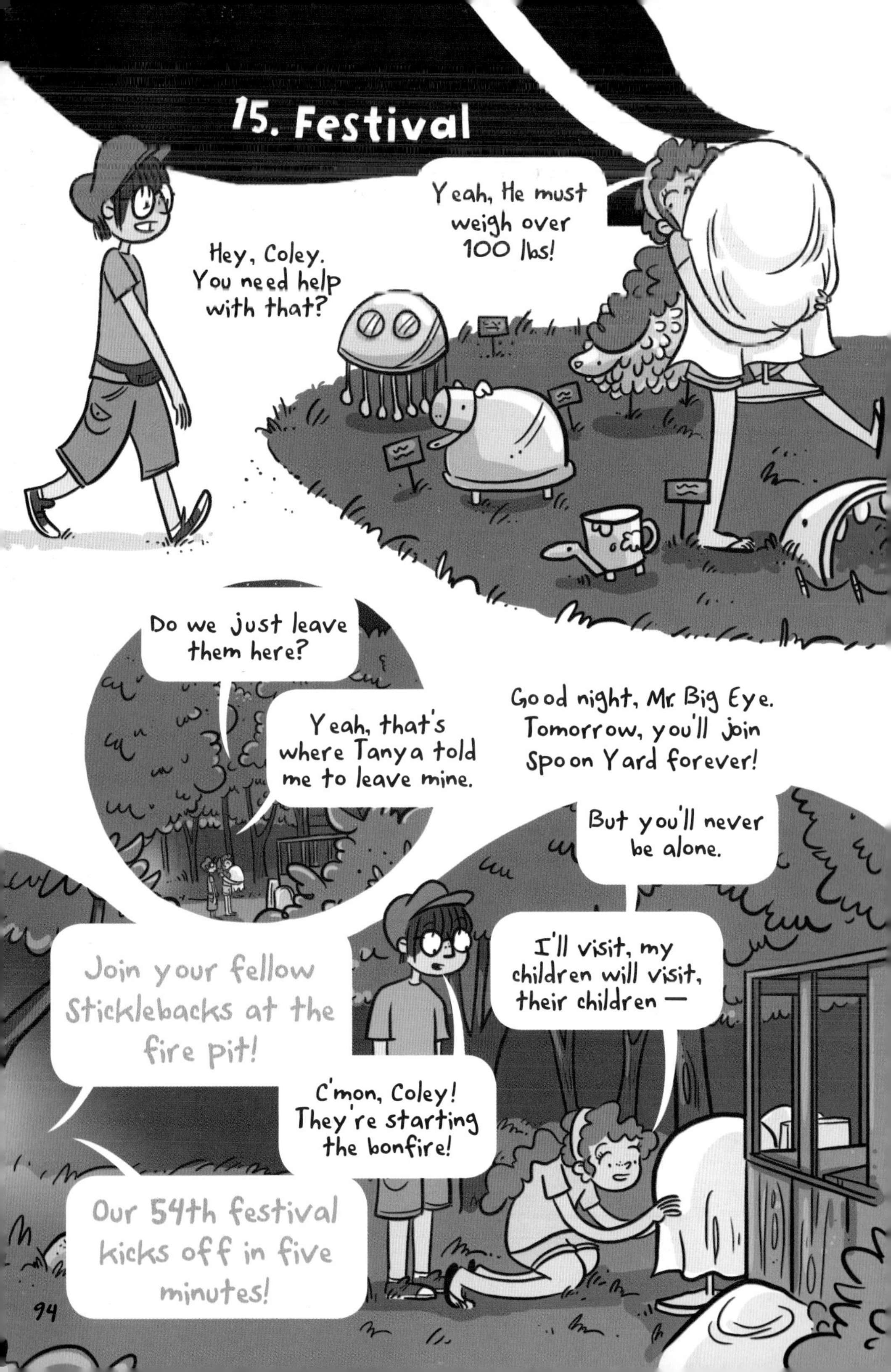
Hey, Coley. You need help with that?
Yeah, He must weigh over 100 lbs!
Do we just leave them here?
Yeah, that's where Tanya told me to leave mine.
Good night, Mr. Big Eye. Tomorrow, you'll join Spoon Yard forever!
But you'll never be alone.
I'll visit, my children will visit, their children —
Join your fellow Sticklebacks at the fire pit!
C'mon, Coley! They're starting the bonfire!
Our 54th festival kicks off in five minutes!

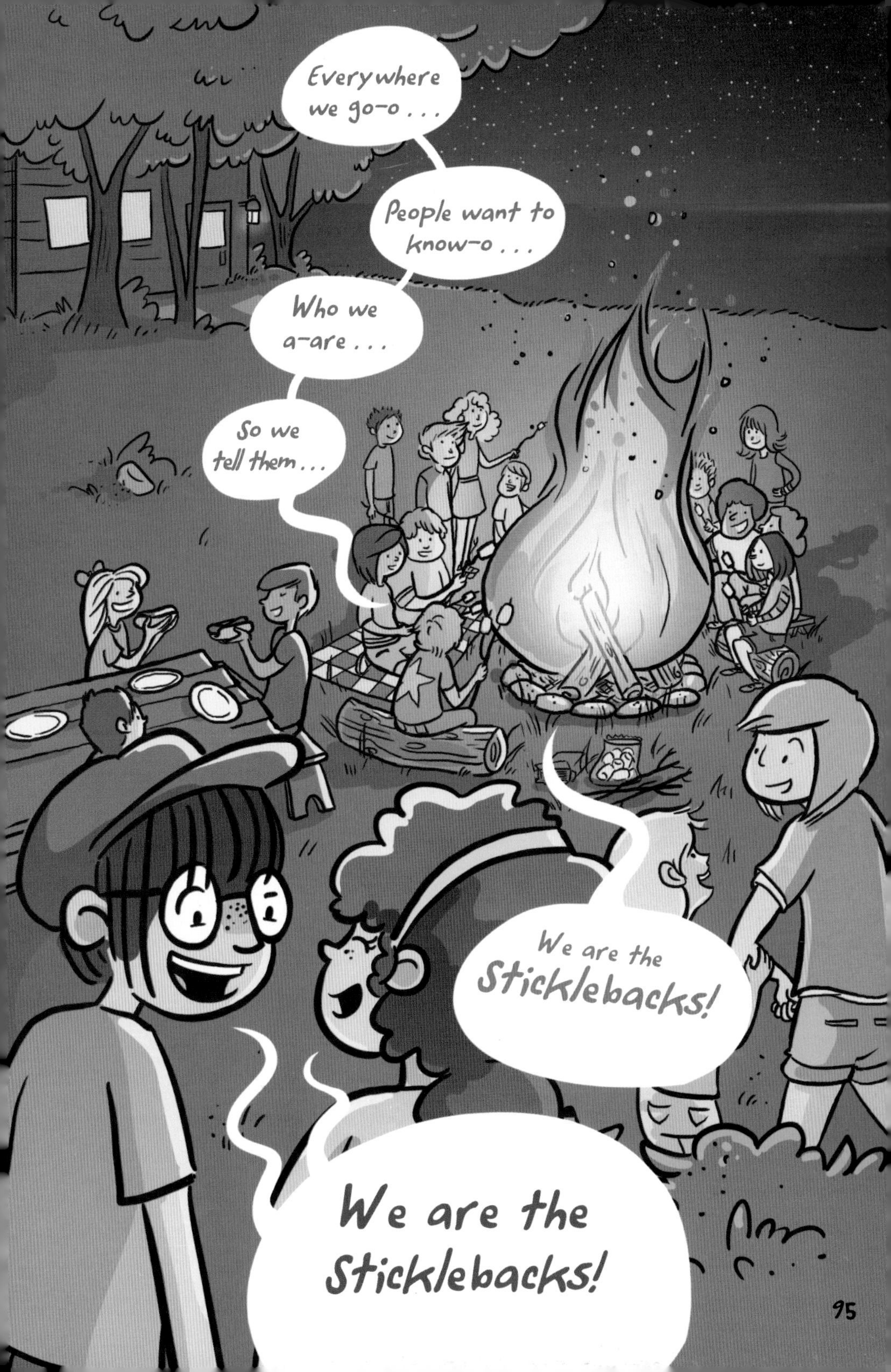
Everywhere we go-o . . .
People want to know-o . . .
Who we a-are . . .
So we tell them . . .
We are the Sticklebacks!
We are the Sticklebacks!

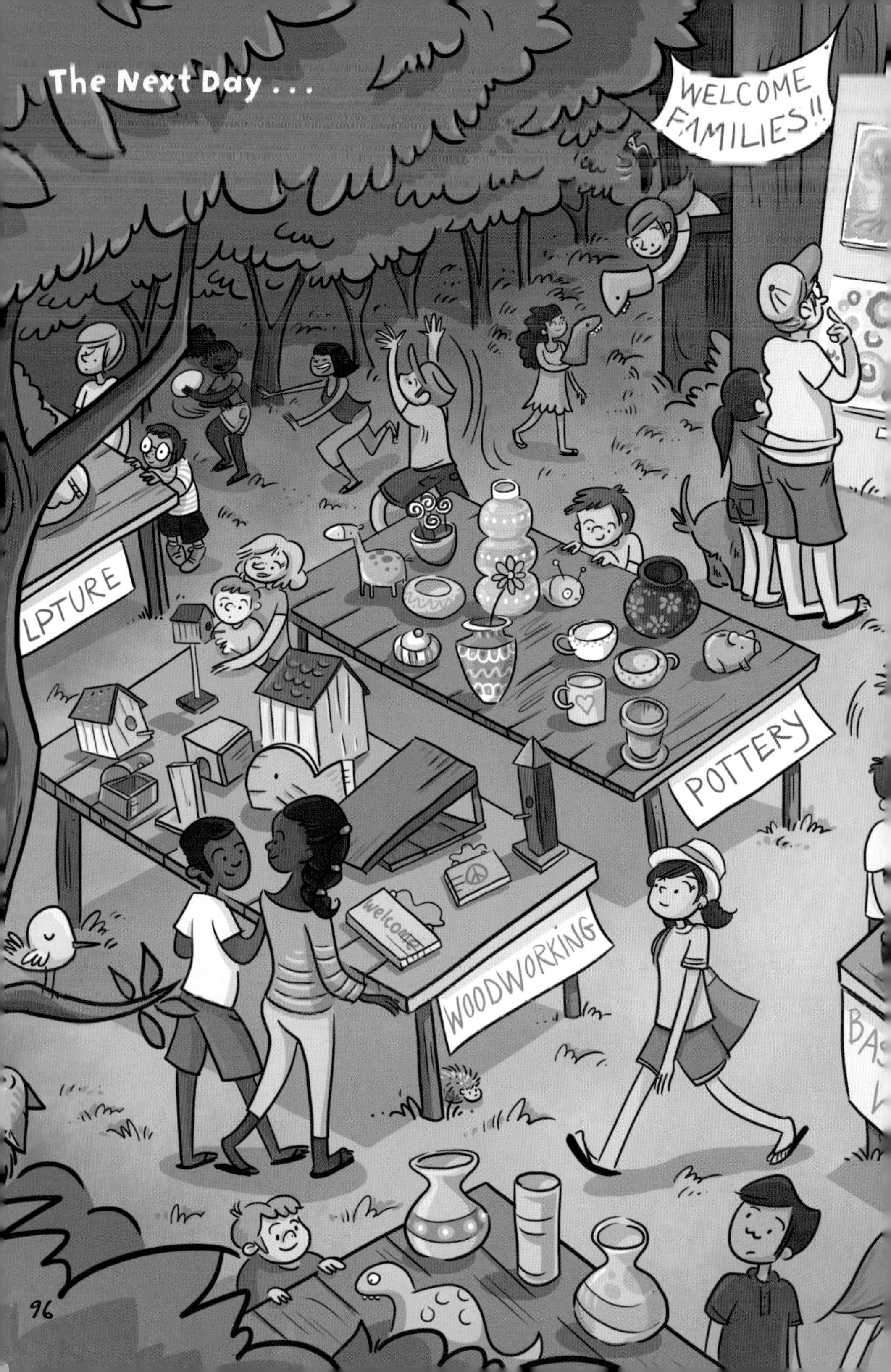
The Next Day . . .
WELCOME FAMILIES!!
LPTURE
POTTERY
WOODWORKING
welcome
BAS

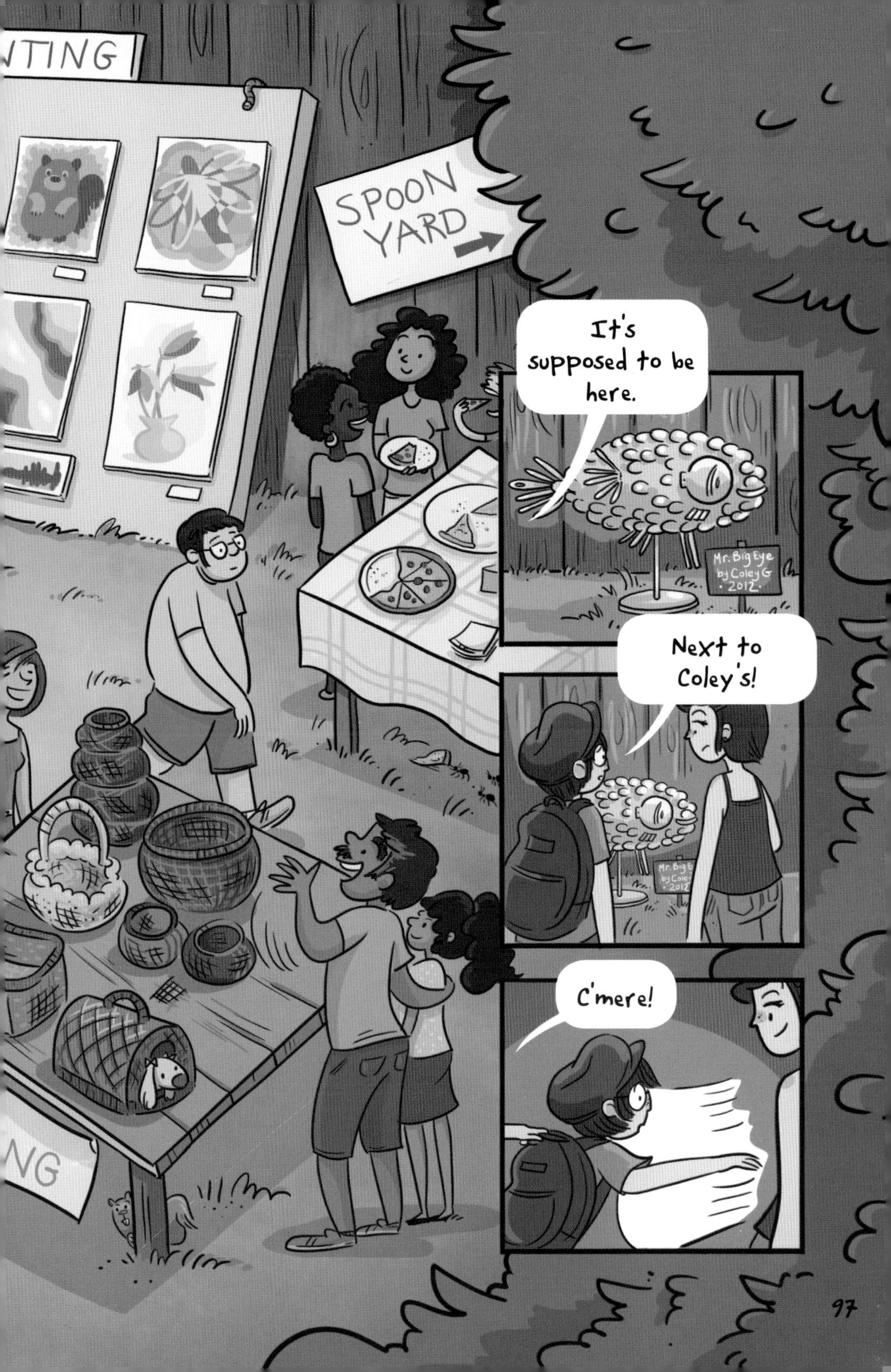

...NTING
SPOON YARD
It's supposed to be here.
Mr. Big Eye by Coley G 2012.
Next to Coley's!
C'mere!
...NG

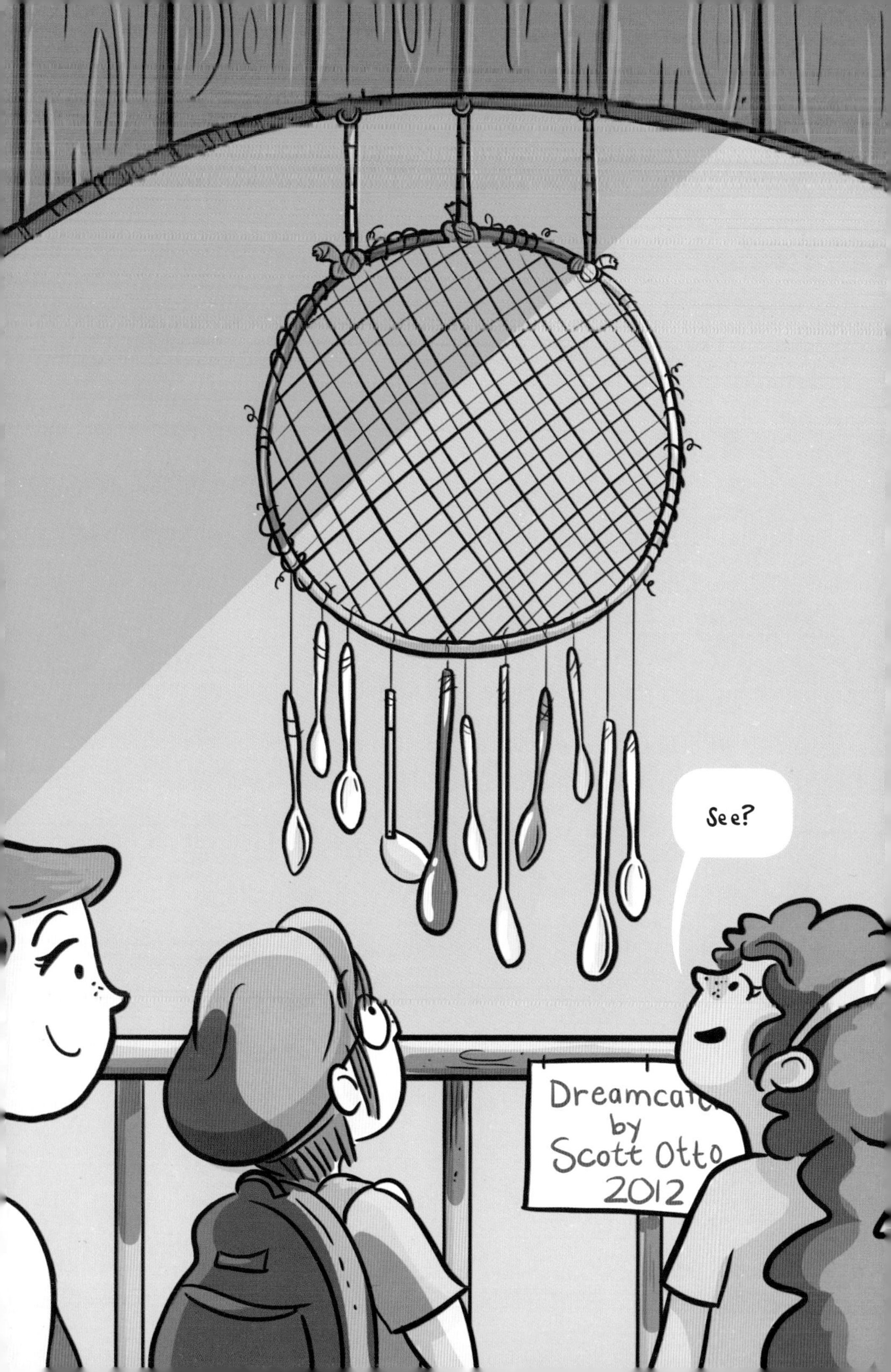
See?
Dreamcat
by
Scott Otto
2012

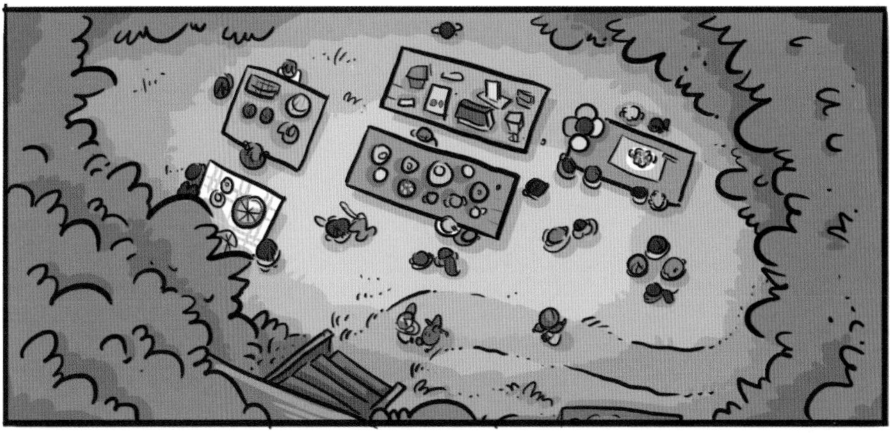

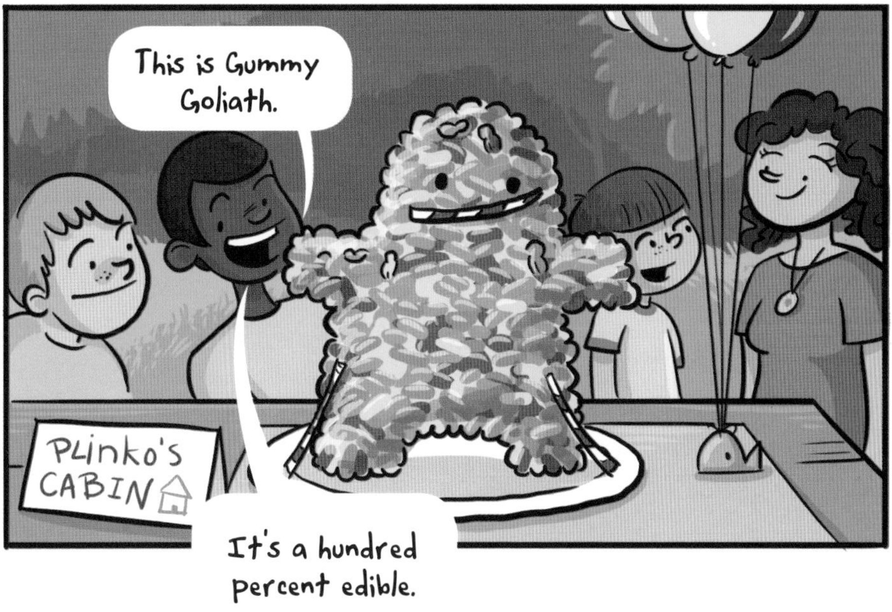
This is Gummy Goliath.
PLINKO'S CABIN
It's a hundred percent edible.

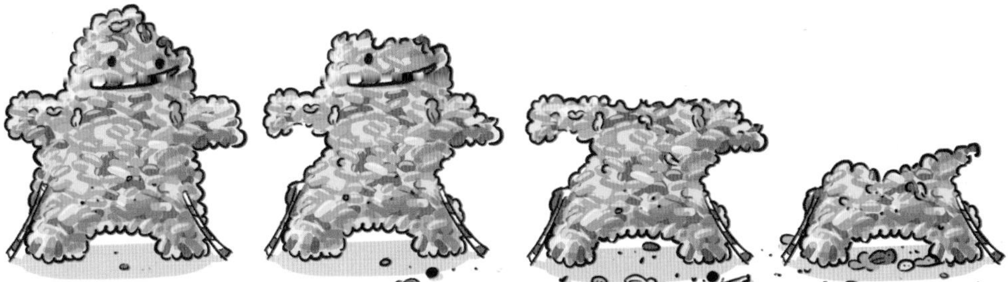

The Next Day . . .

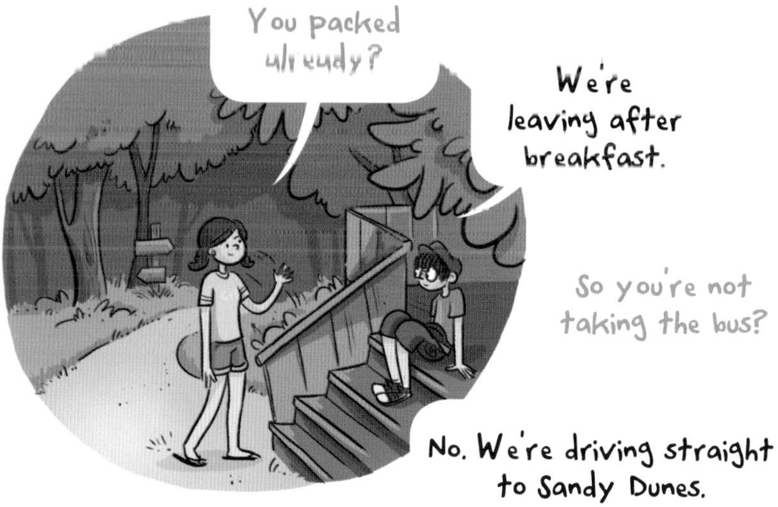
You packed already?
We're leaving after breakfast.
So you're not taking the bus?
No. We're driving straight to Sandy Dunes.

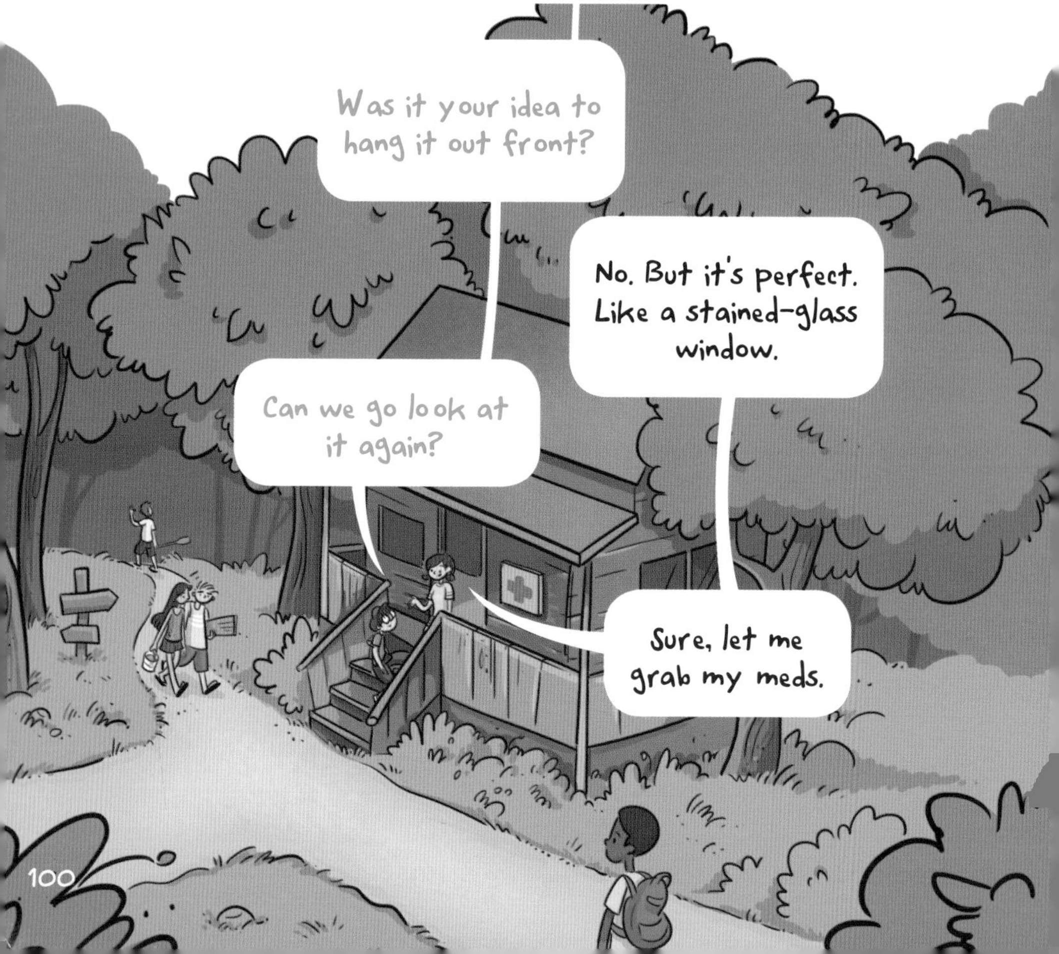
Was it your idea to hang it out front?
No. But it's perfect. Like a stained-glass window.
Can we go look at it again?
Sure, let me grab my meds.

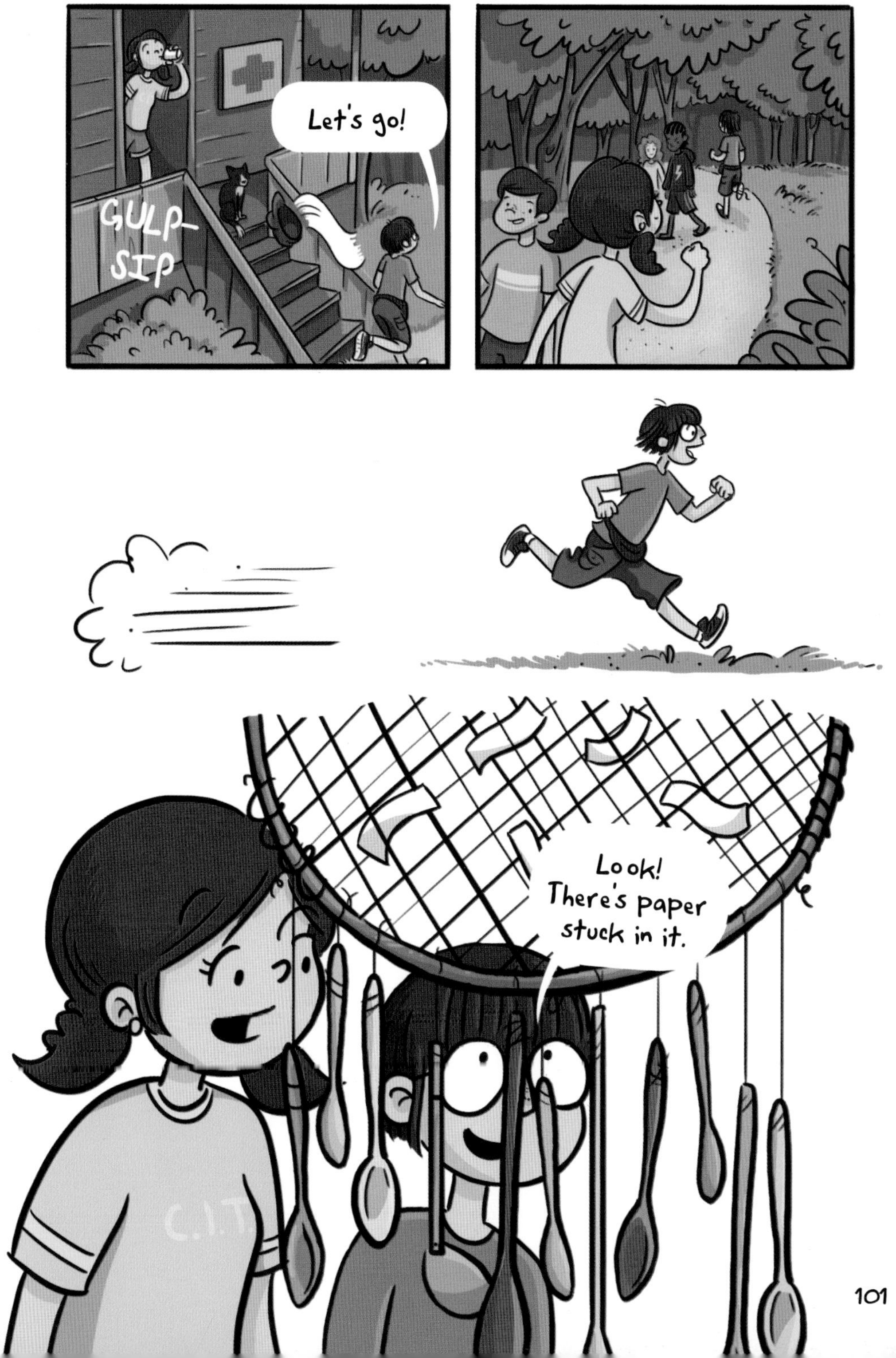
GULP-
SIP
Let's go!
Look! There's paper stuck in it.
C.I.T.

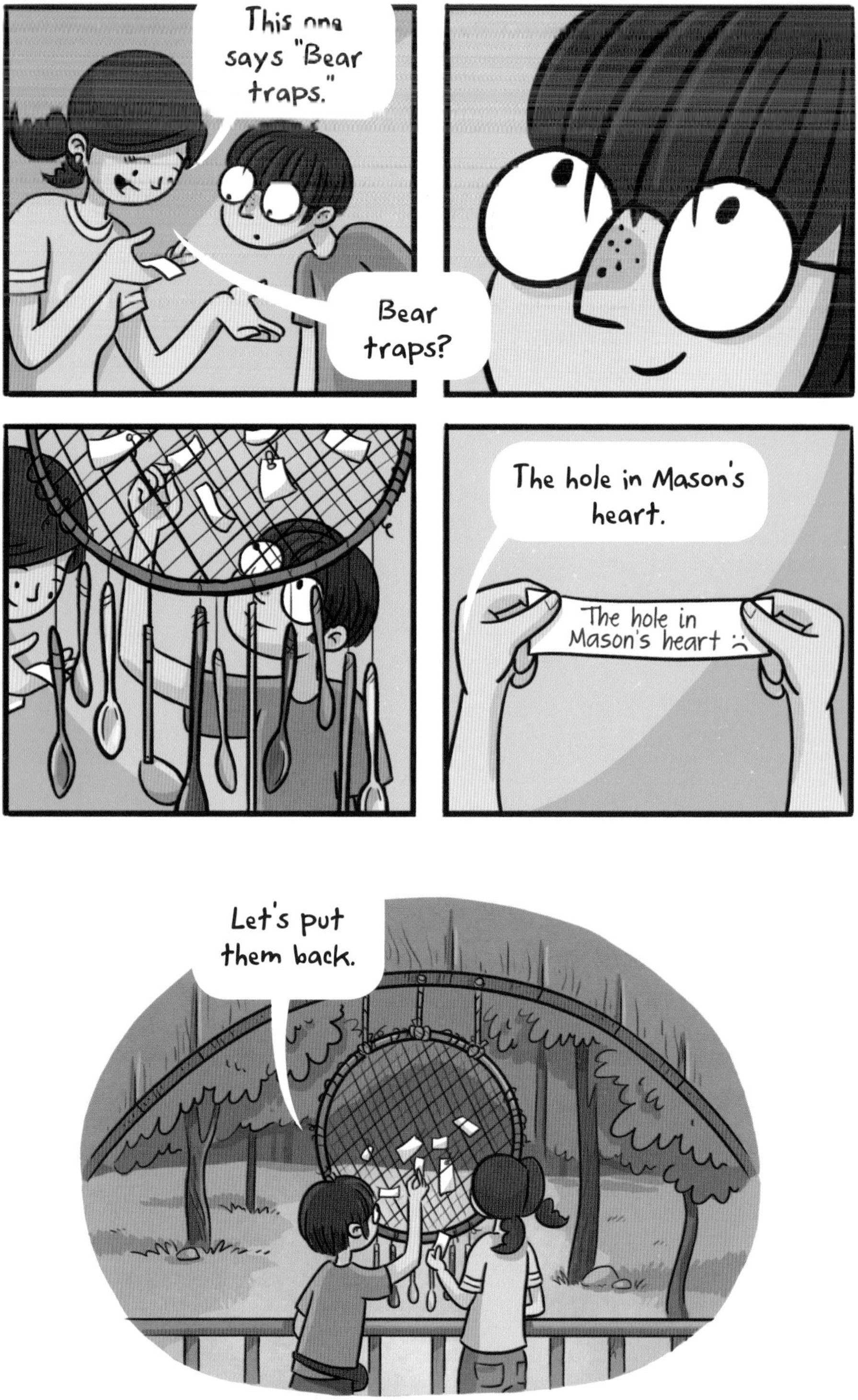

This one says "Bear traps."
Bear traps?
The hole in Mason's heart.
The hole in Mason's heart :(
Let's put them back.

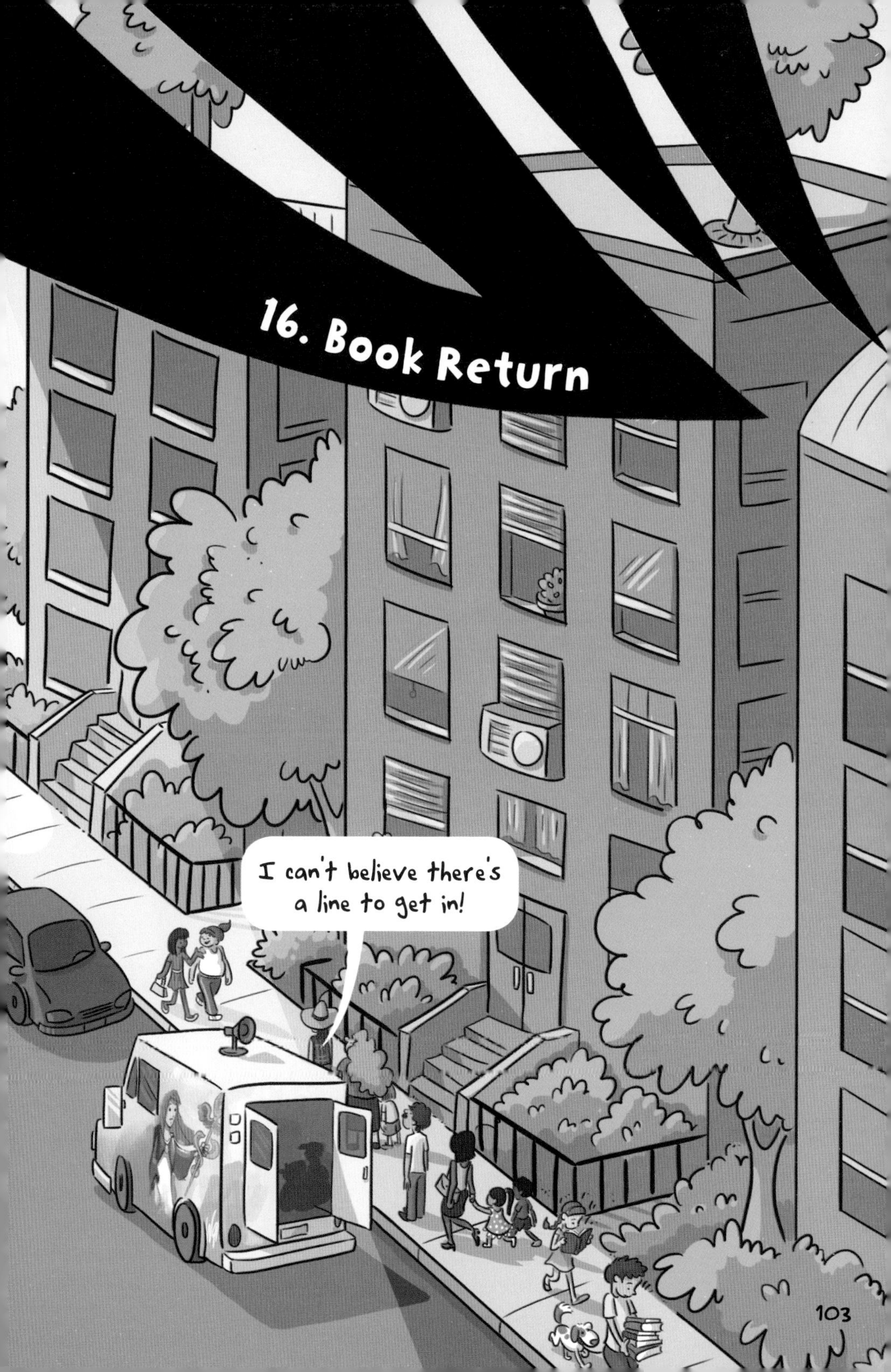
16. Book Return
I can't believe there's a line to get in!

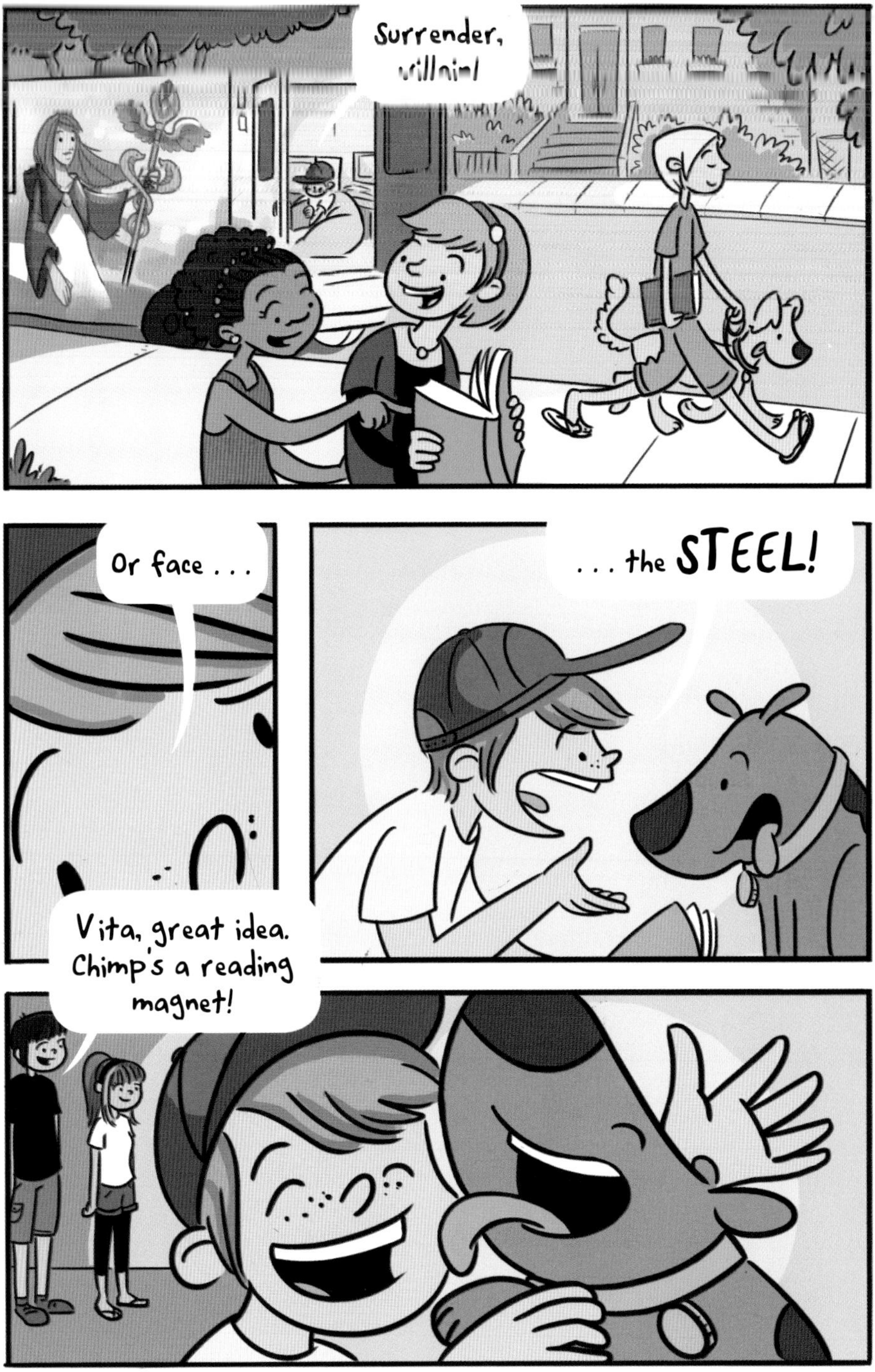
Surrender, villain!
Or face . . .
. . . the STEEL!
Vita, great idea. Chimp's a reading magnet!

Thirty Minutes Later . . .

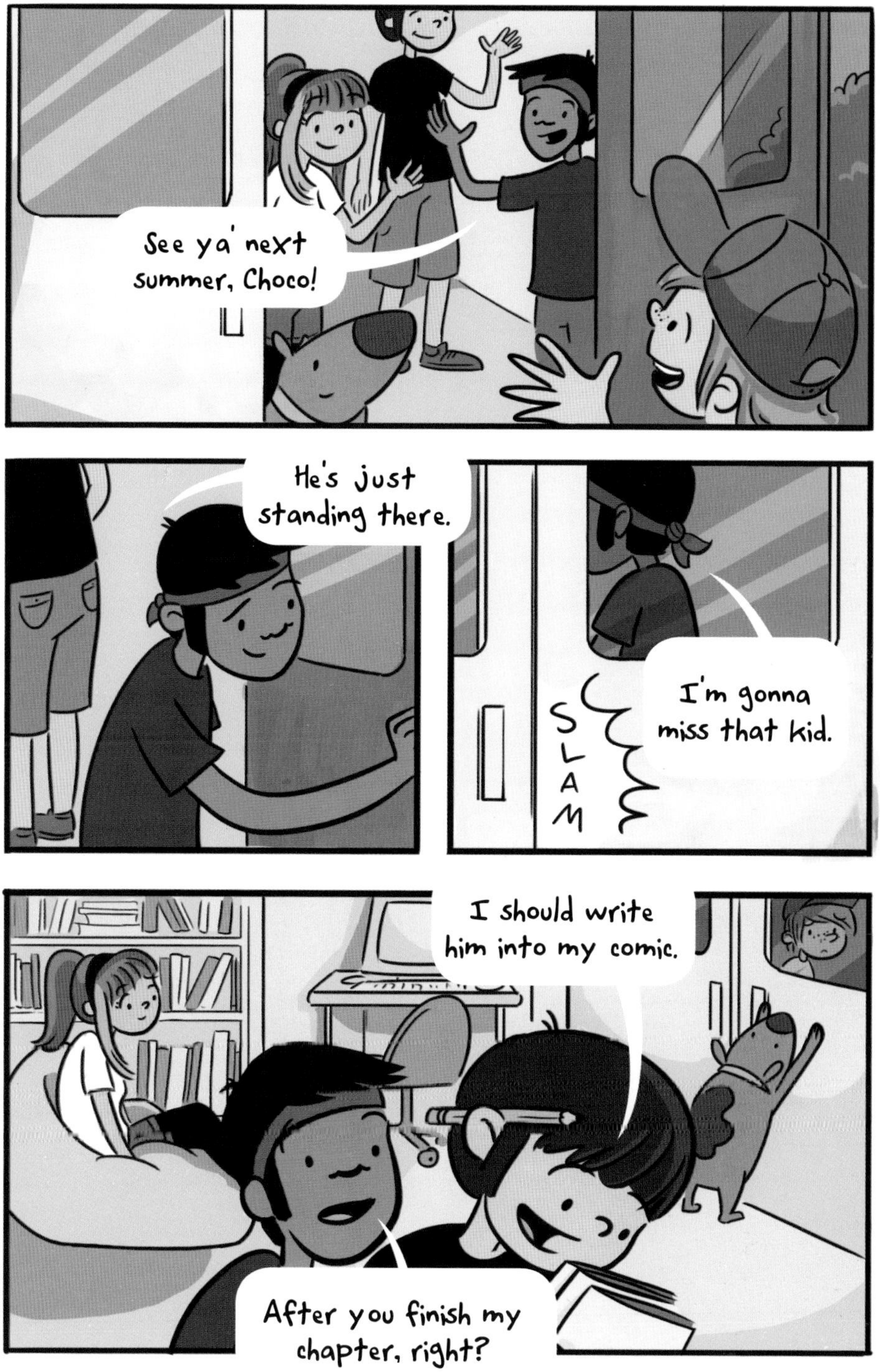

See ya' next summer, Choco!
He's just standing there.
SLAM
I'm gonna miss that kid.
I should write him into my comic.
After you finish my chapter, right?

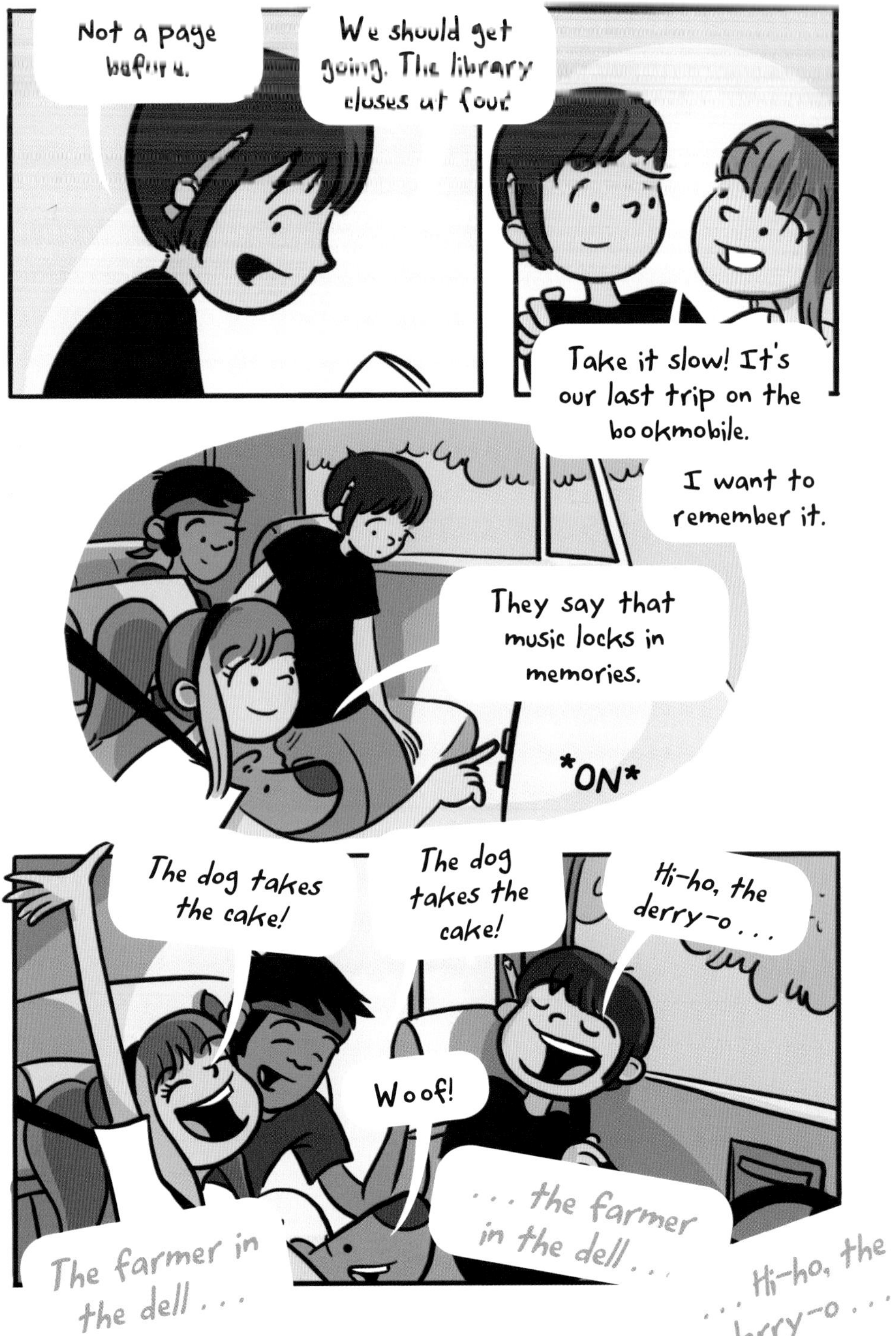
Not a page
We should get going. The library closes at four
Take it slow! It's our last trip on the bookmobile.
I want to remember it.
They say that music locks in memories.
ON
The dog takes the cake!
The dog takes the cake!
Hi-ho, the derry-o . . .
Woof!
The farmer in the dell . . .
. . . the farmer in the dell . . .
. . . Hi-ho, the derry-o . . .

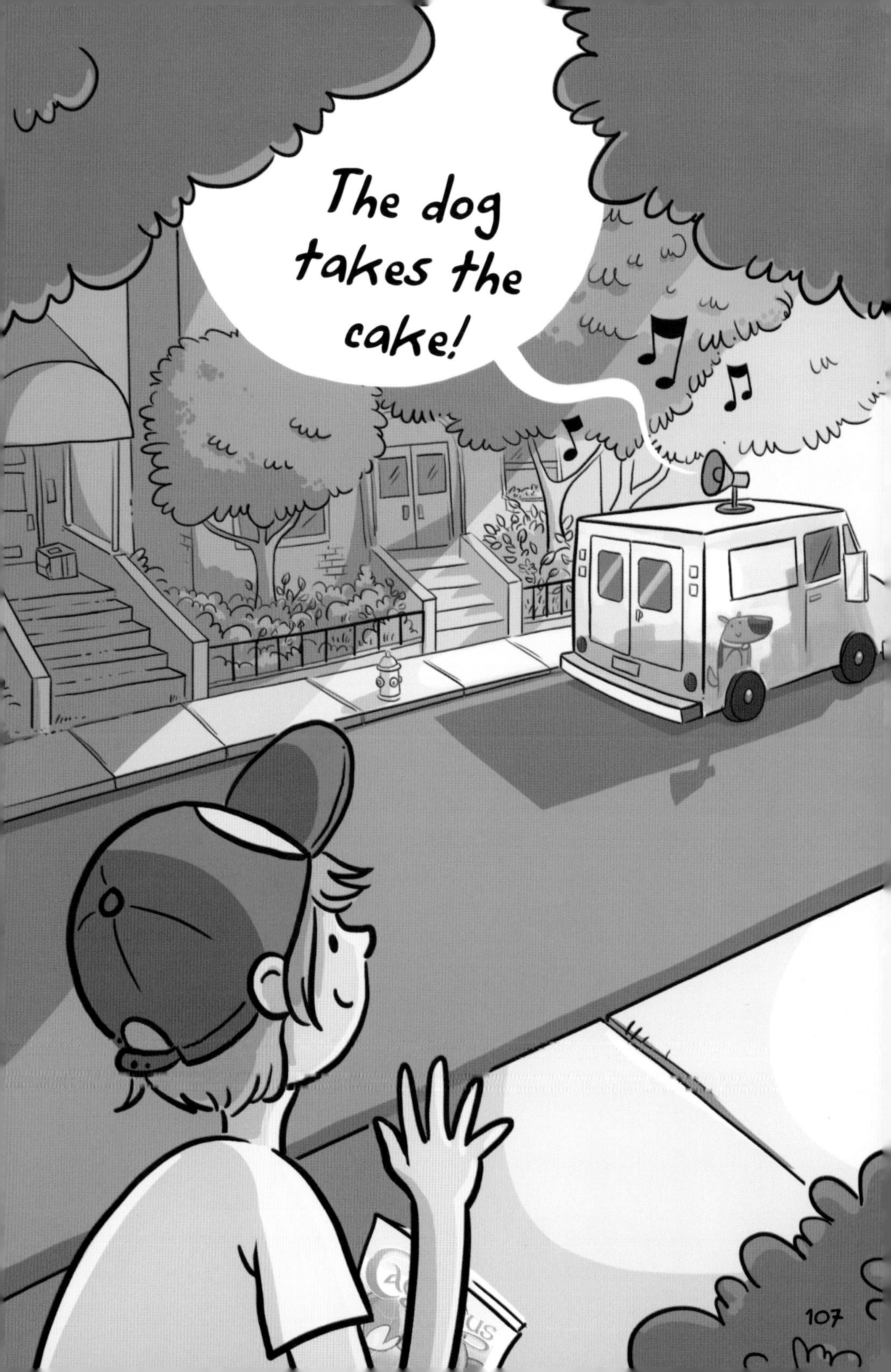
The dog takes the cake!

17. The Day After Dunesday

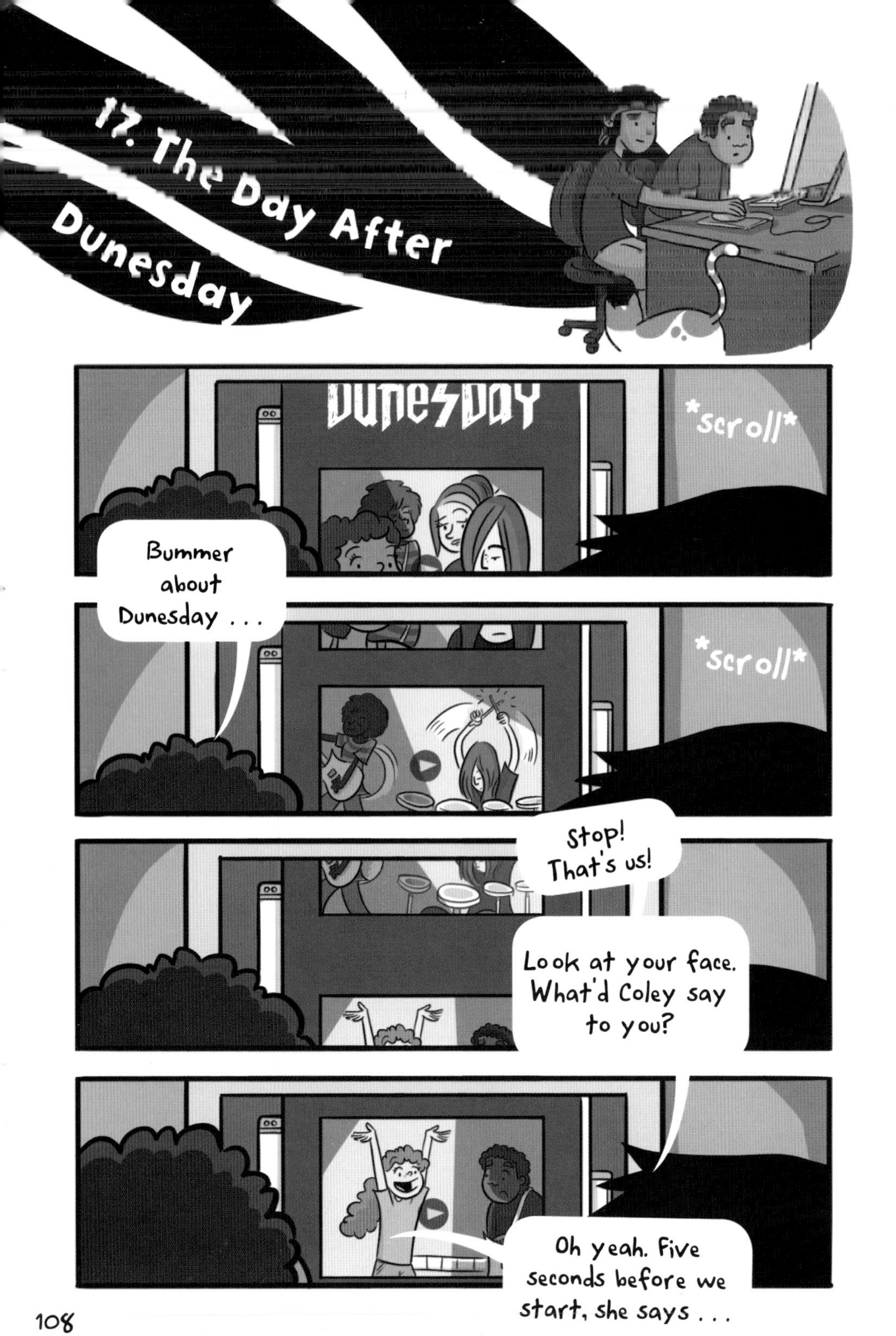

DUNESDAY
scroll
Bummer about Dunesday . . .
scroll
Stop! That's us!
Look at your face. What'd Coley say to you?
Oh yeah. Five seconds before we start, she says . . .

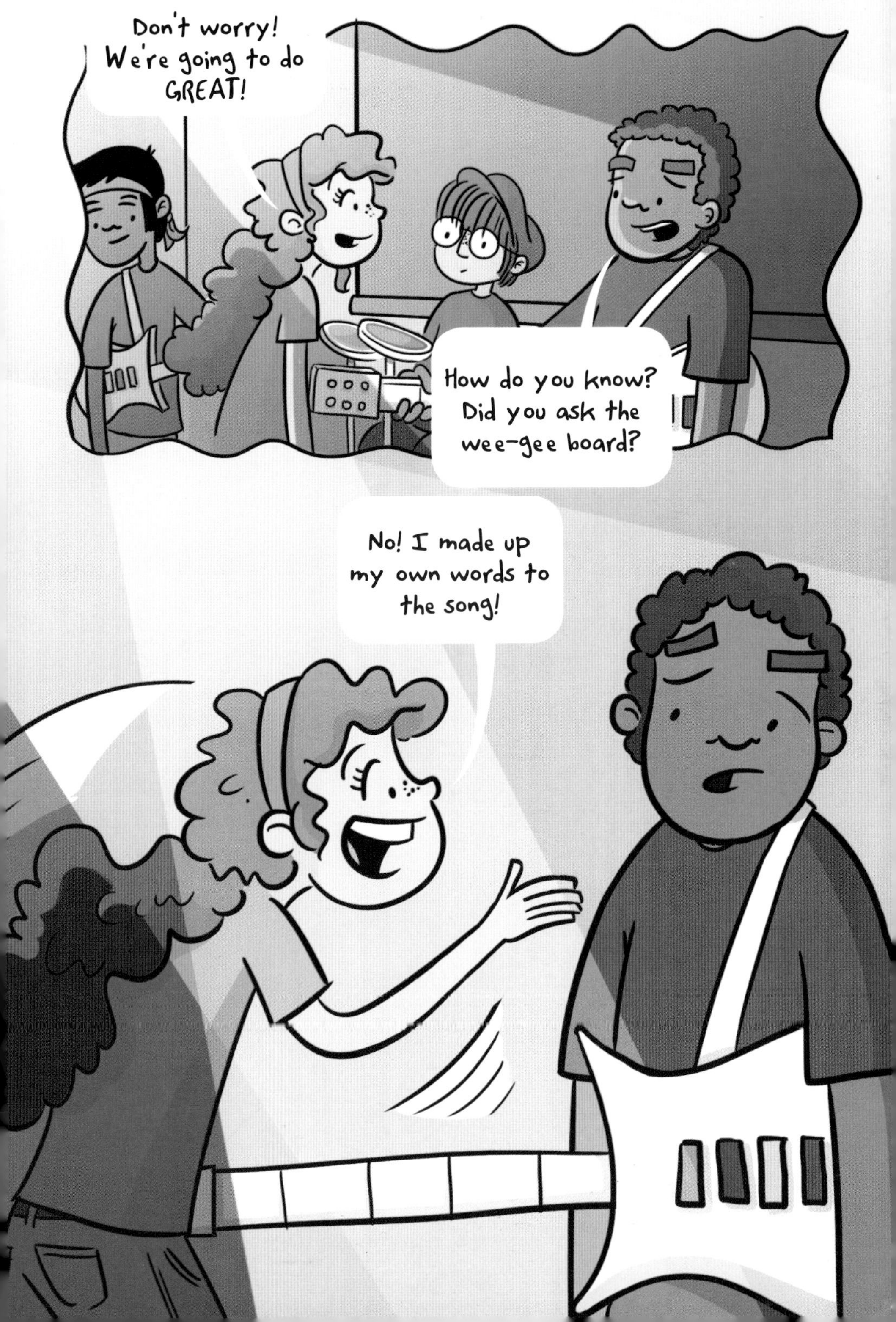
Don't worry! We're going to do GREAT!
How do you know? Did you ask the wee-gee board?
No! I made up my own words to the song!

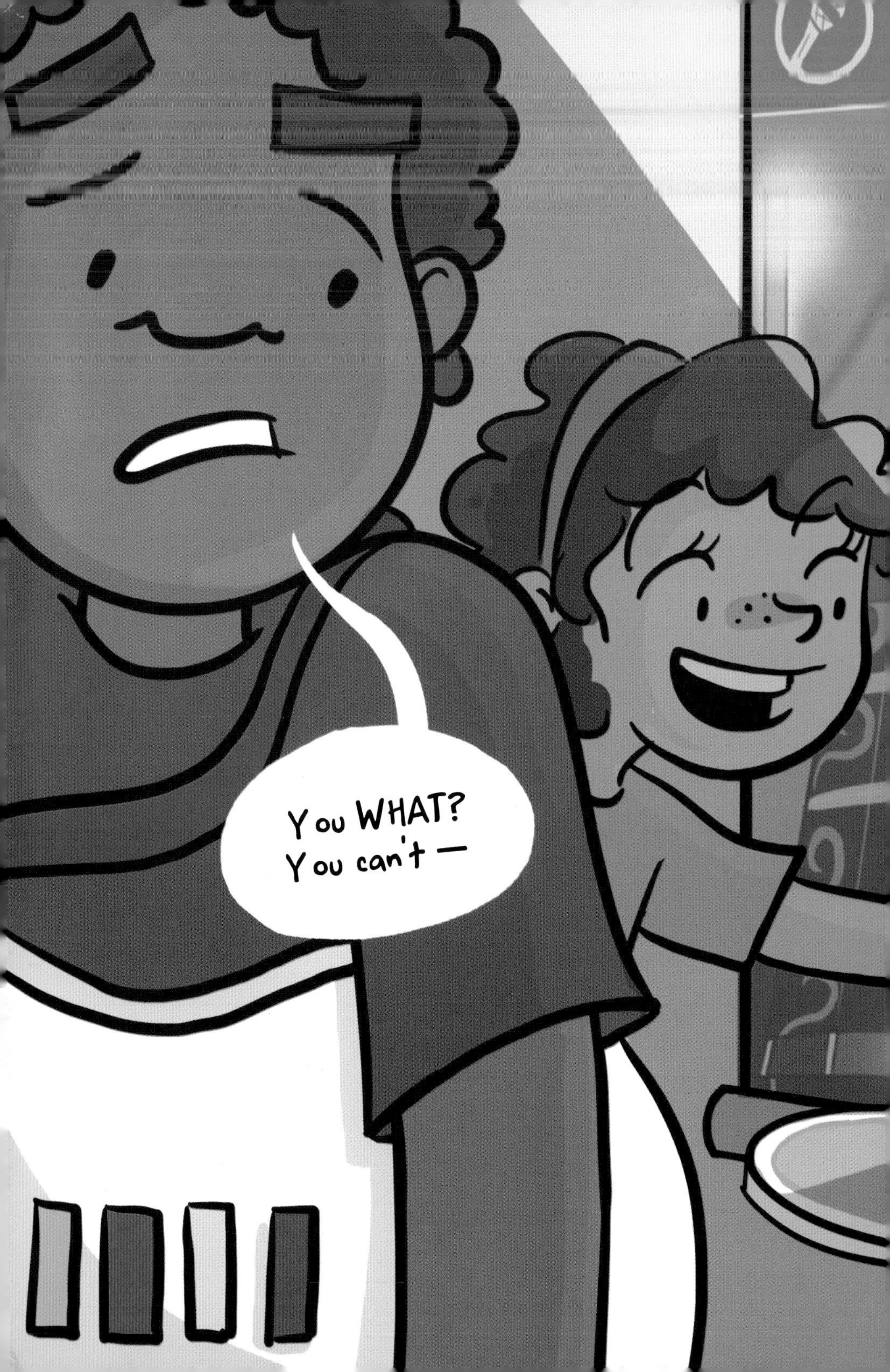
You WHAT? You can't —

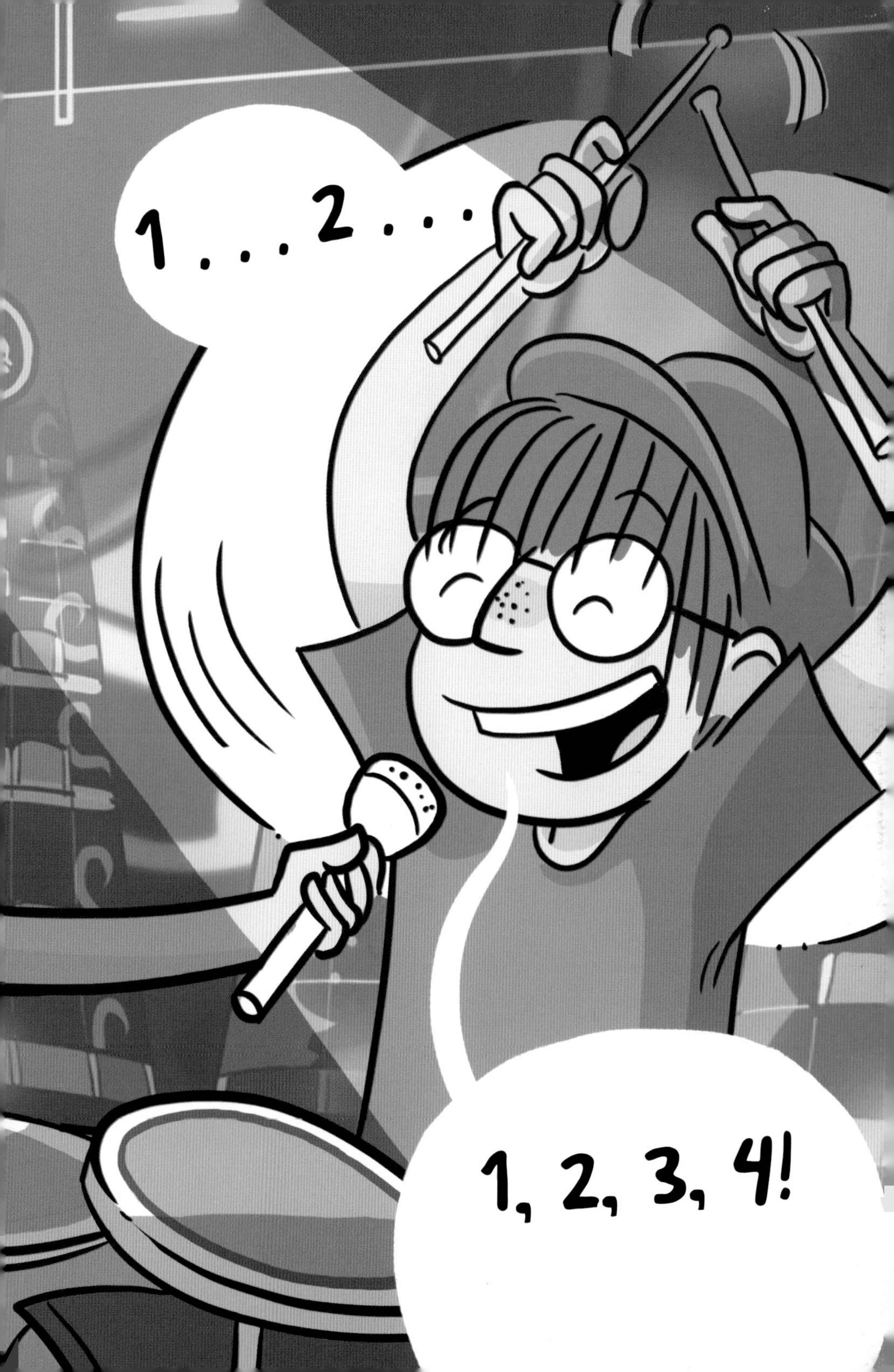
1 . . . 2 . . .
1, 2, 3, 4!

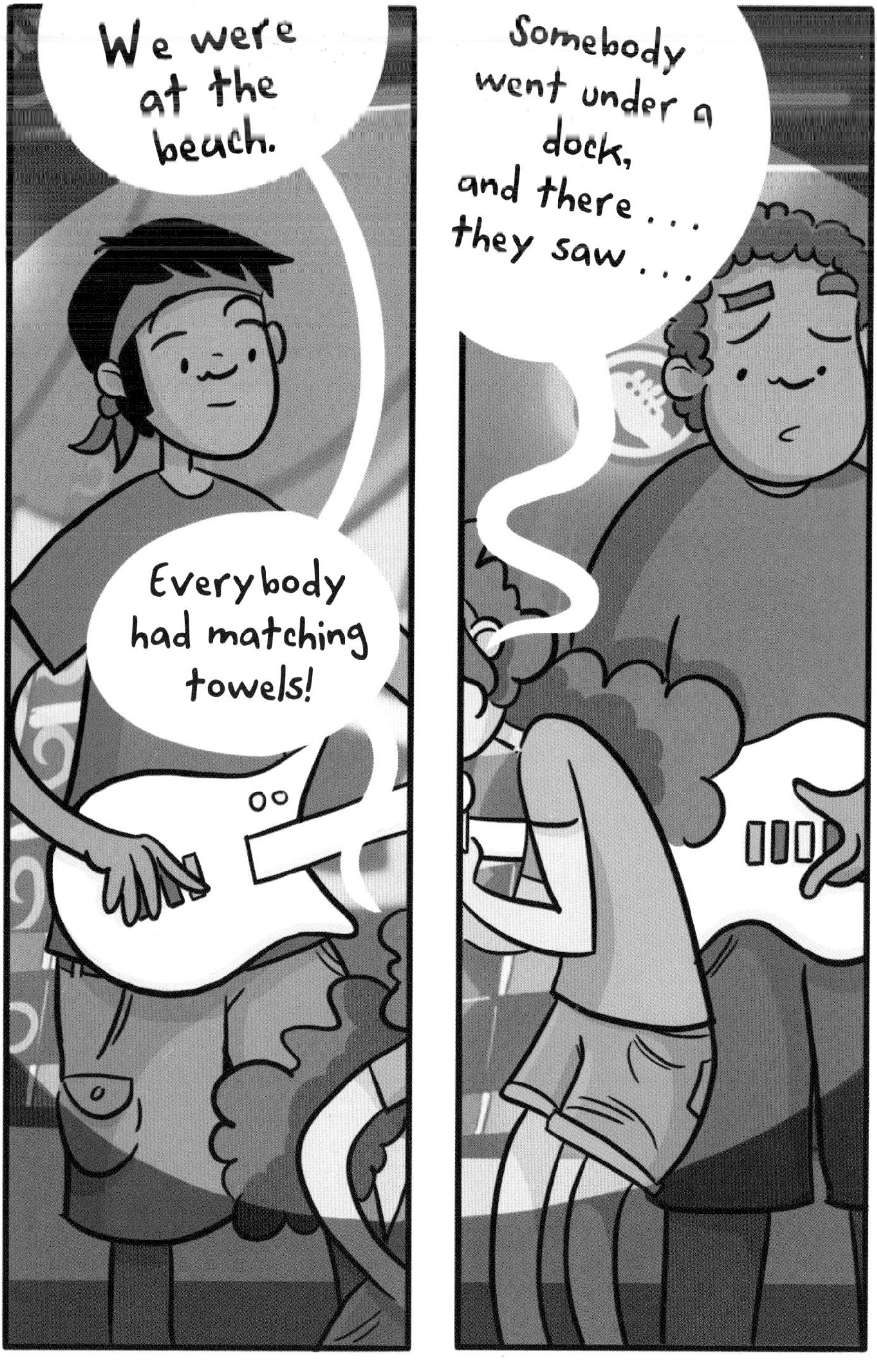
We were at the beach.
Everybody had matching towels!
Somebody went under a dock, and there . . . they saw . . .

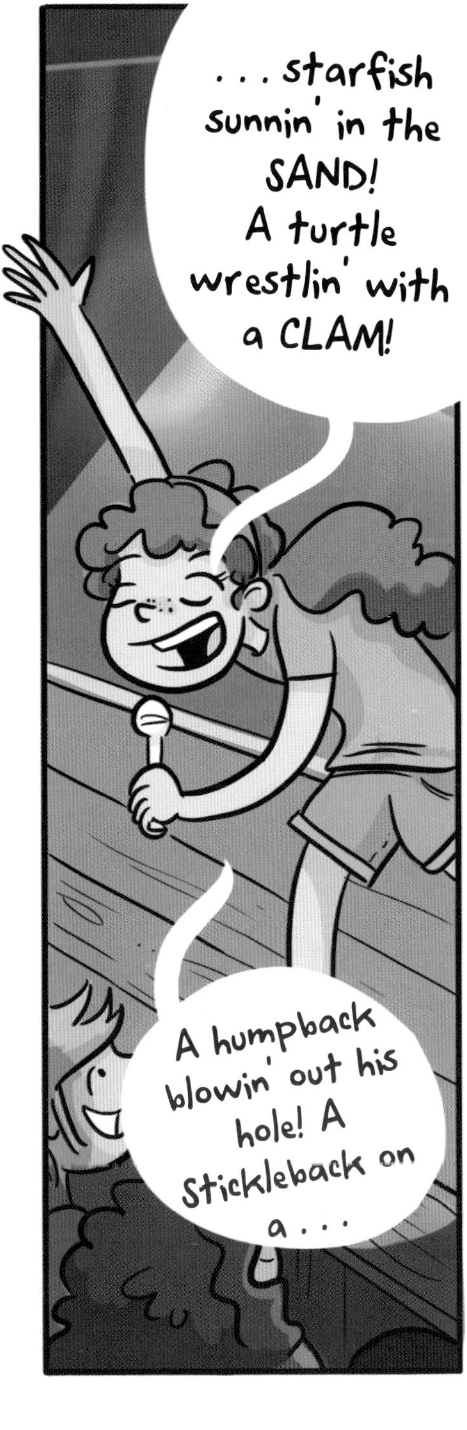
. . . starfish sunnin' in the SAND! A turtle wrestlin' with a CLAM!
A humpback blowin' out his hole! A Stickleback on a . . .

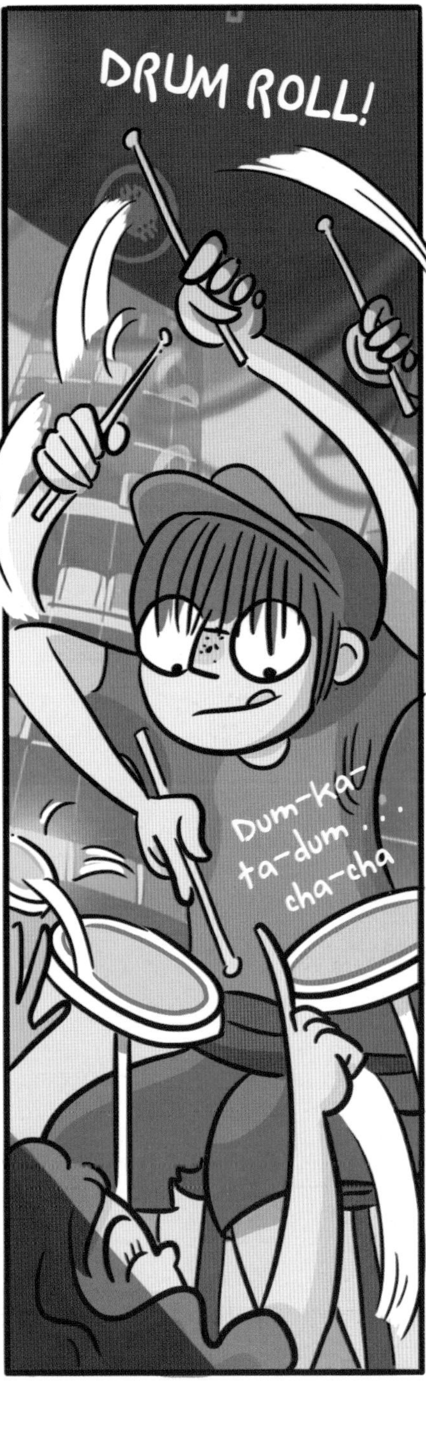
DRUM ROLL!
Dum-ka-ta-dum . . . cha-cha

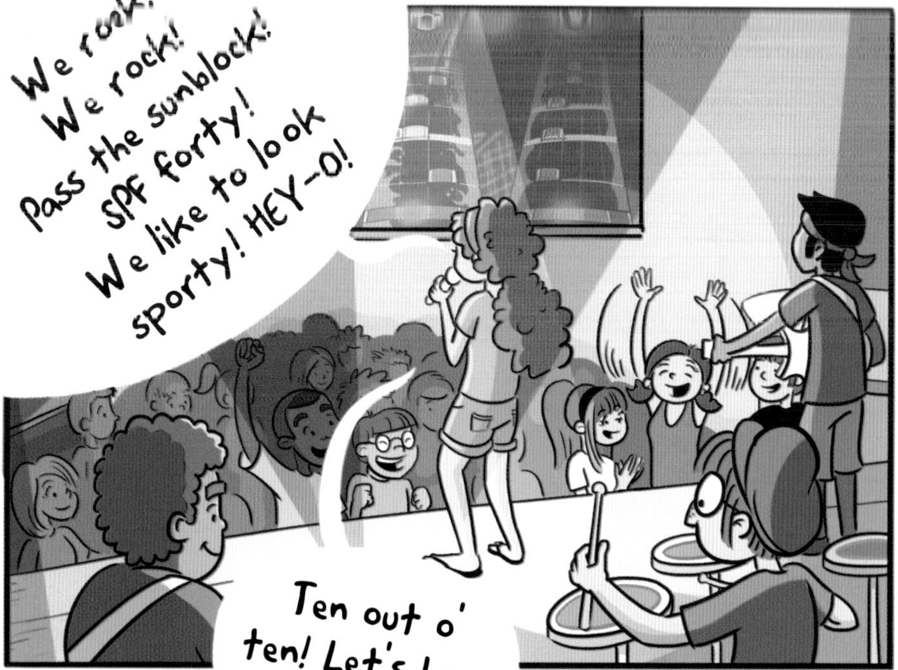
We rock! We rock! Pass the sunblock! SPF forty! We like to look sporty! HEY-O!
Ten out o' ten! Let's hear it again!
SDAY

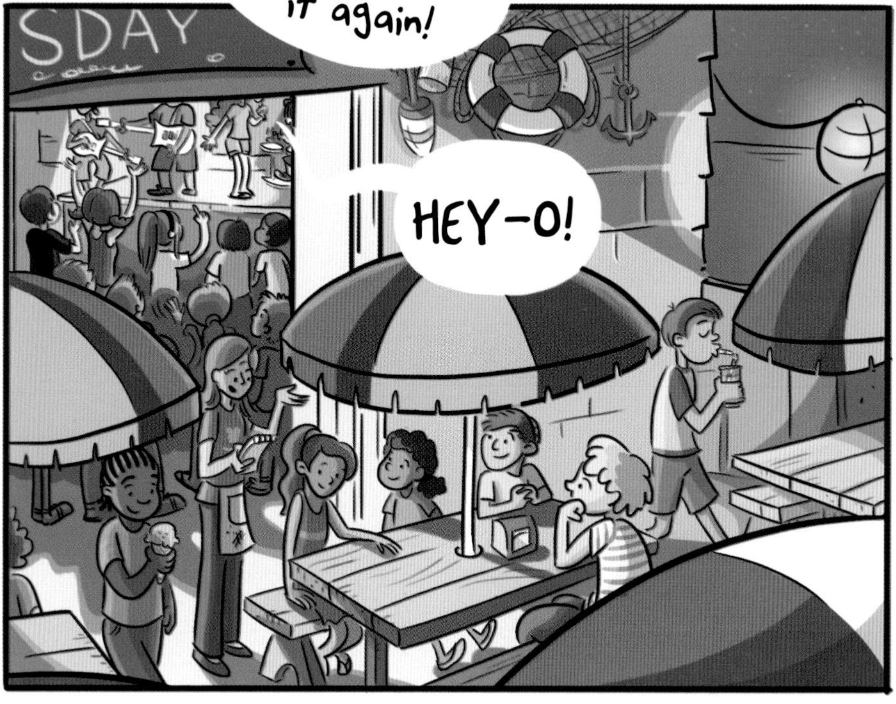
HEY-O!

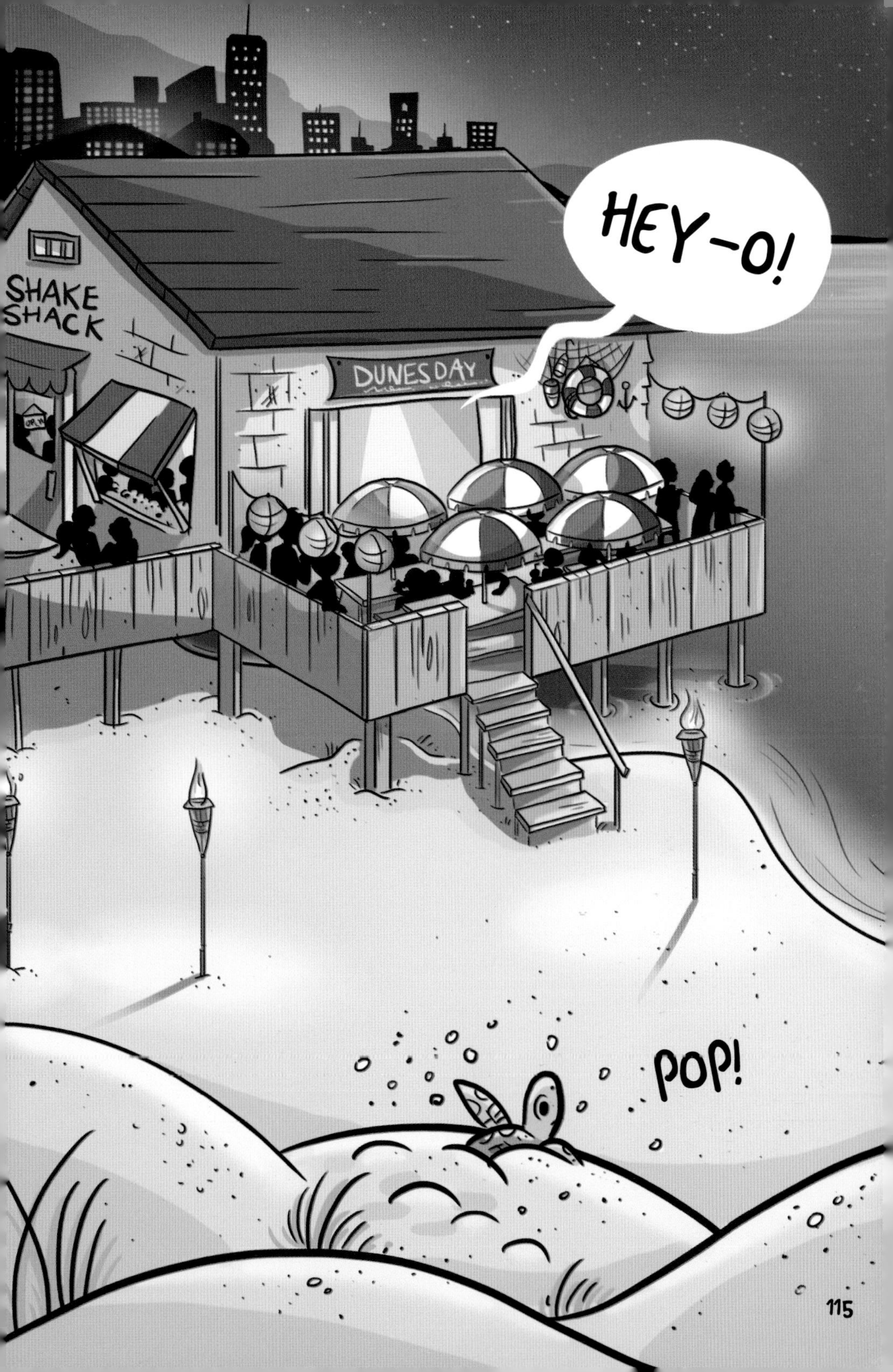
SHAKE SHACK
DUNES DAY
HEY-O!
POP!

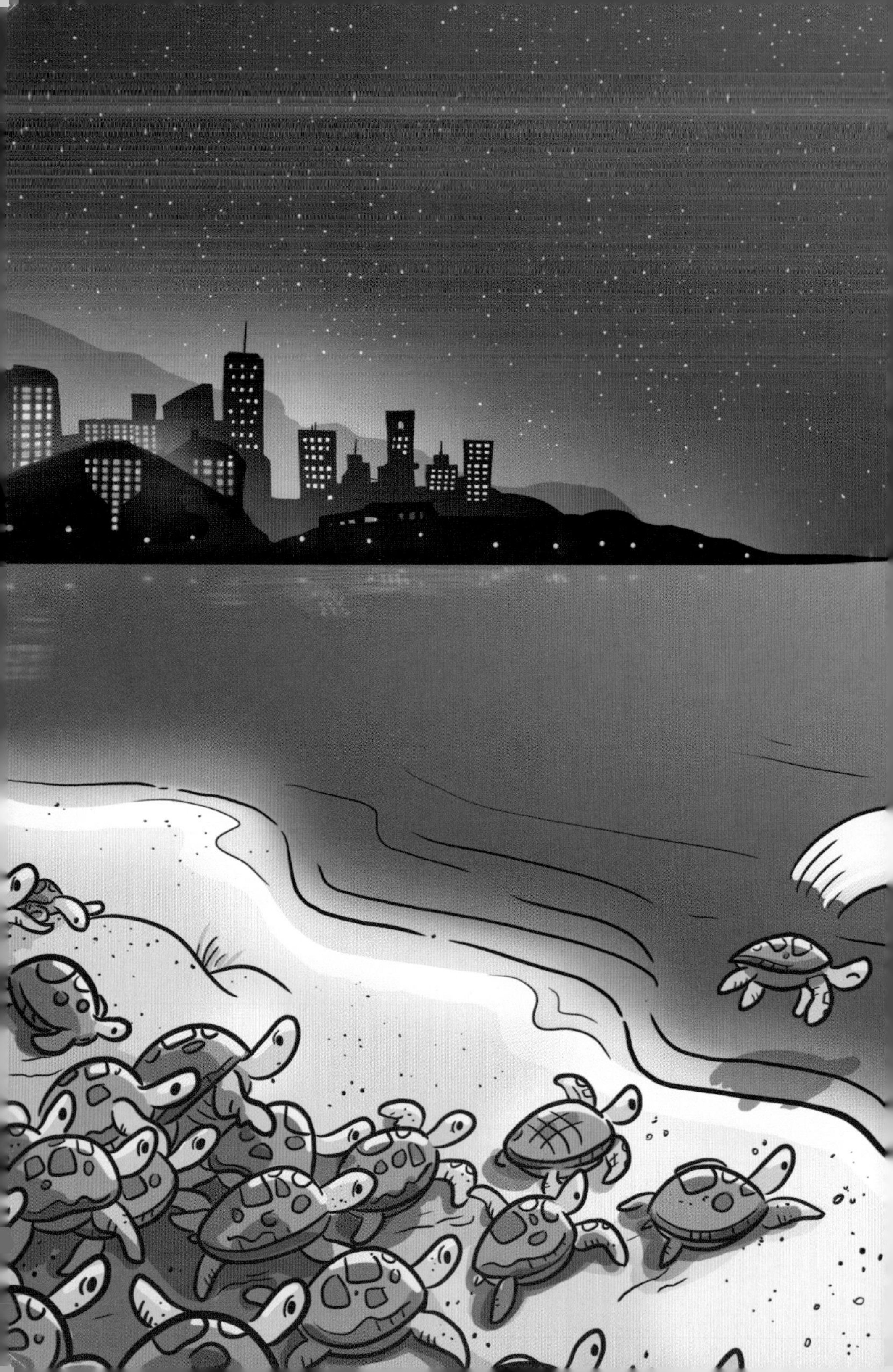

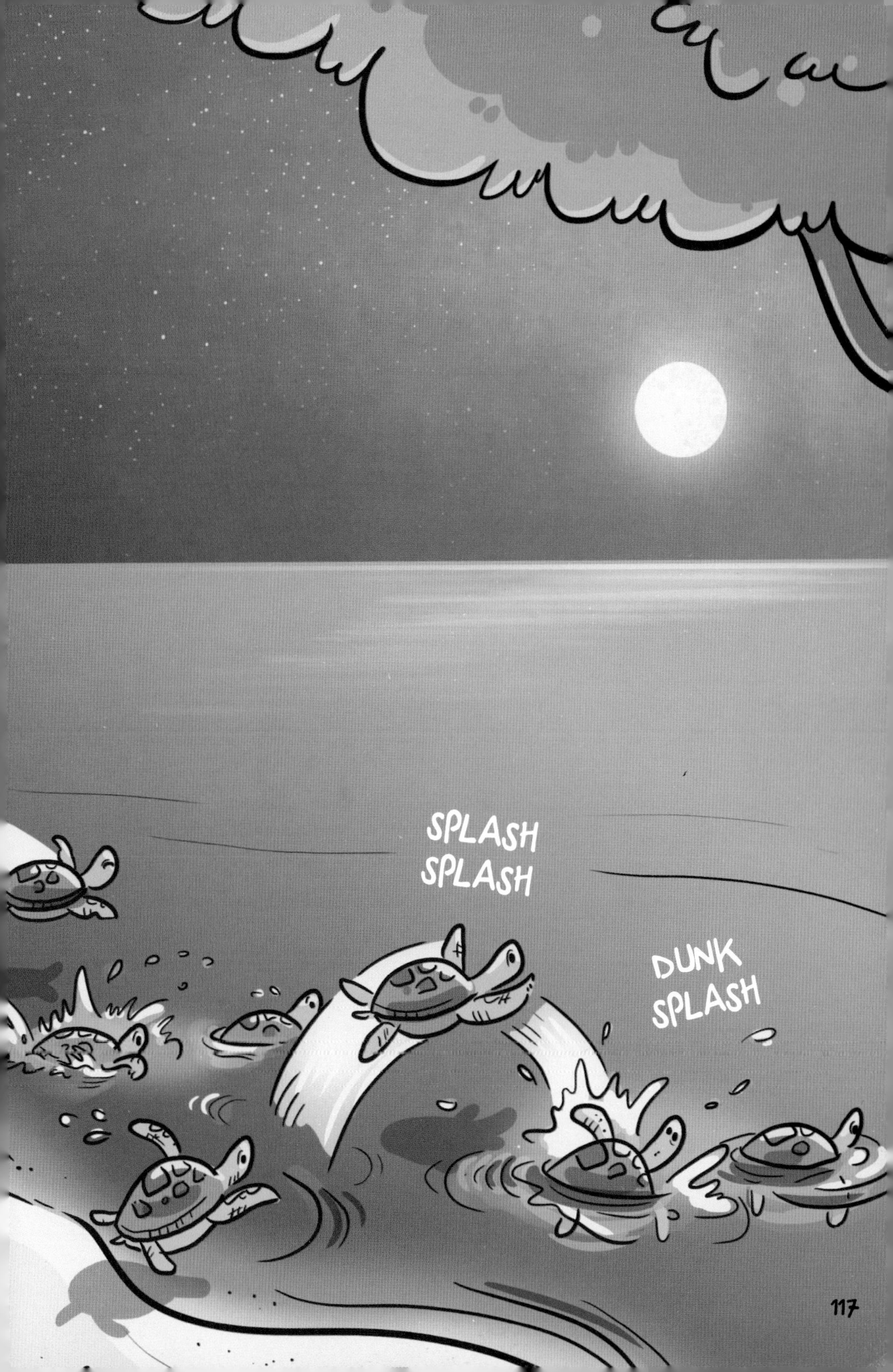
SPLASH
SPLASH
DUNK
SPLASH

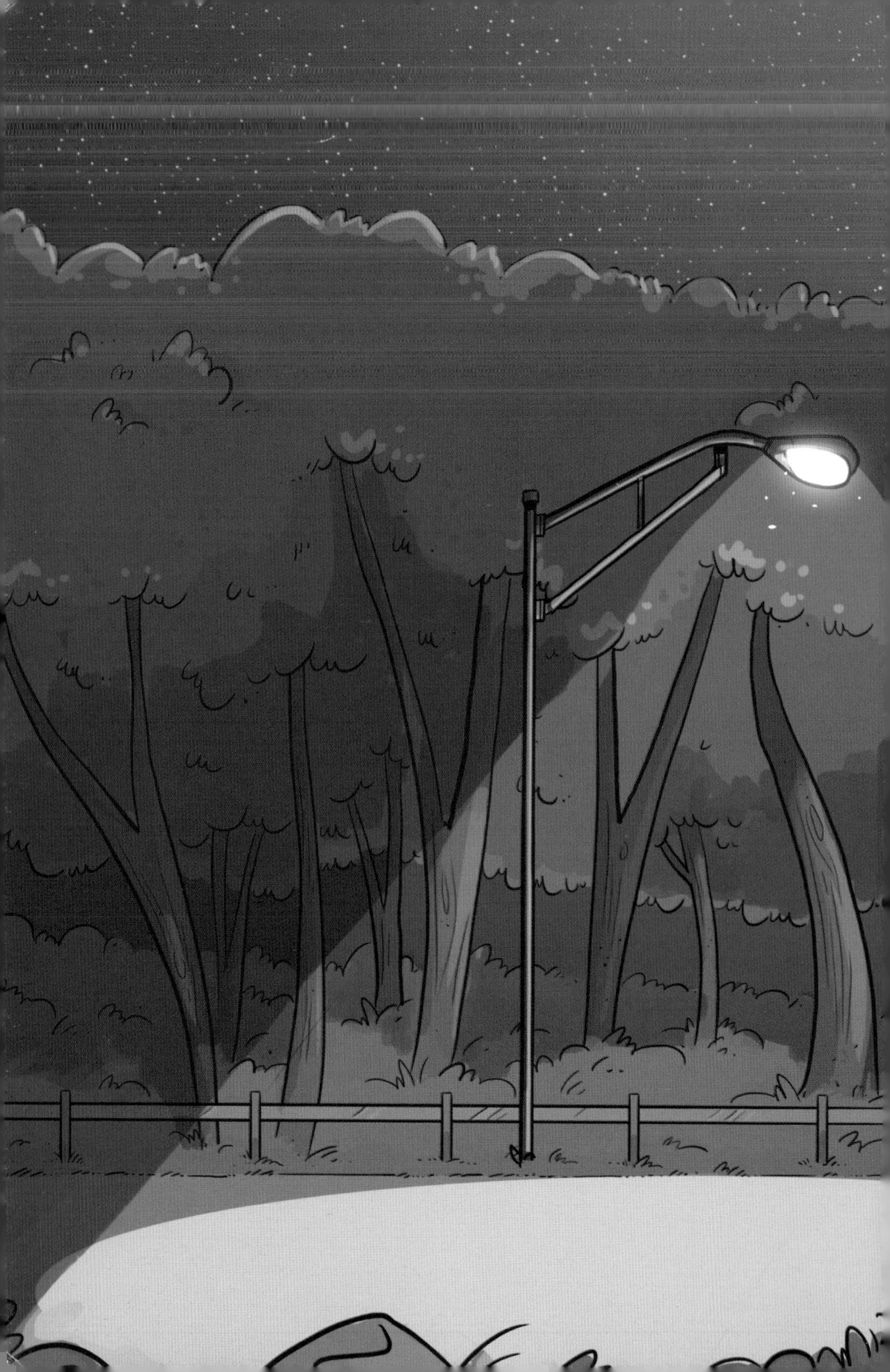

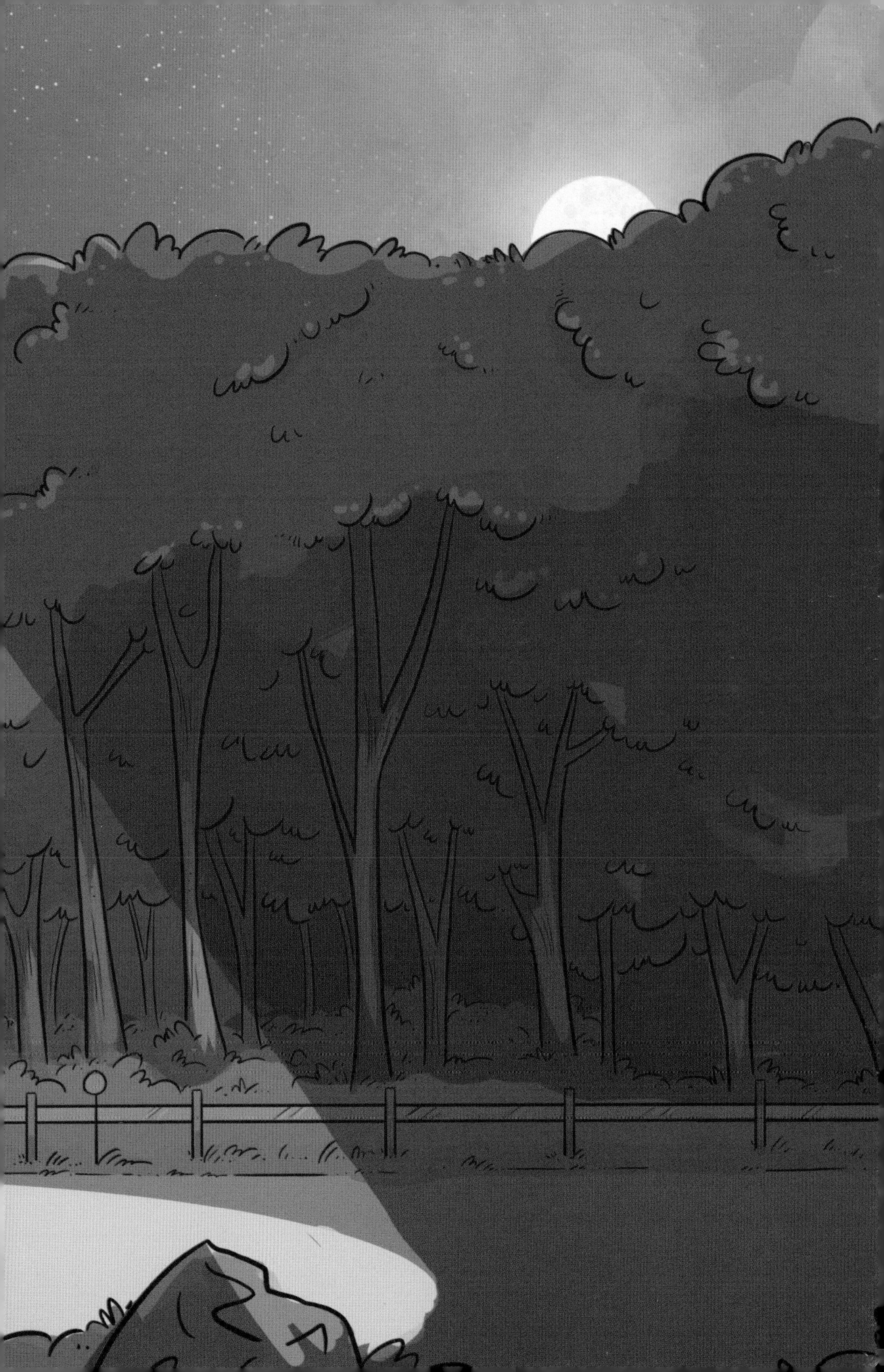